Alex Grecian is the author of the long-running and critically acclaimed comic book series *Proof*. He lives in the American Midwest with his wife and son. *The Yard* is his first novel.

The Yard

ALEX GRECIAN

MICHAEL JOSEPH
an imprint of
PENGUIN BOOKS

MICHAEL JOSEPH

Published by the Penguin Group
Penguin Books Ltd, 80 Strand, London WC2R 0RL, England
Penguin Group (USA) Inc., 375 Hudson Street, New York, New York 10014, USA
Penguin Group (Canada), 90 Eglinton Avenue East, Suite 700, Toronto, Ontario, Canada M4P 2Y3
(a division of Pearson Penguin Canada Inc.)
Penguin Ireland, 25 St Stephen's Green, Dublin 2, Ireland (a division of Penguin Books Ltd)
Penguin Group (Australia), 707 Collins Street, Melbourne, Victoria 3008, Australia
(a division of Pearson Australia Group Pty Ltd)
Penguin Books India Pvt Ltd, 11 Community Centre,
Panchsheel Park, New Delhi – 110 017, India
Penguin Group (NZ), 67 Apollo Drive, Rosedale, Auckland 0632, New Zealand
(a division of Pearson New Zealand Ltd)
Penguin Books (South Africa) (Pty) Ltd, Block D, Rosebank Office Park, 181 Jan Smuts Avenue,
Parktown North, Gauteng 2193, South Africa

Penguin Books Ltd, Registered Offices: 80 Strand, London WC2R 0RL, England

www.penguin.com

First published by Michael Joseph 2012

Published in Penguin Books 2013

002

Typeset in Garamond MT Std 12.75/15pt
Typeset by Palimpsest Book Production Ltd, Falkirk, Stirlingshire
Printed in Great Britain by Clays Ltd, St Ives plc

ISBN: 978–0–718–15967–2

If you wake at midnight, and hear a horse's feet,
Don't go drawing back the blind, or looking
in the street.
Them that ask no questions isn't told a lie.
Watch the wall, my darling, while the Gentlemen
go by!

Rudyard Kipling, 'Smuggler's Song'

I

Two hours since the discovery of Mr Little

Sergeant Kett took a moment to scan the station. Euston Square, the metropolitan terminus of the North-Western Railway, was always bustling. Hundreds of passengers arrived every day for their first experience of the great city, while others fled to Liverpool, Birmingham, Manchester, Nottingham and all points between. Kett knew it was unlikely that Inspector Little's killer had remained at the scene of the crime, but still . . . he held out some slight hope that he would spot the butcher. He stood at the top of the wide double staircase looking south towards the great Euston arch. The grand hall was framed by dark red pillars and sunlight streamed through a domed skylight in the high ceiling, shimmering across the metallic lava floor. The bright blue uniforms of dozens of constables stood out against the grey sea of day travellers, and against the white granite of the station walls. But the presence of so many police in the station, while initially novel, was eventually ignored in the urgent press by commuters to get to their proper destinations.

Irish labourers tramped through the massive entrance along with soldiers on leave and small, dirty children travelling to stay with distant relatives. Beyond the wide green awnings above the gates outside, the lingering morning fog had begun to burn away, but Kett couldn't see far into the mist. He liked the swirling grey and the possibility of newness somewhere inside or behind it.

He scanned the crowd while constables bustled back and forth behind him.

Here was a doctor with his family, headed away on vacation, his elaborate beard losing its curls in the sudden heat of the crowded platform, his black bag clutched tight to his chest. His pretty wife bustled along behind, leading a nurse and a young boy, all of them tired and stressed-looking.

Two tarts loitered against the wall near one of the meeting rooms and, when he caught their eye, he made a quick motion with his head to indicate that they should move along. They strolled past him and smiled.

'We does like a man with a full beard,' the taller of them said.

'Quite masculine,' the prettier of them said. She had a scar that ran from her scalp to her throat, but it somehow added to her vulnerability and attractiveness.

'Keep moving,' Kett said.

'Pity.'

And they were gone, caught up in the crush of bodies.

Prostitution was illegal, of course, and they were a cheeky pair to be plying their trade so early in the day and in so public a place, but they were brave in their fashion, too, and arresting them would have been fruitless. They would be back at it within the day.

Kett shook his head. Murderers, thieves, whores and swindlers were all pressed together alongside that rarest of species, the honest citizen. He could spend the entire afternoon studying the crowds at Euston Square and never sort the decent from the damned.

He turned and watched his men do their work.

The hierarchy of The Yard was unusual in that nobody outranked anyone else. The detective inspectors specialized in certain types of crime, the cases that required the most time to solve. The constables – he never called them 'bobbies', despite the popularity of that nickname among the general public – dealt with London's day-to-day offences and walked their beats, familiarizing themselves with whole neighbourhoods and their people, always with the goal of nipping problems in the bud before they escalated far enough to warrant the attention of the detectives. And the sergeants, Kett among them, facilitated both constable and inspector, working to ensure that everybody on the force communicated smoothly with everybody else, that everyone was at the top of his game.

His constables made him proud. There were times when Kett felt he had to stride up and down among them, barking orders and keeping everyone on their toes, but today, with the gravity of the case before them, every one of the men in blue was bustling, working to do his part. Constable Hammersmith, in particular, seemed tireless and Kett wondered how long it had been since the young man had slept. He was aware that Hammersmith had worked at least two shifts and he made a mental note to send the lad home for a rest before he dropped.

The new inspector, Day, appeared to be up to the job, but Kett knew little about the man. There was an innocence about him that bothered Kett. He had seen idealistic men come and go, the city leaching hope from them too quickly. It was a mystery to Kett whether Day would last at The Yard, but Kett would do what he could to help keep him on the job. There was something immensely likeable about the new detective, a sense of duty and of curiosity as well, that could take him a long way.

Not everyone working around the ominous trunk on the gallery floor was under Kett's watch. Dr Kingsley was an exception as he was not officially a member of the Metropolitan Police Force of Scotland Yard. He worked from a laboratory in the University College Hospital basement and had created his own position as forensic examiner simply because he felt it was necessary. Before he had taken over the police morgue, forensics work had been nearly non-existent. Bodies had been shipped to poorly run storage facilities where they were lost or forgotten. He was a strange little man and the police were wary of him, but his help was invaluable and he was widely respected within the ranks of the detectives.

If Little's killer was smart, he had hopped on the early train and was already far away.

But Kett allowed himself a hard smile. They had lost the Ripper, but lessons had been learned. If Little's killer had been bold enough or foolish enough to remain in London, Kett had utter faith that these men would find him and bring him to justice.

The bald man stood at the edge of the crowd and watched as Sergeant Kett returned to the gallery. The gruff old policeman had glanced right at him without the slightest sign of recognition.

Dr Kingsley passed Kett on the staircase, without a word, and left the station through the arch at the far end. The bald man had never met Kingsley, but he'd heard some of the police talking about the aloof forensics specialist. By all accounts Kingsley was good. Beyond good. The bald man wished he knew what Kingsley had whispered to the dark-haired young detective.

Across the platform, the detective frowned and gestured to two nearby constables.

'Take this trunk up to University College Hospital right away,' he said. 'To Dr Kingsley's laboratory. And be careful with it. The body inside is a detective.'

He spoke too loudly and the crowd gasped. The bald man composed his expression carefully, mirroring the shock he saw on the faces around him. There was a good bit of chatter, people already late returning to work, sharing the excitement of discovery and danger at a safe distance.

The two men struggled with the trunk. The bald man recognized one of the other policemen, a young constable named Pringle. He raised a hand and Pringle noticed him. The constable nodded his head and gestured towards a relatively deserted corner of the platform. The bald man moved quickly through the crowd and joined Pringle there.

'Hello, sir,' Pringle said. 'Bad bit of business this morning.'

'I overheard some of it,' the bald man said. 'A detective?'

'In the trunk.' Pringle grimaced, nodding his head. 'Least that's what he said. Bad for us all, if you ask me. Killing detectives.'

'But I'm sure they'll catch him, whoever did this, they'll catch him straight away, don't you think?'

'I hope so, sir. I certainly do.'

'Well, who's that over there? Who's in charge of it all?'

Pringle glanced over at the men shuffling across the platform, the trunk swaying between them, the detective following behind.

'That's Day, sir. Detective Inspector Day. He only joined us here last week. Come up from Devon, I think. You wouldn't have met him yet, I'm sure.'

'Day, eh?'

'William's his first name. William or . . . no, it's Walter. Walter Day, that's it.'

'Good man?'

'I'm sure I wouldn't know, sir, but I hope he's up to the task. Can't have nobody running around offing detectives. Next thing they'll be takin' aim at us working men. Can't have that.'

'No, no, of course not.'

'Bad bit of business,' Pringle repeated.

'Well, I'll leave you to it, then. Work to do, you know.'

'Of course.'

'Don't worry, Pringle. I'm quite sure your new inspector will do the job up right.'

Pringle nodded.

'Sure he will. Bad bit of business, though.'

'Yes. Good day, then.'

The bald man turned up the collar of his coat and glanced at the sky as he left the building. Grey clouds were rolling in quickly. The crowd would disperse as soon as the rain started and he didn't want to get caught up in the rush.

He hurried across the street, avoiding a fresh pile of horse manure, and repeated the detective's name under his breath. Detective Inspector Walter Day would bear watching.

But the more immediate problem was Dr Kingsley. Kingsley had shown something to Inspector Day, but the bald man had been too far away to see it. Had he left a clue?

The bald man regretted what had happened. He admired the Metropolitan Police, admired them and tried to help them in his own small way. But Inspector Little had stumbled on to his secret and there had been no choice.

Kingsley and Day. The bald man muttered their names again and spat at the hard-packed dirt of the street. He would have to keep an eye on Kingsley and Day. If they discovered his secret, too . . . The bald man shook his head, dismissing the thought for now. He would follow the investigation and if Inspector Day came too close to learning the truth . . . Well, Day might just disappear.

Constable Pringle brushed imaginary lint from his trousers and straightened the cuffs of his crisp, starched shirt. He realized he had a question for the man he'd been talking to and looked across the street, scanning the backs of the departing crowd. Too late. Pringle would have to drop in on him later.

He turned and hurried across the platform. Constables Hammersmith and Jones were shuffling along, the trunk swinging between them.

'Oi, Nevil,' Pringle said. 'You fancy coming with me? Got some things to pick up.'

Nevil Hammersmith looked up and grunted.

'Depends on how long Dr Kingsley keeps us. If he's got nothing for us there, I'll be off-duty, but it was a long night, Colin.'

'Won't take long. I could use the company. Bit nervous today, you know.'

Hammersmith chuckled and switched the handle of the trunk to his other hand.

'Forgot you were taking Maggie out tonight, old man.'

‘It’s dinner. Nothing more.’

‘How very casual of you. May I assume you won’t be returning to the flat until late? I won’t wait up for you, but wake me when you arrive in the morning, would you?’

Pringle pursed his lips in a mock frown.

‘The morning? You scandalize me, sir. And you besmirch Maggie’s good name.’

‘Get on out of here, Pringle,’ Jones said. ‘Hammersmith’s got work to do.’

Pringle wagged a finger at Jones, but hastened away before anyone could ask him to help with the trunk. He didn’t want to get dirt on his new jacket. He would pick up Hammersmith at the college before stopping at the tailor’s.

The thought of Inspector Little, broken and mutilated in the bottom of the trunk, passed through his mind and he swept it away. He’d just got a glimpse of the dead detective before Day had closed the trunk, but it was enough. He hadn’t known Little well. The detective had never even looked at Pringle, just muttered orders at him. Little had undoubtedly run across trouble on an investigation and been killed for it. But that would never happen to Pringle. He had joined the force strictly for the dapper uniform and the pretty girls who noticed it. He kept his nose out of the detectives’ business.

He smiled and stepped into the street, promptly planting his foot in a pile of horse manure.

2

The dancing man was already outside the back hall at Number Four Whitehall Place when Detective Inspector Walter Day arrived. Day wondered at the fact that the dancing man had thus far avoided the workhouse, but he had visited that place and had no desire to send anyone there, if it could be helped. At least a head taller than Day, with massive hands and feet, the dancing man looked intimidating, but he kept his distance from people and bowed his head when he spoke. He worked, in a way, for his daily bread and Day, who thought himself a good judge of character, found him somehow touching. Today he had found the top half of a broken broom and was displaying it proudly as he gyrated atop an overturned milk crate, blowing kisses to passersby. Day gave him a ha'penny and went inside.

The Metropolitan Police Force was headquartered in the rear of a massive building located off Great Scotland Yard and the entrance was commonly called the 'back hall', though there was no corresponding front hall. Day nodded to the sergeant on duty at the desk in the small receiving area and then passed through a short hallway.

The main room on the ground floor was segmented. To Day's right as he left the hallway was the largest and most accessible section. It housed most of the detectives of the Metropolitan Police Force, along with numerous constables, all of whom hurried in and out, day and night, struggling to deal with wearying numbers of cases involving burglary, assault, prostitution, missing persons and muggings.

Day did not even glance in their direction. Instead, he turned to his left and walked past a row of communal desks, used by police and solicitors to talk to suspects before taking them back through yet another hallway to a walled-off holding area. He passed through a swinging gate in a low wooden railing and into the common office set up to accommodate the select group of detective inspectors who were referred to by the rest of the force as the 'Murder Squad'.

Prior to that, detectives working murder cases had used the same shared desks that were used by constables on the beat. But the Ripper case had changed all that. The railing had been installed and new desks had been brought in. A dozen of The Yard's best detectives were moved over and given all of the murder cases in all of London.

They were not relieved of the many other cases they were already working on.

Day hung his jacket and hat on hooks against the far wall, then went to his desk in the large central area. The room was quiet and he didn't yet feel comfortable there. He hadn't done anything to personalize his desk, sure that he'd be sent back down to Devon when it was discovered that he had no talent as a detective. He'd been a good constable, energetic, strong and ready to serve, but detective work was daunting. He had seen something in Dr Kingsley's eyes back at the railway station.

Day was sure Kingsley knew he wasn't up to the job, positive that everybody knew it except Claire.

Michael Blacker waved at him from an identical desk halfway across the big room. Inspector Blacker's desk was messier, papers piled everywhere, a teapot half buried under a scrapbook and a solitary left boot – evidence gathered from some bizarre case that had consumed his time for the past three days.

'Another day, eh, Day?'

Blacker enjoyed the sort of puns and wordplay that Day found most tedious.

'Blacker, when was the last time you saw Mr Little?'

'Little? Sometime yesterday. But not for long, just for a little. A "little", right?'

'Right. I don't suppose you're familiar with any of his cases?'

'Sure, and I've got time galore, don't I?'

Day nodded. He'd known the answer to that question before he asked it. Last month, ninety-six corpses had been pulled from the Thames, more than half of them with their throats cut. It hadn't been an unusual body count for a city where the annual number of arrests topped sixty thousand. The twelve working inspectors of Scotland Yard had no time to deal with their own caseloads, much less each other's. And now, without Little, they were eleven. This half of the common room was quiet because everyone except Day and Blacker was already out dealing with London's crime.

'I'll need to see his files.'

'Don't know if he'd like that. Wait for him. He should be here soon.'

'He's not coming in today.'

Colonel Sir Edward Bradford emerged from his office in the corner and motioned with his good arm.

'Day. See you in here?'

'Yes, sir.'

Day crossed the room, through the labyrinth of desks, ignoring Blacker's puzzled stare. Inside, Sir Edward's office was small and dim, crowded with heavy furniture. A stuffed tiger's head, the only souvenir on display of Sir Edward's time in India, was mounted on the wall behind the desk. The commissioner closed the door and gestured to an empty chair.

When both men were seated, Sir Edward stroked his white beard and closed his eyes.

'How long have you been with us now, Day?'

This was it, Day was sure of it. Sir Edward had decided that the younger man wasn't cut out for detective work and was planning to move him back to Devon. It would be a relief, but Day had no idea how he would explain it to his wife. Claire would be so disappointed in him.

'Almost a week, sir.'

'When I took this post, Mr Day, it was with the expectation that I would be working with the legendary Inspector March, the greatest detective on the greatest police force in the world. You can imagine my dismay upon arriving in London to find that Mr March had already tendered his resignation from the Murder Squad.'

With a long and illustrious career behind him, Inspector Adrian March had been among the men put in charge of the Ripper investigation. He had failed to catch the wily killer of at least five women, and the public knew it.

March had retired early from the force. Day had been brought up to replace him and he still didn't understand why.

'Yes, sir,' he said.

'I suspect you share my dismay.'

'Yes, sir.'

'And so I have missed my opportunity to work with those great Scotland Yard detectives Adrian March and Dick Tanner and Frederick Aberline, but now I have you.'

'I apologize, sir.'

Day avoided the commissioner's eyes. Sir Edward was an intimidating man. He had stepped into the job of police commissioner in the month before Day's arrival and already had the complete respect of the men under his command. He was a veteran of the Indian Mutiny, about which Day knew very little, and had lost his arm in an encounter with a tiger. Perhaps the same tiger whose head now surveyed the office from a wooden plank nailed to the wall. It was rumoured that Sir Edward had accepted no anaesthetic during the amputation of his mutilated arm.

'There's no need for apologies. This isn't a dressing down, Mr Day. But I like to acknowledge the reality of a situation, rather than pussyfoot around the way you lot do over here. You have little experience as a policeman, is that correct?'

'Sir, I acted as constable for four years in Devon.'

'I'm aware. But you have never lived in London until quite recently.'

'I've visited many times.'

'And you have no experience whatsoever as a detective.'

'No, sir.'

'And yet you were handpicked by the great detective himself as his replacement.'

'I am as surprised as you are, sir. If you'd prefer, of course, I'll tender my resignation immediately.'

Sir Edward waved the suggestion away like a bad odour.

'That's not at all what I'm getting at, Mr Day.'

He took a handkerchief from his breast pocket and blew his nose with remarkable one-handed dexterity, tucked the cloth away and pointed to an umbrella stand in the corner behind the door.

'The brown ivory one,' Sir Edward said. 'See it there? Bring it to me, would you?'

The stand was crowded with umbrellas. Day ran his fingers across the bouquet of handles: smooth mahogany with mother-of-pearl inlays; burnished white ivory; brass and silver and semi-precious stones; tortoise shell; carved animal heads, and scrollwork. One handle was less ornate than the others. It appeared to be of humble, unworked wood, but the surface was smooth and buttery, unlike any wood that Day had seen. He assumed it was brown ivory, so he pulled it from the stand and handed it across the desk.

'Have you seen mammoth ivory before, Mr Day?'

'No, sir, I don't believe I have.'

'It's worth far less than the ivory we see from elephant tusks, but I place great value on it, nonetheless. This was once the tusk of an animal that is long since extinct, an animal that thundered across the land in great herds, larger and heavier and more impressive than anything it encountered. And it's now as if that animal had never existed but for this bit of bone. Neither you nor I will ever see a mammoth, but here is the proof of its life, here in this simple umbrella handle. An elephant tusk may be worth more on the open market, but I've seen elephants, Day, and to hold an elephant tusk in my hand no longer impresses me.'

'Were there many of them in India?'

'What, elephants? There were some, yes.'

'I've never seen one.'

Sir Edward nodded.

'Thank you. Yes, it's easy to forget sometimes just how extraordinary that continent is. I do miss the sun, Mr Day. Since I arrived here, the sky has been grey and my nose has become increasingly raw. I appear to have come down with something or other.'

'I'm sorry to hear it.'

Sir Edward waved his hand, dismissing the sentiment.

'I shall improve. Nothing has killed me yet and a bit of wet weather won't do the job where bullets, blades and a scorpion's sting have failed.'

He smiled and held the furled umbrella up to the light.

'These things, these bones of something that will never be seen again, are dug up by the bushelful every day in Siberia. I wonder how many are left under the ice there.'

'I wouldn't imagine there's a never-ending supply of them.'

'No, of course there isn't. So why do we value the elephant ivory so much more?'

'Elephant ivory is a good deal whiter than mammoth ivory, isn't it, sir?'

'Hmm. Yes, it is.'

He laid the umbrella on the desk between them and leaned forward.

'I value experience, Mr Day.'

'I understand, sir. Inspector March would naturally be of greater value to you than I am. And of greater value to The Yard.'

'You're not following. Yes, of course Mr March would be of great value to me but, as I said, he's picked you as his successor. His experience has told him something about you which I have not yet seen. But I must rely on Mr March's instinct. On his experience. And that means that I must trust you to be up to this job.'

'Thank you, sir.'

'You grasp what I'm trying to get at?'

'I believe so, sir.'

'Good,' Sir Edward said. 'Now, you're at a decided disadvantage here today.'

'Sir, I hope to have more time to prove myself.'

'So, you want to continue on this case?'

'This case?' Day had thought they were still talking in broader terms.

'Yes. This is perhaps more than you should have to shoulder so soon after arriving. The murder of one of your fellow detectives . . . I can assign someone else and there would be no shame in it for you. Blacker or Tiffany can do it. They knew Little better than you did.'

'Sir. With all due respect, and thank you for your generosity, but it could be that not knowing him might make it easier for me to investigate his death. I have no previous attachment to Mr Little.'

'You have the attachment of a fellow officer.'

'Of course, sir. I didn't mean . . . what I mean to say, sir, is that it might be more difficult for one of the other men to deal with the hard facts of a friend's murder. I would not be troubled in quite the same way.'

Sir Edward pursed his lips and stared at a corner of the office. Day watched him, growing more nervous by the second. Finally, Sir Edward blinked and turned his gaze to Day.

'Perhaps you're right,' he said.

'Thank you, sir.'

'Is there any indication yet, any evidence, pointing to a culprit?'

'Dr Kingsley found needles and thread at the scene, sir. Obviously, they were used to . . . well, to sew Little's mouth shut. It might be worthwhile to track the manufacturer. And there's the trunk itself. Kingsley has the body now, and the trunk as well. I'll be paying him a visit later in the day. Meanwhile, Sergeant Kett and three of the other men are still questioning everyone who was on the platform when the trunk was found.'

'What about the porter who found it?'

'He's being brought over.'

'Good. Let me know what resources you need. Anything at all. This takes precedence over everything else you may have going. Every man here is to be considered at your disposal.'

'Sir, that may not sit well with everyone. I haven't proven myself to be one of them yet.'

'I don't care whether you're one of them or you're a Turkish pasha, they'll jump when you say jump or they'll answer to me.'

'Yes, sir.'

'One more thing . . .'

Sir Edward hesitated and Day braced himself for the question he knew was coming, the question that had plagued his own thoughts since he'd stood looking down at Little's mutilated body.

'Is it him?' Sir Edward said.

'Sir?'

Day knew who 'him' was, but he didn't want to be the one to say it out loud.

'Is it Jack? Is it the Ripper again?'

'No, sir. I don't believe so. Whoever killed Little . . . well, it doesn't match anything we know about Jack or his methods.'

'Good.'

Sir Edward rummaged in a drawer behind his chunk of a desk.

'I nearly forgot. He left something behind for you. For me to pass on to you.'

'Inspector March did?'

Sir Edward nodded and pushed a small, flat, black leather pouch across the desk. Day hesitated before picking up the pouch and opening it. Tucked in against the threadbare velvet lining, a dozen long iron keys were held in place with fabric loops. A single smaller key sat loose on top of the others, clearly added as an afterthought.

'His skeleton keys,' Day said.

'He asked me to tell you that these are the most useful

tools he could give to you. They served him well in the line of duty. I'm told he had quite a collection of keys.'

'What's this smaller key? Is it different?'

'It is. One moment, please.'

Sir Edward turned his head and sneezed. He held up a finger for a moment then turned back to look at Day.

'Excuse me. I thought I might sneeze twice.'

'God bless you.'

'Thank you. The smaller key is for a unique structure at the south-east corner of Trafalgar Square.'

'I can't think of what you mean, sir.'

'You're familiar with the Square?'

'I've been through it a time or two now.'

'It goes unnoticed by most who pass it, but there is a stone column there with a miniature door and window. It looks very much like a large lamppost, but there is enough room inside it to fit a man.'

'And to lock him in?'

Day held the small key up so that Sir Edward could see it.

'Yes,' Sir Edward said. 'It is the smallest jail cell in the whole of England.'

'But of what possible use is it?'

'I don't know that it's ever been used and Inspector March was apparently the only detective to hold a key to it. My guess is that the key served as a totem for him. He wanted you to have it. Perhaps as nothing more than a keepsake. Or perhaps he thought you might see the same symbolic importance in it that he did.'

'I'm honoured.'

Sir Edward turned his head and sneezed again.

'There it was,' he said. 'I knew there was another sneeze coming.'

He blew his nose into his handkerchief and wiped his eyes with the heel of his hand.

'It will be my sad duty to visit Inspector Little's widow this morning,' he said. 'She will have questions and I have no answers for her.'

Day was quiet.

'Go on, then,' Sir Edward said. 'Get out there and bring me a murderer.'

'I will, sir.'

'Remember, detective work is as much about logical deduction as it is dogged footwork. Follow your train of thought and see where it takes you. And Day?'

'Sir?'

'If you don't yet believe in yourself and your abilities, at least believe in Mr March's opinion of you.'

'Yes, sir.'

Day fumbled with the knob before he managed to get the door open and slid out into the common room. It felt bright and airy compared to the close atmosphere in the commissioner's heavy mahogany office.

As Day closed Sir Edward's door behind him, he saw Sergeant Kett entering from the other side of the room, pushing a large man ahead of him. This would be the porter who'd found the trunk on the station platform.

'Got 'im here for you, Inspector,' Kett said.

'Good man, thank you.'

'What's the fuss about?' Blacker said. He stood up from his desk.

'You'll find out soon enough,' Day said. 'I'd appreciate

it if you could gather Little's things for me. I'll want to sort them after I speak to this man here.'

Blacker squinted. He was a short, wiry man with limp, ginger hair and a moustache that curled over his upper lip into his mouth.

'What's happened to Little?'

Day gestured for Kett to take the porter to his desk and he moved his body so that he could talk in semi-privacy with Blacker.

'He's been killed.'

'No.'

'I'm afraid so. There's a strong possibility it had to do with one of his cases.'

'Which one?'

'I don't know. It could be any case, current or old.'

'Who's working it? You?'

'I am.'

Day braced himself, waiting for an argument, but Blacker nodded.

'Whatever I can do to help, you let me know and I'm on it right away. I can't say Little was my favourite, but he laughed at my jokes often enough.'

'Thank you, Inspector.'

'Can't have them killing us out there. Job's hard enough as it is.'

Day watched Blacker walk to Little's desk and open the top drawer, then he turned his attention to the porter and took a deep breath. It was going to be a long afternoon.

3

It was a beautiful afternoon.

The rain had swept out as suddenly as it had swept in, leaving fresh, blue skies behind. The bald man had closed up shop for a bit and now he sat on a bench and watched the children play. St James's Park was crowded with children and their nannies strolling the paths that circled the canal. The bald man watched the little boy at the water's edge. His pocket was full of biscuits and a flock of quacking ducks waddled after him. The boy ran this way and that, stopping when he ran out of breath, letting the ducks catch up while he giggled and hiccupped. He tossed a biscuit and the fat ducks ran after it, competing for the crunchy morsel, their bills clacking. Then it was gone and they were after him again.

The bald man smiled. It was good to see the boy enjoying himself. He looked like he had the first time the man had seen him. So much more pleasant than the boy's more recent tears and bargaining.

A breeze blew through the lime trees and the bald man tucked his hat down lower on his forehead. An unpleasant odour wafted over from the sheep enclosure, but even that was tolerable on such a fine day.

A carriage rolled down the path between the bald man and the boy he was watching. One enormous wheel turned up a stone and chucked it into the bark of a tree behind the bench. The bald man looked with alarm at the fresh scar in the tree trunk. So close that the stone might have injured him. When the carriage had passed, the bald man glanced back at the canal and the boy was gone.

He stood, nearly frantic, and scanned the small clutches of Londoners enjoying the fine, dry weather. There. The boy was at the far curve of the water's edge, talking to a little girl. She was dressed in what looked like her Sunday finery, but the lace at the hem of her dress was worn and the collar was too tight around her pretty throat.

The bald man strolled in their direction, trying to appear calm, forcing himself not to run. His beating heart drowned out the sound of the gravel crunching under his feet. He was still too far away to hear what the boy and the girl were talking about. What was the boy saying?

'Here now,' he said.

He was close enough that his voice carried to the children and the boy looked up at him, his eyes wide. The girl looked up too and followed the boy's gaze to the imposing man as he finally drew near them.

'What are we on about, then?'

'Nothing, sir,' the boy said.

'He doesn't know where he lives,' the girl said. 'Are you his papa? You should teach him his street.'

'I should, shouldn't I?'

'I know mine. Wanna hear it?'

The bald man imagined pushing the little girl into the canal and holding her under the water. He could clearly picture her struggling against him, her eyes magnified by the water as they dimmed.

His fingers tingled and his hands shook with the imagined thrill.

Killing the detective had been a necessary evil, not anything he would have considered doing before the accident. But now he thought of it often, relishing the details.

He closed his eyes for a moment, remembering the thick needle as it pierced Inspector Little's lips, the tip of it pressing the skin above the detective's beard then thrusting through, a dot of blood following the black thread back through the dead man's flesh. He pushed the thought away, took a deep shuddering breath and glanced at the clusters of women and children around him.

He looked down at the girl and smiled.

'Aren't you a pretty thing.'

'I am, aren't I? Do you like my dress?'

'I do very much.'

'It's my best one. I have a puppy.'

'That's wonderful.'

He turned his attention to the boy, who was standing stock still, staring at the bald man's shoes.

'Are you ready to go, boy? I should get back to the shop soon.'

'Yes, sir.'

The bald man smiled once more at the little girl. The skin around his eyes crinkled agreeably when he smiled. He gave the appearance of a nice man and, for a moment, he wondered what had become of him. It wasn't his fault, he thought, that he had been driven to such acts. He had once been exactly what he seemed to be: a nice man. His life had been perfect. All he wanted, all he had ever wanted, was to regain that perfection. The boy would help. Oh, how he needed the boy.

He reached for the boy's hand and had to stoop to grab it. The boy didn't squeeze back, didn't actually hold his hand, left it loose in the bald man's grip, but he didn't pull it away either. They were making progress.

'Good day, young lady.'

'Good day, sir. Goodbye, Fenn.'

The boy raised his free hand, but didn't look at the girl.

'Perhaps I'll see you again soon,' the bald man said to the little girl.

'I'm often here in the early afternoon,' the girl said. 'My governess brings me here before tea almost every day unless her gentleman friend comes to call.'

'Then I will make every effort to visit you as soon as I'm able. And perhaps you can tell me your street then.'

He nodded and led the boy away. When they had passed out of the girl's sight, he frowned and gazed down at the top of the boy's head.

'You told her your name?'

'Yes, sir. I thought there wouldn't be no harm in it.'

'Hmm. From now on, you'll keep your name to yourself, unless I tell you it's all right to share it.'

'Yes, sir, I will.'

'Good lad. We're getting along just fine, aren't we?'

'Yes, sir,' the boy said.

The bald man saw a tear fall from the boy's downturned face and splash in the dust on his shoe. The man sighed and said nothing, looked away into the branches of the trees as they passed down the path.

He would work harder to make the boy happy. A little more work, a little more time, eventually the boy would accept his new life as if he had always been with the bald man. The boy was young and he would forget his old life.

But what if it never happened? The bald man tried to push the unwelcome doubt from his mind. It would happen. The boy would be happy again and smile at the man. He was sure of it.

The thought of having to find another boy was almost unbearable.

4

The detectives stopped chattering and all heads turned towards Sir Edward, who stood in his office door holding a cigar box.

'Thank you all for taking the time to meet today,' he said. 'Most of you have no doubt heard that Detective Inspector Little has been found dead. He was murdered.'

Sir Edward waited for the wave of excited murmurs to subside and then set the box on an empty desk in front of him and held up his hand.

'The first question I know you all have – in fact, the question I had – is whether this is the work of the Ripper. Our own Inspector Day assures me that it is not.'

Sir Edward gestured at Day, who nodded.

'But,' Sir Edward said, 'although it may not be Jack himself, it may very well be the work of that dissatisfied citizenry who routinely jeer at us in the streets. It's true that the frightened people of London have begun to calm. After all, there has been no renewed activity that we're aware of from the Ripper. But there is still anger directed towards you, towards us, I mean, for our inability to solve that most important mystery. And I'm afraid a very great deal of anger was directed towards Mr Little's corpse.'

'Why are we here?' Inspector Tiffany said. 'All due respect, sir, why aren't we out there hunting the blighter down?'

Sir Edward nodded. 'We are, all of us, inclined towards a certain degree of disorganization. This job requires us to be out and about in the city and it's a rare occasion when we gather. This needed to be such an occasion. One of us lies dead.'

Inspector Tiffany looked down at the top of his desk as if in mourning, but Day suspected he was simply embarrassed by the mild rebuke.

'It would behove us all,' Sir Edward said, 'to pay respect to Mr Little. If you've the means to contribute a bit to Little's family – and there's no shame in it if you haven't – I'm sure they would appreciate your generosity. This box on Inspector Gilchrist's desk will be here for the rest of the day and if you've something you can spare to put in it I'll take it round to his widow.'

He drew a five-pound note from his waistcoat pocket and placed it in the box as if it were made of porcelain.

'Meantime, Inspector Day will be heading up this investigation.'

At that, there was an angry swell of voices and Sir Edward held his hand up again.

'I know,' he said, 'that you are anxious to cooperate with him, but please save your comments until I've finished.'

Day felt a warm blush spread up from under his collar. He hoped it wasn't noticeable. Of course, nobody in the room was anxious to cooperate with him. Every one of them, he was sure, wanted to work the case and every one of them was justifiably unhappy that the youngest and least experienced of them had been put in charge.

'Because you are all so busy and because we are so seldom gathered together like this,' Sir Edward said, 'many of you may not have made Mr Day's acquaintance. I'm afraid I have not taken the proper time to make formal introductions, but I would like to remedy that oversight here and now. Detective Inspector Day was a constable, and then briefly a sergeant, in Devon and was brought up by Inspector March upon his retirement. He has been with us for a week and, so far as I have observed, he is an exemplary addition to our Murder Squad.'

Day felt the blush move to his cheeks.

'He has every qualification necessary to solve Mr Little's murder and I have chosen him to do so. If you disagree with my decision, you may take it up with me, not with him. I will take your comments now.'

There was a low rumble that passed through the room, but nobody spoke up.

'Good. Now, all of you knew Mr Little. Some of you may have something of value to contribute to Mr Day's investigation and, if so, I would like you to speak with him when we're done here. Mr Day . . .'

Sir Edward turned to Day and held out his hand, then swept it across the room.

'This is your squad. These men are at your disposal. I trust you will not take them away from their existing cases if you don't need to, but if you do decide it's necessary . . . well, then, I'm sure they will cooperate without complaint. Do you hear me, Mr Tiffany?'

'Yes,' Tiffany said. 'I hear you.'

'Have you met Mr Tiffany yet?' Sir Edward said.

Day nodded.

'Then you have no doubt already decided how best to put him to use.'

Sir Edward looked out over the room and drew a deep breath. He let it out slowly and his beard fluttered.

'There are eleven of you now. The loss of Inspector Little hurts us. It hurts us a great deal. You all depend on each other. You cannot function as single police officers any more. Whether you've realized it yet or not, you are soldiers, and soldiers work as a unit. Mr Boring.'

Oliver Boring sat up straight and his ample stomach pushed his desk an inch away from him.

'Sir?'

'I just said that there are eleven of you, but I only count ten. Where is Inspector Gilchrist?'

'Patrick, sir? I don't know, sir. He's always busy, always hopping, you know.'

'Apparently so. I have just realized that Mr Gilchrist is the only one of my detectives I've yet to meet.'

Day glanced at Gilchrist's desk. It was the cleanest of all the desks in the squad room. In fact, Day was sure nothing had been moved on that desktop in the past week.

Sir Edward's brow creased and he sniffed. He turned his back and drew a handkerchief from his trouser pocket. The detectives looked around the room at each other and Day recognized that there was something being silently communicated between them. After a moment, Sir Edward turned around to face them again.

'I apologize,' he said. 'I've got a bit of a chill and thought I was going to sneeze just now. What was I saying?'

Tom Wiggins cleared his throat.

'You was sayin' Patrick Gilchrist is the one you ain't met yet,' he said.

'So I was. That, in itself, is bothersome, but it is particularly so on a day such as this. Are we sure he's quite all right? Has anyone seen him in the past twenty-four hours?'

He held up a finger and turned away again, his handkerchief flying to his nose. Day watched the detectives. Every man in the room looked at Inspector Gilchrist's spotless desk. Then they all looked at one another again. He had met barely half of them in the course of the week and spoken to maybe three of them. They were busy, in and out of the building at all hours, and there had been no time for niceties. But he knew them by their desks. He had memorized where each of them sat, so that he would be able to talk to them in the future without confusion. He knew Oliver Boring, of course, and Jimmy Tiffany. He knew Michael Blacker and tiny Crockett O'Donnell. This was the first time he'd laid eyes on Tom Wiggins. He glanced at the other desks, doing his best to associate these faces with the names he already knew: Inspectors Alan Whiteside, Waldo George, Waverly Brown. There were so few of them. And there was so much death for them to deal with.

And he suddenly understood something about them.

If there was one thing Day felt he was good at, it was reading people. He had an honest face and most people opened up to him easily but, even when they didn't, he was able to read their expressions, no matter how they tried to compose themselves. This ability made it easy for him to trust others and that often led to the mistaken belief that he was naïve.

But he wasn't naïve.

He waited for Sir Edward to turn back around.

'That sneeze won't leave me,' Sir Edward said. 'While we wait for it to present itself, who has seen Mr Gilchrist?'

'I have, sir,' Day said. 'He was by earlier this morning. Hot on the trail of a dangerous criminal. He asked me to tender his apologies.'

'A dangerous criminal, you say? I suppose there's no better excuse. But please tell him that I'd like to see him at his earliest convenience.'

Sir Edward looked down at the cigar box on Gilchrist's desk. He drew in a deep breath before looking up at the room again.

'You are my Murder Squad,' he said. 'You were all chosen for this unit because you have demonstrated exemplary skill in solving crimes. You are among the best that Scotland Yard has to offer. Therefore, you are the most qualified to solve the worst crimes in London. Many of you are still carrying cases having to do with robbery, missing persons, assault, and the like. For eleven of you to try sorting out all the murders in London is a difficult task. Perhaps an impossible one. But for you to take on the burden of every crime is ridiculous. Your morale is already low and Mr Little's fate can do you little good in that regard. In addition to helping Mr Day with this case, if he so deems, you will also sort through your files and remove anything that doesn't have to do with murder. You are to deal with no cases that are not to do with murder. You are experts on murder now.'

'What makes us experts on murder?' Oliver Boring said.

'I do,' Sir Edward said.

'Now, when I arrived here,' he said, 'I asked that you limit your duties and take on no work that wasn't to do with fatalities. It was my expectation that you would gradually work your way through your cases and be left with nothing but murders. That has not happened. Your workloads are simply too large. And so I now ask you to take every case that is not a murder across the hall and give it to the sergeant on duty there. He will pass those cases along to the other detectives. Or to the many constables whose job it is to deal with common crimes.'

'Sir, the other detectives've got their hands full with the dockworkers' strike. They ain't got no more time than us.'

'No. You're right, they don't. But murder trumps all. You are my elite detectives, the select few chosen to excel at solving the most heinous of crimes. And, beginning today, you will act the part. A member of my Murder Squad has himself been murdered and that will not do. You will find the man responsible for this crime and he will pay.'

He waited for his words to sink in, nodding almost imperceptibly to himself.

'Take care,' he said. 'I cannot afford to lose another man.'

He opened his mouth as if to say something more,

but then turned without another word and closed himself in his office.

A moment later, Day jumped at the sound of a hurricane-level sneeze that shook the walls of Sir Edward's office.

5

'Well done, old man. But how did you know?'

Day turned to see Inspector Michael Blacker staring up at him, a mischievous grin at play beneath the limp ginger moustache.

'How did I know what?'

'That won't do, old boy. Nobody's seen Gilchrist round here since he upped to Wolverhampton last year. Heard he's a bona fide shopkeeper there now. But you knew he wasn't here and you carried on our little joke with Sir Edward. How did you know?'

'Intuition, I suppose. The behaviour of everyone since I arrived as regards Mr Gilchrist and his empty desk. You might want to make it look like it's being used if you want to continue pretending he's here.'

'But that's just it. Patrick was the most cleanly of the lot of us. That desk looks just the same as it was when he was here.'

'I think that's why he left us,' Tom Wiggins said. He walked over to stand with Day and Blacker. Oliver Boring and Ellery Cox followed behind him. Boring reached out and clapped Day on the shoulder.

'Work here was too untidy for the likes of him.'

'A nice little shop in the Midlands is what a personality like his calls for,' Cox said. 'Probably serving tea to old ladies at this very moment.'

‘Discussing the weather, they is.’

Wiggins minced about the room and pitched his voice high, mimicking an old Black Country woman.

‘Oh, it’s quite brisk out today, don’t you think, Mr Gilchrist.’

‘If it’s brisk you want,’ Crockett O’Donnell said, ‘then you’ll want a holiday in London right about now.’

‘Oh, did you know I used to be a London policeman?’ Boring said. Day was sure Gilchrist couldn’t possibly have sounded like Boring’s lisping impersonation. It was more likely a sign of contempt. One of their own had packed up and left, his tail between his legs. Gilchrist had failed. There was probably a certain amount of fear in Boring’s mimicry: *There but for the grace of God go I, and do I have what it takes for the long haul?*

‘Why, let me tell you about a grisly murder I saw there, Mrs Dalrymple,’ O’Donnell said. He, too, had pitched his voice high and sounded much like a teenage girl.

‘Oh, my, no. That sounds dreadfully . . . well, dreadfully dreadful, Mr Gilchrist.’

‘More tea, then?’

‘Yes, please. And some for my dog as well.’

By now the other men were laughing despite themselves at the impromptu play being enacted by Boring and O’Donnell. They were all exhausted and worried and they had lost a colleague. The laughter eased the pressure in the room. Day was laughing along with them, despite never having met Patrick Gilchrist. A small part of him, the part that was always the outside observer, felt silently pleased to be included.

'But why you?' Wiggins said. His voice had returned to its normal pitch.

The laughter gradually died and the detectives' eyes all turned towards Day.

'Pardon?' he said.

'Why did Sir Edward choose you for this one? You didn't even know Little.'

'I was first at the station when the trunk was opened. I don't think there's more to it than that, but I have to think it's something of a relief for you, since all of you are so overworked. I don't have many cases yet and have more time to dedicate to this.'

'There's time and there's skills,' Ellery Cox said. 'The one's of no use if you haven't the other.'

'Go to it, then,' Tiffany said. 'Just don't come to me when you get stuck. I've plenty enough to deal with.'

'Little was one of our own, Jimmy,' Cox said, 'and he still deserves the best we've got. Not a fresh-faced kid. No offence intended.'

'How do we know Day's not the best we've got?' Blacker said. 'He could be.'

The others stopped arguing and looked at Blacker. There was a long silence. Finally, Tiffany cleared his throat.

'I suppose we'll find out, won't we?' he said.

He walked back to his desk, sat down and began sorting files. One by one, the others followed suit, returning to their desks, until Day and Blacker were left standing in the middle of the squad room alone.

'Thank you,' Day said.

Blacker shook his head.

'Don't prove me wrong,' he said.

6

Nevil Hammersmith lit a cigarette and took a deep drag. He blew the smoke upward and inhaled the scent of it. Across the room, Dr Kingsley arranged a freshly laundered sheet on the bare wooden examining table. The table had been washed down countless times with lye and water and the timber gleamed in the light of a nearby electric lamp before the white sheet settled gently down on top of it.

A girl leaned against the far wall of the laboratory hugging a large pad of paper to her chest. Hammersmith estimated her age at somewhere between twelve and fourteen. Her long hair fell straight past her shoulders and her dress was too short; she had clearly outgrown it. She kept her eyes on Kingsley. The girl had not responded to Hammersmith's greeting and Kingsley hadn't made any attempt to introduce them.

The odour in Kingsley's laboratory was almost unbearable, but neither the doctor nor the girl seemed to notice. Detective Inspector Little's body had spent a night and the better part of the next day inside a trunk in a warm train depot and there were no windows in the cramped lab. Hammersmith couldn't blame Constable Jones for leaving immediately after they had delivered the trunk. It would be up to Hammersmith to assist the doctor with his examination.

'Here now, we're ready for him,' Kingsley said.

Hammersmith took another drag of the cigarette and ground it out against the inside of a spittoon next to the door. He positioned himself between the trunk and the girl and made a point of looking the other way as he reached into the trunk. Little's body was solid, heavy like a river rock. The detective hadn't been a thin man in life, and death had somehow added weight. Hammersmith struggled with the legs while Kingsley lifted the dead man from the other side, his hands hooked under Little's armpits. The two men shuffled sideways and gave a great heave. Little flew through the air, bounced once and settled on the table. Maggots plopped loose on to the wood and wriggled around looking for shelter while Kingsley scurried about, straightening the sheet under the body.

While Kingsley busied himself, Hammersmith stooped and peered into the empty trunk. There was a shoe, flattened and wet. Reflected light glistened on the laces. Something small and round, about the size of his thumbnail, was partially hidden beneath the toe of the shoe and Hammersmith poked at it. The object moved. He got a fingernail under its edge and peeled it away from the bottom of the trunk. A thick dollop of congealed blood clung to his finger and a sticky black web stretched out towards him as he lifted the object. He wiped it on the leg of his trousers. Under the green light of the laboratory, the object appeared to be a smooth button, wrapped in fabric and stained with blood.

'Fascinating,' Kingsley said. 'Come here, Constable.'

Hammersmith reluctantly approached the table,

where Kingsley had already removed Inspector Little's jacket. The doctor was carefully cutting the dead man's shirt off. The shirt was rigid and stained brown with irregular patches of its original white showing here and there. Hammersmith noticed a small mustard stain on Little's shirtfront and focused intently on it.

'I may have found something, sir.'

'Something?'

Hammersmith held out the round object and Kingsley peered at it. He picked up a pair of metal tongs from a nearby table and plucked the object from Hammersmith's hand, holding it up to the light.

'It's a button,' he said.

'It doesn't appear to match Mr Little's clothes,' Hammersmith said.

'Very good, Constable. No, I'd say this is a furniture button. From a sofa or a chair, perhaps, or possibly even a mattress.'

'Not from the trunk.'

'No, the trunk is riveted, not buttoned. This may be relevant, Mr Hammersmith. It's a good find.'

'Thank you, sir.'

Kingsley plunked the button into a shallow enamelled dish and turned back to the corpse on the table.

'Now, let's see what Mr Little's body can tell us, shall we?'

'Yes, sir.'

'You're going to be looking for an amateur, I think, Hammersmith.'

'An amateur, sir?'

'Yes, look at the sheer number of wounds here.'

Kingsley paused and looked at the ceiling. He smiled. 'Sheer. Remember that, Hammersmith, sheer. I'll want to come back to that in a moment. What was I saying?'

'Sheer?'

'No, the other thing.'

'The number of wounds.'

'Yes, the number of wounds. This wasn't the work of someone who's killed before. This person was desperate or very angry. I count . . .'

Kingsley stopped talking while he rolled the body on its side. Little's arms and legs remained twisted and stiff. Kingsley rummaged around on a side table until he found a magnifying lens and he stooped over the table, scrutinizing Little's back. Hammersmith craned his neck, surprised that the rolls of fat around Little's midsection hadn't moved when the body did. The back of the corpse was bruised a deep purple, mottled with black around a ring of pale white where the body had rested against the bottom of the trunk. Already the sheet covering the examining table was sticky with old blood.

The girl followed Kingsley around the table and he murmured under his breath at her, pointing out areas of interest on the body which she seemed to be sketching in her pad.

Kingsley jabbed his finger in the air repeatedly, silently counting, and turned to Hammersmith with a scowl.

'There are at least twenty-two separate puncture wounds here, most of them non-fatal.'

'Lord.'

'Indeed. Little was in the fight of his life. Many of these wounds were shallow and occurred perhaps at the beginning of the altercation, before the killer had committed to the deed. There's a great deal of distortion in the wounds, as well, most likely from Little twisting and turning his body as he struggled with his attacker.'

Kingsley demonstrated by twisting and turning his own body, holding his arms up as if to ward off an unseen assailant.

'I believe this was not a premeditated attack. If I were to guess, I would say the killer made up his mind to murder Little on the spur of the moment and followed through with increasing determination as they fought.'

Hammersmith lit another cigarette and noticed that his hand shook as he tried to hold the match steady. He took a small black notebook from his pocket and endeavoured to take down what Kingsley was saying. Detective Inspector Day would get a report from the doctor when his examination was complete, but early information might help in the investigation.

'Now, I asked you to remind me of something,' Kingsley said.

'You did?'

Hammersmith looked up from the notebook. Behind the table, with its ghastly banquet, a gasogene bubbled quietly. The green liquid inside it cast a faint sickly glow over the immediate surroundings. An enormous jar on the back counter held a pair of thick rubbery babies, joined at the skull. A man's face floated in another jar, the skin pulled taut with nearly invisible wires. Hammersmith could see the man's eyelashes and upper teeth, all carefully preserved.

The girl, seemingly oblivious to the horrors surrounding her, was bent over her pad of paper, a chunk of charcoal in one hand. Her light-coloured hair shimmered with green highlights. Hammersmith felt seasick.

'Yes,' Kingsley said. 'I distinctly remember asking you to remind me of something.'

'What was it?'

'I put it out of my head because you were going to bring it back up.'

'Oh.'

'Well, come on, man.'

'Sheer,' the girl said. 'You mentioned the word "sheer" as you rolled the policeman over.'

Her voice was flat and soft and she never looked up from her pad of paper. Hammersmith moved closer and peered over her shoulder. She had sketched the body and was carefully noting the positions and sizes of Little's wounds on her drawing. Hammersmith thought the likeness was amazing.

'Yes. Yes, thank you, my dear. That's what you'll be looking for, Hammersmith. The weapon.'

The doctor stared at Hammersmith, who shifted his weight to his right foot and licked his lips. He wasn't sure what Kingsley wanted from him.

'The weapon?' Hammersmith said.

Kingsley smiled and nodded.

'Just so,' he said. 'Of course, it's generally impossible to determine the type of instrument used in a stabbing death. I can often tell you how long a blade was, if there happens to be a secondary wound made by a hand guard.

That sort of thing can point conclusively to the length of the blade.'

Hammersmith nodded, but he didn't write in his notebook.

'But this,' Kingsley said, 'this is a slightly different matter. First, you've no doubt seen for yourself that there are no incision wounds.'

Kingsley's eyes gleamed in the room's greenish glow and Hammersmith didn't see any point in correcting him. Hammersmith hadn't noticed anything about the wounds because he had tried hard not to look directly at them. Kingsley went on.

'Every wound on the inspector's body is a stab wound. No blade was ever drawn across his flesh. When we couple that fact with my theory that this was a first-time killer, it becomes remarkable. Was there no hesitation on his part, no stuttering of the blade before it plunged in? And there is ample evidence of a struggle, so why aren't Little's hands cut? We know he tried to stop his attacker.'

Kingsley indicated Little's right hand, gesturing for Hammersmith to lean in for a better look.

'You see? But that is only our first clue as to the murder weapon. Now here . . .'

Kingsley swept his hand across the small table behind him until he found a short ruler. He measured several of the larger wounds. He set the ruler down next to the body and pried one of the wounds open with his fingers, bending over Little's torso.

'Rigor should leave the body within the next few hours and then I'll be able to get in there and tell you more, but even now . . .'

He worked a finger deep inside the body and nodded to himself.

'As I thought. Here, we have our second clue. Those wounds that measure the same width across – in other words, those that were inflicted late in the attack and were the deepest, using the entirety of the blade – those wounds taper within the body. Do you see?'

Hammersmith shook his head.

'No. I'm sorry, I don't understand.'

Kingsley sighed and frowned at Hammersmith. A teacher addressing a slow student.

'The weapon used here was shaped like a spade, sharp at its pointed end, but widening as it neared the handle. And it had no blade. Or, if it did have a blade, that sharp edge was covered or otherwise protected, which is why we find no slashes on the detective's body, only stab wounds.'

'So he was killed with a spade? No, he was killed with a pair of shears, wasn't he? That's what you're getting at.'

Kingsley beamed at him.

'Exactly. The detective inspector was stabbed repeatedly with a pair of shears. They were closed at the time.'

He picked up the scissors he had used to cut Little's shirt off and turned them around to hold them under the handles, bringing his hand down above the body in a stabbing motion.

'Like this,' he said.

Hammersmith wrote in the little black notebook, his pencil flying across the pages.

'So what do you think? We're looking for a gardener perhaps?'

The doctor smiled.

'No,' he said. 'Well, yes, it's possible, but I believe that if you couple the discovery of the shears with the needle and the two colours of thread that were found with the body . . .'

'Yes?'

'The killer was not gardening, but was sewing something right before the attack.'

'Of course. Sewing. Could it have been a woman, do you think?'

'It's possible. A great deal of force was used, but a woman's fury may sometimes increase her strength to an amazing degree.'

'So, Little might have surprised his killer while she was darning something, or otherwise going about her household chores?'

'I've only just started examining the body, but I wouldn't discount the notion. Though we mustn't forget that button you found. It would seem to point to someone who was making or repairing a piece of furniture.'

'A furniture maker?'

'Or an upholsterer, perhaps. It's not definitive by any means. The button may have been in the bottom of the trunk before Mr Little was placed there. Or he might have grabbed at an upholstered chair as he fell, pulling a button off. There's really no way to say.'

'It's a clue, nonetheless.'

'I will try to have more results for you as soon as I can, but at the moment we've narrowed the list of suspects to furniture makers, tailors, seamstresses, nurses . . .'

'Doctors.'

'Hmm. Yes, I suppose so. And virtually every housewife in London.'

'Thank you, Doctor. I'm afraid there are too many wives in the city to question them all, but I will recommend that someone pays a visit to Detective Inspector Little's widow right away.'

'It's a place to start.'

7

The house in Kentish Town, at the edge of London proper, was well beyond the salary of a Scotland Yard detective. It had been a gift from Claire's parents, a belated wedding present, bestowed upon Mr and Mrs Day upon their move to London. Day hated it. He wanted to provide for his wife, not take handouts from his in-laws.

Day often wished, for his wife's sake, that she had married a man who might provide for her in ways Day knew he never could. A man of wealth and taste and social standing. He knew that she had been wooed by better suitors than himself.

There had, as usual, been no available police wagons when Day had left The Yard and so he had stood on the footboard of an omnibus for more than an hour. His legs hurt and the muscles in his left arm were sore from clenching and unclenching against the railing as the horses had clomped their way across ruts in the dirt and cobblestones.

When he arrived home, his forehead immediately beaded with sweat and he removed his hat and his jacket. The weather was unseasonably warm, but Claire had recently learned to light a fire and practised the new skill every day. The parlour was stifling. Claire sat in a high-backed chair, facing the hearth. When she heard the door, she dropped her sewing and ran to him.

'I've missed you today.'

'I'm afraid I'm only home for a meal and a quick wash-up. I'll have to go back out. There's a new case . . .'

He sensed a shift in her attitude. The small vertical worry line between her eyebrows deepened and her chin dipped just enough that her starched collar dug into the flesh under her jaw. Day drew a breath and braced himself for unpleasantness, but Claire surprised him with a quick hug.

'There's always a new case, Walter.'

She stepped away from him, but kept her hands on his elbows. She frowned at him, but he knew that she wasn't angry. She looked perfectly composed from the top of her sculpted blonde hair to the tip of her high-buttoned boots and he wondered at her ability to withstand the parlour's suffocating heat all day.

'Is there anything on the fire yet?'

'Mrs Dick was here. She made mock turtle soup and I watched, but I'm not sure I can make it myself yet. I'll learn.'

Day made a face.

'There was no real turtle available?' he said.

'Don't be ridiculous. We can't afford turtle. But mock turtle tastes almost the same, doesn't it?'

Day winced. The price of live turtle was two shillings a pound and even the pre-packaged variety of the fatty green meat was two pounds a tin. Turtle was for special occasions. Day would have preferred to leave mock turtle out entirely. It was made from gelatinous mutton and didn't truly resemble the taste and texture of the meat it mimicked, but he kept his dislike of it to himself, since

Claire seemed to find the stuff agreeable. He hoped the calf's head had already been removed from the soup. He'd seen enough gore for the day.

'So Mrs Dick has left already?'

It was Claire's turn to make a face.

'I don't like her.'

'Why?'

'She does the bare minimum to keep the place up and she laughs at me when I ask her to show me things. It's not my fault I don't know how to properly mend a shirt.'

Claire had grown up in a wealthy household with a phalanx of servants ready to cater to her every whim. Marrying Walter Day had plunged her into a world where she was expected to take care of her husband and household without the aid of much staff. Day made barely three hundred pounds a year. They could afford Mrs Dick, but there were no servants' quarters in the little house at Kentish Town. Mrs Dick came once a day to help cook and clean and Claire trailed along after her, hoping to absorb some of the knowledge dribbled out by the older woman.

'Did she sew it, then? The shirt?'

'No, I did it myself, but she peered over my shoulder every so often to spy on my progress.'

Claire smiled and went to the chair where the shirt in question was draped, perilously near the fire.

'I've only just finished. Try it on.'

Day removed his shirt and collar and let Claire help him on with the shirt she'd mended. She had a handful of buttons and poked them through, but the holes didn't line up on both sides of the shirt. It bunched and puckered along his chest and felt tight across the shoulders. He hunched himself forward to avoid letting Claire see how short the sleeves were now.

He smiled at her, but she scowled back.

'Don't you pretend to me. Look at this. It's awful.'

'Well, it fitted better yesterday, but it didn't button at all. So we've made some progress, haven't we?'

Claire kept the scowl for a few seconds and then relaxed, smiling back at him.

'Progress, indeed. Just don't tell Mrs Dick. I'll hide this in the bottom of your bureau and we'll never speak of it again.'

'Agreed.'

He reached for her and held her for a long moment. He knew she was unhappy; knew she was bored. The only way he could think to make her happy was to become a success. It was what she wanted for him. Then he could expand their household staff and she could return to the life of privilege she'd grown up with. Not completely, not on a detective's wages, but things would improve. Day knew he could never return to his life in Devon. He needed his wife to be proud of him.

'Why did you marry me, Mrs Day?' he said.

'As I recall, you'd taken a blow to the head. I considered it my duty to keep an eye on you so you wouldn't get into too much trouble.'

'Good of you.'

He winked at her and she smiled.

He let go of her and turned away to put his old shirt back on. Claire took the 'mended' shirt from him and folded it carefully. He was sure it would disappear into the rubbish pile before the week was out.

'Lead me to the dinner table,' he said. 'I'm famished and I have a long night ahead of me.'

8

Constable Pringle was waiting outside when Hammersmith left University College Hospital. Hammersmith's stomach growled and he realized that he hadn't eaten since early that morning. He'd missed both lunch and tea.

'A quick stop at the tailor's and we'll grab a bite,' Pringle said.

'You spend more time at the tailor's than you do on the job.'

'It's been two or three days. Stopping there isn't a daily occurrence.'

'Close enough.'

'Yeah? When's the last time you were there?'

Hammersmith looked down at himself. His blue uniform was dingy and greying. Blood was smeared across the front of his right trouser leg. He reached for his handkerchief, thinking he might at least wipe some of the blood away, but his pocket was empty. His handkerchief had been used to wrap evidence at the scene of the crime.

'I don't remember the last time I was there.'

'Well, it's high time. You have a single uniform and it's seldom cleaned or pressed or cared for in any way. You pay absolutely no attention to your general appearance and it won't do. No woman will want a scarecrow for a husband. You'll grow old in that flat, long after I've moved out.'

'I'm not worried about it, Colin. I suspect I'd be a bad husband anyway.'

'Well, it's true that you'd have to spend more time at home than you do now. A wife will want attention paid to her.'

'Exactly right,' Hammersmith said. 'And who has time for it when there's so much work to be done?'

Colin Pringle opened his mouth to reply, but before he could speak a cry came from behind them.

'Hoy! Coppers! Over this way!'

A huge bearded man who looked as if he'd been left out in the sun too long strode across the road towards them. Up close, the man's green eyes shone brilliantly through the surrounding dark hair. They twinkled with intelligence, belying the man's thuggish appearance.

'You bluebottles is hard to come by, ain't you?'

'Is there something we can do for you, sir?' Hammersmith asked.

As the man drew closer, Pringle took a step back, no doubt concerned about his spotless uniform.

'Can I show you a thing?' the man said.

'What's your name, sir?'

'Blackleg.'

Hammersmith smiled. The name was more likely the man's job description. It meant that he was willing to cross picket lines for work during a union strike. Hammersmith suspected Blackleg had long since forgotten the name he was born with.

'What have you got for us, Mr Blackleg?'

'It's this way. C'mon with me, then.'

They waited for an omnibus to roll past, the horses chuffing and foaming at the mouth, then crossed the road and followed Blackleg to the mouth of an alley halfway down the other side of the street. Pringle leaned close to Hammersmith and whispered.

'Nevil, my shift's long since over. And so's yours. I've got an appointment. Where's the man on the beat?'

It was a good question. London was divided into fifteen-minute segments, meaning that every beat constable was within fifteen minutes' run from every possible spot in the territory he patrolled. Hammersmith still had one of the big wooden wheels that had been used to measure distance and determine the size of each beat within the sprawling city.

'Did you encounter any constables before us, sir?' he said.

'No, sir, an' I looked, you believe me. You're the first I seen.'

'I can't ignore him, Colin.'

'Let him keep looking. He'll find someone else.'

'And if he doesn't?'

'Don't change the fact we're off duty.'

Hammersmith grimaced. He was never off duty.

'Tell you what, you go on and I'll see what's what. I'll catch up to you soon enough.'

'I wouldn't feel right leaving you. What if this bloke decides to take you on?'

They both looked at Blackleg, who stood patiently at the alley's mouth, waiting for their conference to end. At rest, he still seemed coiled and ready to spring. Blackleg looked like he was no stranger to violence and

Hammersmith wondered what other shadowy work the man was involved in, besides crossing picket lines.

'I believe I'd be up to the challenge,' he said.

Pringle raised his eyebrows.

'You're sure?'

'Go on, Colin.'

'You'll be right behind me?'

'I imagine I'll arrive at the tailor's at the very moment you do, if you dawdle a bit along the way.'

'Right, then. I'll see you.'

And Pringle was gone, hurrying back across the street to disappear in the maze of fruit vendors and fish peddlers that lined the walkway. Hammersmith chuckled and joined Blackleg at the alley.

'What happened with him?'

'He had a pressing engagement. Lead on.'

Blackleg nodded and gestured for Hammersmith to follow. Hammersmith hesitated before plunging into the alley after Blackleg. He could make out shapes in the dark, but no details. He drew his billy club from the loop on his belt and stepped into the shadows.

Blackleg was far ahead, silhouetted against the light from the other end of the alley, but Hammersmith knew better than to chase blindly after him. He walked carefully, peering into every dark corner and skirting the crannies in the buildings on either side of him. There were people in here, sleeping away the daylight hours. Perhaps they would awaken at dusk to ply whatever unsavoury trade they practised. Or perhaps they wouldn't ever wake up again. Hammersmith left them where they lay and moved forward.

He emerged unscathed at the other end of the alley, blinking in the sudden light. Ahead of him, Blackleg impatiently beckoned Hammersmith forward.

The East End had been a prosperous neighbourhood, but had fallen on hard times over the past decade. Once handsome architecture was no longer maintained or repaired and the London poor – the working class, the beggars, the pickpockets, swindlers and drunkards – had all begun to claim it for themselves. There were oases of elegance to be found among the homes, and the nearby medical college still brought doctors to the area, but fewer doctors lived here now. Dignified old houses endured an uneasy proximity to some of the seediest pubs and opium dens in the city and students who couldn't afford homes in the suburbs were being edged out by vendors and streetwalkers.

Blackleg led Hammersmith to a row of imposing terraced houses skirted by a black wrought-iron fence. The slate-grey building was dotted helter skelter with small windows and there was a garden area below street level, sunken behind the fence.

Blackleg pointed down at the garden. It was accessible by a series of stone steps that were partially hidden by potted plants on the walk.

'I was settlin' in for a doze down there, right?'

Hammersmith squinted at the other man and pursed his lips. It was a credible lie and Blackleg sold it well, but Hammersmith didn't believe for a moment that he slept on the street or in sunken gardens. No, in all likelihood, Blackleg was an 'area diver', a criminal who broke into homes through their below-ground-level servants' entrances and burgled the lower rooms. There was little doubt Blackleg had been casing the townhouse to make sure nobody was home.

Blackleg didn't miss the accusation in Hammersmith's expression.

'God's truth, yer honour. Any rate, I was down there and I happened to spy a thing through the window that's unsettled me.'

'Looking through the window, were you?'

'Just glanced is all. I'm not a peep. Just had a little glance as I rolled over on me side to get a good sleep.'

'Of course. Go on.'

'Well, look for yerself. Me, I don't quite know what to make of it.'

Hammersmith kept his eye on Blackleg as he descended the steps to the sunken area. It was an ideal spot for the criminal to mug him, but if Blackleg intended to harm him, Hammersmith suspected the attack would have come in the alley.

He squatted on a bed of cedar mulch and peered into the room beyond the window. Within the semi-gloom he could make out furniture: three chairs, a small table, a sofa, all covered in heavy white cloths. The wall to the left was dominated by an enormous fireplace with a marble hearth that jutted into the first third of the room. Above the mantel and dotting the other walls was a collection of recent Impressionist paintings that looked valuable to Hammersmith's untrained eye. A Turkish rug was rolled up in the far corner, unfurled at the end so that the deep blues and reds of the carpet's pattern gleamed in a shaft of sunlight that shot past Hammersmith's shoulder. He turned and Blackleg was standing by his side, watching the policeman anxiously.

'It appears uncommonly well-appointed for a servant's room, if that's what it is,' Hammersmith said. 'But that's hardly cause for concern.'

'Look harder, sir. Look over there.'

Hammersmith frowned and looked again at the massive fireplace. The grate was folded to one side and a set of fireplace tools stood neatly against the stones. Hammersmith counted a bellows, tongs, a poker and a shovel. A selection of ladles and spoons hung from an iron bar bolted to the bricks, and a toaster, its rectangular slots rusted and black with soot, rested by itself on the right-hand side of the hearth. Something worked at the periphery of Hammersmith's vision and he turned his gaze to the black maw of the fireplace itself. *There.* He drew back and looked up at Blackleg, who nodded.

'Now you see it.'

'What is it?'

''Fraid it's a chavy, sir. Too small to be aught else.'

'Why did you go for the police? Why not sod off and leave it be?'

'Told you, sir. I'm right sure it's a chavy. That ain't proper.'

Hammersmith nodded and pushed at the pane of glass in front of him. It gave way. The window was unlocked. He felt along the edge of it for damage and ran his fingers over splintered wood. It confirmed for him that Blackleg had broken into the house, but

Hammersmith kept that knowledge to himself. There was no sense in scaring the criminal away. Blackleg might still prove to be a useful witness.

Hammersmith swung his legs over the windowsill and dropped down into the room. Dust swam aimlessly through the solitary beam of sunlight. Hammersmith was sure that Blackleg had rolled up the rug in the corner of the room, planning to cart it away, before he made his lurid discovery.

'Hello?' Hammersmith said.

He raised his voice and hollered again, louder this time.

'Hello. Is anybody home? Police.'

Silence answered him. The house had the feel of a long-abandoned place.

Behind him, Hammersmith heard Blackleg drop to the floor. He turned and Blackleg nodded at him. The two men walked to the fireplace and Hammersmith knelt on the hearth. He reached out towards the shoe that dangled from the chimney and prodded it with his billy club. There was clearly a foot in it. A body was stuck up inside the chimney.

Hammersmith paused and glanced back again at Blackleg. The other man's expression mirrored his own. The shoe hanging down below the top edge of the fireplace's mouth was small enough to fit in the palm of Hammersmith's hand. They were looking at the foot of a chavy: a dead child.

Hammersmith grabbed the child's ankle in both hands and pulled. Nothing happened. The body was wedged in tight. He braced himself and pulled again. He felt something shift above him.

'Come here and help.'

Blackleg squatted on the marble slab next to Hammersmith and the two men pulled together. The child's trouser leg ripped and the shoe thumped into the ashes below. Both men fell backward on their rumps and coughed as a cloud of ash and dust billowed out at them. A rasping sound echoed through the room and a moment later the entire body dropped from the chimney and tumbled out on to the hearth.

Hammersmith pulled his shirt over his mouth and nose, shielding himself from the swirling ash, and scrambled forward until he was leaning over the body. He wiped soot away from the blackened face and stared heavily down at the face of a boy who could not have been a day over five years old.

Interlude 1

Collier, Wales. Eighteen years ago

Nevil Hammersmith was the smallest boy in the village of Collier. With a piece of coal, he had marked his height on the doorpost of the room he shared with his three sisters and each morning he stood against it. He held his palm flat against the top of his head and moved carefully away to see whether his hand had risen higher than the black smudge on the wood behind him. Each morning his hand was even with the mark. He was almost five years old and he had not grown since his fourth birthday.

His morning ritual of measurement was a hasty thing. His father shook him quietly awake before dawn, six days a week, and Nevil was expected to stumble into his clothes (generally left in a heap on the floor the previous night) and sneak out of the room without waking his sisters. They had housework and chores to tend to on the small farm, but he let them sleep.

Nevil and his father left by the front door. The back door was for the girls. The pigs were kept behind the main house and it was bad luck to see a pig before the day began. His father hung an arm over his shoulder as they walked and Nevil felt proud, grown-up. He pushed away thoughts of the day ahead and focused, instead, on the moment, basking in his father's easy camaraderie.

At the mine, they lit candle stubs and entered the huge main chamber. The overman wasn't anywhere to be seen and Nevil was glad for that. The last time he'd seen the overman it was for a whipping with the yard wand.

Nevil's father checked in for them both and then left the chamber without looking back, headed for the tunnel he'd been working the day before. When he had gone out of sight, Nevil turned and scampered into his own tunnel.

The interior was hard-packed dirt, shored up on both sides by thick wooden beams hammered into the walls at regular intervals. Side tunnels branched out every few yards and ponies trotted past Nevil, pulling coal carts from deep in the mountain. As Nevil hurried forward, the ceiling of the shaft ahead of him grew lower and the walls gradually pushed inward until there was no room left for a pony to travel. He blew out his short candle. There was always the danger of gas pockets down here and the candle wouldn't last long anyway. He moved forward in the dark, feeling for trapdoors ahead of him, closing them behind him before crawling on to each new door. Soon, the ceiling was too low for a grown man to stand upright and, as Nevil neared his post, even he had to crouch and then crawl forward. The walls narrowed until there was barely room for a coal cart in the tunnel.

Nevil hated the dark and hated the cramped tunnels, but he felt pride, knowing that his job was important and that nobody else could do it. No adult in the village could fit in these tunnels when a cart rolled through. And, as the smallest four-year-old (almost five) in Collier, Nevil could squeeze into the smallest spaces of anybody. There wasn't much value in being small. This would have to do.

He reached his post behind a trapdoor and whispered. 'Hello?'

'Is it you, Nevil?'

'It's me.'

'The night's done, then?'

'It's nearly dawn.'

'Did you hear?'

'About the South Drift?'

'Yes. I thought maybe you hadn't heard yet.'

'I heard.'

Nevil's father had broken the news carefully over supper. Three children from the village, barely older than Nevil, had died in a shaft collapse the day before. Nevil hadn't known them well and death was not yet a concept he completely understood, but he had gone to bed shaken and the trio of ashen children had haunted his dreams.

'Have a good day then, Nevil,' Alice said.

He scrunched against the wall as she passed him. Alice was six and would soon be moving to a bigger tunnel. When she was gone, he searched for the warm spot where she had been sitting, but the floor was cold everywhere in the small chamber and so he found a spot of his own and settled in.

It took a few moments for his body heat to warm the damp wall enough that he didn't notice the cold any more. He could feel, rather than hear, the rumble of carts rolling through distant shafts, and he listened for one of the carts to move towards his own tunnel. If a cart came through this tunnel, Nevil would have to quickly open and shut the trap so that the tunnel would remain properly ventilated. That was the entirety of the job: twelve hours of opening and closing this trapdoor, six days a week, for tuppence a day. As he grew, he knew he would move on to larger tunnels. By the time he hit puberty, he would be on his hands and knees pushing coal through these same shafts every day and smaller children would have taken his place behind the doors, listening for his cart.

But he knew that he would never take his father's place in the newer shafts, pounding out the black nuggets and loading them into empty carts to be rolled away down the tunnels by someone else's children. Nevil had no idea how he would escape the mine, but he had no intention of spending his entire life there the way that his grandfather had and the way that his father would. Nevil could see the cycle of life and death that took place down in the dark below the village and he was determined to break it. It could be done. His uncle George had run off to London and joined the navy when he was sixteen. Nevil had never met him, but George had become a family legend, a whisper passed around among the children. Someday, Nevil would go to the city himself and he would find a job he could be good at and he would never return to Collier.

And when he had children of his own they would spend their days in the sun.

He listened to the dark. Water dripped from the ceiling, plonking on to the dirt beside him. Rats scurried somewhere to his left, coming closer then scuttling away whenever he moved his legs. He closed his eyes (there was no point in keeping them open), but he was careful not to fall asleep. If the mine's deputy caught him sleeping, it would mean ten lashes from the overman's yard wand again.

When his stomach began to rumble, he opened his pack and felt for the jam sandwich he'd brought with him. One of the braver rats crawled up his leg, attracted by the scent, and Nevil dropped a few sandwich crumbs on to his lap. The rat was warm and Nevil didn't mind its little claws. He ate slowly, aware that the sound of his own chewing could drown out the noise of an approaching cart and cause him to miss his cue.

When the sandwich was gone, the rat left him and Nevil went back to listening. Listening and waiting. The day ground forward and Nevil opened his trapdoor four times, closed it again each time and returned to his thoughts until he heard a voice on the other side of the door.

'Nevil?'

'Alice, is that you?'

'It's me.'

'Is the sun still up?'

'It's already gone down. I'm late, Nevil. I'm sorry.'

'It's okay.'

'I'll see you in the morning.'

'Have a good night, Alice.'

'You too, Nevil.'

He crawled past her and moved up the tunnel. His father would be waiting for him.

As they left the main chamber, Nevil searched the sky

for Orion's belt and gulped the fresh night air. He listened to the crickets in the stubbly grass beside the road. His father's knobby fingers, black with coal dust, closed on Nevil's shoulder and squeezed gently. Nevil smiled and enjoyed the moment while it lasted. There were still chores to do on the farm before supper and bed, but it hadn't been a bad day. Nevil had been luckier than the lost children of the South Drift. He might still escape the tunnels.

9

French Upholstery and Fine Furniture was a small shop on Charles Street, between Euston Station and Regent's Park, and perhaps a quarter of a mile from University College Hospital. Day had chosen it for its proximity to the scene where Inspector Little's body was found. On his way there, he stopped at the hospital and collected Dr Kingsley, who brought the button found in the bottom of Little's trunk.

A tiny bell over the doorway jingled as they entered. Inside, the shop was dim but pleasant. Two graceful armchairs with high oval backs and brocade seats were displayed on a low wooden platform near the door. A small Gothic Revival table sat between them as if in preparation for tea. The place smelled of sawdust and furniture varnish. Day smiled. The odour reminded him of his father's carpentry shed behind the family house.

At the sound of the bell, a small round man scurried out from a back room. He sported enormous mutton-chops, perhaps to compensate for the sparse growth on top of his head. Wire-rimmed spectacles perched on the tip of his nose. Day resisted the urge to reach out and push them up on to the man's face.

'Gentlemen, gentlemen, gentlemen,' the man said, 'to what do we owe this honour today?'

'Good afternoon, sir,' Day said. 'This is Dr Kingsley and I'm Inspector Day of The Yard. We'd like a moment of your time, if you wouldn't mind.'

'Oh, dear me. Oh dear. Is there any possibility you've only come here for furniture? Any chance at all?'

'I'm afraid not, sir.'

'No chance, you say? You know, I also reupholster older items. Older and newer items. I can reupholster new items to make them look like they was much more dear than they cost you. Much more dear.'

'Thank you, no. We'd like to ask you a few questions. About your working methods and where you may have been last evening. Last evening.'

Day pretended to scratch his nose, covering his mouth so that the furniture man wouldn't see him smile. He had inadvertently picked up the little man's method of speech and was repeating himself.

'Oh, my. My, my, my. I was here, right here working into the wee hours, I was.'

'Of course you were,' Kingsley said. 'You mentioned just now that you are in the habit of reupholstering furniture? I suppose you use needles, thread, that sort of thing in your work?'

'Of course I do. Of course. Needle and thread are the very foundation of the upholstery trade. And fabric, of course. Fabric and wood and iron. Mustn't forget those. Fabric and wood most especially. Needle and thread and fabric and wood.'

'Yes. I wonder if you might let us take a look at some of the tools you use in your very interesting trade.'

'And iron. Did I forget iron? There's a great deal of it

used in some styles of furniture, you know. Not all, but some.'

'You did indeed mention iron.'

'Oh, good. Wouldn't do to forget. Wouldn't do at all.'

'No, I don't suppose it would. Your tools, sir?'

'Oh, of course. Please, come with me. Certainly, certainly. Come, come.'

The little man disappeared back through the door in the far wall.

'Our furniture maker seems a bit nervous, doesn't he?' Kingsley said.

'He certainly does,' Day said. 'Certainly, certainly.'

Kingsley smirked and held the door open for Day.

In the back was a workroom, much larger than the shop that clients saw.

'Forgive the mess,' the little man said. 'Wasn't expecting you or I'd have tidied a bit. Wasn't expecting anyone at all today. No one at all. Although, of course, one hopes for a smidgeon of surprise if one can get it. If it comes. If it's good.'

'I'm sorry,' Day said. 'We didn't catch your name, sir.'

'Oh, my. Unforgivable of me. Absolutely unforgivable. Where are my manners?'

Day waited. The little man bustled about, picking up bits of material and setting them next to other things without appearing to bring any order to the space. Giant spools of twine were strung on a series of bars that ran across the wall behind the main workspace. Shelves on the west wall of the room were lined with smaller spools of thread and fine chain stuck on pegs. The opposite wall was covered with bolts of fabric, jutting out on long, wooden arms. A sewing machine was bolted to a stained but solid worktable that filled the centre of the room. The rest of the table was covered with a jumble of fabric pieces and pots and brushes, loose springs and dowels and bins full of buttons. Behind the table, partially obscured by it, the corpse of a sofa squatted, its arms and back exposed, bits of cotton batting stapled haphazardly to its naked skeleton.

'Your name, sir?'

'Oh, my name. Oh, of course. My name is Frederick French. French as in "French Furniture", you see, although too many think I work only with French imports. French imports from France, I mean.'

'I see.'

'Oh, no, no, no. I don't mean that I *do* work with imports. Although of course I do. Of course I do. I'm perfectly capable of working with imported furniture and do so all the time. But I named the shop after myself, not after the country of France, you see?'

'We do see. We do.'

'Good, good.'

'You say you were here all evening last?'

'Yes. I'm afraid this poor Chesterfield was rather badly abused by its former owner and it's taking some time to get it back up to snuff. Poor thing. One shouldn't have children if one wants to own fine furniture. Really, one shouldn't. Children are a bane.'

'Are they?'

'Oh, certainly. An absolute bane. Sticky and messy and always jumping about, ruining springs and wearing the texture off everything within sight. An absolute bane.'

'So you don't particularly care for children, I take it.'

'Not at all, not at all. They're darling little things, I suppose. But we mustn't let them on the furniture. Don't have any myself. Children, I mean, not furniture. I have a good deal of furniture, of course. A good deal. But no children.'

'Has another policeman been to visit recently? Another detective?'

'Never! You're the first. The absolute first.'

'Sir,' Kingsley said, 'your tools, please?'

'My tools?'

'You were going to show me the tools you use in your work.'

'Oh, so I was. Come round here to this side of the table, if you don't mind. Come, come. Easier over here on this side of the table. Don't have to lug it all round there when it's all over here to begin with.'

Day looked at Kingsley, who rolled his eyes. Day understood. The upholsterer was amusing, but communicating with him was a tedious process. They stepped around the end of the table and stood back as French lifted a wooden tub of tools up and on to the table, scattering nails and screws on to the floor. The tub sat off-balance, the end of a short bolt of burgundy linen under one corner.

Kingsley peered into the tub and pulled out a number of items, setting them on the table next to him.

'You don't mind, I hope,' he said.

'Not at all, not at all. Feel free.'

Kingsley picked up a white rubber mallet and held it up to the light.

'Why white?'

'Pardon? Oh, you mean why is the mallet white?'

'That is indeed what I mean.'

'Well, not to mar the furniture, of course. A black mallet would leave marks, wouldn't it? I mean, wouldn't it?'

'I suppose it might.'

'Oh, it would. It most certainly would.'

Kingsley set the mallet aside. Day reached past him and took a small hammer from the tub. It was shaped like a miniature pickaxe, with dull metal points on both sides.

'This looks dangerous,' he said.

'Oh, not at all. Not at all. Perfectly harmless. Of course, one must know how to use any tool. In that sense, I suppose you might say it is dangerous. Quite dangerous indeed.'

Day held the hammer out for Kingsley to see.

'Do you suppose,' he said, 'that something like this might have been used to subdue Detective Little before the murder?'

French gasped and his hands flew to his face. He grabbed his muttonchops in both fists and pulled.

'Murder?' he said. 'Oh my Lord. Murder?'

'No,' Kingsley said. 'Please calm yourself, Mr French.'

The doctor shook his head and took the hammer from Day's hand, frowned at it.

'There was no evidence of any crushing blow,' he said. 'So far as I was able to determine, the only implement used was a pair of shears.'

'Like these, you mean?'

Day reached into the tub again and pulled out a pair of shears, angled near the handles. The blades were well worn and had been frequently sharpened. The handles gleamed black.

'Perhaps,' Kingsley said.

He took them from Day and held them up to the light.

'No, sir. No, sir, my shears never were used for no murders, none ever. Oh, my Lord.'

'Mr French,' Kingsley said, 'you may want to ease your grip on your side-whiskers before you pull them entirely from your face. We are here to ask questions of you, not to accuse or incriminate you.'

Day put a hand on the little man's shoulder.

'We really just need your expert opinion, sir. You can be of great service to the Metropolitan Police Force and to all of London.'

French looked at him and let out a long breath. He loosened his grip on his cheeks and nodded.

'Be proud to do what I can then, sir. Proud and honoured.'

'Good. That's settled.'

'Shears very much like these, I would imagine,' Kingsley said. 'I would need to perform some tests on them for blood residue before ruling out this specific pair as the weapon.'

Day held out his hand to stop French, whose hands had flown to his muttonchops again.

'It's quite all right,' Day said. 'Dr Kingsley is speaking in the hypothetical.'

'I don't mind the language, sir. It's the question what throws me. It's the question of murder, don't you know?'

'May I borrow these?' Kingsley said.

'My shears? Well, I do have a second pair, but I prefer those. I prefer them over my second pair.'

'I don't care to inconvenience you. I could arrange to have them back to you by teatime.'

'I'd rather not. I'd really rather not. But, as you say, if I can be of service . . .'

'I'll have them returned to you forthwith. And these, if you don't mind.'

Kingsley held up a set of long, curved needles, each about four inches long and thick through the middle. They were fastened to a plain white card and resembled metal ribs, torn from a spine.

'My needles? Certainly, certainly. I have many of those. In fact, if you don't mind, I'd much rather you took a dull needle. I have many I plan to discard if you don't need one of my sharpest ones.'

'A dull one will do just fine, sir.'

'Excellent. Wonderful. Excellent.'

'One more thing,' Kingsley said.

He reached into his pocket and withdrew the sofa button. He held it out in the palm of his hand for the furniture maker to see. French leaned in and moved his spectacles closer to the end of his nose. Day watched carefully, ready to catch them if they fell from his face.

'What do you make of this?' Kingsley said. 'Anything unusual about it?'

'Unusual? No, not unusual, I wouldn't say. Nothing unusual about it, except perhaps that it's not attached to anything. This sort of button, you know, this sort of button is not the sort one carries about in one's pocket. No, not a pocket button at all, per se, but meant to be attached to a piece of furniture. Most definitely a furniture-type button.'

'I see. Well, there was very little reason . . .'

'I can tell you that the sofa this comes from is quite old and somewhat out of fashion these days. Somewhat old-fashioned. The velvet has been worn down to nothing, hasn't it?'

'I hadn't realized it was velvet.'

'Oh, yes, at one time. And peach coloured, though you wouldn't know it to look at it now. Yes, once upon a time this was a peach velvet button. Most likely from a peach velvet sofa.'

'Yes, most likely.'

Kingsley's sarcasm was lost on the little man. French beamed up at the doctor and pointed at the button.

'May I?'

'By all means.'

He lifted the button from Kingsley's hand and peered at it.

'I'm not at all sure what these stains are. Teeny tiny black stains dotted all about it and this big smudge here on the side. Not at all sure. Perhaps mould?'

'It's blood.'

'Blood? Oh, my. Blood, you say? Well, yes. Now, if you look at the back of it here, you see there's still a bit of thread attached, which tells me almost nothing because thread is thread is thread, don't you know. But it's frayed quite a bit. I imagine this button drooped from the sofa for a good long while before it was plucked off. A good long time. I would absolutely hate to see the state of this piece of furniture. Clearly not cared for in the least. Why, do you know . . . ?'

French snapped abruptly to attention and pushed his spectacles back up on the bridge of his nose.

'Do you know, I would be willing to wager that whoever owns this piece of furniture . . . well, not this piece of furniture because this isn't a piece of furniture at all, is it? No, it's a button. But I mean to say the piece of furniture this button comes from. The couch it was once attached to, if you take my meaning.'

'We do,' Day said. 'We take your meaning entirely.'

'Good, good. I would wager anything that this button comes from a sofa, which comes from a home, which has children. And more than one child, I should think. This sofa has been abused by children.'

'I hear they're a bane.'

'They are. An absolute bane.'

French carefully laid the button back on Kingsley's outstretched palm.

'I only wish I could be of more help,' he said.

'Think nothing of it. You've given us one or two bits of new information.'

'Have I? How wonderful. Wonderful.'

'Thank you very much, Mr French. We'll be taking our leave now.'

Kingsley scooped up the scissors and the card of needles and walked briskly to the door. He turned and nodded and stepped out into the shop. The little bell over the front door jingled and by the time Day exited the back room, Kingsley was already out of the shop and standing in the street.

'We'll send someone round later today with your things, Mr French,' Day said.

'Oh, thank you. I should hate to lose my tools. They're quite necessary to my work. Absolutely essential, really.'

'Of course.'

'I suppose I can make do for a bit. Glad to be of use to The Yard, you know, always glad to be of use.'

'Thank you again, sir.'

Day shook his hand and hurried out of the shop. He joined Kingsley at the kerb.

'You do know he wanted to send you out with a used needle, rather than his new ones,' Day said.

'Why do you think I left so briskly? I don't want an old needle. I want these.'

'Why does it matter?'

'I want to see how easily they puncture flesh.'

'Oh.'

'They're thick, you see. Quite a bit thicker than a normal needle.'

'Do you think this was the type used on Mr Little, then?'

'No. The needles I found at the scene were of a different sort.'

'Then why take these at all?'

'I like to be thorough, my boy. I may learn something from these that will shed light on something else entirely. Solving this crime is important, of course, but crime doesn't stop and the more I know, the better prepared I am. Evidence never lies, but it's up to us to interpret correctly what it says.'

'I see. At any rate, it doesn't look as if our Mr French had anything to do with Little's murder.'

'Not in the least. A more harmless specimen I've never laid eyes on.'

Day nodded.

'Certainly, certainly,' he said.

Kingsley chuckled and waved Day into their waiting carriage.

10

'Dash it all, anyhow,' Constable Pringle said.

Lately, the tailor's shop seemed to be closed more often than it was open. Pringle tried the door again, but it was locked tight and the interior of the little store, visible through the big plate-glass window at the front, was dark. He sighed and rubbed his chin, deciding whether to wait for the tailor to return.

'Was you talkin' to us, love?'

Pringle turned and nearly bumped into two women who were standing directly behind him.

'Pardon me,' he said. 'No, I'm afraid I was talking to myself. Must be going mad.'

He smiled his most charming smile. The two women were clearly prostitutes, but the taller one was pretty, if one looked past the livid scar that ran down her cheek. The other woman, the short one, seemed more aggressive and Pringle liked that. She was the one who had spoken.

'Everybody talks to themself,' the short woman said. 'What separates us from the beasts, don't you know?'

'Perhaps it does at that, ma'am.'

Pringle tipped his hat at them. 'Now, I don't mean to be off-putting, my dear ladies, but you may see by my uniform that I am the law.'

'Yes, but the law's got needs like any man, don't he?'

'True. Very true. And I appreciate your noticing. But my personal needs are filled quite well at the moment, and I'm afraid it's my solemn duty to wag my finger at you and send you on down the road so you may think on the error of your ways. That, or I have to run you in for looking after the needs of strangers. I don't think any of us would enjoy that.'

'Just as well,' the short one said. 'We prefers 'em with beards anyway, don't we, Esme.'

'That we do,' Esme said. 'But you're very nice, anyhow. For a bluebottle.'

Pringle smiled at her again. Her scar was actually a bit fetching. Hinted at a hard life and a stubborn nature. *Character* is what he'd call it.

'Thank you,' he said. 'Likewise, I'm sure.'

'We'll be on our way, then.'

'And I will be on mine,' Pringle said. 'You ladies have a lovely evening.'

He watched the prostitutes walk away from him down the street and shook his head at the unfairness of life. The company of two such interesting women would have been fun. But it wouldn't do to be seen in uniform in their company. The uniform might be taken away from him.

At the thought of his uniform, he glanced once more at the locked door of the tailor's shop and shook his head.

Life, he thought, ought to work itself in a man's favour more often.

11

Constable Nevil Hammersmith stood at the foot of the stairs that led up to the main house. From here he could direct the other police as they arrived. He had explored the entire house without finding anything of interest, but two other constables had rolled out the Turkish rug and were looking for clues. He watched them work, but his mind was elsewhere.

Blackleg had disappeared soon after they'd dragged the boy's body from the chimney. His parting words before climbing back out through the window were, 'Don't you worry, bluebottle, I'll find the man to answer for this.'

Hammersmith felt restless, hemmed in by the crime scene. He wanted to be there when the chimneysweep was found, wanted to confront him, look him in the eye, make him understand his crime.

'The body was found in the chimney?'

Hammersmith turned to see Dr Kingsley descending the stairs. The girl from his laboratory trailed silently behind. The doctor nodded at Hammersmith and glanced at the fireplace.

'You're in charge here?'

'At the moment I am,' Hammersmith said.

'I'm Kingsley. Hope I haven't kept you waiting long.'

'We've met, sir. Just today, actually.'

Kingsley peered at Hammersmith and nodded. 'Of course, Constable Hammersby, no Hammersmith. I apologize. I've been learning about furniture. Far more interesting than you might think.'

'Yes, sir, I'm sure it is. Thank you for coming. The body was wedged in part of the way up there.'

'Well, let's see what we can discover.'

Kingsley crossed the room and laid flat on his back on the hearth. He slid across the marble until his head was in the fireplace. From across the room, Hammersmith could see part of the way up Kingsley's left trouser leg. The doctor's garter was worn out and his stocking had holes. Someone at home hadn't kept up with the mending.

Kingsley's girl had already taken up a post in the farthest corner of the room with her arms folded, clutching her pad of paper to her chest. Hammersmith waved her over.

'Hello, again,' Hammersmith said.

The girl nodded. Her thin hair was light, almost blonde, and her eyes, when she lifted her head to look at Hammersmith, were too large for her narrow face.

'What's your name?'

The girl stared at Hammersmith's shoes.

'Are you a student of Dr Kingsley's? At the college?'

Hammersmith heard a giggle, but the girl's face was hidden behind a golden sweep of hair and the sound was abruptly stifled. He smiled, pleased to have flattered the girl that she might be older than she appeared.

'Ah,' Hammersmith said. 'You're his daughter, aren't you?'

The girl nodded, her hair swinging back and forth between them.

'Why aren't you with your mother? Or at school somewhere?'

'Fiona!'

Kingsley's voice echoed up the chimney and back down, booming from the mouth of the fireplace. The girl jumped and turned around, hurrying to the hearth where her father's legs were still the only visible parts of him.

'My scalpel, please,' Kingsley said. His voice filled the room, causing the other two constables to stop what they were doing with the rug and watch the unmoving legs, waiting to see what would happen next.

The girl, Fiona, opened the black satchel that sat next to her father's legs on the giant slab of marble. She dug around in the bag for a moment before producing a short blade, which she carefully placed in Kingsley's questing hand. The hand disappeared back into the fireplace.

'Paper. Quickly, girl, I can barely breathe in here.'

Fiona opened her sketching pad and tore out a blank piece of paper. It was snatched up by the hand. A faint scraping sound filled the room, then the legs on the hearth began to wriggle and dance as Kingsley slid himself slowly back into view.

Kingsley moved carefully, the torn piece of paper balanced on his chest. In the middle of the paper was a small pile of black dust. As soon as Kingsley's arms were free, he grabbed the paper and folded it over on itself again and again until the black dust was completely contained, then he sat up and took a deep breath. His face was smudged with soot and his wild grey hair was streaked with black.

Kingsley sat for a long moment, staring at Hammersmith. The girl busied herself with the pad of paper, minding her own business.

'It's been a busy day for you,' Kingsley said. 'And your colour's not good. Have you eaten?'

'Thank you, sir. I'm not hungry.'

'The laboratory . . . Inspector Little's corpse. That was unsettling, wasn't it?'

Hammersmith shrugged. 'Murder's never pretty, sir.'

'Of course not,' Kingsley said. 'But that was perhaps a bit worse than other cases you may have seen before. The number of maggots I found in Little's corpse was unprecedented in my experience. Particularly in the region of his crotch. Normally, flies will be drawn to a body's orifices almost immediately upon death, but they're drawn to filth as well. The man's hygiene must have been . . .'

'What's going on here, then?'

Kingsley and Hammersmith turned to see Inspector James Tiffany peering in through the open window at them. Tiffany squinted at the small body on the floor and withdrew his head. A moment later he bustled down the staircase behind Hammersmith.

'Inspector Tiffany,' Kingsley said, 'the constable and I were just discussing venereal maggots and the importance of regular meals.'

'Lovely,' Tiffany said. He turned to Hammersmith. 'Perhaps you would be so good as to tell me why we're here, Constable.'

'Of course, sir.'

'And you, doctor, get up off the floor. You look a fright.'

Kingsley frowned and clambered to his feet. He brushed off his shirt with both hands, smearing more soot down the front of it. The doctor didn't touch his wild streaky hair and Hammersmith thought he might have given up on it in advance as a hopeless cause.

'Sir,' Hammersmith said, 'I was passing by and saw the body of a child – well, his foot at least – hanging from the fireplace here.'

He had decided to leave Blackleg's involvement out of it. Tiffany was the most rigid of The Yard's inspectors and Hammersmith suspected the detective would stop listening as soon as he heard that a criminal was involved in the body's discovery.

'So you sent for an inspector.'

'Yes, sir. It all seemed very suspicious to me. The house is empty and there's something . . .'

'And you sent for the doctor here, as well?'

'I did, sir.'

'Well, you've certainly been busy.'

'Sir?'

Tiffany sighed again and gestured at the floor. Hammersmith turned around and saw Kingsley crouched over the body, probing the boy's throat and chest and armpits, his fingers darting here and there under the boy's shirt. Kingsley angled a mirror so that it caught the dying sunlight in the room and cast it on the boy's face, then he peeled back the boy's eyelids and leaned in close. Twice he turned the boy on his side and pointed out some matter of interest to Fiona, who had her pad open and was sketching furiously.

'Hammersmith, are you aware that Inspector Little was found dead today?' Tiffany said.

'I am, sir.'

'Do you feel that this is making good use of the doctor's time, when he might instead be leading us to Little's killer?'

'Sir?'

'You found this corpse in the chimney, correct?'

'Yes, that is correct.'

'Do you have any doubt, whatsoever, that this was a chimney climber, engaged in cleaning out the flue? That he got himself stuck up there and suffocated to death?'

'I don't see how . . .'

'Well, Doctor?'

Kingsley looked up from his exploration.

'This was most definitely a case of suffocation. I found fingernails embedded in the bricks in there, so I believe I can say that he struggled a good bit before succumbing. I'd guess the boy's been dead for quite some time, but there's very little insect colonization here. The conditions in the chimney have preserved the body and begun the process of mummification, rather than putrefaction. An exact day and time of death will be difficult to pinpoint, but I'm happy to take the body back to my laboratory for further examination.'

'No. Thank you, but that won't be necessary,' Tiffany said. 'None of this is necessary in the least. Constable Hammersmith has exceeded his duties.'

'This boy couldn't have been older than five or six,' Hammersmith said.

He didn't look directly at Jimmy Tiffany, and he kept his voice down. If he betrayed any emotion, he was sure Tiffany would see it as a sign of weakness.

'I appreciate your zeal, Constable. But surely you see your mistake here.'

'My mistake, sir?'

'You must stop thinking of this body as a boy. This is a labourer. A chimney climber, in the employ of a sweep, whose job it was to climb the inside walls of this chimney and clean it out. This person was doing his job and he had that job because of his small size, not because of his age. His age is irrelevant here.'

'Surely not, sir.' Hammersmith was unable to rein in his temper any longer. 'His size is directly related to his age. This is completely illegal. Small children are stolen from their parents by sweeps for this very purpose. They're used and cast aside when they grow too large to do the job properly. This is not some instrument of service, as you say, this is a little boy.'

'No, this is a dead end. His employer didn't care enough about him to pull him from the fireplace, nor did his family step forward to ask for help. Nobody cares about this body and it is not our job to take up lost causes.'

'With all due respect, sir, I believe that is exactly our job.'

'Then I'm afraid you will not last long in the Metropolitan Police Force.'

Hammersmith had had enough of proper protocol.

Tiffany had age and experience, but that didn't earn him automatic respect from Hammersmith.

'If the job of The Yard is to look the other way when we encounter dead children, then I have no interest in lasting long. Sir.'

Hammersmith waited, braced for the dressing down he expected would come next, but Tiffany's expression softened.

'I've been at this a while now, Hammersmith. The job can wear you down if you let it. Look, I have twenty-eight open cases on my desk, right now, and all of them come with family members who desperately want closure. They need justice, something they can hang their hats on. And I really do want to give them that justice. But I can't because there are too many of them. Most of the time, I have to hope for a lucky break. Put simply, our job is to uphold the law. We catch, or we try to catch murderers because murder is against the law.'

He walked past Hammersmith and stood over Fiona, who had completed her sketch of the dead boy.

'It's a good likeness,' he said.

He looked at Hammersmith, then down at his own shoes. Hammersmith noticed that Tiffany still hadn't looked directly at the boy's corpse.

'This boy wasn't murdered, Hammersmith. He died. Everybody dies.'

Tiffany cleared his throat and stared at a point somewhere over the mantel.

'You said that it's our job to chase lost causes. And I suppose you're right. But every case that comes to us is a lost cause because we can't allow ourselves to care about a single one. The ones we care about are the ones that take the piss out of us. They are the ones that kill us by degrees. The dead outnumber us and we have no power over them. Our duty isn't to these bodies, our duty is to the Queen and to the law. To the idea of the law. And to the living. Them's the real victims because they have hope and they look to us.'

Tiffany was clearly talking about things that had weighed on him for a long time and Hammersmith was afraid to interrupt. A window to Tiffany's soul had opened and anything Hammersmith said now might cause that window to slam shut again.

'This boy has no family asking us for justice. It's horrible, but the reality is that no one really cares. No one at all. This is a lost boy and nothing we do will change that fact. Our time and energy are best spent solving the cases that can be solved. I'm sorry, Hammersmith. But you've wasted my time and you've wasted the good doctor's time. Have this room cleaned and go home. Get some rest. Tomorrow this hopeless job will begin again, and it will begin again for you every day until you quit it or retire from it. Unless it kills you first, as it killed Inspector Little.'

Tiffany walked to the stairs and hesitated, but didn't turn around.

'Choose your causes more judiciously, Hammersmith.'

Then he took the steps two at a time up and out of sight.

Hammersmith stared at the Turkish rug as the other constables began rolling it back up against the wall.

'He's wrong, you know,' Kingsley said. 'About your duty to the living, I mean.'

The doctor had stood silent throughout Tiffany's long speech, but now he stepped closer to Hammersmith and put a soot-smudged hand on his arm.

'Your duty is to society and the dead have always been a part of society. How we treat the dead says much about us. Tiffany has never been the best that The Yard has to offer. He's too easily overwhelmed and now he's frightened and cowers at the thought of more work. Don't learn from him.'

Hammersmith shook his head, unsure what to think. It was possible he was letting his own history, his time in the mines, cloud his judgement. But a glance at the tiny body on the floor helped him regain some focus.

'How long? You said he struggled. How long was he up there in the dark before he died?'

'I can't say with much certainty, but it looks as if it took him a long time to finally suffocate. I'll know more when I have a chance to examine the fauna nesting within his body. That is, if you plan to pursue this case.'

He watched the constable patiently, but Hammersmith avoided his gaze. He went to the body and knelt over it, moved a lock of the boy's hair and smoothed it back over his head. The boy's forehead was still smooth and pink where his hair had covered it. Hammersmith licked his thumb and wiped away a smudge of grime. The room was quiet. Kingsley and his daughter stood like statues until Hammersmith finally spoke.

'It was difficult but not impossible to pull him from the chimney. Someone could have done it while the boy was alive, but nobody did.'

'The body has undoubtedly shrunk slightly due to the

heat and the closeness within the chimney,' Kingsley said.

'Maybe. But someone left him there to die. This was murder by neglect and that means the law was broken.'

'Should I remove the body to my laboratory, then?'

'Please do, sir. I have no intention of dropping this case.'

'That's good,' Kingsley said. 'That's a good lad.'

12

Day rummaged through the supply cupboard at Number Four Whitehall Place. It was surprisingly free of clutter. He had assumed that Scotland Yard would be as filthy and hectic as the rest of London, but in the past week he had discovered something quite different. Sir Edward had made sweeping changes upon being installed as commissioner. The place was kept clean and neat and, while detectives, sergeants and constables were expected to stay busy, they were not encouraged to treat the place like a home away from home. Sir Edward preferred that his police be family men and that they spend at least eight hours a day at home. Drinking was tolerated, but tacitly frowned on if it became excessive. And a cleaning service was now employed to keep the premises from looking like a bachelor's flat.

Which meant that Day couldn't find an empty box anywhere in the building. He returned to Inspector Little's desk and leaned on it, staring at the piles of paper he'd gathered, until inspiration struck. He ran down the back hall, past Fawkes, the sergeant on duty, and out into the street. Fawkes looked up from his penny novel and said something, but Day was already out of earshot.

The evening was cool and Day had left his hat and jacket hanging on the back wall of the common room, but he didn't notice. He looked to his right and left without seeing what he wanted and, after a moment's consideration, took off at a brisk pace down the right side of the street. A short while later, he stopped at the mouth of an alley and peered down it. He had just about screwed up his courage to enter the narrow passage when he noticed a bulky shape against the outside wall of the inn across the road.

Day looked both ways and crossed the road. Street lamps cast his shadow out over the cobblestones where it broke apart and flowed back together in increments. There was little traffic and the nearby police station meant that prostitutes and pickpockets were scarce here. But Day knew there was one loiterer who had no fear of the police.

A blanket was draped over the crumpled body against the wall so that nothing of the man beneath was visible. The blanket moved up and down, up and down, as the homeless man breathed. Day knelt and spoke softly.

'Sir?'

There was no answer and Day wasn't sure how to proceed. Although they were on a public thoroughfare, the street was this man's home and Day was intruding. Cautiously, he reached out and poked a spot on the dirty blanket. The dancing man came to life, erupting from the pavement as the blanket went flying off to the side. The man was filthy, but fully alert. He held a knife in one hand, pointed at Day. The knife undulated, back and forth, much the way the man himself did every day in front of the police station.

'Mine,' the man said.

Day held his hands out in front of him and took a step

back. He wasn't worried about the knife. The man holding it clearly didn't know how to use it and Day didn't think he would even try. The dancing man was only defending himself, not trying to harm the detective. Still, Day's errand seemed foolish to him now. He had disturbed someone who clearly didn't need any more trouble.

'Of course it's yours. Of course it is. I'm a detective with The Yard, sir. I'd like to ask a favour of you.'

'A favour?'

'Yes.'

'I'll dance for you.'

'That won't be necessary.'

'I know you. You're the one gives me money. You're the only bluebottle gives me money there.'

'Am I?'

'The only one.'

Day kept one hand up in front of him and reached into his pocket with the other. He pulled out a penny and held it out to the dancing man.

'I'd like to borrow your milk crate, if I may.'

The man's eyes narrowed. He was clearly confused, accustomed to having people pay him to go away, not ask for anything more than to be allowed to ignore him.

'My . . . ?'

'Your platform? The crate you dance on every morning. I'd like to borrow it for the night.'

The dancing man looked down at his meagre pile of belongings, partially covered by the cast-off blanket.

'You want my stage?'

'It's just for the evening and I'll return it. And you will

get another shiny new penny for doing nothing at all but trusting me for a few hours.'

'That's the rub, ain't it? Don't trust no bluebottles no how.'

'Not even the one who gives you money?'

The dancing man stared at Day for a long moment and then nodded, dropping his knife hand to his side. His other hand came up, palm out, thrust in Day's direction.

'You gimme that coin first.'

Day held up the penny so that the beggar could see it clearly in the gaslight and then placed it in the man's hand.

The dancing man sidled over to his belongings without taking his eyes off Day. He moved behind the crate and scooted it to Day with his foot. Wary of the dancing man's knife, Day bent and picked up the crate. He straightened up, holding the wooden box in front of him like a shield.

'You'll give it back?' the dancing man said.

'I'll leave it outside the door when I leave tonight and it will be there in the morning when you arrive to . . . well, when you arrive at your post tomorrow.'

'It's too short for the bodies. The long dead ones won't fit in there. Not with their legs on.'

The dancing man stared at Day, waiting for a response. Day nodded as if he understood and took a step backward.

'Ain't crazy, you know.'

'I'm sorry?' Day said.

'I ain't touched in the head like some folk out here is.'

The dancing man nodded his head in the direction of the street behind Day, in the direction of all London.

'Don't got nothin' else is all. Don't wanna go to the workhouse.'

Day nodded and turned to leave.

'I was there already. The workhouse. I was there and they sent me to work for you lot.'

Day turned back.

'For The Yard, you mean?'

'For the long dead. I worked for the long dead. Like you.'

Day felt suddenly tired. Only a week into the job and the amount of craziness was already swamping him. He felt a momentary twinge of homesickness for the narrow lanes of Devon, for whitewashed shopfronts and bicycles and birds.

'They brung the bodies to the place, the place where the long dead wait.'

'The morgue?'

'That's what they called it, but it weren't nothing but tables on tables, rowed up through the place and all too short for them long, long bodies. Their legs all hung down over the edge. Hung down to the floor, but they didn't walk out of there and they didn't dance no more. They never did dance for me.'

'I can't imagine Dr Kingsley would allow you anywhere near his work.'

'Weren't no doctor there. Just us as was rounded up from the workhouse and we cut on them bodies and they was still.'

Day looked at the man. The knife hung at his side,

held loosely as if forgotten. The energy Day saw in the dancing man every morning was absent. The man's effort to find a connection to his life and memories had drained his spirit.

'Rest,' Day said. 'In the morning you'll dance and this fever dream will be forgotten.'

'I'll dance for you, bluebottle. I dance for 'em all, all the dead. Just like you do. Just like you. You and me.'

'You're nothing like me. Go to sleep.'

'I got a choice, is all. Keep me out of that workhouse and I'll show you how to dance. You watch me and you'll learn. See if you don't. Dancin's good. And you gotta do it now 'cause the dead don't remember how.'

Day turned and trotted back up the street as quickly as he could, but he could still hear the dancing man behind him long after he returned to The Yard.

'Dance, bluebottle, dance.'

13

Day was only a quarter of the way through the enormous pile of papers on his desk when Inspector Michael Blacker swung open the gate and entered the detectives' warren of the common room. Blacker had his topcoat draped over an arm and he stopped at Day's desk on his way to the coat hooks at the back wall.

'Still here or returning?' Blacker said.

'What time is it?'

'Coming up midnight. I'd have been back here sooner if there were any police wagons to spare tonight. Always a shortage of those, it seems. What about you? Thought you had a pretty young wife to go home to.'

'I do. I mean . . .'

Day sat back and tossed a sheaf of papers at the larger stack on his desk. The impact made a few of the topmost pages slide off the desk on to the floor.

'There's so much here.'

'Little's files?'

'Yes.'

'That's why I came back. Couldn't sleep knowing someone's out there killing detectives.'

'I had no intention of being here this late. I thought I'd move Little's papers over here and perhaps organize them so that I could start in on it all tomorrow morning, but I had no expectation that there would be so much to deal with.'

'No shortage of crime around here, Day. And no extra time in the day to deal with it all. Never any extra time in the day.'

Blacker waved a finger at Day and grinned.

'Your name is a blessing, Day. I've made a crack without even realizing it.'

Day sighed and bent down to pick up the fallen papers while Blacker finally hung up his coat and hat. Blacker came back to Day's desk and pulled a chair up to the other side of it.

'You want some help with this?'

'Well, I wouldn't turn it down.'

Blacker sat and pulled a folder from the stack.

'You're still assuming Little came upon something in an investigation and that it led to his death, then?'

'I have no idea. This is a place to start. I thought I'd give his family the day to mourn before I call on them tomorrow.'

'Good of you.'

'They may know something, but it would be indecent to intrude upon them today.'

'Of course. What about the scene?'

'The railway station? Kingsley seemed quite certain that he wasn't killed there. I doubt very much I'd find anything more than the doctor already did.'

'If we could determine where he was killed . . . '

'Yes. Or who did it.'

Blacker smiled and nodded.

'Point taken. This is a place to start,' he said.

He opened the folder and began to read. Day rummaged through the papers until he found the sheaf he'd been looking at and resumed where he'd left off. Little's filing system seemed to be completely random. His case files had been shuffled together in no particular order. Day skimmed through case after case, trying to impose order on them, trying to find some possible connection between Little's job and his death.

'What is that stench?'

Blacker was sniffing the air in the closed room.

'I didn't want to sit at his desk, so I moved the files over here.'

'Right.'

'But I couldn't find a box to do it. There's so much here, I didn't want to spend the night going back and forth. There are no boxes anywhere in this building.'

'Sir Edward likes to keep a clean workplace.'

'Clearly. I had to borrow a box.'

He pointed to the milk crate on the floor.

'How can a box stink up the entire room?' Blacker said.

'Its origins are dubious.'

'Well, we don't need it now.'

'I promised the owner I'd leave it outside for him.'

'Outside is a good place for it.'

Blacker stood and picked up the crate. He left the room by the back hall and returned a minute later wiping his hands on his waistcoat.

'We need a window,' he said. 'It'll take all night for this odour to leave us.'

'In hindsight I should have left the box where I found

it. Once I was committed to getting it, I felt I had to follow through.'

'Good trait in a detective. Shall we get back to the business at hand?'

'There's just . . . How could any one man possibly hope to solve so many cases?' Day said.

He waved his hand over the stacks.

'How many do you have? How many cases have collected on your own desk in the week you've been here?'

'Including Little's cases?'

'Just your own.'

'More than a dozen. I'll never solve them all.'

'No, you won't,' Blacker said. 'So which case is most important? Of course, that's been decided for you. The murder of another detective has to come first. But when you've solved that one, you'll have to choose the next most important case from the stacks.'

'But how? How do you decide that?'

Blacker shrugged.

'You just do. Give it time and you'll get a feel for it.'

'And if I don't?'

'Then you'll go back to wherever you came from and probably live a much happier life.'

Day stared at the papers in front of him without seeing them. He looked up when Blacker began talking again and realized that the other detective had been watching him.

'Being an inspector with The Yard is a responsibility and an honour,' Blacker said. 'You keep that front and centre in your mind and it all tends to seem a bit more manageable.'

Blacker grinned his lopsided grin and bent his head to read. Day sighed and did the same.

Judging by Day's preliminary count before moving the files over to his own desk, Little had been working on at least a hundred cases at once and had made almost no headway on any of them. Day tried to organize the files as he went along, creating three separate stacks on his desk.

In the first stack he put Little's notes on cases that seemed to Day to be solvable, things he could follow up on once Little's own unfortunate case was resolved. That first stack, the stack of cases Day wanted to look into, was the largest of the three by far, but as the night wore on, fewer case files made their way there. Day became jaded as he went. There was too much crime for any one man to care about it all.

A rash of burglaries in Highgate had stumped Little for some time. The intruder had entered through half-open windows, often two or three storeys up, only to take small trinkets and baubles. The circumstances seemed to rule out all but an extremely agile child, but a smudged handprint on one window frame had led Little to conclude that a trained monkey was involved. The task of rounding up every organ grinder in the vicinity had apparently been too daunting for Little and, after forming the idea, he had abandoned it. Day made a note to follow up on the case to see if any organ grinders had been contacted and filed the case in his 'probably solvable' stack. But it seemed to have no bearing on Little's death.

The second stack of papers on Day's desk was for

cases that seemed on the surface to be dead ends. Either there were no witnesses or the injured parties were criminals themselves or, in many cases, Little had hit upon a false trail and Day could not see from his scant notes where to go from there. At first, few case notes went into this pile, but it grew disproportionately larger as Day grew more tired and disillusioned.

The remains of a newborn baby had been found behind an apartment wall, again in Highgate. It wasn't uncommon for a couple to hide the miscarried evidence of a tryst, but Kingsley's preliminary examination had led him to believe that the baby was buried after it was born, which made it murder. The couple currently living in the flat didn't seem suspicious and there was no evidence that they'd ever had a child. Moreover, they'd brought the matter to the police after discovering the tiny body, which would seem to point to their innocence. According to the landlady there had been a young woman living in the apartment some years before, but Little had found no leads on her current whereabouts. Day initially put the file in the stack of cases to be looked into, but as the evening went on, he withdrew it and moved it to the 'Dead end' pile.

Many other cases joined it there . . .

A boy named Fennimore Hubbard had been stolen from in front of his home while playing. There were no witnesses and Little had made a notation indicating that he might make enquiries among local chimneysweeps to see if the boy had been nabbed as a climber. Day couldn't see that Little had ever followed up on his own suggestion and the case seemed hopeless, considering how many children disappeared every year.

A prostitute had been cut and strangled to death in the East End and Little had made an alarming one-line notation: 'Ripper?' But there was nothing to indicate that Jack the Ripper had returned to haunt the city and the modus operandi was entirely different. The woman's purse had been stolen, never a motivation for Saucy Jack. The case was clearly unsolvable unless Day wanted to devote all his energy to it.

A third pile was for cases that might have some bearing on Little's death. This was the hardest criterion to judge for, but it was the reason he and Blacker were there.

'I might have something,' Blacker said.

'Little's killer?'

'I don't know. Listen, this man, John Robinson, was found in his bathtub with his hands and ankles bound and his beard shaved off. The razor was also used to slit his throat and was then left in the washbasin, covered in blood.'

'Good Lord.'

'Indeed. The man's whiskers floated all about him in the bathwater.'

'Was he shaved before or after he was killed?'

'I think that would be impossible to say except that . . . wait.'

Blacker paused to continue reading the notes Little had left behind.

'Kingsley cut the victim up and determined that Robinson was already dead when his throat was slashed.'

'How was he killed?'

'His lungs were full of water. He drowned.'

'So the killer slashed the throat of a corpse.'

'And, here, your question is answered. Bits of his whiskers were found in his lungs as well. So he was shaved before he was drowned.'

'And he was drowned before his throat was cut.'

'Someone bound him, shaved him, pushed him under the water and then cut him open from ear to ear with the same razor used to shave him.'

The two men looked at each other across the cluttered desk. Blacker's eyes were wide with excitement.

'Did Little have a clue?' Day said. 'Was he on the trail of the killer?'

Blacker went back to reading, moving quickly through the file, flipping pages over as he read. Day waited patiently. It didn't take long. Little had only left them six pages of notes on the case.

'There isn't a lot here. A bloody handprint on the bathroom tile and a smashed pocket watch that was stopped at midnight.'

'Bizarre.'

'And attention-seeking, don't you think?'

Day nodded. 'Quite. So if Little was close to finding this killer . . .'

'Even if he wasn't, whoever did this might have been watching Little, rather than the other way around.'

'And killed him.'

'Both bodies were ill-treated.'

'In different ways.'

'But strange ways.'

Day tapped on a stack of case files.

'Let's keep looking.'

'This is it, Day. Don't you think so?'

'It could very well be. But we should sift through the rest of this just in case.'

Blacker pursed his lips and returned to the files in front of him, but he appeared reluctant and Day could tell that he wasn't really reading any more. Finally, Blacker stopped and leaned forward.

'I want to talk to Kingsley about this,' he said.

'As do I, but Kingsley is most likely home in bed.'

'True.'

'And if we can sort out the rest of these files, we can both go home to our own beds.'

'Point taken.'

The two detectives read in silence for a few more minutes.

'The killer may have changed his methods because he wasn't able to lure Little near enough to a bathtub,' Blacker said.

'Pardon?'

'I can't stop mulling it over, the possible connections between the two murders.'

'What do you mean?'

'There was a reason Little's desk was located far from mine.'

'Was Little . . . was he disliked?'

'Disliked? I wouldn't say so. But few of us associated closely with him. It was unpleasant to be too near him.'

'In what way?'

'He was somewhat . . . odiferous.'

'He smelled bad?'

'Quite. When I first found you here this evening I

thought that Little had returned from the grave. That box you had in here smelled very much like him.'

'Could he have been killed for that? For a lack of hygiene?'

'What, by someone with hyperactive nostrils?'

'Perhaps by a neighbour who tired of his scent?'

'A neighbour who was so tired of his scent that he killed the man, sewed shut his eyes and his mouth – but not his nose, mind you – and pounded his limp body into the bottom of a steamer trunk, then dragged that trunk to the railway station.'

'It does sound ridiculous.'

'No, I agree that it might be worth following up with the neighbours. After all, I'm the one who brought up his body odour in the first place. I'm simply laying it all out to look at. There's no part of this case that isn't ridiculous in the most morbid way. A foul body odour is as likely a motivation as any, I suppose.'

'Not for a sane man.'

'What sane man does any of these things?' Blacker indicated the mounting stacks of case files on the desk. 'If all men were sane, we would be blacksmiths.'

'I believe I would be a lord to the manor born.'

'Ah, well, if we have that much choice in the matter . . .'

Blacker chuckled and they hurried through the rest of their files. There was nothing else in Little's files as promising as the beard-hater who had killed John Robinson twice in the same bathtub.

'Listen,' Day said, 'whoever killed Robinson, if he killed Little too, what if he killed others? There are dozens of unsolved murders here.'

'You mean he's like the Ripper, he kills again and again?'

'I know it's a horrible thought, but . . .'

The idea of someone who killed from habit and need was a relatively new one and something the detectives weren't prepared to deal with. Murder was usually between spouses or involved money. Crimes of passion were frequent. Prostitutes were killed, bankers bludgeoned, landladies buried alive. Madness was sometimes a factor, but madmen were most often public and demonstrative about their crimes. The Ripper had been something new. He had killed in secret and for no apparent reason. He had done it again and again with impunity.

'No, you're right. If it isn't the Ripper, it's possible there's someone else like him out there, though I shudder to think.'

'We need to look at other cases. It's possible another murder committed by this same person has been looked at by one of the others.'

He swept his hand over the room, indicating the three rows of four desks each. There were nine other detectives in the big room who might be working other murders and have clues that, separately, added up to nothing, but could be put together in a useful way.

'I'll go to Sir Edward first thing in the morning,' Blacker said.

'Let's not bother him yet. He gave me leave to do what I needed to solve Little's murder. I'll use my authority and get everyone to look through whatever they've got.'

'There'll be some who won't like it.'

'I know it.'

'I'll throw my weight behind you. I may not be the most respected peeler in the room, but I think I'm well liked. If I vouch for you, I'm sure the others will cooperate.'

Day smiled.

'Thank you. It means a lot that you're willing to trust me. I'm not sure I trust myself on this.'

Blacker nodded, but he didn't smile.

'I'll be honest with you, Day, there are men here that I'd rather were looking into this. But I trust Sir Edward and if he picked you for it then there must be a good reason and I'll go along. I'm behind you on all this, but I'm not blindly following.'

He stared pointedly across the desk until Day had to look away. When he looked back, Blacker's scowl had dissolved into his trademark grin. The atmosphere in the room was lighter again.

'But you'll find no more loyal hunting dog than me,' Blacker said. 'You point me in the direction of the bird that did this and I'll bring the bloody bastard back to you with his head hangin' out me mouth.'

He winked and Day laughed.

'What say we get a couple of hours' sleep and freshen up? We've got a lot to do in the morning.'

'I think morning is already in progress.'

'If you're willing, once the sun's up and the milk's delivered, I think it would be best if you questioned Little's family, while I handle the neighbours,' Day said. 'You've got a lighter touch and the family might be more open with you.'

‘Will do.’

‘One other thing. Are there any constables we could trust? Smart men who can be discreet?’

‘There’s one or two I can think of.’

‘We may want to enlist them. There’s a lot to track down here and some help would be welcome.’

‘I’d go to Hammersmith first.’

‘Hammersmith? He was at the crime scene this morning. Good man?’

‘He rarely laughs at my jokes, but he’s a born police officer.’

‘Hammersmith it is, then. I’ll see about getting him reassigned when Sergeant Kett comes on duty.’

‘I wouldn’t want to be Little’s killer right now,’ Blacker said. ‘We’ll have the noose ’round his neck by sundown tomorrow.’

Day nodded, but he didn’t smile. He stood and got his hat and jacket from the hooks on the wall and left without a word for the duty sergeant. On his way out, he saw that Blacker had left the dancing man’s wooden crate on a pile of rubbish at the end of the block. He picked it up and carried it to the back door of The Yard and left it there.

14

Constable Nevil Hammersmith didn't return home until after midnight. The flat was empty. Colin Pringle was still out courting with the shop girl, Maggie.

Hammersmith and Pringle shared a two-bedroom flat above a confectioner's shop. The aroma of chocolate and sugar filled the rooms day and night, and they were locked in a constant battle with rats that migrated upstairs and skittered around inside the walls. The entirety of the floor above them was leased by a young man who received a yearly stipend of five hundred pounds from his grandmother. He didn't need to share rooms. Hammersmith and Pringle, being eligible men of no social standing and of limited means, struggled to make their rent each month.

Despite the hour, Hammersmith started a fire. His thoughts returned to the dead boy and he unconsciously studied the dimensions of his own fireplace. It was, he thought, too small for even a child to fit in, too narrow for anyone of any size to shimmy up the chimney. When the fire was going, he put the kettle on to boil. He lifted the teapot and a small tin of tea from the mantel and spooned green leaves into the pot. Pringle generally filled the tin with 'renewed' tea from a street vendor who collected used leaves from people in the neighbourhood. The damp tea leaves were dried, spiced and coloured green with copper. It was weak, but affordable. When the water began to boil, Hammersmith poured it from the kettle into the teapot and put the lid back on. While the tea steeped he paced back and forth through the small parlour.

A piece of paper, disturbed by the breeze he was creating, fluttered at the edge of his vision as he passed by the door to his bedroom. A note was tacked to the wall there and he pulled it down, leaving the tack where it was. He read it and tossed it into the fire. He rubbed the back of his neck and forced his thoughts to return to the case at hand.

He was startled from his reverie by irregular footsteps in the hall and, a moment later, Pringle staggered into the flat and tossed his hat on the well-worn chair by the door.

'Hello, old boy.'

Pringle's face was red and Hammersmith could see a smudge on the knee of his flatmate's trousers. A sober Pringle would never be seen in soiled clothes.

'How's Maggie?' Hammersmith said.

'Oh, my dear Mr Hammersmith, Maggie's fine, all right. Quite fine, indeed.'

'Good to hear.'

'And what are you doing awake and prowling about at this beastly hour?'

'I've made tea.'

'Thank you. I'll have some.'

'Good.'

Hammersmith strained the tea into two cups and set them on the small table under the window. The curtains were drawn back and, outside on the street, sweepers were already hard at work, shovelling horse dung into their foul carts, trying to get a head start on the coming day's traffic.

'There's no milk.'

'Did we drink it all?'

'It was spoiled.'

'You threw it out?'

'Should I have kept spoiled milk?'

'Well, I suppose we'll have more in the morning.'

'Not long, now. Still, there's no milk.'

Pringle shrugged and burned his tongue on the tea.

'Let it sit,' Hammersmith said.

'Easy for you to say. I've already burned myself. Say, did you get the note I left? There was a message sent over from a doctor at St Thomas's this morning. Dr Brindle, I think his name was.'

Hammersmith blew across the surface of the tea and took a sip. He could taste the sharp tang of copper and wished again that they could afford fresh tea.

'I got it,' he said.

'You ought to visit him. Sounds like the old man's not long for this world.'

'There's no sense in it, Colin. He doesn't know me any more.'

'It might do you some good to say your piece to him. Whether he knows you or not.'

'If I get the time.'

Pringle nodded and tested his tea with a finger. Hammersmith was grateful that his flatmate didn't press the issue. He hadn't visited his father in months. The last time he'd been to St Thomas's Hospital, his father had called him a stranger and cursed at him, the stream of invective finally halted by a spasm of coughing and a spray of blood across the dirty white sheets in the consumptive ward. Hammersmith wanted to remember his father as a tall strong man with a ready smile and quick hands, not as the shrunken angry old man who had to be tied to a bed so that he wouldn't bite the nurses who fed him.

'It's not just him eating at you, is it?' Pringle said. 'I can see by that faraway dreamy look on your face that there's a case boiling away inside your skull.' He sat forward in his armchair and scowled at Hammersmith. 'Was there something in that thug's story, then?'

Hammersmith nodded, glad to put his father out of his mind for the moment.

'A child,' he said. 'A dead boy in one of the homes along the row there.'

'Damn it all, I should have gone with you.'

'Nothing you could have done to change things. The boy was long since dead and stuffed up a chimney.'

'Stuffed up?'

Pringle gazed into his tea for a moment before looking up.

'Stuffing a body up a chimney's no easy feat. Could the boy have been dead in advance and stiff. If he was rigorous stiff, it might have made it easier to push him upward.'

'I may have misspoke. Stuffed isn't the right word for it. It appears the boy crawled up the flue of his own accord. Got stuck and was left there.'

'Oh, so it was a climber.'

Pringle sat back again and took another sip of tea.

'Yes, I think the boy was a climber,' Hammersmith

said. 'But climbers shouldn't be abandoned in chimneys.'

'Of course not. But the job does come with risks and it follows that croaking in a chimney is one of them risks.'

'No five-year-old should be made to face those risks. What five-year-old would even understand that kind of risk, let alone agree to it?'

'Whoa,' Pringle said.

He waved his arm at Hammersmith and tea sloshed out of his cup, dotting his shirtfront.

'Oh, damn,' he said.

He stood and Hammersmith handed him a cloth from the table. Pringle dabbed at his shirt, shaking his head.

'Too much drink, I think.'

'It'll come out.'

'I'm sure. Never mind the shirt.'

'Never mind the shirt? Who am I talking to? What's happened to Colin Pringle?'

Hammersmith smiled weakly and Pringle shook his head again.

'No, look, I've given the impression that I don't care about a dead child.'

'I'm sure you do.'

'I do. I really do. Every death is a tragedy, but I don't understand what makes this one so special.'

Hammersmith looked down at his shoes. Hammersmith's own shoes were old and worn and cracked. They had never been polished. He looked over at Pringle's shoes, which reflected the room's ambient lamplight. He and Pringle shared mutual respect, but had nothing in common. They had been thrown together simply because they'd started as constables on the same day at the same station. Pringle cared deeply about the trappings of life. Being a policeman allowed him access to material privileges and opportunities that Hammersmith cared nothing for. The job mattered to Hammersmith. The job and the people who needed him to do that job properly. He had never been able to make Pringle understand.

'It's not . . .' he said. 'It was a child, Colin. He was used and discarded.'

Pringle nodded, but said nothing. He waited for Hammersmith to continue.

'It's true, we do see bodies often enough. This was different.'

'They'll put a detective on it.'

'No. They won't.'

Pringle was silent for a moment. When he spoke, he kept his eyes on the floor.

'Did they tell you to let it go?'

'Yes.'

'Are you going to let it go?'

Hammersmith took another sip of tea. It was cold now.

'No.'

Pringle nodded at the floor.

'I'm going round to Kingsley's,' Hammersmith said. 'To see if he has any more information about the body yet.'

'Nevil, no. It's the middle of the night. He's a family man. Probably as sound asleep as we should be.'

'He might be awake.'

'He might be, but he won't want to see our ugly mugs. Let 'im be till morning.'

'I feel restless. I need to act.'

'Well, Kingsley won't have cut on the body yet, anyway. And besides, what'll he tell you that you don't know?'

'You're right. I know how the boy died.'

'And you know there's nobody to bring in on this. Nobody killed him. He died of natural causes.'

'Not natural causes.'

'He stopped breathing of his own accord. Nobody held a pillow over his face. There's nowhere to go with this.'

'And the people he trusted? The ones who abandoned him?'

'What can you do? They've broken no law.'

Hammersmith ran a hand over his chin. He needed a shave.

'I can scare them.'

'You're scaring me right now, Nevil.'

'I need to do something about this. You needn't involve yourself, but if I sit on my hands here it will eat away at me until there's nothing left.'

'You could lose your commission. You might as well toss your entire career with the Met on the rubbish pile. You'll be shovelling horse manure in the street.'

'It's honest work.'

Pringle shrugged.

'It is at that. All right, I'm in.'

'You don't need to . . .'

'What's a mate for, then? I'm in it. But I'd like about three days of sleep first.'

'What about *your* career?'

'As long as I get to keep the uniform, I'll be fine.'

Hammersmith grinned and finished his tea. He hardly noticed the metallic aftertaste.

15

Inspector Day walked up Charing Cross, away from The Yard. His heels clicked on the road and echoed back from the high walls of the hotels on either side of him. There was a hole in the bottom of his left shoe and he could feel the cold of the paving stones under his feet. The bulk of The Hotel Victoria loomed out of the fog to the left of him and, to the right, The Hotel Metropole, tall and elegant. Ahead, a cab rank split the street. In the morning it would be filled with hansoms and buses and growlers, queued up in the median between the great hotels, letting off and picking up and waiting, but now the rank was empty. An omnibus rattled past him, its yellow sides dull in the lamplight, a feedbag hung over the horse's nose. Day moved aside and watched it disappear into the mist.

The road widened out and Day crossed the Strand to Trafalgar Square. On a clear day he would be able to see the National Gallery on the other side of the square, but tonight he could barely see fifteen feet in front of him. A tide of mist rolled over and past him. He thought he could make out the pillar of Admiral Lord Nelson's statue against the pale night sky, but it might have been nothing more than a thin distant layering of fog upon fog. The square was silent, the fountains shut off for the night and the hugeness and the openness of the space seemed cathedral-like to Day, who still thought of the intimate marshes and woodlands of Devon.

He was at the south-east corner of the square. He oriented himself and walked diagonally towards the far end. Soon he came to the outside of a low wall that encircled the nearest fountain. He followed it, walking slowly. This close, he could hear the breeze shaping ripples across the water.

After a few yards the wall angled back north, towards the fountain, and Day stopped at the corner where a massive lamppost squatted, joining the two ends of the wall. He had passed this lamppost before, he thought, but had never noticed how much bigger it was than the others that were dotted about the square. The lantern globe atop its pillar was dark. Day ran his hand over the smooth stone of its base. In the centre of the structure was a door, two steps up from the flagstones beneath, and in the centre of the door was a small round knob. Now that he was looking directly at it, it was unmistakable, but he knew that the door went unnoticed by hundreds of passersby every day.

Day turned the knob. Nothing. He stepped up to the windows set into the tiny door and cupped his hands on either side of his eyes. Peering in, he saw only darkness.

He turned and squinted into the mist. London seemed empty of any other human soul. He felt utterly alone, but the Ripper was out there somewhere in the grey city. Or perhaps the Ripper was dead and gone, having destroyed the confidence of The Yard and of the citizens who no longer trusted The Yard to protect them.

Whether he was gone or not, it hardly mattered. Saucy

Jack had gifted them all the idea of himself. Others like him circled like lions around the herd. The city was changed.

Day reached into the inside pocket of his overcoat and drew out the flat leather pouch. Atop the array of heavy skeleton keys on their velvet bed was the tiny brass key to the kiosk. He picked it out and turned back to the door. Under the knob was a small keyhole. The key fitted perfectly and Day heard a click when he twisted it. The knob turned under his hand and the door swung open without another sound. He stepped inside.

There was enough space within the pillar for two men to stand upright. Aside from the wooden door with its small window, the interior was all of the same stone that made up the outer wall. Day closed the door behind him and passed his hands across the walls. There was a shallow ledge that circled the room at waist level. Perhaps wide enough for a candle. Day reached up and felt along the ceiling. It tapered in the middle, leading up to the lamp outside. He put his hands down and stood, looking through the window at the fog.

There was nothing here.

Whatever this lamppost-stationhouse had represented to Inspector Adrian March, it eluded Walter Day. This was a tiny room in a vast city and, perhaps, that was all it was meant to be. One of the many secrets concealed beneath the day-to-day business of the mightiest empire in the history of the world. A place of safety and hidden potential for a policeman who had ultimately been defeated by a killer of women.

Day left the kiosk. He locked the door and put the key

back in its pouch. He didn't know what he'd hoped to find here, but if Detective March had left a message, its meaning was a deeper mystery than Day was prepared to solve.

He walked away from the square and turned towards his home and his wife and his bed.

16

Hammersmith and Pringle sat on a short wall under the drooping branches of a willow tree. They were across the street from the house where Hammersmith had found the dead boy in a chimney. The street was completely deserted and Pringle was slumped into Hammersmith's left shoulder, snoring softly.

The moon hung low in the sky and Hammersmith could feel the cold stones of the wall through the seat of his trousers. He thought, not for the first time, that it would have been nice if he and Pringle had the funds to sit in a hansom cab in the shadows and watch the house in relative comfort, but cabs were expensive.

Pringle shifted in his sleep and a wet strand of drool seeped from the corner of his mouth on to Hammersmith's arm.

Hammersmith had taken care to let no doubt show on his face while discussing the matter with Pringle, but alone in the dark, watching an empty house, and with his shift due to start in four hours, he could feel his confidence ebbing. Pringle was right. So, for that matter, was Inspector James Tiffany. Hundreds, maybe thousands of children died or went missing every year in London. The police lacked the resources to pursue every case, particularly if there was no evidence of a crime.

But he had once been that little boy. He had spent

long hours alone in the dark doing a job he didn't entirely understand. His own circumstances had been different, of course. He had been sent into the mines by his family to earn the money they needed for groceries and medicine. He had felt proud to contribute, useful and grown up. But the fear and the loneliness had been there with him every minute of every day.

He was certain the boy had shimmied up that chimney on the promise of no greater reward than a smile or a pat on the shoulder or an extra biscuit. To Hammersmith's way of thinking that made the chimneysweep, and maybe the people who hired the chimneysweep, criminals no different from highway robbers or pickpockets. Maybe not murderers in any technical sense, but people who should be taken off the streets and locked up for society's good.

And that was Hammersmith's job.

From far away he heard the *clip clop* of hooves on cobblestones. He leaned back into the shadows of the willow and shook Pringle awake.

'Wha– ?'

'Shush. Someone's coming.'

Pringle nodded and wiped his cheek with the sleeve of his jacket, then frowned at the silvery streak of drool and tried to brush it away.

'Is it them?'

'Don't know yet.'

'We don't know anyone's ever going to return to this place.'

Hammersmith ignored Pringle. It wasn't the first time he'd said it that night.

The two of them retreated behind the wall and watched as a patch of darkness blacker than the night moved up the street towards them. A pinprick of light bobbed along in time to the sound of the horses' hooves. When it drew closer to them, the light resolved itself into a lantern on a pole affixed to the side of a great black carriage. Two sweating chargers pulled up the carriage alongside the row of houses and stopped by the wall, snorting and stamping.

After a moment, the driver hopped down from his perch and opened the door on the other side. He fetched a stool from the seat above and placed it on the cobblestones. Hammersmith could see under the carriage, as first one foot lowered itself and then another, and a man's weight eased forward. The feet touched ground and the man turned, apparently to help a woman down because a pair of dainty ankles were briefly visible before the hem of a frilly dress settled down, obscuring the view. Another woman followed, then a child. The four pairs of feet moved away from the coach and the driver jumped back up on to his seat and whipped his reins across the horses' backs. The carriage moved on up the street.

Hammersmith stood and stepped over the wall. He felt a drop of water hit his arm and he looked up. Another drop hit him in the eye and he gasped. He wiped his face with his sleeve and looked out across the street where the man from the carriage had also felt the rain coming. He was hurrying the two women and the child up the steps to the house. He was carrying a black leather overnight bag and one of the women was struggling with a much larger suitcase.

Hammersmith walked briskly across the street. He felt Pringle keeping pace. More raindrops splashed on his head and shoulders as he strode, his heels clicking against the cobblestones.

The man hadn't noticed them yet. He was busy unlocking the front door. Hammersmith put his right foot on the bottom-most step and cleared his throat.

'Excuse me, sir.'

The man visibly jumped and dropped his bag. The two women turned to look at Hammersmith, but the little boy stared up at the man, perhaps surprised to see his father caught unawares. The man turned slowly towards Hammersmith, looked down the steps and pursed his lips, but said nothing. He had an elaborate beard that had been groomed into four outward-jutting curls that beckoned the eye, drawing attention from the rest of his long, horsy face.

'Are you the homeowner here?'

The man nodded, his curls bouncing on his chin.

'May I ask your name, sir?'

'Why, I'm Dr Charles Shaw.'

He said it as if the two police should already know him, as if everyone should know him.

'My colleague and I are with the Metropolitan Police. We'd like a word with you, please.'

Charles Shaw turned back to the door and opened it. He ushered the two women and the boy inside and closed the door behind them. He looked up at the black sky.

'It's late, Constable, and it's beginning to rain. Perhaps you'll come back at a proper time?'

Hammersmith ignored the irritation in the doctor's voice.

'Beg pardon, sir, but you don't seem to be home much of late and I'd hate to miss this opportunity to talk to you.'

Shaw stared at Hammersmith so long that Hammersmith thought the doctor might come down off the porch and hit him. He watched Shaw's hand curl into a fist, relax and then curl up again. Behind him, Hammersmith could hear Pringle shift from one foot to the other. They were all getting wet.

'And what if I decline to talk to you?' Shaw said.

Hammersmith shrugged. That was certainly an option. From the tone in his voice when he gave his name, this man was apparently prominent in the community. Hammersmith and Pringle were at least several rungs below him in social status and, if Shaw chose to pursue a grievance with Sir Edward, he might cost them their jobs. The two constables were well over the line and they all knew it.

'Then I suppose we'll wait, sir. It's no problem at all. We'll still be right here, outside your home in the morning.'

The implication was clear. When the neighbours awoke and looked out of their windows, they would see two wet and miserable police officers sitting outside Dr Shaw's home. It wouldn't be good for the doctor's reputation. It would require endless visits, up and down the street, by both Shaw and his wife, to smooth things over and quell the rumours.

Shaw sighed.

'Very well,' he said, 'I wouldn't want to appear rude. Please come inside, but I'll ask you to refrain from dripping on any of the rugs.'

Hammersmith and Pringle followed Shaw through the door and into a well-appointed antechamber. Shaw didn't know it, but Hammersmith had been here before, had explored the entire house for clues when the boy's body was found. He looked around as if it were his first time there. A bench with an embroidered cover sat under a huge gilt-framed mirror to their left as they entered. On the opposite wall was a series of brass hooks beneath a small chandelier. Hammersmith took off his overcoat and hung it on one of the hooks. He hung his hat next to the coat. Pringle hesitated, then followed Hammersmith's lead. Shaw looked stricken, but said nothing.

It was the custom, when visiting for a short while, to leave one's coat and hat on unless the visit was expected to last more than fifteen minutes. Often, neighbours would take a stroll after dinner and call on their nearby friends and acquaintances. If they left their coats on, it meant that their host shouldn't worry about serving tea or dessert. To take one's coat off signalled a prolonged obligation and was avoided unless there was a clear invitation to stay.

Hammersmith had not been invited to stay.

One of the women appeared at the arched doorway between the entrance hall and the rest of the house. She smelled faintly of lavender and apples, and she was the better-dressed of the two women Hammersmith had seen outside. He guessed she was Shaw's wife and the other woman was probably a governess or maid.

'Charles,' she said.

'Penelope,' Shaw said, 'please have Elizabeth put on some tea for our guests.'

Shaw didn't sound pleased about it. The woman, Penelope, looked like she wanted to say something, but then turned and walked out of sight. Hammersmith rummaged in the pocket of his hanging coat until he found his notebook. He turned to a fresh page and wrote *Dr Charles and Mrs Penelope Shaw* and then below that: *Elizabeth – Housekeeper?*

'What are you writing?'

'Nothing important, sir. Your names, that's all. How long has Elizabeth been with you?'

'I'm sure I wouldn't know. My wife hired her, of course, and it's been many years now. At any rate, it's none of your business. What's this all about, then?'

'Have you been informed that there was a break-in at your address?'

'Here, you mean?'

'Yes, sir.'

Hammersmith watched Shaw's eyes. He had assumed that Shaw knew about the boy's body and had a good reason to want to avoid talking to the police, but when he heard that his home had been burgled there was genuine surprise and concern in his eyes. It was gone almost immediately, but Hammersmith had seen the emotion there for one unguarded moment.

'Why wasn't I told?'

'We had no way to reach you.'

'I was . . . we were in Birmingham on holiday.'

'Birmingham?'

'Family there.'

'I see. May we?'

Hammersmith gestured towards the rooms beyond the hall and Shaw looked at the floor. He rubbed the bridge of his nose, sniffed loudly, then nodded, seemingly to himself rather than to his uninvited guests. Without looking directly at the constables, he led the way into the drawing room and they followed.

Pringle grabbed Hammersmith by the arm and they let Shaw get a few steps ahead of them. He gave Hammersmith a look and Hammersmith nodded. Mentioning the break-in to Shaw was a dangerous move. Hammersmith hadn't even told Inspector Tiffany about Blackleg's involvement in finding the boy's body. There was no official record of any burglary. If Shaw went over their heads and enquired at The Yard, Hammersmith might lose his job. But he was certain Shaw wouldn't contact the police. And scaring the doctor was the only surefire way he could see to get his attention.

Shaw's drawing room was tastefully decorated. There was nothing gaudy about it: the stag's head on the wall looked, to Hammersmith's untrained eye, to be real and the furniture was old but elegant. The large round table in the centre of the room was scratched and scarred, but crafted of a single piece of wood and had surely cost more than Hammersmith's entire annual salary when it was new. There was a low armchair with a high back and Penelope Shaw was sitting in it, waiting for them. She rose and greeted them as if they hadn't just met her at the front door.

She held out her hand and Hammersmith took it. He looked from it to her face and noted the way her dark hair framed her high cheekbones. Her eyes were wide and a blue so pale they appeared frozen. She smiled and looked away from him.

She waved them all to chairs and they sat. Hammersmith saw Charles Shaw bristle silently as he and Pringle sat down. The housekeeper Elizabeth entered with tea and set the table for them. The scones appeared to be several days old, but Hammersmith assumed it was the best she could do for unexpected strangers at three o'clock in the morning. He refused a scone, but took a cup as Shaw explained the situation to his wife.

'They say we've had a break-in while on holiday.'

'Oh, my. Was anything taken?'

'You might be able to tell us that, ma'am,' Hammersmith said.

'Well, I haven't . . . I mean, we've only just arrived home. I wouldn't have any idea yet.'

'They're lying,' Shaw said.

His face went white and he blinked quickly. He clearly hadn't meant to speak out loud.

'Pardon me?' Hammersmith said.

'I apologize. I'm quite tired.'

'Of course. We're very sorry to intrude like this. It's just that with you being such an important figure in the neighbourhood, we assume that your neighbours might also face some danger of burglary. We want to nip this in the bud as quickly as possible. I'm sure you understand.'

'Of course,' Penelope said.

Hammersmith could feel the doctor sizing him up, but he didn't look at him. Instead, he focused his attention on the wife. Penelope was much younger than her husband. Her face reminded Hammersmith of a fox: long and lean and smart. There was something hungry about her, hidden behind a façade of perfect respectability. He shifted his attention to the husband.

'Dr Shaw, have you noticed anyone unusual in the neighbourhood of late?'

'We've been out of the city.'

'For how long?'

Shaw hesitated and Hammersmith watched the doctor's eyes. Shaw met his gaze and straightened his shoulders.

'Just the night. We ran into bad weather and had to turn around.'

'So you weren't gone long at all.'

'I didn't know how recently you meant.'

'Before you left, then?'

'No. I think I would have attached some importance to anyone who appeared . . .'

'I'm sure you would. But we mustn't rule anyone out. What about your staff?'

'Elizabeth is beyond reproach.'

'I understand. And this is a difficult question to be faced with, but how well do you know the rest of your household? What about your laundress, or your chimneysweep?'

Pringle spat his tea back into his cup.

'Hot,' he said.

Shaw glared at him.

'Our chimneysweep?'

'Or anyone who might have access to this place in your absence.'

'Well, I'm sure he seemed perfectly respectable.'

'Do you have a name for him?'

'I believe his name may have been Robert,' he said.

'Excuse me, Charles,' Penelope said, 'but our chimneysweep's name is Sam. I'm sure of it.'

'Don't interrupt. You have things you could be doing, don't you?'

'Of course, Charles. I apologize.'

She rose from the table and walked slowly to a door that led to the kitchen. She looked back at the table before passing from the room. Hammersmith was surprised to realize that he wanted her to look his way, but she didn't. She didn't look at her husband either. After she was gone, the scent of lavender lingered and the three men were silent for a long moment.

'So,' Shaw said. 'You're of the opinion that our sweep stole something from this house?'

'Perhaps. Later in the day, would you be so good as to make up a list of anything that might be missing? If we track this man down, we may find some object, something belonging to you about his person, and that would be all we'd need to ascertain his guilt in the matter.'

'Do you have any idea what time it is?'

'Of course, sir. That's why I said it might wait until later in the day.'

Shaw stood and Pringle followed his lead, standing up too. Hammersmith remained seated.

'I have entertained this matter as far as I am willing

to,' Shaw said. 'I'll ask you to leave this house and not return.'

'You don't want us to find the man who burgled you?'

'I don't care. What I want is to go to bed and enjoy a few hours of uninterrupted sleep, free from thoughts of sweeps and burglars and nosy police.'

'Nosy, are we?' Pringle said. 'And aren't we trying to help you?'

'I'm sure I have no idea what you're trying to do, but the hour is inappropriate and your questions seem unusual.'

Hammersmith was unperturbed. For Shaw to be so openly rude meant that he was hiding something from them. Knowing that there was something hidden was the first step towards finding it.

'Could you give us some indication, at least, of where we might find this sweep?'

'No, I could not. Leave now.'

Hammersmith concealed a smile and stood.

'Of course,' he said. 'We apologize for disturbing you.'

'Well, I don't apologize,' Pringle said. 'I think you've been bloody rude.'

'Please excuse my friend,' Hammersmith said. 'We're quite tired ourselves.'

'Just get out.'

'Would it be permissible for us to return later?'

'Not at all. I very much hope never to see you again.'

'A crime has been committed here, sir,' Pringle said, 'and we are duty bound to follow . . .'

'You are duty bound to do what your betters ask of you. Now go. If there's been a crime committed – and

I've seen no evidence of that, only your word – then I will investigate it myself.'

'Very well,' Hammersmith said. 'Have a good night, sir.'

'I shall have a very good night indeed just as soon as you are both out of my sight.'

Shaw ushered the two policemen out of the door. Hammersmith paused on the step and turned back towards the doctor.

'Please tell your lovely wife goodnight for us,' he said. 'And apologize to her on our account for the beastly hour.'

'I shall do nothing of the kind.'

And with that, Shaw slammed the front door.

'Well, I never,' Pringle said.

Hammersmith rubbed his hands together and bounded down the front steps. Pringle hurried to keep up with the longer strides of his friend.

'So, that's the end of it, right?' he said.

'Not at all,' Hammersmith said. 'We know the name of our sweep.'

'He said it was Richard, didn't he? No, Robert.'

'Yes, he said Robert. But the name of the man we're looking for is Sam.'

'Oh, yes. That's what the wife said, isn't it?'

'Penelope. Yes.'

'She's a lovely thing.'

'I hadn't noticed.'

'You hadn't? How could you not?'

'Perhaps that accounts for the good doctor keeping her out of sight.'

'I would, if I were married to her.'

‘She may have more to tell us, if we could talk to her alone.’

‘Well, I’m willing to make the attempt.’

‘It might be better if I have a go at her myself, Colin.’

Pringle smiled and clapped Hammersmith on the back.

‘Oh, I quite understand.’

Hammersmith shook his head.

‘We should hurry,’ he said. ‘The sun will be up soon and we have a long walk ahead of us.’

17

Esme whimpered in her sleep.

Liza rolled over and traced her fingers lightly down the length of Esme's scar. The puckered red line began under Esme's hair and ran diagonally across her forehead, jumped over her left eye and exploded in a starburst on her cheek before commencing down over her chin, her throat, and disappearing under the top of Esme's loose-fitting nightgown. The endpoint of the scar was a crater where Esme's left breast had once been.

She leaned in and brushed her lips against the coarse fabric of the nightgown, gently kissed the absent breast.

Esme stirred and smiled. She wrapped her arms around Liza and groaned.

'You was havin' the dream again,' Liza said.

'Did I wake you?'

'I was awake already.'

'You ain't slept, have you?'

'I'm fine, love.'

'You should sleep.'

'I will.'

Esme mumbled something that Liza couldn't hear and slipped back into her dreams. Liza watched her for a long while after. Watching her beautiful girl Esme was all that Liza ever wanted to do. The one time she hadn't watched, hadn't been there, Esme had met Saucy Jack.

And now they both dreamed of Jack when they slept.

Liza wasn't there when it happened. Liza never saw the Ripper. In her dream, as in reality, she was too far away to help poor Esme – Esme who went down a dark alley with the Ripper. Him with his midnight cloak and his yellow teeth.

And his wild black beard.

Esme had been working – both women had been working that night – and she had chosen the alley herself.

In hindsight, of course, taking a strange man into an alley was a foolish, even fatal mistake. But the Ripper hadn't arrived in the popular press as yet and going down alleys with men was what Esme, Liza and countless other women in Whitechapel had to do in order to put food on the table.

And so Esme got lost in the dark with the man and his knife.

Liza wasn't there when it happened. Liza was with a different man, down a different alley. But Esme had told her everything and Liza's dreams replayed for her what had happened as if she had been in that alley on that night. And night after night ever since.

She imagined the scent of the Ripper as he pressed against her, briny and rank. The feel of his beard against her face, wires in her eyes, blotting out the gaslight from the street so far away. The sting of the knife on her face, on her throat. On her breast. The sound of her blouse ripping open and the warmth of her blood trickling down her ribs.

She screamed and he pulled her face into his chest so that she breathed in the hair of his beard. She beat against him and she pushed against him and he didn't seem to notice. Her strength left her more quickly than she would have dreamed. She let her arms fall to her sides and she shut her eyes and she waited for the end.

Jack held her like a father might hold a bawling infant and he spoke a single word. Through his beard, his mouth smelled of metal and fish and old rope.

'Slowly,' he said.

And then there were other voices, the voices of women, far away at the alley's mouth. She felt herself fall to the stones as Jack disappeared. There came the sound of boot heels on cobblestones and then she felt soft hands on her skin and she heard a soft voice in her ear.

'Don't die,' someone said.

And so she didn't die.

Instead, she slept.

Liza woke again for the third time that night and gasped at her false memory of Esme's ordeal. She watched the ceiling of the tiny rented room they shared and, when that proved unsatisfying, she rolled on to her elbow and went back to watching Esme.

And Esme whimpered in her sleep.

18

The bald man woke with a start. He lay listening to the dark house and the rain beating against the roof above, unable to pinpoint what had awakened him. He fumbled along the bedside table for his spectacles and put them on, then went searching for the box of matches he kept next to the candlestick. He was a firm believer in the old ways of doing things and a candle would do just fine. There was no electricity in his house. He felt strongly that mankind had grown too arrogant and had harnessed an elemental force that would eventually turn on its master. He waited nervously for all of London to burn to the ground, done in by the fiery electrical wires strung here and there over the city.

He struck a match and contemplated the sudden blue flame for a moment before lighting the tallow candle and snuffing the match between his fingers. He felt a sudden cramping in his bowels and, jamming his feet into the slippers on the floor beside his bed, he hurried out of the room and down the hall to the water closet. Not all of the new ways of doing things were bad. Indoor plumbing, for instance, was marvellous.

When he had finished, he pulled the chain to flush and took his candle back out to the hall. The house was old and the floor creaked under his weight. He walked against the wall where it was quieter and eased open the boy's door.

At first he didn't see anything amiss. The candle's glow didn't penetrate far into the room. He crept closer, just wanting a look at the boy before heading back to his own bedroom. He had given

Fenn a room of his own after they'd returned from the park. The bald man had been proud of the boy for obeying him in public. There had been no shouts for help or attempts to run away. The bald man was sure that Fenn was beginning to think of him as his natural father and to think of this house as his own. Of course, the bald man wasn't stupid. He had still tied the boy to his bed.

The flickering candlelight played over the boy's bed, chasing shadows into the folds and curves of the blankets. Too many folds and curves. The bald man approached the bed. He swallowed hard and reached out, grabbed a corner of the topmost blanket and yanked too hard. The blanket flew at his face and he almost dropped the candlestick. He let the blanket fall to the floor and pulled at the other blankets. The ropes he had used to tie the boy were tangled at the foot of the bed.

Fenn was gone.

Panicked, the bald man rushed to his own room and pulled on a pair of trousers under his nightshirt. He used a snuffer to put out the candle and hurried into the hall and down the creaking stairs to the front door.

How had the boy made it down the stairs without the sound of those dry old boards awakening the man?

He cursed himself for a trusting fool. He hadn't double-checked the ropes before going to bed, hadn't taken out the slack. He had been too kind. Of course, the boy wasn't ready yet to accept his new family situation. It would take more time. The bald man had rushed things, trying to recapture his past. He hesitated, trying to remember his first son's name, but it wouldn't come to him. He shook off the sudden twinge of sadness and regret. It hardly mattered now.

Outside, the rain fell steady, but not hard. The bald man left the front door open and went to the middle of the street. He looked *both ways, trying to decide where the boy might have gone. The rain beaded on his head and ran in rivulets down the back of his neck. Within minutes the thin fabric of his nightshirt clung to his skin and his slippers had absorbed enough water to triple their weight.*

He hunched his shoulders and shut his eyes, trying to imagine himself as a young boy in a strange neighbourhood. He opened his eyes again and looked around. Rain clouds blotted out the moon. A carriage swept by, a gas lamp swinging back and forth from the pole next to the driver. The bald man's gaze followed the carriage down the street and watched as it turned on to a broader lane where firefly clusters of street lamps struggled to penetrate the gloom. The bald man's street was completely dark, no lamps here, and the streets to the east were also residential, but to the west there were more thoroughly travelled streets which were lit up with gas. He felt sure the boy would have been drawn to the light, dim as it was.

The bald man set himself on a westerly course and followed in the wake of the carriage.

19

Kingsley stared into the dying embers of the night's fire, not focused on the coals or his surroundings. Outside, rain pattered against the roof. A small noise in the room woke him from his daze and he slowly shook off his malaise and turned his head. Fiona was standing in the doorway watching him.

'How long have you been there?' he said.

'Not long. Do you feel all right, Father?'

He smiled and nodded.

'Of course I do. Why aren't you asleep, Plum?'

'I heard a noise. A carriage going by outside.'

Kingsley sniffed and glanced up at the clock on the mantel above the dead fire.

'It's early yet. Or late. You should try to sleep a bit more.'

'I'm awake. Should I get you something? Tea?'

'No, thank you.'

'Have you slept yet?'

'You know, I don't think I have,' Kingsley said.

Fiona padded across the room and sat on the arm of the chair. Kingsley put his hand on her back. He wiped his other hand across his face and tried to remember what he'd been thinking of. Fiona spoke as if she could read his thoughts.

'Were you thinking of Mother?'

'I don't know. Maybe I was.'

'I was thinking of her even before the carriage woke me.'

'You were dreaming, you mean.'

'Yes. We were all together at Hyde Park, gathered around the fountain. You know the one I mean, with the statue of the angel in it.'

'I think I know the one, but I'm not sure that statue's meant to be an angel.'

'I think it is.'

'Fair enough.'

'You and Mother were holding hands and Beatrice was there, too, home from school, I think.'

'We should visit her soon.'

'I'd like that.'

'Then we'll do it.'

'Do you still dream about her?'

'Beatrice?'

He knew what she meant. She wasn't talking about her sister.

'Mother.'

'Yes, Plum, I still dream about her. I suppose we always will.'

'Do you think she dreams of us?'

'No.'

'Not ever?'

'She doesn't dream any more.'

'How do you know that?'

'Because I have seen countless dead people, I have cut into them and removed their organs and I have weighed their brains and not one of them has ever told me anything about them that wasn't concrete and physical. When people die their minds no longer work. They can't dream.'

'What about their souls?'

'I have never seen a soul nor found a repository for such a thing in any body I've examined. There is no soul.'

Fiona was quiet and Kingsley realized he'd upset his daughter. He was too tired to be of any use to her. He rubbed his hand clumsily up and down her back. He wished he could offer her some comfort, some assurance that her mother lived on, but since he didn't believe it himself he had no way of convincing her. She wiped her eyes, but her hair had fallen over her face and Kingsley couldn't see her.

'Well, I believe we all have souls,' she said, 'and you just can't see them.'

Kingsley nodded. He was afraid to contradict her.

'I believe my mother is in heaven and I will see her again some day.'

Kingsley smiled, but it was a sad smile.

'I sincerely hope that day is a long way off,' he said.

'I mean that we'll see her when we both die of old age, hundreds and hundreds of years from now.'

'It's a pleasant thought, at least.'

'Maybe she's looking at us right now. Maybe she's smiling at us and making nice things happen for us.'

'That would be an excellent dream for you to have.'

'It would, wouldn't it?'

They sat in companionable silence, staring at the embers in the fireplace and, eventually, Fiona slid off the arm of the chair and into her father's lap. He smoothed her hair away from her face and she shifted slightly, mumbled something unheard, and began to snore quietly.

Kingsley sat in the dark and watched the crackling remains of the fire until he fell asleep.

He didn't dream about anything at all.

20

Walter Day laid his head on his wife's pillow and closed his eyes. Beside him, Claire swept a lock of hair from her eyes and propped herself on one elbow, her other hand on her husband's chest.

'Let me lie here a moment and I'll return to my room,' Day said. 'I should have stayed there. You need your sleep.'

'But your room is miles away from mine,' Claire said.

'Only down the hall.'

'That's still too far. And I sleep too much as it is. I hardly see you any more.'

'It's this case.'

'I know that. I'm not complaining. What is the case, Walter?'

'I shouldn't say.'

'But I would love to hear about it.'

'It might upset you.'

'I'm no flower, you know.'

Day sighed.

'I heard Percy Erwood still hasn't married,' he said.

'Are you changing the subject, Mr Day?'

'You must have been the only woman for him.'

'I was never for him.'

She took her hand off Walter's chest and moved away, staring in the dark direction of the ceiling.

'Why did you ever marry me and leave poor Percy in the lurch?' Day said.

'I declare,' she said. 'You're not going to worry about Percy Erwood for the rest of our long lives, are you?'

'I wouldn't say I'm worried about him.'

'If you had your way, Percy Erwood would come here right now and carry me away.'

'Right now?'

'In the morning, then.'

'I would rather he didn't.'

'As would I.'

Day smacked his lips and mumbled something Claire couldn't make out.

'What's that, dear?' she said.

'I asked if you remembered the first time I saw you.'

'Did I see you too or were you hiding behind a bush to see what Percy Erwood would do first?'

'It was in church. That's the only place I ever saw you. No, that's not true. I saw you passing in the street sometimes and once in the post office, but church was the only place I thought I could talk to you.'

'What a lovely story.'

'You were wearing a yellow dress the first time I saw you. And a bonnet.'

'You remember the colour of my dress?'

'And you wore gloves that nearly reached your elbows.'

'Did you like me then?'

'You were the prettiest girl I had ever seen and I knew you would never marry me because I wasn't good enough.'

Claire smiled, though she knew Walter couldn't see her.

'I prefer to decide that sort of thing for myself.'

'And so,' Day said, as though he hadn't heard her, 'though I knew it was a hopeless cause, I tried every day to be the best person I could be, to be good enough for you, whether you noticed or not.'

'You were always good enough, Walter Day,' she said. But she wasn't sure whether she'd spoken loud enough for him to hear.

They lay there, side by side, for a long time then, Claire straining to see the ceiling. She thought her eyes would eventually adjust to the darkness, but they didn't. Before long, Walter began to snore and Claire curled up with her back along his side. She knew he would be gone by the time she woke in the morning.

'I married you,' she said, 'because you're the sort of man who remembers my yellow dress.'

She closed her eyes and waited for sleep to come.

'Humph,' she said. 'Percy Erwood indeed.'

21

Constable Nevil Hammersmith paused with his hand on the knob and took a deep breath before opening the door and entering The Brass Tankard. It was the seventh pub he'd visited since parting ways with Pringle and they were getting more squalid as the hour grew later. The only pubs still open were the places that catered to serious drinkers and criminals. Unless he found what he was looking for soon, he feared that he would get no sleep before the morning's shift.

He had a long day ahead of him.

DAY TWO

22

Seventeen hours since the discovery of Mr Little

The sun climbed over the rooftops of Kentish Town, glancing through rain clouds and windows as it rose. Claire Day stood in front of her mirror, but she didn't watch herself. She had enough experience that her fingers remembered what to do now; she didn't need to see them.

She pulled the corset over her head and tugged it into place above her hips. She tightened the top set of laces below her shoulder blades and moved down, rung by rung, until she reached the middle of her back where two loops hung down. She grabbed them and pulled the top half of the corset tight, whalebone biting into her sternum.

She took a shallow breath and started again at the bottom of the corset, just below her waist. Again, each set of laces was yanked taut until once more she reached the middle of her back. The loops, longer now, were crossed over each other and stretched again until they were long enough to wrap around to the front of Claire's waist. She pulled as hard as she could and tied the ends into a discreet bow over her navel.

She looked down at her handiwork, what she could see of it, and frowned. Her maidservant had always made a prettier bow. Claire had resigned herself to the fact that she would never have a staff like the household she'd grown up in. Her husband was the loveliest man she'd ever met, and money meant nothing to him. They had little enough of it, but Walter routinely gave it away to anyone he met who appeared to be needy. Claire had no regrets.

She backed up and sat carefully on the edge of the bed, still avoiding her reflection in the mirror above the vanity.

She panted like a small dog, shallow breaths in and out. The inevitable suggestion of a deep breath presented itself to her and she tried to ignore it, but the thought grew until she felt she had to yawn.

Of course she couldn't yawn.

Instead, she felt her stomach turn over on itself, cramped though it was down there, and she ran to the bathroom, barely making it to the basin against the far wall before her gorge rose and she vomited water. It splashed her chin and dribbled from her nose. Thankfully, there was nothing else in her system, but still she continued to heave.

Finally, her body calmed itself and she slid to the floor, her eyes closed, her breathing slow and steady.

She sat there until the light of the dawning sun filtered through the curtains and turned the insides of her eyelids orange. Then she grabbed the edge of the basin and stood.

Claire wiped her face and rinsed out her mouth. She pulled on a long, lacy gown over the corset and left the bathroom. Her husband's room was just down the short hallway and she could hear water splashing in a basin; Walter getting ready for the day. She hurried her steps. He would need a freshly pressed shirt for work.

Her stomach turned again and she pushed against the wall until the sensation passed. She closed her eyes, took a short breath, and when she opened her husband's bedroom door she was composed and smiling.

There was no need to trouble him.

The bald man returned to his house when the street vendors started setting up their stalls for the day. Traffic had begun to pick up, curious passersby glancing in his direction, and the bald man realized that he was still wearing his sopping nightshirt and slippers.

He bathed quickly and changed clothes.

In Fenn's room, the bald man examined the ropes that had held the boy to his bed. They were still intact, still knotted. Fenn must have spent hours wriggling his way out of them. The bars on the window looked sturdy, but when the bald man checked them, one bar slid out of place. It swung to the side and the bald man stooped to look at the window casing. The mortar there was crumbled and loose. When he scraped at it with a fingernail it sifted down the wall like sand. He moved the bed and there was a pile of grit on the floor. Clearly he had done a shoddy job installing the bars, hadn't mixed the mortar well enough and left a dry pocket that the boy had been able to scratch away at, loosening a single bar just enough to squeeze through.

Below the window, a floodwall ran the length of the block. Fenn could easily have hopped down to the top of it, then over and away.

The bald man had an idea of where the boy might go. Fenn had a head start, but he was probably still on foot and had miles to travel. The bald man kept a private hansom on retainer and would be able to overtake the boy soon enough.

His shop was on the way. He would stop there first to get some supplies and to put a sign in the window. It was a shame to have to close the place down for the day, but the bald man had his priorities.

Family should always come first.

Constable Colin Pringle couldn't decide whether to wait or to go home and try to get an hour's sleep before his shift. But after a long, sleepless night outside, his clothes were a mess, wrinkled and dirty. Maybe the tailor would be at his shop early. And maybe he would have new clothes that Pringle could wear off the peg. It would be good to show up for his shift looking fresh, even if he didn't feel awfully fresh.

But it was clear that the tailor still wasn't in. There was a sign in the window, carefully printed in red ink on stiff white paper: *Will Return Soon.* Pringle cupped his hands against the glass and peered into the shop. It was dark and still. There was no sense that anyone was working within and there was nothing to indicate how 'soon' anyone would return.

Pringle assumed that if he left now, the tailor would immediately return to the shop. But if he waited, he might be here all day. That was the way the universe worked. He regretted not waiting at the shop on his previous visit. If he had, he might have a fresh new uniform waiting for him at home right now.

He tried the doorknob. He didn't expect it to turn, didn't expect the door to swing open, it was just the thing you were supposed to do before giving up. But the knob did turn and the door did swing open, and Pringle stepped inside.

Now that he was here, he might as well wait.

He walked through the shop and sat in an overstuffed chair that was positioned near the back room for clients who were being fitted. He would give the tailor fifteen minutes and then he would leave.

Just fifteen minutes.

It was a comfortable chair and the shop was quiet and it felt good to sit.

He closed his eyes and was instantly asleep.

23

Walter Day woke up early and rolled out of bed with the cobwebs of a bad dream clinging to him. He splashed cold water on his face from the basin and ran a wet cloth over his chest and armpits. He shaved quickly, pausing to smile at Claire when she entered his room.

By the time he finished, Claire had set kindling in the small fireplace. Day's trousers from the night before were draped over the board to be pressed. He checked the walk-in wardrobe and was pleased to find that he had three fresh shirts.

'I didn't hear you leave my room last night,' Claire said.

'I was quiet. I'm glad I didn't wake you.'

'I wish you had stayed.'

'What would the housekeeper say?'

He chuckled, but Claire acted as though she hadn't heard him. The kindling began to blaze and she carefully placed a handful of thin logs on the new fire. She stood and aimed a pointed stare at him.

'I swear I don't know what to do with myself, Walter. Except for the housekeeper, I know none of the women in the neighbourhood. They don't come round. They haven't warmed to me.'

'How could they not? You are, I'm sure, the most charming woman in all the city.'

'Detectives' wives are not universally beloved here.'

Day grimaced. It was another reminder that the man on the street had no great love for the police. There was too much crime that went unstopped and no one felt safe. Everyone in London knew that the Ripper was still out there in the fog and that the police were helpless to stop him.

'Then don't tell anybody what I do.' He winked at her.

Claire smiled and put the press on the fire. It was a flat rectangle of iron with a wooden handle bolted to one side. She used a pair of sturdy tongs to move it into place on the logs.

'Shall I tell them you're a vendor? I'll say you sell dolls from a cart in the West End. I'm fabulously proud of the work you do with dolls.'

'Hmm. Perhaps I drive an omnibus.'

'The other wives shall embrace me and raise me on their shoulders when they find out.'

Day laughed.

'They'll carry me through the streets,' Claire said.

'Until I run over them all with my omnibus.'

'You and your bus will ruin my best day.'

'You are the best Day.'

'Oh, that's terrible.'

'It is. There's another detective I'm working with. His name's Blacker. That's the sort of joke he makes.'

'You've made a friend?'

'I believe I have.'

'I'm glad.'

'Now we need to find some friends for you,' Day said.

'Perhaps Mr Blacker has a wife.'

'I believe he's a bachelor.'

'Poor man.'

Claire used the tongs to lift the hot iron from the fire and wrapped a cloth around her hand before picking it up by the handle. She dipped her other hand in a small dish of water and sprinkled it over the ironing board. When she pressed the iron against her husband's trousers a cloud of steam and a loud hiss filled the air around her. She moved the iron over the trousers quickly, repositioning them as she went. In seconds, they looked fresh and presentable again.

'I should go round to the tailor for another pair of trousers,' Day said.

'Mrs Dick will be in today and I'll have her launder your other pair.'

'There you have it. Right under your nose. Mrs Dick shall be your bosom companion.'

'That sort of friend I'm sure I don't need.'

'Perhaps if you were to . . .'

'Walter.'

'Yes?'

'Walter, you're a dear man and I'm touched that you concern yourself with my affairs, but I shouldn't burden you with my silly complaints. I have this fine house to look after and I am content to know that my husband is a brilliant detective with the famous Scotland Yard.'

'Even so. If you wanted to go back . . . I mean if you should ever wish to return to Devon, to your family, I would understand.'

'You mustn't worry about that when you have so many

important things to do. Now, let's get you dressed and off to work.'

She held out his trousers to him and he put them on. They were still warm.

24

The sky was the palest of greys and street vendors had begun setting up tarps and awnings to protect their wares from the drizzling rain. The city's nightlife had wound down and the pubs had emptied out. Hammersmith's eyes were grainy. He needed sleep, but the coming day beckoned.

He had been in every pub and opium den in the area surrounding the Shaws' home and, in the last hour, had extended his search several streets out, but with no luck. He decided he had time to visit one more establishment before returning to the flat and getting ready for his shift.

The place in front of him was drab and run down. The timbers of the steps were split and rotting, but a yellowed paper sign in the window read 'No Griddling', meaning that beggars and peddlers weren't allowed inside. The peeling sign above the door read 'The Whistle and Flute', which was Cockney rhyming slang for a gentleman's suit. Hammersmith imagined the original proprietor had started out with more optimism than the neighbourhood had finally permitted.

He pushed the door open and stepped inside, stopping long enough to let his eyes adjust to the cave-like darkness. When he could see well enough to move forward he approached the long bar that imposed itself before the back wall. It was really nothing more than a few well-worn planks that had been nailed to four uprights. The barman, a heavy-set man with a wild beard and thick, tattooed arms, nodded to him from behind the counter. The barman's eyebrows met in the middle and struck out from there across his forehead. Pink cheeks and beady eyes were the only features of the man's face still visible through the thickets of hair.

Hammersmith ordered a pint and stood surveying the room. Two worn-out tarts hunkered at a small table near the end of the bar. They weren't looking his way. No doubt they were ready to turn in for the day without company. At the other end of the room a handful of shadowy figures hunched over four tables that had been pushed together. Hammersmith could hear cards being shuffled and bets murmured through the smoke. The barman set a mug on the counter and backed away. Hammersmith took a courtesy sip. He had no intention of drinking the ale, but he didn't want to appear out of place. The people in this pub weren't here early in the morning. They were here late at night, heavy drinkers who didn't want to stop.

The ale tasted of ashes. Hammersmith set the mug back down and wiped his mouth with the back of his hand. He noticed he needed a shave and wondered if he had time for one before his shift.

As he reached for his wallet, he felt a hand on his arm and he turned, ready for a fight.

The girl in front of him was no more than fifteen years old. She wore a low-cut white blouse and a skirt that was immodestly tight. Her long, dark hair hung loose over her shoulders and she leaned in towards Hammersmith, breathing heavily, the tops of her breasts visible under the blouse's scooped collar.

'You look lost,' she said.

She giggled, covered her mouth and looked up at him with her head lowered.

'Would you be wantin' some company?'

Hammersmith understood. He looked towards the end of the bar and saw the two worn-out whores watching them. The girl was bait. She was a working girl, but it was her job to lure men outside or upstairs or to wherever business was done. Once a man was committed to the deed, a switch would be made and one of the others would take her place. The young woman would then sidle up to the bar once again to be dangled in front of the clientele. Hammersmith assumed that in another year, maybe just a few months, this girl would assume her place with the harder-working women and a fresh young girl would be recruited to act as the bait. It was a sad fate awaiting her and he wondered how much of her future life she was aware of.

'No, thank you,' he said.

Her face turned red and ugly.

'Well, you're a ponce then, aintcha?'

'Hardly.'

He put the girl out of his head and frowned at the mug on the bar. The Whistle and Flute had yielded no results and he didn't have time to visit another pub this morning. Besides, most of them would be closing soon if they weren't closed already. Only the least reputable places were still open, which was why Hammersmith was still out looking. The least reputable places were the places most likely to attract his quarry.

'Oh!'

Hammersmith turned in time to see the girl fall to the floor.

'You didn't have to get rough,' she said.

He didn't see anyone else around and the men at the card table across the room hadn't budged. Hammersmith realized he was about to fall into yet another trap arranged by the same girl and he moved quickly away from the bar just as the giant hand of the barman came crashing down where he had been leaning.

'What's this, then?' the hairy brute said.

Hammersmith felt like a fool. Evidently, if the girl couldn't coax a man upstairs where the older women might gain a shilling from him, then she'd fake an insult and the barman would beat or intimidate the hapless victim for a few coins. The entire establishment was set up to swindle anyone who wasn't in on the game.

Hammersmith took another step back and reached for his club. It was strapped to his side, under his jacket. He brought it out as the barman produced his own club from beneath the counter. It was three feet long and had iron spikes set into it. Next to it, Hammersmith's club looked like a toy. The barman raised a hinged portion of the bar's surface and stepped out from behind the counter. In one smooth move he was standing in front of Hammersmith.

Hammersmith glanced towards the other end of the room. The two older prostitutes had disappeared, presumably into a back room or up the stairs. The card players had left their table and were ranged out across the wall, their features still hidden in the shadows, waiting either to resume their game or to head Hammersmith off if he ran for the door.

Hammersmith raised his hands, showing the barman his pitiful truncheon. The barman blinked and punched Hammersmith in the nose. Blood poured out across the front of Hammersmith's shirt and spattered the floor.

He swung his club. It hit the barman on the shoulder and bounced off. The barman grinned. His teeth were uneven and brown, crumbled nuggets of bone. The young prostitute grabbed Hammersmith from behind and he shrugged her off, but he was distracted long enough that he almost missed seeing the barman's club as it whistled towards him. He ducked and the club sailed over his head, thunking into the stool behind him. One of the spikes on the big man's club stuck in the wooden seat and the barman braced the stool with his foot to try to pry it out.

Hammersmith seized the moment and turned to run, but the girl hung on to his jacket and blocked his retreat. He swatted her hands away, but by now the barman had freed his club from the bar stool and was taking aim again.

Hammersmith turned to the side, hoping the club would hit him in the arm, rather than the head, but he tripped over the girl's leg and fell back. The girl fell the other way and the club clipped her shoulder. She screamed and Hammersmith hit the floor rolling. He jumped up, but the barman had already dropped the club and was hovering over the girl, who had pulled herself into a ball under the seats, her legs drawn up to her chest and her back against the counter. Blood flowed freely down her left arm and she was trying to stop it by batting at it with her right hand.

The barman squatted down in front of her and grabbed her flailing hand, trying to get a look at the damage. Hammersmith was frozen in place. He knew he should run, but he was riveted to the spot, unable to look away.

'Hush now, little one,' the barman said. 'Let me have a look at it.'

'Daddy, make it stop.'

Hammersmith felt sick. The barman had put his own daughter to work swindling the customers.

The barman looked up from the girl and snarled.

'Don't you move, mister. You give me one minute here and I'll kill you good.'

Hammersmith felt a hand on his arm and jumped. He turned, his club raised. The only other people in the pub were the card players and they had him outnumbered. He was ready to do his worst, but the man behind him was familiar, now that his features weren't hidden in shadows.

'Best we get out of here now,' Blackleg said, 'afore Big Pete gets his hands on you.'

Hammersmith nodded.

'I've been looking everywhere for you,' he said.

25

Fennimore Hubbard sat on the kerb and examined the soles of his feet. They hurt badly and his pace had slowed in the last hour. Blisters had already formed and burst and blood mixed with rainwater beneath him to create pale pink tributaries that crossed the divides of his toes and trickled away into the gutter. He wished now that he had taken the time to put on a pair of shoes before dropping from The Bald Man's window, but what was done was done.

He took off his sopping pyjama shirt and twisted it in his tiny fists, trying to rip it in half. The fabric was too strong and he used his teeth. It was a well-made shirt, probably fashioned by The Bald Man himself. Once he got it started, it ripped easily enough up the back, but he had trouble with the collar and had to remove it completely, tossing it into the street.

He wrapped the shirt-halves around each of his feet and knotted them at the top. He stood. The fabric bunched under the balls of his feet and threw off his balance, but his feet felt a little better.

Now, of course, he was bare-chested and cold. He was seven years old and not large for his age. His ribs sat on his flesh like umbrella tines. The best way to keep warm, he thought, was to keep running.

Fenn had a good sense of direction and he was certain

he was headed towards home, his real home, the house he'd been born in and the house where his parents, he hoped, still lived and waited for him. The Bald Man had told him that his parents and three sisters had moved away, that they had sold Fenn to The Bald Man and that there was no birth-home to return to. But Fenn didn't believe anything The Bald Man said. The Bald Man had also claimed to love Fenn as his own son, but Fenn's father, his real father, had never tied him to a bed or shut him up in a dark cupboard or screamed at him. Fenn wasn't a baby, he could figure things out for himself and it hadn't been hard to figure out that The Bald Man was dangerous. The Bald Man was something that Fenn had heard his father refer to as 'touched in the head'. Which meant that he did things that made no sense.

Fenn was also certain that The Bald Man had killed other children. He had heard the man say several times that Fenn was 'another chance' for him, that Fenn would be better than 'the others'. And so Fenn *had* tried to be better than he imagined the others had been. He was smart – his real mother always said so – and he had understood that fighting The Bald Man, or disobeying him, was futile. He had known to bide his time.

His one big mistake had been in not talking to the policeman who had come round to The Bald Man's shop. The policeman, who had not worn a blue uniform like the other policemen Fenn had seen, said his name was Little, but he was big and fat, which was funny. The Bald Man told Fenn to be quiet when the policeman came, but Mr Little had looked right at Fenn and said that his parents were looking for him.

And right then Fenn should have told Mr Little that The Bald Man was touched in the head. He should have shouted it as soon as he saw the scissors in The Bald Man's hand. But he didn't. The nice fat policeman was dead now and Fenn believed it was his fault.

He came to a wide junction in the road and stopped. The sky was growing brighter and the fog was burning off. It would be harder to run and hide in the daylight. People would see him, shirtless and dripping, tattered fabric wrapped around his feet, and they would stop him. And if they didn't listen to him, they might take him back to The Bald Man. They might think that The Bald Man was really Fenn's father, like he said he was.

But he recognized a building across the street. It was a department store, specializing in tartan weaves. A big restaurant jutted from the side of the shop, the street-facing wall a single huge piece of bowed glass. Fenn's mother had taken him and his sisters there for tea one day more than a year ago. It had been a treat, a rare day out, and Fenn remembered the window, remembered the wonder of it: a single pane of glass so big and yet somehow curved. Food had been served on fine china, the platters pearly and nearly translucent, nothing like the dishes used at home. The tiny cakes they ate were fresh and moist and sweeter than anything Fenn had tasted in his life. That day they had walked to the department store and walked home after tea, burdened with heavy shopping bags filled with sundries for the house.

Fenn was in his own neighbourhood. Close to his real house.

The department store was closed this early in the

morning, but Fenn could see a shopkeeper moving around behind that magical window, readying the place for today's business. A donkey carrying sacks of brick dust trotted past Fenn. The dust would sell for a penny a quart and be used to clean knives and ironwork. A peddler trudged beside the donkey, leading it to the first stop on his daily rounds, and he didn't even glance in Fenn's direction.

Down at the other end of the street, a news vendor was shouting out the morning's scandal while waving the latest tabloid over his head. 'POLICE KILLER AT LARGE,' the boy called out, his voice much deeper and louder than seemed possible for his size. He couldn't be very much older than Fenn. 'IS THE RIPPER BACK?' the boy shouted at nobody in particular.

Fenn took a moment to orient himself and then crossed the street, away from the other boy and his frightening speculation. Fenn picked up his pace as he passed more little shops and houses that he recognized. Ahead, he knew, was his own house, maybe three or four streets away.

'Here now, what's this, then?'

Fenn stopped, his heart in his throat. He turned, just as a meaty hand grasped his shoulder. A constable with a bushy orange moustache glared down at him from under his high blue hat.

'This's a respectable neighbourhood, little man.'

'Sir.'

Fenn could barely breathe.

'Where's yer master?'

'I don't have a master. My parents are waiting for me.'

'Ye look like a sweep's boy to me.'

'No, sir.'

'Don't talk back, boy.'

'No, sir. Sir, I need help. Somebody's after me. He's gonna hurt me.'

The policeman drew back and released Fenn's shoulder.

'Don't be playin' games with me now, son.'

'No games, sir.'

'What're ye sayin'?'

'There's a man and he took me to his house and he tied me up and I think he'll hurt me if he finds me again.'

The policeman stared down at Fenn for a long moment. Then he reared back his head and laughed. It was a deep, booming roar of a laugh that made Fenn's chestbone vibrate. Finally, the policeman wiped his eyes and settled his hat low on his forehead.

'Aw, get along home with ye then,' he said.

'But, sir, I need help. Please.'

'I'm bein' patient with ye, boy, but don't test me. Ye'll be gettin' somewhere fast, either yer home or the workhouse, ye make up yer mind right quick about it.'

The policeman raised his hand as if to hit Fenn and the boy backed away a step. He ducked, but the blow didn't come. The constable turned his back and ambled away, back on patrol. Without looking back, the policeman rumbled a warning.

'If I see ye about when I come round this way next, it's the workhouse fer ye, and that's a promise, boy.'

Fenn blinked back tears and sighed. Behind him was a high wooden fence, painted green long ago, faded and peeling and nearly grey in the half light. He clambered up it and dropped to the other side, out of sight of the street and of the policeman, should he turn back around. Fenn hunched his shoulders and trotted alongside the fence, headed again in the direction of his parents' home. It didn't matter whether the policeman believed him, Fenn's father would believe and would protect him from The Bald Man. And when The Bald Man was caught and put in prison, the unhelpful policeman would be sorry and maybe even apologize to Fenn.

Birds began to chirp in the treetops that lined the street and a dark hansom chugged past Fenn, unseen on the other side of the fence. Rainwater sloshed off the wheels and heavy beads ran like dew off a monstrous black beetle's back. The cab rolled past and turned the corner.

Fenn cut through an opening in the fence and sprinted to the end of the street. He was on his own road. The solid terrace of houses lined the street ahead, queuing up in a row that led right to Fenn's front door. He could see the windows on the ground floor, twinkling with gaslight. His mother was awake and no doubt cooking breakfast for Fenn's father and sisters. A door opened at the far end of the street and Harriet Smith stepped out on to her doorstep. She was far away, but he could see her yellow pigtails. Another door opened and a second child, young Robert Harrison, emerged. Fenn hated Robert Harrison, but he had never been so glad to see anyone in his life. Robert and Harriet waved to each other and ran into the street, already picking up a game they'd clearly left off the previous evening. It was still too dark out. They didn't see Fenn and he was afraid to call out, afraid the policeman might still be nearby.

He untied the bits of pyjama shirt on his feet and left them in the road. He could run faster barefoot and he didn't care about the pain any more.

He ran past the first house on the corner, joined to the next, but more squat, a dwarf beside stone giants. To his right, the black hansom cab sat idle, the horse sniffing the morning air, the coachman hidden in a blanket of shadow. The cab looked familiar and Fenn slowed as he drew near. The hansom's windows were covered by dark curtains and Fenn saw one of them move.

Realization dawned and Fenn swallowed hard. He had to pass that cab to get to his door. He decided to put everything he had into one mad dash down the street. He was too close now to do anything else.

26

The bald man sat in a hansom cab on Cheyne Street watching the passive expanse of brick and iron, an entire street's worth of one building divided up into multiple homes. The patter of rain eased and the sky began to turn a pale shade of pink. Children emerged from their townhouses and resumed the previous evening's play without benefit of grass or trees. They raced here and there, shrieking and whooping, making ingenious use of hoops, balls and sticks.

The bald man had sat in this same spot many times before, watching the children. He liked to single out the most beautiful or charming of them and concentrate on him. Or her. Today, a pretty blonde girl, thin and graceful and calm, directed a playmate in his effort to keep a metal barrel hoop rolling along. Ordinarily, the bald man wouldn't have been able to tear his eyes away from her and her fetching pigtails, but this morning he was there for a different reason. He had already selected his ward and had lost him. Now he was waiting for Fenn, certain that he would return here to his first home, the home he'd had before the bald man had rescued him from this perfect ordinariness.

The coachman was well paid and had proven trustworthy on past expeditions. The bald man didn't worry about him, but didn't care to engage him in conversation. They had a long, silent wait ahead of them. The boy had surely been walking half the night, but the bald man had travelled faster and was certain he'd got there first.

He thought about his shop and he wondered whether he had

remembered to lock the front door after putting up the 'Back Soon' sign in the window. It would gnaw at him, he knew, if he didn't return to check on it. But this was not the time. Once he'd found the boy, it would be a quick stop on their way home.

He needed to find the boy before he could do anything else.

There was always the possibility that Fenn had gone to the police, but the bald man doubted it. He felt sure that the boy was already beginning to love him, to think of him as his new father, and what son would dare to call the police on his own father?

The bald man smiled to himself. When he caught Fenn again, he would be well within his rights to be angry. No one would think less of him for beating the boy. After all, he'd caused his father a long night of worry. But their little family of two was going through a difficult time and so he would show mercy. Oh, there would be changes at home, that was certain, but the bald man could turn the other cheek this time and the boy would see how much his new father truly loved him.

He was snapped out of his reverie by the sight of Fenn himself, bedraggled and dirty and bare-chested, still in his pyjama trousers, staggering up the hill at the far end of the street. There was no mistaking him. The bald man was so filled with relief and fatherly love that, for only a moment, he was unable to move.

The bald man was sure the boy saw the cab and he must have suspected who was inside, but he kept coming anyway, tried to run right past. The bald man smiled. Fenn wasn't making much of an effort to get away. The poor boy was clearly exhausted and running to his new father.

The bald man stepped out of the cab just long enough to scoop his son up and lay him on the empty seat, then he clambered back in, sat across from the weeping child and pounded twice on the cab's ceiling.

He looked back as the cab moved down the street and saw that the children were still playing their pointless games. No one had noticed anything.

He smiled, thrilled by his own cleverness and courage. And by his extraordinary good luck.

He passed a note up to the coachman. They would need to stop at his shop so the bald man could check the locks. And then he would take the entire rest of the day off work.

Clearly, he needed to spend more time with his son.

27

'I promised you another penny, didn't I?' Day said.

He held the coin up so that it caught the light. The dancing man reached out for it, but then drew his hand back.

'I know you,' he said. 'You were in my dream last night.'

'It wasn't a dream,' Day said.

'I'll dance for you.'

'No need. Take the penny. Get yourself a loaf of bread.'

Day tossed the penny in the dancing man's direction and walked quickly away, past the upturned milk crate and in through the back door of The Yard. Behind him, he heard the coin clink against the stone pavement.

Inside, Michael Blacker was already hard at work, along with two other detectives, Tiffany and Wiggins, who were at their own desks across the room. Neither of them looked up as Day entered. The piles of paper on Day's desk had grown. Day could barely see Blacker on the other side of it, his legs crossed, a foot-high sheaf of notes in his lap.

'I thought I might beat you here this morning,' Day said.

Blacker grinned at him. He put down the notes he was reading and wiped his eyes.

'No chance of that, old man,' he said. 'I never left.'

'You've been here all night?'

'Hasn't been so long since you went home. Anyway, I've nothing to go home to. Not like you.'

'Well, I should have stayed. Had I known . . .'

'Better one of us should be fresh. There's a joke in here somewhere about it being a bright new day or somesuch. Too tired to find it myself, so if you could work it out on your own, I'd be grateful.'

Day stared at the piles of paper that covered every inch of the workspace. Yesterday morning his desk had been pristine.

'Where did all this come from?' he said.

'I've been rounding up our colleagues as they arrive and commandeering their notes.'

'You? But I was going to . . .'

'And you should. By all means. Not stepping on your toes at all, old man. But we're all so in and out, I was afraid we might miss a chance to talk to some of them if I didn't seize these bulls by the horns, as it were.'

'And have you found anything?'

'Oh!'

'What is it?'

'I can't believe it slipped my mind to tell you. First thing as you came in I wanted to tell you, but I let it go right by me.'

'Yes?'

Blacker beckoned and Day leaned over the desk, resting his hands on the papers there.

'He's struck again,' Blacker said.

'What? Not another detective.'

'No, none of us this time. But another man with a beard was found dead last night. We only received word a few minutes ago.'

'A man with a beard?'

Day straightened back up, annoyed.

'Men with beards are killed every bloody day, Blacker. This is London, for God's sake.'

'Well, that's true enough. You're beginning to sound like an old hand at this.'

'I'm sorry, but I thought you were going to tell me that we were being stalked and picked off, one by one.'

'The body that was found . . .'

'Yes?'

'His beard was trimmed and his throat was cut.'

'Just like Robinson.'

'Exactly like Robinson. Except that this bloke was found with his head in a toilet, not in a bathtub. But otherwise it's the same, through and through.'

'Has Kingsley had a chance to look at it yet?'

'I rather doubt it. Sir Edward's assigned this new murder to Waverly Brown, but I believe we can wrest it from his grip with very little effort. "Little effort", right? Not bad. I haven't lost my wits entirely.'

'I'm not convinced this means what you hope it does,' Day said.

'What do you mean? What do I hope?'

'If anything this murder, done up in exactly the same fashion as Robinson's, says to me that we have two completely different murderers. This one continues to kill, doing in bearded men right and left, while the man we're after did the one killing. It's something to do with Little specifically, not with any beard.'

'But surely you can't ignore the bizarre features of the three murders when looked at together.'

'Little's beard wasn't shaved.'

'But Little didn't have a beard for the killer to shave in the first place.'

'Exactly.'

'If he'd had a beard, it would have been shaved.'

'If he'd had a beard? It doesn't matter what would have happened if he'd had a beard. He didn't have a beard. There's no beard and it's not a clue that there's no beard since there never was a beard.'

'Listen, we're both tired. You're getting upset.'

'I'm not upset. I'm simply . . .'

Day sat down. He picked up a pile of papers from atop another pile and tossed it back down.

'I'm at sixes and sevens. I feel as though I've missed out on a great deal of activity and conjecture because I went home.'

Blacker sighed.

'I owe you an apology.'

'No, not at all.'

'But I do. Perhaps I should have waited for your arrival before launching enquiries within the ranks here.'

'No, you were right to set things in motion. I'm struggling to find a foothold here and you're already firmly established. I suppose there's a touch of envy in me this morning. That's all it is.'

'No need for envy. You're off balance. Let me tell you

a secret. That feeling never goes away. We're in the dark here, utterly hated by the people we're trying to help and blindly seeking things we'll absolutely never find. It's a miserable experience that I wouldn't wish on my most intimate enemy.'

'Then why are you here?'

'Because it's the only game in town, old man. This is the best and only way to feel you've got the inside track. Because what you'll eventually come to realize is that everyone out there is groping around in the dark, too, but in here we know it. Gives us a leg up.'

He winked at Day and, after a long moment, Day laughed.

28

'I was outnumbered.'

'Course you was. Otherwise you could've handled Big Pete, eh?'

'Well, he was rather fierce.'

'Fierce. That's Big Pete.'

'Thank you for stepping in when you did.'

'Don't mention it.'

'Pete seemed to calm down as soon as you spoke up. I'm curious, why did he let us leave so easily?'

'Don't fret about it.'

'He seemed a bit frightened, really.'

'I have a reputation, is all.'

'A reputation?'

'I've been known to do a bit of violence in my day.'

'Oh.'

'Best if you don't know much about that, being as you're a bluebottle.'

'Why help me at all?'

'Don't know, really. Strikes me you might be a different sort than the bluebottles I run up against. You coulda pinched me at that posh house yesterday, but you didn't. You cared about that chavy more'n you cared about lookin' the big man and impressin' me. S'pose that meant somethin' to me.'

'I see.'

'I'll let you go on about your business, now you're not gettin' yerself killed.'

'Wait. Are you looking for the chimneysweep? The one who left that boy?'

'I put out the word I'm lookin' fer 'im. Somebody'll point 'im out soon enough.'

'Don't approach him yet. I want to be there.'

'Stay out of trouble, bluebottle. And getcher nose fixed up or it'll heal crooked like mine.'

'Did you hear me?'

'Don't you worry. I'll find you again when our friend shows 'isself.'

29

Walter Day took a deep breath and knocked on the door. He glanced to his left where Michael Blacker shifted from foot to foot. Neither of them spoke.

After a pregnant moment Day heard shuffling footsteps behind the door and the metal-on-metal rasp of a chain being drawn. The door opened a crack and dull brown eyes peered out at them from a woman's heavy, grey face. Day thought of raisins pressed into a lump of clay. From somewhere in the flat behind her a strange wailing sound drifted out to them, rising and falling like an animal crying out in pain. It was accompanied by the more familiar din of a baby crying. The wailing noise would occasionally stop on an up-note and then begin again.

'What is it?' the woman said. 'Got some more dead you wanna tell me 'bout?'

Her lips barely parted when she spoke, her mouth an unmoving slit.

'Mrs Little?' Day said.

The woman nodded. 'Yeah.'

'We're sorry for your loss, Mrs Little,' Blacker said.

'Yeah? Well, you lot done your duty by me. That one-arm bloke come an' tol' me last night, so I got nothin' I need from you 'n' yours.'

Day held his hands up in a gesture of peace and calm.

'We'd like to ask you some questions if we may, ma'am.'

The Widow Little turned from the door and it opened wider, but she held on to the edge of it, not letting them in yet. Ropes of loose skin and fat swung from the underside of her arm and slapped against the jamb.

'Gregory, I tol' you already you better see to yer brother. That singin's just made the baby worser. You see to him right now, you unnerstan' me?'

'Yes, mama.'

It was a boy's voice, followed by the patter of small feet on wood. Mrs Little turned her attention back to the two detectives in the hall and pursed her lips as if trying to remember who they were.

'What's in it for me if I answer these questions you got?'

'Could we come in, ma'am?' Day said.

Blacker widened his eyes and shook his head at Day. He was on the other side of the doorway, his shoulder pressed against the outside wall of the flat, and thus was out of Mrs Little's line of sight. Day had no way to respond to him without Mrs Little seeing. He had no more desire to enter the flat than Blacker did, but he smiled at her and nodded as if she'd already agreed to let them come in.

She shrugged and turned and they followed her inside. Her grubby housecoat ended well above her thick ankles. Day looked up at the water-stained ceiling.

The stench of old food and human waste hit them like a physical force as soon as they entered the dingy flat. The floorboards were worn so smooth that the men could have skated across them but for a faded threadbare rug in the centre of the front room. A battered dun-coloured sofa, buttons dangling like fruit from its back, hunched against the wall under a curtainless window where a single ray of sunlight fought its way through the smeared glass. Three chairs stood upright, grouped around a barrel. A large, pearl-coloured doily was draped over the barrel in a vain attempt to make it look like a table, and peanut shells and dust were scattered across it. Day recognized a cigar box in the centre of the table as the same one Sir Edward had brought to the squad room. A fourth chair was tipped over on the floor, its upholstery unravelled from the top, cotton batting spilling out. A baby lay on the chair-back, its arms and legs stretched out towards the ceiling. It hiccoughed and coughed when it heard their footsteps, then began to cry again.

A naked, moon-faced boy was strapped to a wooden chair in the corner of the room. Drool ran in rivulets over the boy's chin and down his chest. He rocked back and forth, the leather straps digging into his flesh, his eyes rolling wildly in their sockets as he gibbered and howled at the baby. A smaller child, wearing nothing but a filthy pair of knickers, was attempting to silence the monster-boy, patting his arm and clucking at him. Day realized that the boy in the chair was singing to the baby in some strange, unrecognizable language.

Day drew back.

'Good Lord,' he said.

The woman chuckled and her black eyes sparkled.

'Hard to look at, ain't he?'

'Let that child free from there, right now.'

'I undo 'im and he'll fall straight on to his face, see if he don't.'

'But this is barbarous.'

'Only looks to be. He's a happy boy, ain't you, Anthony?'

At the sound of his name, Anthony let out a fresh wail and bounced up and down in his seat. The other boy, Gregory, whooped and danced around his brother's chair, which excited Anthony even more. The baby fell suddenly silent. Day and Blacker stared, entranced and disgusted, as the two boys worked themselves into a contained frenzy, colonial natives dancing for rain.

''At's enough,' the woman said. 'Enough, I say. Gregory, you settle 'im down now.'

The smaller boy stopped hopping about and laid a hand on Anthony's head, which seemed to calm him. In the fresh silence, Day could hear the baby wheezing.

'Gregory, see to that baby.'

Gregory scampered over to the infant and stuck a dirty finger into its mouth. He fished out half of a peanut shell, dripping with spit. The baby let out a long wail and immediately began to snore, which excited the boy in the corner. Anthony began rocking his chair once more, beating his head against the wall behind him.

Gregory threw the shell on the ground, where the baby could presumably pick it back up when it awoke, and ran back across the room. While the others watched Gregory stroke his older brother's head, Day reached down and picked up the wet peanut shell. He slipped it into his pocket and wiped his fingers on the leg of his trousers.

When Anthony had calmed down again, Mrs Little turned her attention back to the detectives. Day nodded towards the boy in the corner.

'What's . . . ?'

'What's wrong wiv 'im? Hell if I know. Come outta me that way and been that way ever since. But he's a good boy.'

'Has he seen a doctor?'

'Course he seen a doctor. Ain't savages, is we? Too much fluids, says they, too much blood. They bled 'im near dry, cupped 'im and leeched 'im and left 'im so's he couldn't hardly move no more. Ain't takin 'im to no more doctors. He's happy here and, anyway, he ain't likely to live too much longer. Money's better spent than on doctors.'

Day was filled with a mad passion to run from the room.

'Gregory, you seem like a responsible young man,' Blacker said.

The boy blushed and looked down at his feet.

'But I don't see how you can hear anything with that growth in your ear.'

Gregory looked up, wide-eyed. His hands flew to his ears.

'I don't feel nuffink there,' he said.

'Come here, lad.'

Blacker dropped to one knee and reached out to the boy. Gregory came to him, his expression frightened.

'Nothing to fear,' Blacker said. 'We'll have you fixed up in no time.'

He looked at the boy's left ear.

'Well, that's odd,' he said. 'I was mistaken. That's not a growth. Now why would you keep money in your ear?'

Gregory gasped. Blacker grinned at him and his fingers flitted through the air next to the boy's head, barely grazing his ear. He brought his hand up to Gregory's eyes and produced a shiny penny.

'I think you'll be able to hear much better now.'

Gregory gulped and stared at the penny in Blacker's hand.

'Well, go on and take it,' Blacker said. 'It was in your ear so it must be yours.'

'Cor, that's magic, that is,' Gregory said.

'I'm sure I have no idea what you're talking about.'

Blacker winked at the boy and Gregory finally smiled back at him. The boy took the penny from Blacker's hand and goggled at it.

The Widow Little took two steps towards them and snatched the penny from her son's hand. She made it disappear somewhere within the folds of her housecoat.

'Any money comes into this flat is mine,' she said.

She glared at the detectives, daring them to contradict her. Gregory shrugged and smiled at them. Blacker patted him on the head and stood back up. He frowned and cleared his throat.

'When's the last you saw your husband, Mrs Little?' Blacker said.

'Can't recall. Maybe a week, maybe more.'

'Is that unusual, not to see him for a week?'

'He hardly never come home no more. The sight of Anthony made him sick to his stomach.'

Anthony wailed again and Day noticed that the tonal shift he'd heard before was present again in the boy's voice.

'He done assed you where our daddy's at,' Gregory said.

'You understand him?'

'Sure. He ain't dumb. Just different's all.'

'Don't matter where yer daddy's at. Hush now and let these gennlemen talk. They's friends of yer daddy.'

'He was a fine man, your father,' Blacker said. 'One of the best The Yard ever saw.'

Gregory switched his gaze from Blacker to Day and stared unblinking at him.

'He only come home most times when he got his pay,' Mrs Little said. 'Left enough with me for the groceries and such. He dint spend much time 'ere though.'

Hardly a surprise, Day thought.

'Did you talk to him? Did he discuss any cases with you or anything that might have been bothering him? Anyone who may have threatened him?'

'You lot'd know better'n me. He was up there alla time. Never tol' me nothin'. One of them killers he was after most likely done 'im.'

'I see. Well, thank you for your time, ma'am.'

'Where I'm gonna get paid from now?'

'I'm sorry?'

'Without Mr Little's pay, how I'm gonna take care of these young'uns? You think on that. Without food money, I'm gonna have to take young Anthony and drown 'im in the river.'

'I don't . . .'

The Widow Little suddenly smiled and her face re-arranged itself. She looked almost pleasant. Day realized that she was much younger than he'd first supposed. It was unlikely that she'd ever been a great beauty, but Day could see the ghost of the spirited bride she once was.

'I'm havin' a laugh on you boys is all. I know you don't have nuffink to do wiv it. The money, I mean. I done talked it over wiv your man there, the one's got no arm. He'll see to it, see I get Mr Little's pinchins.'

'His pension? How wonderful.'

'He's a good man, that one. He brung that box, too,' she said. More'n five pounds there. Thanks to you an' yours gonna do a bit o' shoppin' later in the day.'

'Yes, of course,' Day said. 'Well, we should . . .'

'Was Inspector Little planning to grow a beard, by chance?' Blacker said.

Day scowled at him and Blacker shrugged.

'Don't think so. Beards is filthy, all full up with food and dust and such. Won't have no beard near these lips, I tell you. Mr Little was allus considerable about such things. Knew how them whiskers scratched and kep' hisself tidy for me. Allus kep' hisself tidy, he did.'

Without warning, the widow burst into tears. Her lips opened wide, trailing stringers of grief, a cobweb of spit connecting the two halves of her face. She seemed suddenly vulnerable in her ugliness and Day wanted to put an arm around her, but Gregory reached her first and patted her jiggling arm.

'There, there, mama. Don't cry.'

Across the room, Anthony began to bounce in his chair again, howling, and Day could almost make out words. The back of the wooden chair beat against the plaster wall as the hideous woman and her strange children celebrated their grief. The baby woke then with a start, its tiny arms windmilling against the floor, and joined its voice to the Little family's horrible wailing.

Day took a pound note from his waistcoat pocket and slid it under the top of the cigar box. He laid a calling card atop the barrel and grabbed Blacker by the arm. The two of them left, pulling the door closed behind them.

'I need a drink,' Blacker said.

'So do I. How could . . . ?'

'I don't know. But if I were married to that, I'd spend all my time at work too. Sir Edward's admonition to the men to spend more time with family must have gone hard with poor Little.'

'Well, I don't only feel sorry for him. Look at them. What kind of life is that?'

'That's why I'm not married,' Blacker said. 'I'm sure she wasn't like that when he met her.'

Day looked back at the door. If Mrs Little had changed over the years, how had her husband fared? Had he once been an idealistic young detective? Or had he always avoided his work and his family, just waiting for the inevitable end?

'The magic trick,' Day said. 'That was kind of you.'

'He seems like a good boy,' Blacker said.

'You know you can't have children if you don't first find a wife.'

'Who said I want children?'

'Don't worry. You'll find the right woman.'

'Who said I was looking?'

Halfway down the stairs, they could still hear the chorus of misery behind them. The wailing and howling seemed to keep time with the regular beat of the chair banging against the wall.

'That boy should be taken away.'

'You think he'd be better cared for in an asylum?'

Blacker sighed.

'No. I wouldn't wish the asylum on anyone.'

'Thank God they'll get Little's pension.'

Blacker stopped as they reached the door to the street. The sorrowful music wasn't heard down here so much as it was felt, a fog seeping through the walls and the floor.

'Little's pension?' he said.

'What?'

'Little didn't have a pension any more than you or I do. And it doesn't look like he saved much over the years.'

'Then what was she talking about?'

'Sir Edward.'

'You mean?'

Blacker nodded.

'I have to think so. After witnessing all that, the man's doing what he can.'

'Bully for him.'

'He's a better man than I am, that's a sure thing.'

Blacker pushed open the door and the two stepped out into bright daylight. Day breathed deep and let the sun fill his lungs. He took the peanut shell from his pocket and tossed it into the street. Blacker saw but didn't ask.

'I say live every day as if you're Walter Day,' Blacker said.

'And what does that mean?'

Blacker smiled. He shook his head and put an arm around Day's shoulder.

'What say we find a murderer?' he said.

Day nodded and allowed himself to be led down the rain-damped street. The bright morning sun shone on his face and London beckoned. He listened to the birds calling to each other above, to the costermongers hawking their wares by the side of the road, to the healthy children shouting from the windows, and everything he had seen and heard and smelled in the Little flat began to recede like the tide, leaving only the faintest trace of black silt behind.

30

'You're covered with blood,' Kingsley said.

Hammersmith was surprised to find Kingsley in his laboratory so early. He had left Blackleg after arranging a time and place to meet later that evening and had rushed to the college, stopping briefly at stalls along the way to grab a penny pie, a ginger beer and something to read.

'I'm sorry?' he said.

He looked down at his shirt, which was permanently ruined by a wide brown swathe of blood.

'Oh. Yes, you might say I had an adventuresome night.'

'Does your nose hurt badly?'

Hammersmith shrugged. He had stopped paying attention to the low throbbing pain that surged outward from the middle of his face.

'Come,' Kingsley said, 'Let's have a look at you. If it's broken we'll need to set it.'

Hammersmith allowed himself to be led to an empty table in the middle of the laboratory. There were ten tables here and all but two of them were currently occupied by corpses. Fiona was standing near one of the tables, sketching the body that lay on it. Hammersmith didn't see Inspector Little's body anywhere in the room. Nor did he see the dead chimney climber.

Fiona looked up from her pad and gasped when she saw Hammersmith.

'Is it that bad?' he said.

He smiled at her, but she didn't smile back.

'You look a fright,' she said. 'As bad as these 'uns on the tables.'

'I'm more lively than they are. Though not by much.'

Kingsley dipped a clean rag in cold water and began dabbing at Hammersmith's face, gently around the nose. Hammersmith could feel dried crumbs of blood falling past his lips.

'Here,' Kingsley said. 'Blow your nose.'

He handed Hammersmith a second rag and stood back. Hammersmith tried to squeeze his nose with the rag, but his vision went suddenly dark and pinpricks of light danced behind his eyes. He steadied himself, then held the rag against his upper lip and blew gently out through his nose. A great clot of blood and snot slid out on to the rag.

'Oh, good lord,' he said. 'That's horrible.'

'Not even the worst thing I've seen this morning,' Kingsley said. 'What's this you've got here?'

He took the balled-up bloody rag from Hammersmith and pointed at the magazine rolled up under his arm.

'I expected to have to wait for you,' Hammersmith said. 'I came prepared.'

'You read,' Kingsley said.

Hammersmith nodded.

'May I?'

Kingsley dropped the rag into a bucket under the table and held out his hand. Hammersmith gave him the magazine. Kingsley unrolled it and frowned at the cover.

'*Punch*?'

'It's quite popular and I like to keep up.'

Kingsley flipped through the magazine.

'What's this? "Mr Punch's Model Music Hall Songs"?' He smirked and handed the magazine back to Hammersmith. 'Amusing, I'm sure.'

Hammersmith smiled, embarrassed. 'Well, there's a variety of subjects. That's only one snippet. But anyway I'm sure you must read more . . .' He stopped, at a loss for what the doctor might read.

'Any reading is good for the mind,' Kingsley said. 'And I suppose even a humorous magazine may stimulate the imagination.' He smiled. 'We have some of these same weeklies around the house, don't we, Fiona? I've seen this before.'

The girl blushed and made a show of concentrating on her drawing. She spoke as if to the pad of paper.

'I quite like the illustrations in it,' Fiona said. 'Did you see the new one by Mr Tenniel in that one?'

Hammersmith was surprised. It was the most she'd said in his presence. 'I'm afraid I haven't had a chance to look it over yet,' he said.

He turned the pages until he found the cartoon she'd mentioned of two men who apparently represented Capital and Labour. They were playing a card game called Beggar My Neighbour. The meaning of it eluded Hammersmith entirely.

The girl smiled at him.

'Well,' Kingsley said, 'Mr Hammersmith, I would like you to think very hard about model music hall songs and Mr Tenniel's illustrations. I'm going to reset your nose and it's going to hurt a great deal. You should have come to me immediately instead of poking about newsstands. By now the tissue has swelled all round the break. It would be best for you to cast your mind on something else.'

'But now that you've told me how painful it's going to be I doubt I'll be able to think about anything else.'

'I apologize. I'm used to dealing with the dead. They never complain.'

'I certainly hope not.'

Kingsley brought his hands together on Hammersmith's cheeks and placed his thumbs on either side of the bridge of his nose. Hammersmith closed his eyes and felt the doctor drag his thumbs down across his face. Pain exploded through Hammersmith's skull and he jerked away from Kingsley. Fixing his nose hurt infinitely more than breaking it had. He braced his arms against the back edge of the table, his elbows locked straight, and breathed deeply through his mouth.

When he opened his eyes Kingsley was holding the bucket out to him.

'If you need to vomit,' he said.

Hammersmith swallowed hard.

'Thank you, no.'

'It will be crooked, I think. Noses aren't my speciality. But it should set well and you'll be able to breathe through it in the near future. Just be careful about your face for the next few days. Sleep on your back. The nose will most likely be tender for some time to come. Use a steak on it to reduce the swelling.'

Hammersmith couldn't afford steak, but he smiled as well as he was able.

'I will. Thank you.'

'Well, I don't think you came here to have your nose fixed. And I'm sure you didn't come to discuss popular literature,' Kingsley said.

'Right,' Hammersmith said. 'I'm here about the boy, of course.'

'Yes, I thought you might be anxious for results. I got to him first thing. Unfortunately, there's not a lot to tell. The boy basically baked to death in the chimney.'

'But the fire wasn't lit.'

'No, but the intense heat that built up inside the structure was enough. His lungs weren't able to process the air around him and he slowly suffocated. There is evidence that his organs began to break down before his death, so I imagine it was a long and painful process.'

Hammersmith's jaw clenched.

'Was there any . . . did you find anything on the body that might provide a clue?'

'The boy's elbows and knees were bloodied and scarred from repeatedly rubbing against bricks over a period of time. At some point, I would say within the past week or so, salt water was rubbed into his wounds to clean them. The soles of his feet had been burned repeatedly. His master might have given him incentive to climb faster by lighting fires beneath him. He also had a small burn on his left wrist. It was up high and covered by the sleeve of his jacket. Possibly inflicted by a cigarette or a fireplace ember, but of an unusual shape.'

'I drew a picture of it for you,' Fiona said.

'You did?'

'Yes, so you wouldn't have to look at the body again. You were so upset yesterday I didn't think . . .'

'That's awfully considerate of you.'

The girl was holding her pad of paper and had already turned to the proper page as the two men were talking. She tore the page out and handed it to Hammersmith. The picture she'd drawn was of a child's arm with a dark, mottled half moon centred between the wrist and elbow.

'Thank you very much.'

Fiona smiled.

'You look horribly sore and tired, but you smell like chocolate,' she said.

'I do?'

Kingsley leaned in and sniffed Hammersmith's jacket.

'You do,' he said.

'It must be . . . I live above a confectioner's shop.'

'It's not unpleasant,' Kingsley said.

'It's nice,' Fiona said.

'Dr Kingsley?'

A young woman wearing a starched white hat stood in the doorway of the big room.

'There are two more gentlemen from the police here to speak to you.'

'Well, show them in, of course. No, wait. I'll accompany you.'

He turned to Hammersmith and lowered his voice so that the nurse wouldn't hear.

'Clean yourself up. I'll keep them in the vestibule for a few moments. Fiona, please fetch a clean shirt from my wardrobe in the back. Mr Hammersmith can't wear this thing.'

He waved his hand at Hammersmith's bloody shirt.

'I wouldn't want to put you to any trouble,' Hammersmith said.

'It's no trouble at all.'

Kingsley followed the nurse from the room. Fiona gave Hammersmith a shy smile and disappeared through a second door at the other end of the room.

Hammersmith stood up from the table and had to grab the edge of it to keep from falling down. He felt lightheaded and the room tried to swim away from him, slowly receding and being brought back by the tide, then leaving again. He moved carefully to the worktop against the side of the room, holding the table until he was close enough to put his hand on the worktop. He worked his way to a mirror on a high stand in the corner. It was angled towards the floor and he swivelled it so he could see his face.

His nose was a huge misshapen beetroot and the skin around his eyes was deeply purple with flecks of yellow fading into the flesh of his cheeks. His face had puffed up to double its ordinary size and resembled a bad cheese.

There was a basin of clear water beside the mirror and a stack of small white towels. Hammersmith dipped a towel in the water and dabbed it carefully over his face. He dipped it into the water again and repeated the process. Looking at his face, he couldn't see a difference, but the water turned pink the second time he dipped the towel, so he supposed he was making some kind of progress.

The towel was rough and it caught on Hammersmith's

whiskers. He cast about the worktop for something he might use to shave. There was a drawer under the basin and he pulled it out. There, amid a selection of alien tools, was a razor. Hammersmith didn't think Kingsley would mind if he borrowed it for a few quick swipes at his chin. He used his hands to pat some of the pink basin water on to his cheeks and jaw and then drew the razor over them as gently as he could, scraping away hair and crusted blood, swishing the razor in the water again and again until it had turned a dark muddy brown.

He was finishing as Fiona re-entered the room with a shirt in her hands. He saw her in the mirror and turned to greet her. He moved too fast, almost fell and she rushed forward to steady him. He noticed that it was the first time he had seen her without her sketchbook.

She drew away from him quickly, as if he had burned her, and gasped when she saw the open razor on the worktop behind him.

'You didn't,' she said.

'I'm sorry. I thought your father wouldn't mind.'

'Oh, no. It's not . . . I mean, I think he's used that blade on a corpse this morning.'

'Of course. I didn't think.'

Hammersmith suddenly needed to sit down.

'I shouldn't have taken so long,' Fiona said. 'I wanted to finish my drawing.'

'It's entirely my fault.'

'Here, put this on.'

She held out the shirt and turned her back to him. He peeled off his old shirt. It was stiff with sweat and dirt and blood, and it was torn under the right armpit. Fiona held out her hand without turning around and he gave her the old shirt. She put it in the bucket with the bloody rags from his face. He put on Kingsley's clean shirt while Fiona rinsed the razor and put it back in the drawer where Hammersmith had found it. She dumped his brown shaving water from the basin into her bucket.

Kingsley's shirt was snug through the chest and shoulders, and the sleeves were too short, but when Hammersmith put his jacket on over it he didn't think anyone would notice.

He didn't hear Kingsley enter the room, but when he turned around the doctor was there, showing Inspectors Day and Blacker into the laboratory.

'Good God,' Day said.

'Is that Constable Hammersmith?' Blacker said.

'Sir. Yes, it is.'

'You look a fright.'

'I apologize for my face.'

Day stood quiet, looking at Blacker.

'What?' Blacker said.

'I thought you might make a comment about someone taking a hammer to Mr Hammersmith's face.'

'Why would I do that?'

'I imagine you haven't many opportunities to make puns about his name.'

'It would be insensitive for me to begin now, wouldn't it?'

'Well, of course it would be.'

'Then why would I do it?'

'My apologies,' Day said. 'And to you, Constable.'

'No need,' Hammersmith said. 'My appearance is inexcusable.'

'Well, what happened, man?'

'Nothing I couldn't deal with.'

'I'd like to see what the other fellow looks like now you're through with him.'

Hammersmith decided not to mention that the worst he'd done to the barman was upset him.

'At any rate,' Day said, 'we were hoping to connect with you before the morning was out, so it's good luck for us running into you here. Detective Blacker says you're among the best men we've got, dedicated and serious. We could use the assistance of a man like that. Clearly you've anticipated us, though. I assume you're here about the body too?'

'Yes, but . . .'

'Yes,' Kingsley said. 'You mean the man's body that was brought in late last night. Or, rather, early this morning.'

He gave Hammersmith a pointed look. The investigation of the little boy's death was unofficial. Day and Blacker were there on a different matter.

'Yes, of course. And I wonder if I might take another look at that button found in Inspector Little's trunk?'

Kingsley raised an eyebrow and patted his pockets. He found the sofa button and handed it to Day.

'You have an idea?'

'It occurs to me that I may know where this comes from.'

'Do tell.'

'Let me check into it first. I think this button may be immaterial to our case, but I'm not ready to decide that just yet.'

Kingsley nodded. He brushed past Hammersmith and walked to the counter.

'Well, if you find anything, I'd like to know about it. Meanwhile, I haven't had a chance yet to do a thorough examination of this new body, but I can tell you a few things. To begin . . .'

He trailed off as he seemed to be looking for something on the worktop. Then he brightened and opened the drawer underneath.

'Forgot where I'd put this,' he said.

He brought out the razor Hammersmith had used to shave.

'I'm quite certain this was the murder weapon,' he said.

The room began swimming again and Hammersmith grabbed the table behind him to keep from passing out.

Interlude 2

Pyworthy, Holsworthy District, Devon. Three years ago

'Wake up, Constable!'

Walter Day heard the voice as though from a great distance and struggled towards it. He opened his eyes, immediately felt an ice-pick stab of light and closed them again. After the briefest moment, a shadow blocked the light and he was able to open his eyes again. The shadow resolved itself into Claire Carlyle's lovely face. She seemed concerned and Day tried to reach for her, to comfort her, but he couldn't move.

'Walter? Can you hear me?'

Seeing Claire, knowing she was alive and well, gave him strength. He had known Claire his entire life and admired her from afar, but had always understood that she was too good for him. She came from money and he was the son of a valet. He was surprised she even knew his name.

He blinked and found his voice. It sounded far away, as if someone else were speaking.

'I'm awake,' he said. 'Don't worry about me.'

It came out *Doane wurbit meeh.*

'Oh, thank God. The inspector said you would recover, but I was afraid . . . Your head's bleeding horribly, you know.'

'M'uh kay.'

He could feel his arms and legs now, heavy and useless, but it was an improvement. He moved his head and saw that he was lying flat on his back on a church pew.

'What's happened?'

'Mr Sanders hit you.'

'Where is he?' Day said. *Whurzee?*

'He ran right out after he hit you in the head.'

'Where's Inspector March?'

'He chased after Mr Sanders. But he stopped first to be sure you were breathing.'

Day worked one marionette arm and grabbed the top of the pew. His body gradually came unstuck and he pulled himself up. The air in the church's nave smelled hot and dusty and he wanted to lie back down, but he fought the temptation and stood on wobbly legs. Blue and yellow light streamed through the stained-glass windows around them and pressed painfully on Day's eyeballs. His stomach churned and he swallowed hard.

'Are you sure you're all right?'

'Fine. I'm fine.'

The world began to come into focus. His skull was filled with broken glass and his legs still wanted to quit under him, but every second that passed brought a little more resolve. Day touched his temple and stifled the urge to cry out. When he looked at his fingers there was blood on them.

'You say Sanders hit me?'

Day looked down at the pew. A broken pitchfork lay on the floor beneath it, the two halves of the handle splintered. He realized that his skull must have sustained a terrific blow. It explained why he couldn't remember anything that had happened since he'd entered the church. He could remember chasing the imposter stable-hand, Sanders. He remembered Sanders grabbing Claire, snatching her right off her feet and dragging her into the church. Day had given chase and then . . .

Then he had opened his eyes here in the nave.

'You saved me,' Claire said.

'Of course I did. I love you.'

'You do?'

Day blinked. *Had he spoken out loud?*

'What?' he said.

'Perhaps you should sit back down.'

'No. I need to help the inspector.'

'He has had years and years of experience in catching the likes of Rex Sanders.'

'Still . . .'

'I love you too, Walter Day.'

Day sat. He closed his eyes and inhaled slowly, exhaled and then drew another breath. When he opened his eyes again, she was still there. He looked away, at the high windows in the clerestory above them. A shadow flitted past, blocking the sun, a pitter-pat of feet on the roof. There was a dreamy quality to the air and when Day spoke his voice seemed to him to come from somewhere else.

'Marry me,' he said.

Claire drew back from him.

'Your injury . . .'

'I'm sorry. I don't know why I . . .'

'No, don't be sorry.'

'Entirely inappropriate of me. Percy Erwood has his eye on you, I know. It's an excellent match.'

'I can't stand Percy Erwood. I can't stand any of the men my father wants for me. They're all spoiled little boys who care for nobody but themselves. They love their money and they love the way other people look at them. I am not an accessory.'

'Yes, Erwood's an excellent match,' Day said. 'My head is simply . . . Again, I apologize most sincerely and I hope you'll mention nothing of this to your father.'

He stood again and lurched past her, out into the centre aisle. He stumbled, regained his footing and walked steadily past the sanctuary and out the back door into the vestibule. When he looked back through the small window in the door, Claire was standing by the far pews under a stained-glass window, blue light shimmering in her hair. She wasn't looking in his direction, hadn't watched him leave. He wasn't sure he would ever be able to speak to her again.

Outside, he took a moment and leaned his hand against the cool stone of the church wall. Far away, across the marshes, he could see a figure moving slowly towards him. The air in front of him wavered and the figure split into two men, moving side by side, then merged back into one. He closed his eyes again.

When he opened them, Inspector Adrian March was standing over him.

'You look unsteady, Constable,' March said. 'Your head's still bleeding.'

'Did you catch him?'

March snorted and stretched his hand out to indicate

the marshes behind the church. Green and brown, they extended as far as the eye could see. Day could smell the rotting plant life and hear the desperate insects calling out to each other. Their lives amounted to a handful of days in which to find love and leave their legacies.

'Sanders could be almost anywhere by now. I can find no sign of him out there. He knows this territory far better than I,' March said.

'If you hadn't stopped to check on me you might have caught up to him.'

'I couldn't very well leave you to die.'

Day's knees went out from under him and he fell back against the wall.

'You need to lie down, Day. You saved that girl's life, you know.'

March leaned in close to him and Day grabbed his shoulder as if he were steadying himself. He put his lips close to March's ear and whispered.

'He's on the roof. I saw him run past the windows.'

March nodded, but he didn't look up. He gazed across at the marshes and spoke too loudly.

'I wish we had more men like you at The Yard,' he said. 'It's too bad about Sanders, though. What's behind those marshes?'

'The river.'

'He could be anywhere, then. No doubt he'll have taken a boat by now. Let's get you back inside.'

March put his arm around Day's shoulders and they entered the vestibule. Inside, out of earshot of the man on the roof, March set Day down on a bench. Across from the bench was a single door. Day pointed at it.

'Inside that cupboard there's a ladder to the roof. Sanders has to come back through here to get down. He's trapped himself.'

'I'll bring him down.'

'Give me a moment to get my bearings and I'll go with you.'

'You stay here. If he gets past me, stop him in this room.'

'He might still be a danger. You shouldn't face him alone.'

'You forget you've already disarmed him. You broke his weapon in two with your rock-like head.'

March jiggled the cupboard doorknob.

'Locked.'

'Where's the parish priest? He must have a spare key.'

'He's outside. We cleared this place out. If I go out to get him, Sanders will know we're on to him.'

March knelt in front of the door and pulled a flat leather case from his jacket pocket. Inside was an assortment of odd-looking keys. He tried each of them in turn and the third key fitted the lock. He turned it and a soft click echoed through the tiny room.

'Skeleton keys. I collect them. When you become an inspector, remember to have them on your person at all times. You never know when they'll be handy.'

'I'll never be an inspector, sir. I'm content here.'

'It is more important to use your gifts well than to settle for being content. You were the only one who saw the significance of the missing horseshoe. You'd make a fine detective.' March smiled. 'And the bump in salary you'd receive would make that young lady happy.'

'Which young lady do you mean?'

'You may observe things that others miss, Constable, but I'm still better at it.'

He disappeared through the door. Day could hear his footsteps fading up the ladder to the roof.

'Constable?'

The voice came from outside. For a moment, Day thought it was March, already calling down from the roof, but then it came again.

'Walter? Where are you?'

Day stood up too fast and had to steady himself with a hand on the wall. He stared at the forest-green pillow on the bench and waited for the swimming sensation to stop. When the world around him came back into focus he noticed that the green was newly dotted with thick wet splashes of burgundy. He turned the pillow over to hide the blood and hurried outside.

'Claire?' he said.

He heard a noise from above and took a few steps back from the building. He looked up in time to see Adrian March heave into view through the trapdoor on the church's roof. He scanned the length of the roof that was visible on that side and saw nothing but a portion of the clerestory which jutted out at the front of the building. It was the only place Sanders could be hiding. He nodded his head, gently, in that direction and saw March nod back.

'Walter?'

When he turned and saw Claire, everything else disappeared.

'Miss Carlyle, you must leave. Sanders is still at large.'

'I don't care about that.'

'Well, I do. Leave before you're hurt.'

'I will not. You asked me a question and it would be rude to leave without answering.'

'I apologize for that. I've had a blow to the head.'

'Don't apologize. We've known each other since we were children. You have every right to ask me a simple question.'

'Not the one I asked. It was unforgivable of me.'

'You didn't wait for my answer.'

'I don't require an answer.'

'I think you do.'

'Your father has already arranged things with Mr Erwood.'

'My mind is made up on that matter. I am not some chit to be traded back and forth over a business matter.'

'Of course you aren't. I never meant to . . .'

'Stay back, March.'

Day looked up. Sanders had emerged from behind the stones at the front of the church roof and was pulling himself up the rusted downpipe bolted to the side of the clerestory. There was nowhere to go from there. March had a gun in his hand, but wasn't pointing it at Sanders.

'Stop where you are, Sanders. You're under arrest, on Her Majesty's authority, for the murder of Zachariah Bent.'

'I'm innocent. I never did it.'

'I will never marry Percy Erwood,' Claire said.

Day pulled his attention back to the girl in front of him and took a step towards the shadow of the church where she stood.

'Please, Claire,' he said, 'it's dangerous here. You must leave.'

'Come back to London with me, Sanders,' March said. 'You'll get a fair trial.'

'I'll hang for it and you know it, March.'

'I've always admired you,' Claire said.

'I didn't know,' Day said.

'I've done everything short of throwing myself off a horse in front of you, but you never so much as glanced my way.'

'It would have gone better for you if you'd cooperated, Sanders,' March said. 'You shouldn't have run.'

'They'd have carted me off to prison. You don't know what it's like there.'

Day was growing dizzier trying to keep up with the conversation between March and Sanders while talking to Claire at the same time. Too much was going on and all of it was of vital importance. He held a hand to his head and shut his eyes. Above him, metal scraped against stone and a great wrenching noise filled the air.

'Sanders!'

Day rushed forward, his hands out, ready to push Claire out of the way. An instant later, Rex Sanders landed in Day's arms and the weight of him pushed Day back against the church wall. A broken section of the downpipe thunked into the ground where Day had been standing.

'I see you've caught our villain,' March said.

Day looked up and March peered at him over the edge of the roof. Day dropped Sanders in the dirt. Sanders tried to gain his feet, but Day tripped him and grabbed his arm.

'You're under arrest,' he said.

'I'll need help transporting him to London,' March said from above him. 'Care to come along?'

Day looked at Claire and she smiled. The sun flashed across his eyes and he smelled sunshine and honey and warm grass.

'Go,' she said. 'I'll be here waiting for you.'

Day smiled back at her and felt his knees buckle under him as the world turned dark again.

31

Hammersmith grabbed the worktop before he could fall. He held up a hand.

'Please, go on. I'll be fine.'

'Are you sure, man?' Day said.

'A dizzy spell. Nothing to trouble yourself over.'

He had used a murder weapon to shave his face. He decided not to mention it unless it had some bearing on the case. He would try not to think about the fact that he had just mingled his blood with that of a dead man.

'If Mr Hammersmith is quite all right,' Kingsley said, 'I have a notion regarding how you might identify one of these many killers we seem to have running loose about the city.'

'The Beard Killer, you mean?' Blacker said.

'The Beard Killer? A beard is made up of unfeeling hair, Inspector, and can't be harmed in the least.'

'Of course. I know what a beard is, Doctor. But this person seems to target men with beards. Therefore, I call him the Beard Killer.'

'Blackly humorous, I suppose, but inaccurate all the same.'

'You were about to say, Doctor?' Day said.

'Yes . . .'

Kingsley glanced around the room before going on.

He held the straight razor up so that the other three men could see it.

'This will sound fantastic, I'm sure, but there is a theory and I believe it has some credence. I have been following the advancements of the French regarding scientific identification of the criminal class. Although I find him odious in all other respects, Alphonse Bertillon has made great strides in the field. He has begun recording certain physical measurements of those arrested within his jurisdiction. The French are now measuring the length of a man's arms, the colour of his eyes, the size of his shoes, all manner of things which might be altered individually, but when taken together add up to a positive identification. A man may shave his beard or don a pair of spectacles to disguise his appearance, but he cannot make himself taller or shorter or alter the length of his middle finger without, I suppose, a great deal of difficulty.'

'Are you saying that you can somehow deduce these things from that razor?' Day said.

'No. Certainly not. But there is an additional characteristic that the French are not using yet. They are considering it quite seriously, but there has been some opposition.'

He hesitated and Day urged him on.

'Bear with me,' Kingsley said. 'This will be hard to credit, but perhaps a demonstration will help. Fiona? May I borrow your charcoal, dear?'

The girl jumped at the mention of her name. She had been standing unnoticed in the corner of the room, leaning against the long worktop and quietly drawing.

As she passed by him, Hammersmith glanced at her pad and saw the sketch she had been working on. It was a remarkable likeness of Hammersmith himself.

Fiona handed the piece of charcoal to her father. Kingsley looked at her portrait of the policeman and scowled at Hammersmith. Hammersmith shrugged.

'What was I saying?' Kingsley said.

'We haven't the slightest idea,' Blacker said. 'But it had something to do with a razor and a piece of charcoal.'

Hammersmith had never worked closely with Blacker and he found that he didn't like the detective's flippant attitude. Inspector Day seemed like a serious fellow, though. He was new, but he was clearly determined to do the job properly.

'Ah, yes,' Kingsley said. 'The razor. And not so much the charcoal itself, but the dust from it.'

'The dust?'

'One moment, please.'

Kingsley opened a drawer under the worktop and rummaged through it. Hammersmith glanced over at Day and Blacker, who were talking quietly to each other. He couldn't hear what they were saying, but Blacker seemed angry about it. Finally, Kingsley straightened up with a frustrated grunt and closed the drawer. He pursed his lips and looked around the room.

'I just need something that will . . . something coarse,' he said.

Blacker and Day stopped talking and looked up.

'Coarse? Some sort of fabric?'

'Of course not,' Kingsley said. 'That wouldn't . . .'

He smiled and pointed at the back wall of the room.

Hammersmith turned to look as Kingsley hurried past him and slapped the bricks.

'Coarse, like bricks,' he said. 'These ought to do the job. Now you're going to see something amazing.'

He began to rub the charcoal across the bricks, back and forth, up and down, darkening the wall. He kept one hand cupped under the charcoal to keep the dust from drifting to the floor.

'I have been corresponding,' Kingsley said, 'with a man named Henry Faulds. He's Scottish, a missionary who has spent some time in the Orient. Faulds has been petitioning The Yard of late with a notion he's brought back with him.'

As he spoke, Kingsley continued to rub the charcoal against the bricks. He had his back to the room and might almost have been talking to himself.

'There are faster ways to darken the wall,' Blacker said.

'Darkening the wall is beside the point,' Hammersmith said. 'He's gathering charcoal dust.'

'Exactly right,' Kingsley said. 'Now watch.'

He returned to the worktop, his fingers wrapped around a fistful of black dust, and carefully picked up the razor.

'Hammersmith, would you please bring that basin to me? No, not the metal one. We'll want the white porcelain. The one with the fewest stains, if there is such a thing.'

Hammersmith selected a likely candidate from the table behind him and carried it to the worktop.

'You others gather round here,' Kingsley said. 'But breathe softly. Don't scatter my dust. You too, Fiona.

I've only read about this, never performed it, but I think it will be very instructive.'

He took the basin from Hammersmith and set the razor in the bottom of it.

'Now, look at the handle,' he said.

Hammersmith leaned in. The razor's handle was bone, darker than the porcelain it sat on, almost yellow by comparison. There were two red smudges near the end of it where the blade opened out, a similar-looking streak of red across the middle of it, and a crack where it might have been dropped at some point in the past.

'Blood,' Day said.

'Yes,' Kingsley said. 'Blood. You see here where the blood splashed against both the blade and the handle as it exited your victim's throat. Arterial pressure forced it out quite violently, pushing it past the razor, which is why there's so little to be seen here. But that's not the most relevant point. These two smudges . . .'

'The killer got blood on his hand.'

'He did,' Kingsley said. 'See how rough the outlines of these smudges are?'

'Sort of jagged.'

'Indeed. That tells us that the killer probably wasn't wearing gloves.'

'Could have been wearing suede,' Day said.

Kingsley pursed his lips and nodded, but he didn't look pleased.

'I suppose so. That's a good observation, Inspector. But let's suppose for a moment that the killer wasn't wearing suede gloves and that the roughness of these marks was caused by variations on the surface of his skin. If that's the case, then these marks won't be the only ones on the handle. We simply can't see the other marks.'

'Can't see them?'

'Sweat. Our skin exudes all manner of liquids and those liquids leave a residue.'

'But if we can't see them . . .'

'Watch.'

Kingsley leaned in over the top of the basin and opened his hand. He exhaled quickly, blowing charcoal powder over the razor's handle. The bone white surface turned grey. He grabbed the razor, holding it with his fingertips near the end where the handle tapered, and tipped it up, shaking loose dust off it. He set it on the worktop and blew on it, scattering more of the excess charcoal dust. He turned around and smiled at his daughter.

'You see?' he said.

Fiona nodded, but Hammersmith didn't see anything unusual about the dirty razor. He leaned in closer and almost bumped heads with Day, who was leaning in at the same time.

'There are black smudges now,' Day said.

'Yes,' Kingsley said. 'But they're more complete than the blood smears were. Look at them closely.'

Blacker, who stood back from the others, cleared his throat.

'I think I understand,' he said. 'If we catch the man who did this, we can compare the size of his fingertips to these smudges and prove that he held the murder weapon in his hand.'

'I should think a great many people would have the same size fingertips,' Day said. 'I appreciate your diligence, Doctor, but I fail to see . . .'

'You didn't look closely enough,' Kingsley said. 'Here.'

He drew a magnifying lens from his waistcoat pocket and handed it to Day. Day looked at the glass for a moment before using it to examine the razor's handle. His expression made it clear to everyone that he was humouring the doctor.

'Oh,' he said. 'I see a pattern in the dust.'

'Yes,' Kingsley said. 'Now look at your own fingertips. You don't even need the glass to do it. Hold them up to the light.'

'Of course,' Hammersmith said. 'Skin isn't smooth.'

'That's right, Constable. But what's fascinating is that the minute patterns of the skin on your fingertips is different from those of our friend, Inspector Day. Or from those of anyone else in this city. Quite possibly the entire world, although I don't know how we would verify that.'

'Impossible,' Blacker said.

'I know,' Kingsley said. 'It seems hard to reconcile, particularly when one takes into account how very small a fingertip is. But Faulds has done extensive research and experimentation on the subject and his findings are quite exciting. I have heard that authorities in India are considering the use of these fingertip patterns in identifying criminals. And there are other jurisdictions that may follow suit.'

'Excuse me,' Day said. 'Please forgive me but, interesting as this is, I fail to see how it helps us find the murderer,' Day said.

'Oh, it doesn't, of course. But once found, his fingers might be compared to the smudges found on this weapon. You could prove that he held the razor and that he used it.'

'He might only have shaved with it,' Hammersmith said.

Hammersmith tried to keep his manner casual, but he thought his voice sounded higher than normal.

'True,' Kingsley said. 'I don't think this would hold up in a court of law. But you might use it to coerce a confession, might you not?'

Day nodded and looked at Hammersmith.

'A demonstration much like this, perhaps dramatized a bit more colourfully, so as to seem scientifically conclusive, might convince a suspect that there's no hope for him.'

'Unless he's got any sense,' Blacker said. 'If he's got a brain in his head, he'll simply laugh at us.'

Kingsley appeared put out by the lack of enthusiasm.

'It's worth keeping in mind,' he said.

'Yes,' Day said. 'Perhaps we should ensure that nobody else touches this razor until we have someone in custody and can compare their fingertips with these marks.'

'I agree,' Hammersmith said.

'Splendid,' Kingsley said. 'I'll wrap it in paper. Meanwhile, let's have everyone who might have touched this come in here later today so I can eliminate their prints on the handle. I'll wipe my own off of it and those of anyone else who might have come into contact with it, including the victim himself. Those prints remaining will have to belong to the killer.'

'Unless the killer has the same pattern of skin as his victim,' Blacker said. 'Or as any one of us. I still say this is ridiculous.'

'Be that as it may,' Kingsley said.

'Thank you, Doctor,' Day said. 'This may help us catch Inspector Little's killer. And, even if it doesn't, it's been a fascinating exercise in itself.'

'Catch Little's killer?' Kingsley said.

'Yes. We're operating, for the moment, on the notion that this case may be related to that of the inspector's death.'

'Oh, no,' Kingsley said. 'I had no idea you thought that. There's absolutely no chance of it. This killer and that killer are quite obviously different people.'

Blacker snorted, turned on his heel and left the room.

'What's got him upset?' Hammersmith said.

'He's tired is all,' Day said. 'And he had such high hopes that we were on the right track.'

32

'Message here 'boutcher father.'

Sergeant Kett was waiting for them when they returned to The Yard.

'Whose father?' Day said.

'Him.'

Kett pointed at Hammersmith.

Blacker went to his desk, but Day waited with Hammersmith.

'Doctor at St Thomas's, Dr Brindle, wants you up there when you can, Constable,' Kett said.

Kett was usually businesslike, getting through the day on the back of his paperwork and sending the men where they needed to be as soon as they needed to be there. Day hadn't known the sergeant long, but he was surprised to see pity on his long face.

'If you need the time today, that'd be all right with me, lad,' Kett said.

'Thank you, Mr Kett,' Hammersmith said. 'Really, I think there's too much for me to do here today. I can't leave.'

Day held up a hand. He almost touched Hammersmith's arm, but drew back. The constable radiated intensity.

'We can use your help, Hammersmith,' Day said, 'but see to your father. We'll still be here.'

'With all due respect, sir, I'd rather see this through before I deal with a personal issue.'

Kett frowned and handed over the telegram he was holding.

'Suitcherself,' he said. 'I'm notcher mama. But don't be gettin' messages here if yer not gonna do anything about 'em.'

'Yes, sir.'

'And another thing . . .'

'Mr Hammersmith.'

The three men turned at the sound of Sir Edward's voice. The police commissioner was standing across the room, outside his office door, looking their way.

'A moment of your time, please, Constable.'

'Yes, sir.'

Hammersmith looked at Day, who shrugged. It was unusual for Sir Edward to speak directly to a bobby, but not entirely unheard of. Hammersmith pulled on the cuffs of his sleeves. He crossed through the partition and between the desks to the other side of the room. He preceded Sir Edward into the office and the door closed behind them.

'Huh,' Kett said.

'What does he want with Hammersmith?' Day said.

'Not a clue, lad,' Kett said. 'But when you see the constable again, tell 'im I want a word. His mate Pringle's late for his shift again.'

'That's hardly Hammersmith's responsibility.'

'Didn't say it was and didn't say it wasn't.'

'Of course.'

Blacker was standing on the other side of Day's desk

when he got to it. It seemed to Day as if the stacks of files had grown. He couldn't see the surface of the desk at all.

'Looks like we're starting over again,' Day said.

'Kingsley's wrong,' Blacker said. 'He has to be.'

'What makes you say that?'

'If he's right then we're looking at some sort of epidemic.'

'A disease?'

'Not a disease. Just plain evil. You're a thinker, Day. You look at a thing from this angle and then that. You walk around it and pick it up and you don't decide on a thing, you just look at it.'

'I don't . . .'

'Not an insult, old man. It's good what you do, for this kind of work. But I'm not like that. I find a purchase in a thing and I dig in. I don't look at it inside and out, I go at it. Do you understand?'

'Not in the least. You've entirely misapprehended me.'

'Last year it was Saucy Jack. Now we have Little's killer. And, if Kingsley's right, we've got this other thing, this Beard Killer. If they're not related . . .'

'I was never convinced that they were related. The only link between them was the bizarre nature of . . .'

'Exactly. That's exactly what I'm talking about.'

Day looked around at the other detectives, all of them busy at their desks, none of them looking in Blacker's direction.

'Keep your voice down, Blacker,' he said.

He kept his own voice low and didn't move his lips, hissing the words through clenched teeth.

'They're all listening to us,' he said, 'and you sound like you've lost your mind.'

'Maybe I have,' Blacker said.

But he said it so quietly that only Day could hear him. He leaned forward and whispered.

'You're new here, so take me at my word. This isn't what The Yard is cut out to do. Look, a man loses control and kills his wife, a child is trampled by an omnibus, a woman poisons her neighbour, a bludger takes a man's wallet and slices him up . . . Those things happen every day and that's why we're here. We go in and we grab hold of the killer and we lock him up. We find out why the killing was done and that takes us right to the one that did it.'

'Right. I understand all that.'

'A man cuts the guts out of woman after woman or sews a man's face up or shaves some poor bastard and then cuts his throat for no reason at all, there's no percentage in it. That's killing for the sake of killing. Where do we even start to look for the monster what done that?'

'Little's killing is simple. There's a connection somewhere between the killer and the victim and we seek it out.'

'No. No, this is different. There's no sense to it, and one killer without reason is an oddity, but it seems to me that it's spreading. We had a monster and we couldn't catch him. Now how many monsters are there? It's not just the Ripper any more. Something's changed in this city and everybody knows it. They're all scared, everybody out there's scared, and it's more than we can deal with.'

'You're tired.'

'Of course I'm tired. We're all tired. But this is why I was here when you arrived last night. If there's no sense to this then there's no purchase for me. What am I doing here?'

'You're doing police work.'

'I'm not sure I know what that is any more.'

'I think it starts with putting these files in order. We've made a good run at it and we need to finish up here. We pick the likeliest path and we run it until we can't run any further. When that happens, we come back and take another run down a different path until we've exhausted all the possibilities.'

Blacker nodded. He still looked troubled.

'There's something happening, is all,' he said. 'That's all I'm saying here. I know I'm blathering on, but crime's changing and people are changing. This is just the start, mark my words. I think there's too many of us people and we're too close together and we're turning on each other like rats in the gutter. We're in the biggest city in the world, Day, and I think it's trying to get rid of us.'

Day sat down. From this angle he couldn't see Blacker over the murder reports on the desk.

'London isn't responsible for this,' he said. 'A small percentage of the people in this city are responsible for all of this and if we can find those people and bring them to justice, then everyone else will be safe and free to go about their business.'

'You make it sound as if there's an end to it all. There's no end. And it makes less sense every day.'

Blacker's voice sounded small and strained, drifting

over from behind the wall of cases, and there was no pun to accompany his accidental use of Day's name.

'Even if you're right,' Day said, 'it seems to me that there's only one thing we can do.'

'What's that?'

'Start looking for a killer.'

After a long moment, Day heard Blacker take a sheaf of paper and start turning pages. Day took a deep breath and chose a stack at random. Somewhere, he was sure, there was a clue. He shook off the effects of Blacker's speech and began to read.

33

'Have a seat, Mr Hammersmith,' Sir Edward said.

'Sir.'

Hammersmith sat stiffly on the edge of the straight-backed wooden chair and tried to avoid looking at the stuffed tiger's head on the wall as Colonel Sir Edward Bradford went around his desk and settled into the more comfortable leather chair. Sir Edward gazed at Hammersmith for a long moment before speaking.

'You look rough, Constable.'

'I'm fine, sir.'

'Good. Now tell me, do you by chance know a Dr Charles Shaw?'

'I believe I may have met him, sir.'

'Yes, I believe you have. When I arrived this morning, that gentleman was waiting in ambush for me. It seems you paid a visit to Dr Shaw's home in the wee hours and threatened his family.'

'No, sir.'

'You didn't visit him last night?'

'No, I mean I did, sir. But I never threatened him or his family.'

'You don't seem the type.'

'No.'

'Then why did you go to his house?'

'In the course of an investigation, sir. I was watching

his home when he happened to return from holiday and I took the opportunity to talk with him.'

'In the middle of the night?'

'The household wasn't sleeping. They had just arrived and it was more convenient to approach him at that time than to leave and return in the daylight.'

'I noticed you came in just now with Inspectors Day and Blacker. Were they with you last night?'

'No, sir. I joined them some time after my visit to the Shaw home.'

'He said there were two of you, but the other one was never introduced.'

'No, sir. It was only me.'

'Why would he tell me two if there was only one of you?'

'I don't know, sir. It was me alone.'

Sir Edward stared at Hammersmith without speaking, and Hammersmith returned his gaze. Finally, Sir Edward nodded. He seemed to have made up his mind about something.

'I like a man who stands up for his fellows. Why were you and Pringle there?'

'It was in the course of investigating a case, sir. And, again, it was just me.'

'Which case? Is this related to the matter of Inspector Little's death?'

'I don't think so. This was . . . I found a body yesterday.'

'Why didn't you turn it over to a detective?'

'I did, sir.'

'And?'

'And it was decided that the case was not a priority at this time.'

'Who decided that?'

'Inspector Tiffany, sir.'

'Did he ask you to continue investigating in his absence?'

'No, sir. In fact, he expressly asked me to stand down.'

'But you disagreed.'

'I did.'

'I see. Do you believe yourself to be a detective?'

'No, sir.'

'Then why did you disregard Mr Tiffany's wishes?'

'I don't know, sir.'

'Yes, you do. Go on. Tell me.'

Sir Edward's expression didn't change, but there was something in his eyes that made Hammersmith decide to trust him.

'The body . . . it was a child, sir.'

He had no idea how to explain it better than that. It was enough for Hammersmith.

To his surprise, Sir Edward nodded.

'If Tiffany decided not to pursue the matter, then it's not the business of The Yard to investigate the case. Anything you do, you'll do in your own time. Am I understood?'

'Yes, sir.'

Hammersmith was amazed. Sir Edward was giving him tacit permission to go after the boy's killer, while at the same time disavowing official responsibility.

'While you're on your shift, you will confine your duties to those assigned you by Sergeant Kett.'

'Of course, sir.'

'And don't pay any more visits to Charles Shaw. He's not someone I care to see again before I've had my morning tea.'

Hammersmith almost smiled, but kept a straight face.

'You're dismissed, Constable.'

'Thank you, sir.'

He rose and bowed slightly before turning to the door. Sir Edward cleared his throat as Hammersmith touched the doorknob.

'Hammersmith.'

'Sir?'

'Get yourself a new shirt. That one's much too small for you.'

34

Something touched Colin Pringle's leg. He woke confused and it took him several moments to figure out where he was. The tailor's shop was dim and cold. A shy clique of dressmaker's dummies, draped with dark fabric samples, huddled against the opposite wall. Pringle felt movement against his leg again and he jerked forward, alarmed. He looked down at the floor.

A fluffy white cat rubbed against him, then sat back, waiting to be stroked. Pringle sneezed. He wondered why a tailor would keep a long-haired cat. He imagined it would shed all over the suits and dresses created here. But Pringle had never noticed white hairs on his own suits, so the tailor must have brushed them well before giving them back. Pringle pushed the cat out of the way with his foot and stood up, stretching. The cat returned, purring, and he sidestepped it.

He looked around for a clock, but couldn't see one. He didn't think he'd been asleep long, but he decided he couldn't wait any longer. He was late and Sergeant Kett was sure to reprimand him. Pringle was searching the table in the middle of the room for a piece of paper and pencil so he could leave a note when he heard carriage wheels roll to a stop outside.

A deep voice said something that Pringle couldn't

make out and footsteps approached the shop across the hard-packed dirt pavement. Pringle suddenly realized the tailor would think he was trespassing. He looked around, but he didn't know what he was looking for. He hadn't really done anything wrong. And he was a police officer, after all.

The door opened a couple of inches, as if someone was testing it, and the deep voice he'd heard a moment before said, 'Damnit, unlocked.' Pringle sat back down in the chair so as not to present a threat. He didn't want to frighten anyone.

The tailor opened the door wider and stuck his head inside, looking around, but apparently didn't see Pringle in the shadows. The door closed again and Pringle heard the bolt turn. He was being locked in!

Pringle ran to the big plate-glass window by the door and pounded on it. He could see the tailor getting into a hansom cab at the kerb. There was someone else in the cab. The tailor stopped and turned his head, listening. Pringle slapped his open hand against the glass and the tailor turned to look directly at him. He squinted at Pringle and drew back, alarmed. Pringle smiled and spread his hands out at his sides. He shrugged.

The tailor jumped back out of the cab, reaching into his pocket. He produced a large iron key and approached the door again. The bolt turned and Pringle pulled the door open from inside.

'What's going on here?' the tailor said.

'I'm so sorry, Mr Cinderhouse. I came in here looking for you and I suppose I fell asleep.'

'Looking for me? Why?'

'You were working on a new uniform for me. Surely you remember.'

'Oh, of course, Constable Pringle. I apologize. I had a . . . a family emergency this morning and wasn't able to open the shop. Is there any way I can ask you to return tomorrow? Or even later this afternoon?'

'Well, you can see the state of my current uniform.'

'Yes. Unfortunately, I'm just on my way somewhere and couldn't possibly . . .'

'Then perhaps just a quick steam and press?'

'But I . . .' The tailor sighed. 'Very well, sir. Give me a moment, would you?'

Pringle smiled and Cinderhouse went outside. He spoke to the driver of the cab and handed him a coin. The driver nodded. Pringle moved to the open door and leaned against the jamb, waiting. A small boy emerged from the darkness of the cab and looked at Pringle. The boy's face was red, as if he'd been crying, but when he spotted Pringle his eyes swept up and down the constable's uniform and his expression changed. He opened his mouth wide as if to shout, but the tailor had turned away from the coachman and now he clamped his hand over the boy's mouth before he could make a sound.

Pringle narrowed his eyes and moved away from the jamb. He had no idea what was going on, but there was something about the expression on the boy's face that alarmed him.

The tailor yelped and pulled his hand away from the boy's face. It was clear that the boy had bitten him. He shouted before Cinderhouse could get his hand over his mouth again.

'Help!'

Pringle moved towards them, but the tailor held his free hand up, smiling.

'He's playing a game with you, Constable. My son's a mischievous child.'

'Let me talk to him directly, please.'

'Of course, of course. But let's go inside where we won't draw a crowd. Someone might misunderstand.'

Pringle nodded, but he kept his eyes on the boy. He didn't look like a mischievous child, he looked like he was in trouble. He was dirty and half-naked, like some wild animal.

Cinderhouse kept his hand over the boy's mouth and reached out to pick him up with his other arm. He looked up and down the street, then yanked the boy out of the cab and bustled him past Pringle and into the store. Pringle followed. The tailor set the boy down in the same chair Pringle had slept in, then hurried back past Pringle to shut the door.

The boy leapt from the chair and ran to Pringle. He wrapped his arms around Pringle's leg. He was small and frail and his thin pyjama trousers were soaking wet.

'What's your name, son?' Pringle said.

'Fenn, sir. Please help me.'

'Well, Fenn, what seems to be the . . .'

Something slammed against Pringle's back and the impact forced the air out of him. He felt a mild burning sensation somewhere in his back, and there were little echoes of it tingling in his toes and fingers, the way an itch sometimes appears to be in several places at once. He shook his head and smiled at the boy, but Fenn was backing away, a horrified look on his face.

Pringle moved his head. He was trying to nod, but the gesture was loose, as if his head wasn't properly attached to his body. He opened his mouth to speak, but nothing came out and he felt confused. His mouth was dry.

He turned around and something hit him in the chest. Again, there was a burning sensation, but it wasn't as strong as the one in his back had been. He shut his eyes and opened them again as he was punched in the stomach. He doubled over and noticed that his shirt was completely ruined. Someone had got blood all over it.

He looked up at the tailor in time to see Cinderhouse's hand descend again. The tailor's hat came off as he moved into the thrust. Sunlight through the window gleamed on Cinderhouse's bare scalp. Then there was a glint of silver as the tailor punched him in the throat and Pringle's legs finally went out from under him. He tried to hold up his arms, to ward off another blow, but they didn't respond and Cinderhouse's fist fell on him again.

'I won't let you take him from me!'

The tailor was screaming, but the ebbing tide of blood was still in Pringle's ears and he couldn't hear, he could only read Cinderhouse's lips as if from a great distance. Cinderhouse, still silently screaming, dropped to his knees over Pringle and thrust down at him again and again and Pringle noticed that the silvery thing in his hand was a pair of shears. He tried to smile at the bald man to let him know that he finally understood the situation. He was being stabbed to death. Then he frowned. It should hurt more.

From the corner of his eye he could see a pool of blood expanding across the floor and realized that it was his own. Somehow, the thought of all that blood rushing out of his body was worse than the nearly absent pain of the wounds themselves, and Pringle turned his head just in time to avoid soiling his clothing as he vomited on Cinderhouse's shoes.

Cinderhouse stopped stabbing him and Pringle tried to rise, but his body wouldn't obey.

A moment later the tailor returned, holding a spool of black thread and the largest needle Pringle had ever seen. He felt a distant pressure in his lower lip and then Cinderhouse drew the thread up past his eyes and down and there was more pressure in his upper lip as the tailor went on sewing Pringle's lips shut. He tried again to move and felt Cinderhouse's hand on his chest, holding him down. The breath went out of him, but it sounded far away, like wind in the trees. He wanted to tell the tailor to stop pushing on him, that it didn't matter, that he couldn't move anyway, but the only sound he made was a low gurgle, and the thread came back up through his lips, drawing them tightly shut.

The tailor leaned in and whispered in Pringle's ear.

'I'm terribly sorry about this, Mr Pringle. You were always one of my better customers and I hate to lose your business. But I can't let you take my son away from me again. And I can't let you tell anyone about him. You shouldn't have seen him. You shouldn't have come here and put your eyes on him.'

The deadly scissors snicker-snacked and the needle came back past Pringle's eyes with the short thread dangling loose. The tailor pulled it out and expertly rethreaded the needle. Pringle ran his tongue over the insides of his lips. They were sealed shut. The needle dug into his eyelid and the tailor was back at work, closing Pringle's right eye. Pringle rolled his eyes to the other side so that he wouldn't have to watch, and saw the fluffy white cat padding around the pools of blood on the floor. The cat rubbed against Pringle's ear.

Pringle wondered how much of his murder had been witnessed by the boy. A child shouldn't have to see such a thing. He hoped Fenn had turned away before the worst of it.

The needle began its work on his left eye and, as darkness closed in, Pringle's last sight was of a small drop of bright red blood nested deep in the white cat's fur.

He sighed. The air dribbled out of him and he didn't draw another breath.

35

Hammersmith found himself once more in the East End and once more across the street from the Shaws' home. He hadn't set out for the East End, hadn't given Charles Shaw or his wife any conscious thought, but here he was. The house looked different in the sunlight than it had the previous night. Golden bricks shimmered in the heat, and the tree-lined street spoke of generations, of children playing and of families supping in quiet splendour.

Never mind the brothels and the seedy pubs just steps away.

He watched the house for long minutes before crossing the street and pulling the bell. He had no idea what he might say to Charles Shaw, but at the last minute he decided he would apologize for his behaviour. He recognized that he had overplayed his hand with Shaw and had consequently embarrassed both himself and Sir Edward.

When Penelope Shaw opened the door she said, 'I was just thinking about you.'

Hammersmith removed his hat.

'Is your husband home, ma'am?'

'Please come in.'

She walked away from him through the entrance hall and he had no choice but to follow. Her hair was done up in a loose ball on her head and she wore a long green gown that swayed against the floor with each shift of her hips. She turned to him in the archway that led to the great room. A wisp of hair, escaped from the chignon, curled down over her throat. She took his hat from him and hung it on a hook. When her hand brushed against his, Hammersmith noticed that his own fingernails were filthy. He put his hands in his pockets.

'Would you like something?'

'I'm fine, thank you. I'll just wait for your husband, if that's all right.'

'You may have to wait for some time.'

'I'm sorry?'

'He isn't here today.'

'But you said . . .'

He realized that she hadn't told him her husband was at home, only asked him to come in.

'I've made a mistake,' he said. 'I should be going. Please tell Dr Shaw when he arrives home that I . . .'

'Please sit,' Penelope said. 'I'll bring you something to drink.'

'I don't need anything, thank you. I came to apologize for the way I acted last night.'

'I don't recall being offended by you at all.'

'You're too kind.'

'No one is *too* kind, Mr Hammersmith. Everyone wants something. When we get it, we're kind, when we don't . . . well, when we don't, we're simply surviving.'

'I'm afraid I don't understand.'

'You want to apologize to Charles. I know Charles would want you to stay. And I would like some company.

You could make us all happy at once by accepting a cup of tea.'

'You don't mind if I wait?'

'I insist upon it.'

'A cup of tea would be lovely, then. Thank you.'

'No, Mr Hammersmith, thank you.'

She lowered her eyes and walked slowly out of the room. Hammersmith pulled out a chair and sat and watched her go. He was not a patient man, but he was resolute.

36

The corpse on the table grinned at the ceiling. His expression changed to a grimace, then a smile, then a grimace again as Kingsley manipulated his features. The incision under the corpse's chin ran from ear to ear and Kingsley worked his hands up under the skin and along the skull, loosening connective tissue as he went. The corpse had once been named Thomas and Kingsley spoke to him quietly as he worked, as if reassuring a nervous patient.

'There we go now, nothing to it, old boy.'

But he didn't look at Thomas's eyes.

He kept Fiona out of the room for this stage of the autopsy, and for this stage of every autopsy he performed. Although she seemed to handle everything with the same quiet concentration, the dead were so very vulnerable and Kingsley felt they deserved privacy and respect. In this room, they were as naked as anyone would ever be.

Thomas's jawbone was now fully visible, streaked pink with blood.

Kingsley pushed his fingers farther up, tearing thin dense layers of muscle away from Thomas's cheekbones. A little pressure from beneath and the top of Thomas's nose broke, the narrow peninsula of cartilage snapping away from the skull, an arrowhead cavern exposed in the middle of the corpse's face.

'I'm sorry about this, Thomas,' he said.

His voice was barely audible, trace echoes beating back at him from the close walls of the laboratory.

Thomas's ears shifted and the flesh tore loose around his eye sockets. Kingsley removed his hands from under the corpse's face and grasped the ragged whiskered skin that had once sagged under Thomas's jaw but was now stretched across the middle of his head. He flipped the skin over on to itself and pulled towards the top of the corpse's skull and Thomas's face turned inside-out. Now it lay like a hood at the back of the corpse's head, its expression hidden from view.

Some day, Kingsley knew, it would be him on the table, maybe this same table. He hoped he would be treated with respect.

Kingsley picked up a small straight saw from the table beside him and scored a careful circle around the top of the corpse's skull. He sawed back and forth, around and around. He set the saw down and fitted a chisel into the shallow ridge he had made above Thomas's brow. He held the chisel steady and struck it hard with a hammer. He moved the chisel and tapped it again. And again. All round the top of the skull he went, deepening the groove left by the saw.

Sweat dripped from the end of Kingsley's nose on to Thomas's naked skull. He wiped it off with his sleeve.

Kingsley had always imagined that his own death would come as an embarrassment, a sudden interruption as he went about some other task. He would have no opportunity to make plans, or to make his peace, would not suffer the long, wasting disease that had taken his wife. The Dark Angel would come upon him without warning and he would feel an instant of shame, a loss of control. It was that loss and no other that he feared.

He assumed that Fiona would be the one to find his body. He had spent years acclimatizing her to the many forms of Death, so that she would not suffer the loss of him as she had her mother. By then, if there was any mercy, he would be just another corpse in her eyes.

One final whack with the hammer. He held the cap in place and tapped it, gently now, again, again a little harder. Finally, it came free and he eased the bone off, exposing Thomas's brain. Fluid ran off the end of the table and spattered Kingsley's shoes.

'Doctor?'

Kingsley turned to see a one-armed man approaching him. He recognized Colonel Sir Edward Bradford, commissioner of the Metropolitan Police.

'Sir Edward, my nurse didn't tell me . . .'

'Your daughter let me in, sir. She assured me it would be all right.'

Sir Edward caught sight of the body and blanched. Kingsley grimaced and moved himself between the commissioner and the corpse. He stamped the liquid off his shoes and held out his hand. Sir Edward looked at it.

'Generally,' Sir Edward said, 'I try to be carrying something so that I can gracefully avoid this very situation. I hope you understand, but I couldn't possibly shake your hand.'

Kingsley looked down at his hands. They were covered in gore. He nodded and crossed the room, dipped his hands in a basin of reasonably clean water and rubbed as much of Thomas off them as he could.

'Terribly sorry, Sir Edward. I wasn't expecting you.'

'Of course not. I apologize for intruding. I've meant to visit your morgue, but I'm afraid I haven't had the opportunity.'

'Shall I show you around?'

'Your daughter, what was her name?'

'Fiona, sir.'

'Yes, Fiona was kind enough to show me much of the facility. I take it this room is where the most . . . in-depth work takes place.'

'You might say that. This is where our victims give up their secrets to me.'

'Our victims?'

'We're still alive, after all, and they are not.'

'And we must claim some responsibility for that, I suppose?'

'If we choose.'

'How poetic, Doctor.'

'It's often a lonely occupation and my mind travels to strange places.'

Sir Edward nodded and glanced around the room, taking in the long tables and the instruments and the drain hole in the centre of the floor.

'You've been helping the police with these matters for how long now?' he said.

'Nearly two years, sir.'

'Commissioner Monroe appointed you?'

'No, sir, I took this work upon myself.'

'You're a busy man, Doctor. I've seen your laboratory and the classrooms. Why would you choose more work for yourself?'

'I would rather not speak ill of anyone.'

'Ah, you leave that to me, then. Am I to assume that the previous facility was not up to your high standards?'

'One might say that.'

'And so you simply stepped in, took over, and nobody challenged you.'

'Until this moment.'

'This is no challenge, Doctor. I'm here about a different matter. You have never drawn a salary from the Metropolitan Police. I checked.'

'You seem to be well informed.'

'I am endeavouring to manage a great many things that have gone untended. A great many things that escaped the notice of my predecessors.'

'I'm sure they were busy men.'

'I've no doubt. Did you know that one of my detectives left The Yard before I arrived in London? He has disappeared somewhere in the Midlands, and there was no notice taken at all.'

'He's disappeared?'

'I'm being dramatic. He apparently retired. My men have continued the farce that Inspector Gilchrist is still on the job. It's humorous, I suppose.'

'A joke?'

'In its way.'

'You've let them continue with it?'

'There's no harm in it. Perhaps it boosts the men's morale. I don't know.'

'Wouldn't it be better to replace the man and ease their workloads?'

'Of course. And I will, but I'll do it without exposing their prank.'

'I see.'

'My point, Doctor, is that I intend to do things differently than they have been done before and that includes The Yard's relationship with you, sir. It's one thing to take this extra work on yourself, but why not receive payment for it?'

'I don't need the additional income and I thought it might be put to better use. Perhaps helping to prevent this sort of thing in the first place.'

He gestured at Thomas. Sir Edward glanced at the cavity where the top of Thomas's head had been.

'What happened to him?'

'He was mugged.'

'Is it necessary to . . .' Sir Edward waved his hand, taking in the body and the tray of instruments and the exposed brain, mottled and shiny under the lights. 'To do all of this? If we already know that he was mugged, I mean.'

'There's still more that he might tell us. His brain has swollen with the impact of some blunt tool, but the question is, where on the brain did the swelling take place in relation to the site of impact? Had he been hit at a different point on his skull, might he have survived? Thomas is teaching me things.'

'Is he a good teacher?'

'I find that if you're a good student, the teacher hardly matters.'

'Very good. I'll leave you to it, then.'

'Thank you, sir.'

Sir Edward smiled, not unkindly, and turned to leave. With his hand on the doorknob, he turned back.

'These things you learn, they're for the benefit of the police force, are they not?'

'Of course. For the benefit of us all, but primarily for gathering evidence.'

'You shall draw a salary from this day forward. I'll have a cheque sent round.'

'That's not necessary, sir.'

'Doctor, I can't have you gallivanting about a crime scene and engaging in police business if you are not a proper member of The Yard. And The Yard does not pay its people well, but we do pay them.'

'Yes, sir. Thank you, sir.'

'No, Dr Kingsley, thank you. And in future I would greatly appreciate it if you shared the things you learn here with me.'

'You have but to ask.'

'And now I have asked. I'll let you get back to it, but I hope to see you again soon. Thank you for your time, Doctor. And for everything else.'

With that, Sir Edward stepped through the door and pulled it shut behind him.

Kingsley drew in a deep breath and blew it slowly back out. For two years he had dreaded such a visit and now that it had finally occurred he felt relieved and even excited. He ran his hands through his wild thatch of grey hair and belatedly wondered whether he had got all of Thomas's cranial fluid off his fingers. He made a mental note to wash his hair, then promptly forgot when he returned to work on Thomas's corpse.

With long-handled scissors, bent near the tip, he reached in past the brain and snipped blindly, but expertly, and the brain slid into his hand and he drew it out. He held it up like a newborn for Thomas to see, the corpse's eyes still set in the grinning skull.

The brain went into a small basin, a damp cloth to cover it. Kingsley filled Thomas's empty brainpan with cotton and set the skullcap back in place with a bead of thick glue. He manoeuvred the corpse's skin back up over the top of the head and down. It was a tight fit. He smoothed it over the skull, popping the teardrop of cartilage back in place over the nose. He stitched the skin shut at Thomas's throat using one of the upholsterer's thick curved needles and made a mental note to order more of the needles for the lab. They were ideally suited for this type of work. When the flesh was joined again, he moved his expert fingers over the corpse's face, pushing here, pressing there, realigning the features so that the dead man looked like himself once more.

'See there,' he said. 'Good as new. No one need ever know you haven't a brain in your head.'

He smiled.

The door of the laboratory opened again, barely a crack, and Fiona's soft voice floated in.

'Tea's ready, Father.'

'I'll be there directly.'

The door closed again with a sigh and a click.

Kingsley rinsed his bloody hands in a bowl of water, wiped them on a clean towel and left the room. Before he closed the door he looked back at the dead man. Kingsley followed Thomas's empty gaze to the laboratory's ceiling.

'I hope it's all worth it,' he said.

He closed the door, leaving Thomas to sort it out for himself.

37

Mr Pringle was smaller than Inspector Little had been, and he fitted more naturally inside a steamer trunk. Cinderhouse had only two trunks left in his possession and one of them was a hat trunk, half the size of his only remaining steamer, and cube-shaped. Pringle wasn't that small.

Cinderhouse locked the shop door and took Fenn home. He bolted the boy in a downstairs cupboard with a sandwich and a jug of water and then returned to the shop. He took a hatchet with him.

Pringle's arms were separated from his torso. This was easily accomplished, but there was a suspenseful moment when Cinderhouse's foot slipped from where it anchored Pringle's weight and the body rolled to one side. The bald man almost lost a toe.

But without arms, Pringle was easier to pick up and manoeuvre into the trunk. Inspector Little had been a nightmare. The tailor liked to think that he learned from his mistakes. He had given more thought to the disposal of this second body.

Pringle's legs were folded up against his body and tied there with a length of stout twine. The arms were thrown in on top of the rest of the mess and the trunk closed over it all, removing it from sight and memory.

Cinderhouse wrapped the bloody shears in a length of black crêpe and put them in his pocket. He would dispose of them later, anywhere so long as they were far away from the scene of the crime.

He mopped the floor and scrubbed it with an ammonia solution until it glowed.

The coachman was summoned and, for a shilling, he helped Cinderhouse lift Pringle's trunk up into the hansom. The tailor climbed on to the board next to the coachman and, with a snap of the whip and a 'haw', the three of them set out towards the railway station.

38

‘I hope you don’t mind my saying so . . . Your shirt is ridiculous.’

Hammersmith took the cup from Penelope Shaw and smiled.

‘It’s not mine.’

‘Of course it isn’t yours. It doesn’t fit you.’

‘A friend was kind enough to lend me his shirt. Mine was ruined.’

‘How was it ruined?’

‘I spilled something on it.’

‘Spilled something?’

‘Blood.’

‘Oh, my.’

Penelope took a step back and reached for the wall behind her. Hammersmith rose from the chair and reached out towards her, but she waved him away.

‘Did you kill someone?’

‘It was my own blood. I apologize for troubling you.’

‘You haven’t troubled me in the least. I lost my balance for a bare instant, that’s all.’

Hammersmith took a sip of tea and scalded his tongue. He set the cup on the side table.

‘Have you ever killed anyone?’ Penelope said.

‘No, of course not.’

‘I’m sorry, I just thought, perhaps . . . so many villains out there.’

‘Perhaps fewer than you might think.’

‘Well, it’s clear that someone’s been acting up.’

She gestured at Hammersmith’s shirt, then his damaged face, taking in the entire tableau with an up-and-down movement of her wrist.

‘A misunderstanding.’

‘I hope you gave as good as you got.’

Hammersmith smiled.

‘I believe God will eventually even the scales in this particular case.’

‘If that’s so, then why do we need policemen at all, Mr Hammersmith? Why don’t we all simply wait for . . .’

She waved her hand again, this time taking in all of time and space.

‘Because no man should send another to his death. It’s not for us to decide. Police maintain the natural order of things.’

‘Do you?’

‘I try to.’ He shrugged and picked up the cup. The tea had cooled a bit now and he took a swallow. There was none of the bitter tang of copper that he was used to.

‘You’re about my husband’s size. I’ll fetch you a fresh shirt, at least.’

‘No need for that.’

‘It would make my time spent with you more pleasant if I weren’t constantly reminded of violence and death and your “natural order”.’

Hammersmith narrowed his eyes.

‘Where is your boy?’

'He's with his governess. They're at the park.'

'You don't accompany them?'

'I waited here in case you chose to visit.'

'Why did you think I would?'

'I didn't think that you would. But I had hope.'

She stood and left the room. She paused under the arch and turned towards him for a moment.

'I'll be back with that shirt.'

39

'What's he doing here?'

'He's harmless enough,' Day said.

'Let me dance for you,' the dancing man said.

He began to gyrate, waving his broom handle in the air between them, a talisman of something only he understood. A streamer of black crêpe fluttered at his throat.

'Somebody should've moved him along weeks ago,' Blacker said. 'He belongs in the nuthouse. Or at least the workhouse.'

'No,' the dancing man said.

The dancing stopped. He dropped the broom handle and reached into the folds of his clothing. He drew out the knife that Day had seen the night before.

Day took a step back, but Blacker moved forward. The dancing man feinted with the knife and Blacker jumped back then forward, rocking on his toes. He grabbed the other man's arm and twisted. The dancing man made no sound but Day watched as his expression changed from anger to confusion. Day reached out towards Blacker, but the older detective had already disarmed the dancing man in two swift movements and knocked him to his back on the cobblestones.

'Stay there,' Blacker said.

'What made him do that?' Day said. 'I've mentioned

the workhouse to him before without any threat of violence.'

'Look at him. You think he ever makes any sense?'

Day didn't answer. He leaned down and helped the dancing man to his feet. He held the man's elbow tight and steered him towards the back door of Number Four.

Blacker picked up the knife. He held it out to Day then pulled it back and looked at it more closely, letting sunlight play over the silvery surface.

'This is made of wood. It's only painted wood.'

'Surely not.'

'You think I don't know wood when I see it?'

'It's not a real knife?'

'It's a child's toy.'

Day threw his head back and laughed. He couldn't help himself. The anxiety he'd felt since moving to London caught up with him all at once and he let go. Blacker glared at him and then gave in and began to laugh too.

'It looked so real,' Day said. He wiped a tear from his eye. 'In the gaslight it looked completely real.'

'It looks real enough in the sunlight as well,' Blacker said.

'I don't hurt people,' the dancing man said.

'Of course you don't,' Day said. 'But you're in danger of being hurt yourself. This isn't the best spot for you to dance, you know.'

'I have a message for you,' the dancing man said. 'The messenger wants me to show you something.'

'How lovely,' Blacker said.

'The messenger?' Day said.

'He left something for you. He knows who kills the police.'

'Who is this?'

Day was suddenly interested, despite himself. Even Blacker had stopped chuckling and seemed to be listening.

'Come,' the dancing man said.

He took off at a full gallop across the street and down an alley. Day and Blacker followed at a safe distance, keeping the vagrant in sight. At the mouth of a storm drain, the dancing man ducked down and disappeared. The detectives rushed forward and found the dancing man standing hip deep in rippling water.

'I'm not going down there,' Blacker said.

'Nor I,' Day said. 'But thank you for showing us, sir.'

He smiled at the dancing man and turned to go back to The Yard, but the dancing man shouted.

'No, look!'

Day turned back and, with a deep sigh, squatted down to see what the vagrant was pointing at. There was a ledge formed by a cross-piece between two pillars deep in the tunnel and there, shining bright against the dark red bricks, was a pair of shears.

Day pointed and grabbed Blacker by the leg of his trousers.

'There,' he said. 'Go get those.'

'Not me,' Blacker said.

'I'll get them,' the dancing man said.

He splashed into the cave-like tunnel and emerged a moment later holding the shears high. He presented them to Day, who took them and turned them over.

They were streaked with a filmy layer of red. He clenched his jaw and looked at his colleague.

'Kingsley said that Little's wounds were . . .'

'Inflicted by shears.'

'Yes.'

'Let me dance.'

'Come with us,' Day said. 'You can dance inside, where it's warm.'

The dancing man tossed one end of the long strip of black crêpe around his throat as if defying the breeze to touch him.

'My things,' he said. 'I need my things.'

They walked back to Number Four and Day collected the dancing man's things, including the broken broomstick, but left the milk crate where it was against the brick wall. He was conscious of spectators who had begun gathering in the street in the hope that there might be an arrest.

Sergeant Kett was at the desk in the back hall and he stood as the dancing man entered ahead of them.

'Here now, get on out,' he said.

Then he saw Blacker and Day. He scowled.

'Aw, what're you doin' bringin' 'im in here. Smell's worse'n usual today.'

'Sergeant, you've been coddling Little's killer right outside your door,' Blacker said. 'You and Inspector Day both.'

'No,' Kett said. 'It can't be.'

'There is that possibility,' Day said, 'but it seems doubtful at the moment. Don't trouble yourself, Mr Kett. Detective Blacker is getting ahead of himself.'

'If this is the one did Mr Little in, you just put me in a room with 'im for a minute or two and look the other way, lads.'

Day grimaced and pushed the dancing man down the hall and around the corner. The big room was busy, with the bustle of uniformed police coming and going, but the Murder Squad room behind the rail was nearly empty. Only Jimmy Tiffany sat at his desk, writing a report and cursing his pen, which had worn to a nub. Day was too far away to read what Tiffany was writing, but he could well imagine the ink smearing across the page.

'Get him out of here,' Tiffany said, when he saw the dancing man.

The dancing man was quiet, scowling at the floor. Blacker pushed him through the short gate in the railing and guided him to Patrick Gilchrist's desk. Day dumped the dancing man's belongings on the desk and started sorting through them. Tiffany stood up and moved over to Gilchrist's desk.

'Help me go through all this,' Day said.

'I'm not touching any of that,' Tiffany said. 'What's he doing in here?'

'Not sure yet. May be something, may not, but he led us to what looks like our murder weapon.'

'Did he do the deed?'

'Personally, I think not. I think he just found the scissors.'

'Well, take him somewhere else to figure it out.'

There was a small holding cell in the back, but it was only used to keep dangerous or demented criminals temporarily out of the way until they could be moved to the larger and more permanent jail facility at Millbank.

'Since I've no idea what we're doing yet, I can't promise anything.'

Tiffany turned to Blacker.

'Come now, Blacker, you can't expect the rest of us to work while you're parading this creature through here. He reeks. And now the entire room reeks.'

'Then take your work off to Trafalgar Square and make a picnic of it. Or better yet, help us. Have a boy sent round to fetch Dr Kingsley.'

'I've already got more here than I can handle. I don't have time to be your errand boy.'

'Then try to stay out of our way.'

Tiffany glared at Blacker for a moment, but Blacker didn't flinch under his gaze. Finally, Tiffany gave up and went back to his desk. He threw his hands in the air as if to wash them of the entire incident, then turned his attention back to his broken pen and his uncompleted report. Day noticed that Tiffany was now breathing through his mouth to avoid the odour in the room.

Day spread the dancing man's dirty blanket out on the desk and placed each item on the rough fabric as he examined it. There were two mismatched boots, one of them too big to fit the dancing man's foot; a dented tin canteen – Day opened it and smelled the contents, which resembled chicken soup; the toy knife; a handful of grubby rags; and the tattered remains of what might have been a fox-tail stole. Day held this last item up at arm's length and made a face before dropping the bedraggled thing on the blanket. When he looked up, Tiffany was staring at him.

'That's it,' Tiffany said.

He pushed his chair back, stood and went to the back of the room, where he rapped loudly on Sir Edward's office door. Day looked at Blacker, who shrugged and gestured for the dancing man to sit. Sir Edward's door opened and Day heard Tiffany ask if he could enter. A moment later, Tiffany was in the office and the door had shut behind him.

Day gathered the corners of the blanket together to form a loose bundle with the dancing man's belongings inside. It did nothing to cut the stench in the room. He was looking around for an out-of-the-way place to stash the bundle when Sir Edward's door opened and Tiffany stomped out. Behind him, Sir Edward's deep voice boomed.

'Ridiculous.'

Sir Edward stepped out of the office and his eyes swept the Murder Squad desks. He took in Day, Blacker and the dancing man, sniffed the air and nodded.

'Is this man a suspect?' he said.

'We believe it's possible, sir,' Day said. 'He's at least a witness.'

'Then get on with it, Inspectors. Feel free to use the rear store cupboard for your interview. I believe two chairs will fit quite comfortably inside and it might be best to keep him out of sight of Little's peers. We don't want anyone assuming the worst and lashing out at the fellow before we know anything useful.'

He turned to Inspector Tiffany.

'As for you, Mr Tiffany, if you can't help in the investigation, at least stay out of Mr Day's way. I don't want my detectives running to me with every little thing.'

He turned on his heel and went back to his office. The door closed behind him.

Tiffany looked over at Day, his jaw set and his eyes narrowed. Day knew there was a chance Tiffany would never recover from being embarrassed in front of him. Day was still too new on the job to want enemies, even someone like Jimmy Tiffany. He looked over at Blacker, who was politely pretending to be very interested in the scissors they'd brought in with the dancing man. Day walked to his desk and opened the top drawer. Inside, there was an ink bottle and three new pens that Claire had sent with him on his first day. He chose his least favourite of them and took it to Tiffany's desk.

'This might be better than the one you're using.'

He set it there and walked away. At Gilchrist's desk, he picked up the bundle again and sneaked a glance at Tiffany, who was using the new pen. Tiffany looked up. He didn't smile, didn't nod, but he was using the pen.

40

They sat outside Euston Station waiting for the crowd to clear out, but the stream of commuters, in and out through the tall arch, remained steady. At last, Cinderhouse gave up. If they loitered outside the station too long he feared they might draw attention. It would be hard to explain the contents of the trunk under his feet if a curious bobby asked him to open it.

He passed a note up to the coachman to take them round St James's Park. They were sure to find a deserted path there.

He patted the trunk.

'Don't you worry, Mr Pringle,' he said. 'We'll find a place for you yet.'

41

When Penelope didn't return, Hammersmith began to worry. He stood and paced unsteadily about the drawing room. A shared chimney connected all the floors of the house and there was a fireplace here directly above the one downstairs where the dead boy had been found. An embroidered cloth covered the mantel and a large mirror was fastened to the wall directly above it. The mirror was surrounded by gold filigree and two narrow cases with tiny shelves where porcelain ballerinas posed. A gas ceiling lamp hung above the central table and there was a daybed under the only window in the room. Sunlight danced across the rills and glens of its tatted cushions. Glancing at the bed, Hammersmith realized he felt dizzy. The daybed was too inviting. He couldn't wait here any longer. There was work to do and he needed to keep moving or he might fall asleep.

He moved to the staircase and looked up to the floor above. He couldn't see or hear any movement there.

'Mrs Shaw?'

No response.

He pulled his billy club from under his arm and held it ready in his right hand. With his other hand on the banister for balance, he took the steps slowly, two at a time at first, but he stumbled and set out again more slowly. A green patterned runner extended up the centre of the staircase and softened his footfalls. His feet felt heavy and his knees came up with each step as if he were moving underwater. He stopped and took inventory of his body, realizing he could no longer feel any sensation in his fingers or his face.

The hall at the top of the stairs was dark and silent. He leaned against the wall and called again. 'Mrs Shaw?' he said. 'Penelope?'

After a long moment he heard something rustle off to his left and her voice floated towards him down the hall.

'I'm here.'

'I can't see. Where are you?'

There was no answer this time. He turned to his left and held on to the wall, shuffling forward in the dark. Diffuse light formed a halo in the air a few feet from him, but when he moved his head, the halo moved too. He thought he was still gripping his billy club, ready for anything that might jump out at him, but couldn't be sure. His arms were dead weights. He knew he wouldn't make it to the downstairs door and he had come too far into the house to do anything now except keep moving forward for as long as his legs continued to respond.

The halo around his vision grew brighter and resolved itself into a vertical line somewhere in front of him. He moved towards it and put out his hand. With the tip of the billy club, he pushed out and a door swung open.

Penelope Shaw stood in a floating rectangle of light. He wasn't sure her feet were touching the floor.

'What was in the tea you gave me?' Hammersmith said.

Penelope smiled at him and dissolved into a beautiful

swirl of pink light. Hammersmith reached out towards her, stumbled and fell. The last thing he saw before darkness claimed him was Penelope Shaw's bare ankle.

He did not notice the soft hands unbuttoning his shirt.

42

'So we're agreed, then, that the scissors are the murder weapon?'

'I don't think there's much question of that.'

'Nor I.'

Day and Blacker looked at the meagre evidence on Detective Gilchrist's desk. They had only a pair of shears and a button. Day had once more decided that Gilchrist's desk was fair game, since Patrick Gilchrist wouldn't be showing up to claim it. Besides, it made it look as if the absent Gilchrist was contributing to the case.

'It's progress, I suppose, but there's no way to connect them to anybody.'

'Not yet. Anyone could have access to scissors, but that thinking leads us nowhere, so I think we have to continue to act as though the scissors have to do with the killer's profession. The ferocity and strength required to follow through with the murder rules out the possibility of a woman, agreed?'

'Of course. No woman could have done this.'

'So we need not look at seamstresses, nurses or the ordinary London wife.'

'And that leaves us with . . . ?'

'Tailors, doctors, perhaps a cobbler.'

'Or anyone else in the city who happened to pick up his wife's scissors.'

'Yes.'

'Can we connect them with the button?' Blacker said. 'Does that lead us back to the upholsterer?'

'I don't think so. I have a theory about that and, if I'm right, it's entirely disconnected from the case itself.'

'A false clue?'

'Perhaps.'

'In what sense?'

'I'd like you to take another trip out to Little's place with me later, if you're up for it. I'd like to talk to his widow one more time.'

'I'd rather not.'

'Nor I.'

'But if it's unavoidable . . .'

'I'm afraid it is.'

'So do we rule out upholsterers, too?

'Not necessarily. But probably.'

'So then there's the trunk itself.'

'Kingsley's got that. And the needle and thread too. He says the needle used was probably an ordinary one and I don't see how that helps us much. Except inasmuch as the needles used by an upholsterer are apparently of a different sort entirely, which may be another reason to rule out that occupation as suspect. The thread . . .'

Day shrugged.

'I suppose a thread is a thread.'

'Unless we find a length of it covered with blood in someone's pocket,' Blacker said.

'That would be convenient.'

'Time's running out and we still don't have much to

go on. If we don't catch this one soon, it'll be another Ripper case.'

'Come with me.'

'Where?'

'The widow.'

'Didn't I just say no to that?'

'Not specifically.'

'Damnit.'

43

'What on earth is that frightful odour?'

Sergeant Kett looked up at the man standing in front of his desk. He was dressed in an immaculately tailored black suit accentuated by an aquamarine cravat and matching pocket square. He had a tall black hat with an aquamarine hatband and the lines around his eyes and mouth suggested that smiling was something other people did. Kett recognized him as Geoffrey Cinderhouse, official tailor to the Metropolitan Police. Cinderhouse was holding a pair of navy trousers on a wooden hanger. He removed his hat with a flourish, revealing a perfectly smooth bald head that gleamed in the sunlight from the open doors.

'I don't mean to seem rude, but it rather smells as though someone's died in here,' the man said.

'What can I do for you, Mr Cinderhouse?' Kett said.

He realized that he'd become used to the lingering odour of the dancing man, who was in the back room and out of sight, but who nonetheless seemed to be exerting some influence over the atmosphere.

'I've an errand here,' the man said. 'Two errands, actually. I'd like to speak to Inspector Day.'

'You've brought Inspector Day a change of clothing?' Kett said.

'What? Oh, the trousers. No, these are for Constable Pringle.'

'I'm not sure where Pringle is at the moment.'

'He was supposed to pick them up from me, but hasn't been by the shop. So I thought I'd kill two birds, as it were, by fetching them round here and seeing the detective at the same time.'

'Good of you. I'll get Mr Pringle's clothes to him.'

Kett stood and held out his hand.

'Oh,' Cinderhouse said. 'Of course.'

He started to hand over the trousers, but then pulled them back.

'I'm dreadfully sorry, but I really did have my heart set on meeting Mr Day. I've heard so many good things about him and, if I don't take the initiative, I may never have a chance to congratulate him on his recent promotion.'

'I'll let him know you enquired.'

'Is it true he's working to solve Inspector Little's murder?'

'He is.'

Cinderhouse leaned forward over the desk, Pringle's trousers dangling just out of Kett's reach.

'Any progress?' the tailor said.

'I think they're close,' Kett said. 'They have the murder weapon now.'

'Do they? What is it?'

'A pair of shears.'

Pringle's trousers dropped from the tailor's hand.

44

The sound of wood clattering on wood snapped Cinderhouse awake as if from a trance, and he ducked to retrieve the fallen hanger. He felt around under the desk for it, his face hidden from the sergeant for a precious moment or two.

They had the shears. How did they have the shears? And so quickly?

It hadn't been more than a few hours since Cinderhouse had thrown them from the window of the hansom into the road. He'd expected the shears to be swept up by early morning street sweepers, along with the previous day's horse dung. Or perhaps found by some vagrant and whisked away into the bowels of London's tenements.

And yet, here they were, almost immediately at Scotland Yard, in the custody of the new detective.

Was the man that good? Was Detective Walter Day the enemy he had always feared might come for him?

At least they didn't seem to know that Pringle was dead.

His fingers closed around the hanger. He composed his expression and stood up, draping the trousers over the wooden bar to give himself a moment before turning his attention back to the sergeant.

'Are you quite all right?' Kett said.

'Yes, of course. Please forgive me. I'm just so fascinated by detective work that I get too excited sometimes.'

'Quite all right.'

'The shears . . . are you sure they're the murder weapon?'

'You'd have to ask the detectives that.'

'Of course, of course. I only bring it up because I'm so used to working with shears myself. You might call me an expert. I'd be happy to look them over and lend the detective my opinion, if you think it would do any good.'

He smiled, hoping that the smile looked genuine.

Kett looked over his shoulder at the entrance to the big hall and the tiny, fenced-off domain of the Murder Squad.

'I don't think . . .'

'I'm not a policeman myself, of course,' Cinderhouse said, 'but my close association with the force puts me in a unique position, don't you think?'

'I'll leave a message with the detective and have him get back to you.'

'I really think I can help,' Cinderhouse said.

He stepped around Kett and walked down the short hall. He ignored the large area to his right and went straight to the low railing that surrounded twelve cluttered desks in a corner of the big open space. He started to open the gate in the rail but was stopped short by Sergeant Kett's hand on his arm.

'Here, now,' Kett said. 'I'd hate to do anything nasty when we've been so cordial up to this point.'

Cinderhouse put his hands up and smiled again. 'I don't mean any harm,' he said. 'It's the thrill of being able to help these fine gentlemen. You understand. Surely you understand.'

'And I hope you understand that I can't let every citizen off the street in here to muck with evidence in a murder case.'

'I'm hardly a citizen. You might even call me an auxiliary policeman, since I clothe you all. At least, I like to think of myself as such and I'm awfully proud to be of service to you fine gentlemen. Why, I'm practically one of you.'

'Practically ain't reality.'

Cinderhouse nodded. He made a calming motion with one hand to let Kett know that he wasn't dangerous, wasn't going to do anything hasty. He could see the shears sitting out on a desk in there, almost within reach. The only evidence that connected him to the crime and it was right there, and if he didn't do something to get those shears, then didn't he deserve whatever fate the detectives had in store for him?

'Are those the shears?' he said.

Kett shrugged.

Cinderhouse peered at the scissors over the top of the rail. They were his own. He was sure of it. There was a nick in one blade where he'd run up against a snap in a sailcloth jacket. He could see it from here. There were chips flaked off the glossy black handles from long use, one crack in the paint that he'd always thought resembled the shape of Italy. And there was Colin Pringle's blood caked in the crevices where the blades met the handle and where the rivet swivelled the shears open and shut. The blood was still so fresh that it gleamed red in the lamplight.

'Hmm,' he said. 'I suppose they might be of the same sort I use at the shop. A little different, of course.'

'I'm sure.'

'Tell me, how did Inspector Day come by them?'

'In the course of his investigation.'

'Well, yes, but I mean . . . how?'

Kett clucked his tongue and scowled.

'Official business of The Yard. If there's nothing else . . .'

'I have an idea.'

'Yes?'

'Why don't you let me take these with me back to the shop? Then I can compare them to my own shears – I have several

pairs – and to those in the catalogues I keep. I may be able to match them exactly.'

'I've been patient with you,' Kett said.

'Forgive me. Only trying to be of help. And, as I said, I'm practically one of you.'

'It's why I haven't hoisted you out into the street yet. But we're a bit busy at the moment and it's not part of my job to give tours.'

Kett motioned for Cinderhouse to precede him through the back hall. The tailor hoisted Pringle's trousers high so that they wouldn't drag on the dirty floor. He bit his lip. If Day had been in the squad room he might, perhaps, have welcomed Cinderhouse's help. But the sergeant wasn't interested and Cinderhouse couldn't seem to make him interested, no matter how he approached the subject. There seemed to be no way to get close to the investigation and find out how it progressed. He was in the dark and would, it seemed, remain in the dark.

'I s'pose if you really wanna be of help,' Kett said, 'you could bring those catalogues you mentioned and let the detectives take a look at 'em.'

Cinderhouse turned suddenly, sending the heavy end of the trousers swinging.

'I'm sorry,' he said. 'Bring them in?'

'I don't know. That might be a thing they'd wanna see.'

'But of course. I'll rearrange my schedule. I have a few fittings, but they can easily be pushed back until tomorrow, provided I can get a message to my clients in time.'

'Don't mean to put you out.'

'Not at all. Happy to do it. I'll change my appointments, arrange for someone to watch my son and be right back round with those catalogues.'

'No hurry, I'm sure.'

'I wouldn't want to keep Inspector Day waiting. I'll be back with them as quickly as I possibly can.'

Cinderhouse smoothed a leg of Pringle's trousers over the hanger.

'Best take these back with me, anyway. Clumsy of me to have dropped them. Now I'll have to press them again.'

'I'm sure they're fine. You can leave them here for the constable.'

'Ah, you must not know Mr Pringle well. He's very particular about his trousers. No, I'll take them along to the shop. Who knows? Perhaps he'll turn up, after all.'

As he retreated down the back hallway, his eyes darted back and forth, from walls to ceiling to floor, as if he were already caged. Entering the lion's den had been a calculated risk and he still wasn't sure he had made the right choice. But waiting to see if the other shoe would drop was excruciating. He had to know what they knew.

There was one more thing he could do to keep Inspector Day under his thumb.

'Pardon me,' he said. He turned just inside the door. 'This is frightfully embarrassing, but I'm afraid I need some directions.'

The sergeant looked at him without speaking.

'I forgot about Inspector Day's new suit. I was supposed to take it round to his house, but I neglected to ask him for his address. I'd hoped to get it from him today, but since he isn't here . . . Is there a chance I can get the address from you?'

The sergeant frowned and grumbled something under his breath, but he took a piece of paper from the desk next to him and wrote the address down. He handed the note to Cinderhouse without a word and went around the desk. He sat down and was immediately reabsorbed in his paperwork.

The tailor smiled and thanked the top of the sergeant's head. He tucked the paper with the address into his pocket and left, whistling a happy tune.

45

'I'll stay down here,' Blacker said.

'You're not coming up?'

'Not a chance, old boy. It was difficult enough the first time around.'

'Wait for me, then. I'll just be a moment.'

'Take all the time in the world. I shall stand out here and enjoy the sun on my face and pity you up there.'

'I'm sure that will sustain me.'

Day smiled and shook his head. He opened the door and stepped through into the vestibule of Inspector Little's building. The space was so tiny and foul that Day kept his arms tight at his sides for fear they'd brush the walls and come away stained or sticky. To his left was a closed door and, directly ahead, a long, dark staircase that disappeared into the gloom above. He took a deep breath before letting the street-level door swing shut behind him and then trudged up the steps.

'Damn Blacker for a coward,' he said.

He let a small amount of air out through his nose and could taste the old food odours that lived in the hall. The essence of stale spices lodged in the back of his throat and made him want to cough, but he stifled the impulse. He tried to remember the smell of trees outside his home in Devon, but could not.

The landing at the top of the stairs was as small as the

entrance hall and the door to the Little home was open a crack. Day could hear muffled voices inside, accompanied by an occasional high-pitched wail.

He swallowed, took a breath, and rapped lightly on the jamb. After a moment the door swung open wider and Little's boy Gregory appeared in the gap. Gregory immediately turned and disappeared, but Day heard him speaking.

'Ma, it's the policeman again.'

'Get 'im in.'

Day didn't wait for the boy to come back. He pushed the door open and stepped inside.

The flat was much the same as it had been on his previous visit, but there were subtle changes. The window over the sofa was still curtainless, but the glass had been washed. Sunlight streamed into the room, lending it a somewhat cheerier appearance. Gregory, the helpful son, was fully dressed in clothes that looked reasonably clean to Day. The simple son, Anthony, was sitting on the floor, his back against the wall, stacking wooden blocks. His empty chair sat in the corner, the straps hanging loose. Day was so surprised to see the boy quietly playing that he didn't notice Mrs Little until she tugged at his sleeve. He jumped and turned.

'He ain't breathin', mister.'

Day saw with alarm that she was holding the baby and that its skin was pale blue. Without a thought, he took it from her and turned it over, laying it against his arm. He smacked its back with the heel of his hand, once, then again, and a third time.

Something small and brown thumped against the

floorboards at Day's feet and a second later the baby began to cry, haltingly at first, its howls interrupted by hiccoughs, but then building to a startling crescendo.

Day passed the baby back to its mother. She bounced it up and down, her massive bosom jiggling. Day averted his eyes.

Anthony looked up and shouted something that Day found incomprehensible, but Gregory nodded and Anthony returned to his blocks, apparently satisfied.

'Thank you, mister,' the Widow Little said. 'That was a close one.'

He looked at Mrs Little. She was watching him, biting her lip, rocking the baby back and forth in her arms. She looked much the same as she had the day before, but her hair had been washed and combed and her housecoat had been freshly pressed.

The baby's skin had returned to a healthy pink colour. Day smiled at the widow.

'This happened once before when I was a country constable,' he said. 'The rector's son choked on a bit of sausage.'

'This 'un puts every damn thing in 'is mouth. Can't hardly keep up with takin' it all back outta 'im afore he stops breathin'.'

Day decided not to ask why she didn't simply keep small things out of the baby's reach. The drama now ended, he scanned the floor, looking for the object the baby had been trying to eat. Gregory saw him looking and scampered over to the barrel-table. He reached down and picked up the tiny thing, which was hidden in the shadows. Gregory brought it to him and Day took it.

It was a small round button, buff-coloured, stained and smooth.

He went to the sofa under the window where a dozen identical buttons had been pulled loose from the upholstery and now dangled on threads. He took a button from his pocket and compared it to the others. It matched perfectly.

There could be no mistake, now that he was able to make a side-by-side comparison. The button in the trunk had come from this sofa in this flat.

And Day suddenly knew how it had happened.

'Ma'am,' Day said, 'did your husband visit you on the eve of his . . . I mean, when did you say you saw him last?'

'Yes, it was the night afore what was done to him.'

'Did the baby choke then as well? In Mr Little's presence, I mean?'

'This baby chokes damn near ever day.'

Day sighed.

It was clear in his mind. Little had returned home to give his wife money for the household. His infant had choked on a sofa button. Little had got it out of the baby's mouth and absent-mindedly put it in his pocket. He had carried the button with him to his doom, but it had nothing to do with the murder and could lead the detectives nowhere.

Day put the button back in his pocket and then, on impulse, reached out and plucked the remaining loose buttons from the sofa.

''Ere now, what's this?'

'I need these as evidence.'

'Evidence? What's my couch got to do wiv anythin'?'

'It's hard to say now, but these may come in handy.'

Little's widow sniffed and cast her eye on the mangled sofa.

'Don't look no worser now, I s'pose.'

Day pocketed the handful of buttons.

'I see there have been some improvements made since I was here earlier.'

'The money yer one-armed gennleman gave. Got me thinkin' 'bout things might be done round the place now we have that pinchin comin' in.'

'Sir Edward is a good man.'

'Is he married, though?'

The widow winked at Day and he winced.

'He is.'

'Shame, that.'

'I'm sure it is. I'll take my leave now.'

'Welcome to stay. I'll put the kettle on.'

'Thank you, but no. My associate is waiting for me downstairs.'

'Bring 'im up.'

'I'm afraid we've more visits to make today. Still on duty.'

He tipped his hat to her and reached for the doorknob, but Gregory reached it first and swung the door open for him. Day smiled at the boy.

'You're a good boy, Gregory. You're very helpful to your mother.'

'Thank you, sir.'

'When you're older, in another year or two perhaps, come by The Yard. We employ runners there and I would be more than happy to put in a word for you with the sergeant.'

'Thank you, sir. I will.'

'Good day.'

He nodded again at Mrs Little and slipped into the dark hallway. The staircase seemed shorter going down than it had been going up, but when he opened the outside door the sudden light hurt his eyes.

'There he is,' Blacker said.

'Have you enjoyed your fresh air?' Day said.

'Like nothing else. Did you find what you came here for?'

'Yes,' Day said. 'And I'm afraid we've been chasing at least one false clue.'

He pulled a handful of the smooth beige buttons from his pocket and tossed them in the street. One of them had been found with Little's body, but it hardly mattered any more.

'The button's useless,' he said.

Blacker looked at the scattering of buttons in the road and then up at the window above them. He nodded and Day could see that he'd put it together.

'So that lets out upholsterers as suspects, doesn't it?' Blacker said.

'I think so.'

'Which only leaves everyone else in London.'

'True, I suppose, but I feel this is progress just the same, even if it's not awfully encouraging.'

'Leaving aside the button, then, we've still got needle, thread, shears. I still want to talk to a tailor. That feels promising to me.'

'Right. What's the name of the one we use? Kett mentioned him.'

'Cinderhouse?'

'That's him. He might narrow it down for us, rather than running all over the city to every tailor with a signboard in the street.'

'Should we visit his shop, you think, or send for him?'

'Let's go back. We have the dancing man waiting for us.'

'Good.'

Day took a last look at Little's building and followed Blacker across the street. One piece of evidence had been a dead end, but Day still felt he'd done some good. There were no sofa buttons left in the Little home and so Little's youngest child might breathe more easily now. And perhaps live a bit longer.

46

The store cupboard was an approximate three-metre cube. Blacker had dragged three chairs into the room and they filled it so that there was barely enough space to sit in the chairs without touching each other's knees. He lit a tallow candle and set it on a shallow ledge that ran about the walls of the room at wainscoting-height. Blacker steered the dancing man towards one of the chairs and Day set the bundle of rubbish at his feet. Day sat in the chair across from the dancing man and Blacker stood behind him. The dancing man sat quietly, hardly moving, seemingly stifled by the close walls. The detectives took a long moment to light their pipes. The smell of tobacco smoke was infinitely preferable to body odour. Day was mildly amused to see that Blacker smoked a huge calabash that dwarfed his narrow face, but he hid his smile behind his hand as he lit his own much smaller pipe. When both pipes were going, Day glanced at Blacker, who nodded, then began.

'What's your name, sir?' he said.

'Let me out.'

'We will,' Day said. 'But we need to ask you some questions first.'

'Can't dance here. Can't dance. Too tight, too close, no room.'

'Let us help you get back out there so you can dance again. Just tell me your name.'

'Can't dance. Broken legs. Table's too short.'

The dancing man began to rock back and forth on his chair, hugging himself. Day looked up at Blacker, who gestured for Day to step outside.

'We'll be right back,' Day said.

He rose and left the room with Blacker.

'Shall we send him to the workhouse or to the asylum?' Blacker said.

'I'd like to let him get back to his life. He's not causing any harm out there.'

Life seemed to turn and change on a whim, and while Day didn't imagine he could sink as low in life as the dancing man had, he still worried that this might be his own future if he failed as a detective. What had caused the dancing man to slide into invisibility? How did one prevent it?

'You know as well as I that he didn't kill Little,' Day said. 'All he wants to do is dance with a broomstick. We need to know what he saw, but I don't see a need to frighten him.'

'Frightening him may get him to tell us what we need to know. Assuming we can get him to say anything that makes sense.'

'The more emotional he gets, the more removed he'll be from reality.'

'He's already too removed. Whatever information he might have for us is already jumbled up with a lot of nonsense. There's no way I can see to make him useful.'

There was a thumping noise behind the detectives as the gate at the railing slammed shut, then:

'Perhaps I can help with that.'

Bernard Kingsley stood in the middle of the Murder Squad room, surveying the desks. Jimmy Tiffany looked up and saw Kingsley. He stood and grabbed his jacket from a hook, then exited through the gate behind Kingsley and disappeared down the back hall.

'You've changed a few things since I was here last,' Kingsley said.

Blacker shot a puzzled look in Day's direction. He clearly hadn't sent for the doctor.

'What are you doing here?' Day said.

'Inspector Tiffany sent for me. Said there was a suspect in Little's murder.'

Day smiled. For all of Tiffany's bluster and laziness, he had helped.

'Thank you for coming,' Day said. 'As for the suspect, we don't think he committed the murder.'

'I haven't ruled that out,' Blacker said.

'We think, we both think that he may have crossed paths with the real killer,' Day said.

'Well, let's see what we shall see, shall we?'

Kingsley smiled and patted the black bag under his arm.

'Lead me to the evidence, gentlemen.'

47

The three men squeezed into the small storage room where the dancing man still sat. It didn't appear that he'd moved at all since Day and Blacker had left the room. He stared at his feet, his hands clasped on his knees. Day positioned himself between the vagrant and the doctor in case the dancing man suddenly became violent.

Kingsley set his bag on one of the two empty chairs and opened it. The stench was nearly overpowering, but Kingsley appeared not to notice. He glanced over at the dancing man and frowned.

'You look familiar to me, sir.'

The dancing man said nothing, but continued to stare at his folded hands. Kingsley reached into his bag and drew out a bundle of white fabric. He partially unrolled it to reveal the Beard Killer's straight razor, covered with red and black smudges, and held it out to Blacker who took the entire bundle from him. Both men were careful not to touch the surface of the razor.

'Let's see those shears,' Kingsley said.

'They're on my desk,' Day said. 'I'll be back in a moment.'

'Wait,' Kingsley said. 'I'm afraid I'm not as prepared as I'd hoped to be. Could you possibly bring me at least one clean sheet of white foolscap and a bottle of ink?'

'Of course.'

Day left the storage cupboard door ajar and went to

his desk. Across the room, Inspectors Waverly Brown and Oliver Boring had returned and were huddled at Boring's desk, quietly arguing over a report. Brown looked up and nodded at Day, then went back to his murmured discussion with Boring.

Day grabbed the bottle of ink from his desk drawer and set out two sheets of foolscap. He carefully wrapped the shears in one of the sheets of paper and folded the other sheet in half so that it wouldn't wrinkle as easily while he carried it. He put the ink bottle in his jacket pocket and took the paper and shears back to the store.

In Day's absence, Blacker had moved himself between the doctor and the dancing man. Kingsley didn't seem to notice that the two detectives were positioning themselves about the room in order to protect him. Day wordlessly handed over the paper and shears.

'Perfect,' Kingsley said.

He laid the foolscap in his hand and unfolded it to reveal the shears. He took a lens from his bag and scanned the shears carefully. The dancing man was so still that he might have been a statue in the corner of the room.

'Definitely blood,' Kingsley said. 'And I would guess there was a great deal of it in order to produce these streaks across the metal. The blood has dried in layers, do you see? Look here. Two layers, one overlapping the other. The bottom-most coating would have dried very quickly, especially if it were waved about in the air for a minute or two. Then, while it was still tacky, more blood was forced past the surface, covering the first batch here and there, building the layers up from the surface.'

'Is it possible to tell if they're the same scissors used to kill Inspector Little?'

'No. In fact, I'll need to run a chemical test to determine whether this is human or animal blood. I'm afraid that's as much as the blood evidence will be able to tell us. Of course, it's possible this is nothing more than pig's blood. We'll see.'

Kingsley must have seen the disappointment on the detectives' faces because he shook his head.

'The blood evidence is not the end of it. You'll see. Forensic technology is making great strides of late. Very exciting. Look at this.'

He angled the shears in the candlelight so that Day and then Blacker could see the blades.

'There's a small bit of thread caught here between the blades.'

'What does that tell us?'

'Why, absolutely nothing at the moment. But I'll want to compare this thread to those found at Little's crime scene.'

'You didn't bring those threads with you?'

'No. It will have to wait until I return to my laboratory. But,' Kingsley said, 'before I do that, I'll require more. I'll need to gather data from all three of you.'

Blacker looked alarmed.

'All of us?'

'Oh, I don't mean that I suspect you detectives of any wrongdoing. But you have touched the shears, so I'll need your finger patterns to compare them against any evidence left on the weapon. Mr Day, could I have that foolscap? And the ink, if you please?'

Day handed over the paper and produced the bottle

of ink from his pocket. He opened the bottle and set it on the chair next to Kingsley's bag. Kingsley flattened out the piece of paper against the wall and smoothed it with the back of his hand.

'I do wish we had a bit more room,' he said.

'I apologize. The commissioner felt it best to keep him contained and out of the way while we questioned him.'

'That's undoubtedly wise. Here now, Mr Blacker, let's have you go first. Please dip your finger, any finger will do, into the ink bottle and apply it to this piece of foolscap.'

'Then my finger will be dirty.'

'Regrettable, but unavoidable, I'm afraid.'

'I don't see the point of it.'

'I demonstrated this for you in my lab.'

'I didn't see the point of it then, either.'

Kingsley sighed.

'What about you, Mr Day? Will you risk a little ink on your finger?'

Day shot an apologetic glance at Blacker, then ran his index finger around the inside edge of the bottle. He held his finger up to show that it was black. Kingsley grabbed his hand, held his finger and pressed it against the paper. He handed over the lens and Day looked through it at the black loops and whorls on the clean white paper.

'This pattern, this is unique?'

'I believe so.'

'Michael, let's see yours,' Day said.

Blacker stepped forward and looked over Day's shoulder at the smudged sheet of foolscap. Without a word, he stuck his finger into the ink bottle and made his mark next to Day's. The three of them bent over the lens and Day passed it back and forth so they could see for themselves.

'They *are* all different,' he said.

Blacker shook his head and nudged Day. Day looked up to see that the dancing man was watching them.

'Would you like to try it?' Day said.

'Can't move.'

'Why can't you move?'

'No room. Legs broken.'

'I wish I could place where I've met you,' Kingsley said. 'I do know you, don't I?'

'Only the dead know me.'

Day saw his chance and moved closer to the dancing man.

'What was your name? The name you had before the dead began to dance?'

'Doesn't matter.'

'It matters to me.'

'Henry.'

'Good. Henry. Can I call you Henry?'

'Not Henry any more. I am a dancer. I am death.'

'I can't very well call you "Death".'

'Whatever you call me, I remain the same.'

'Can you tell us where you found these scissors, sir?'

He held up the shears, still wrapped in paper, well out of the dancing man's reach.

'London. The city gave them to me. London sent me the gift.'

Blacker rolled his eyes.

'Oh, for God's sake, can we please stop coddling this infant? Tell us where you got the damn shears, you bloody loon.'

'The messenger on his black chariot. He delivered the gift that was meant for me. Not for you.'

'A man in a black carriage?'

'The messenger.'

'And he gave them to you?'

'He cast it at my feet, wrapped in a shroud so that I would know.'

'A shroud?'

'Yes.'

'There was no wrapping when we found it.'

Kingsley cleared his throat and moved cautiously towards the dancing man.

'That scarf,' he said. 'The black crêpe at your throat. Is that the shroud?'

The dancing man clutched at the length of fabric.

'It's mine,' he said. 'The message was for you. The blood is yours, but not the shroud. You would only have cast it off. It's right that I took it. It's mine.'

'Of course it is. But may I look at it for a moment?'

'You can't have it.'

'I won't keep it.'

The dancing man grudgingly unwrapped the crêpe from his throat and held out one end of it to Kingsley. He held the other end of it, wrapping it around his hand so that it couldn't be pulled away from him. The doctor sighed and held up his lens.

'The most useful tool in my arsenal,' he said.

He smiled at the dancing man, but got a wary scowl in return.

Kingsley hunched over the chair and held the shears next to the end of the makeshift scarf, comparing the two items. After a minute or two, he straightened up and nodded.

'I'm reasonably certain the shears were wrapped in this material. There's blood, or something very like it, on the fabric, and the black thread caught in the shears matches those at this frayed end here.'

'That corroborates his story,' Day said.

'So it would seem we're looking for a black carriage of some sort,' Blacker said. 'Not much to go on.'

He turned to the dancing man.

'What kind of carriage was it? What kind of chariot?'

The dancing man shook his head, still staring at the end of the fabric held in Kingsley's hand.

'Was it large or small? Would it hold two people or several?'

'It was small,' the dancing man said. 'The city doesn't crave notice.'

'And neither do murderers, I'd wager. Possibly a hansom.'

'I want my shroud.'

'Of course,' Kingsley said.

He let go of the end of the crêpe and the dancing man wrapped it around his throat again.

'There's nothing else this length of cloth can tell us,' Kingsley said.

'But perhaps giving it back to him has bought us some good will,' Day said. 'What do you say, Henry? Will you make a mark on this paper for us?'

'It is not for me to make a mark. The city makes its mark on us all.'

'True enough. But perhaps, just this once, you could dirty yourself in the furtherance of a good cause.'

Day brought the ink bottle to the dancing man and held it there. He nodded, encouraging Henry to get a little ink on his finger. The dancing man stared at the bottle for what seemed to be a long time and Day could hear Blacker behind him, shifting his weight from foot to foot. Finally, the dancing man reached out and stabbed his finger into the bottle. Before he could draw away, Kingsley had his hand in a vice-like grip and pressed the blackened finger against the paper. He stood back and let go as Day stoppered the bottle.

'We can't let him go,' Blacker said. 'He might disappear.'

'I know,' Day said. 'But I don't want to cage him either.'

'We've no choice.'

'I know that, too.'

'And we can't leave him here in the closet.'

'We'll put him in the holding cell for now.'

'I want my things. You can't take my things.'

'By all means, take them, sir. All but the shears. Those belong to us now.'

The dancing man gathered his bundle and allowed Blacker to lead him from the room. When they were gone, Kingsley lit a cigarette.

'I should have brought my pipe. The odour is rather overpowering, isn't it.'

Day held his pipe up and nodded. They both smiled.

'Now then,' said Kingsley. 'To work . . .'

48

Hammersmith sensed something near his right elbow. A moment later, he heard a small noise, a rustling that lasted a fraction of a second. He didn't open his eyes. His head hurt and he saw red behind the curtain of his eyelids. Behind that was a pattern of winter tree branches and he spent time listening to himself breathe while he tried to decide whether the skeletal branches behind his eyes were red on black or black against a red sky. When the trees began to fade, he found his tongue and spoke.

'Who are you?' he said.

'Who are you?'

It wasn't an echo. The voice that returned his question was smaller, higher, than his own. Hammersmith focused on his body and was able to feel some sensation in his hands and feet, a distant tingling. Something brushed against his hand.

He opened his eyes, blinking rapidly to filter the light, but couldn't keep them open for long. He let them drift shut again and concentrated on breathing.

'What happened?' he said.

But even as he said it, he knew that he had been poisoned.

'Why are you in my mama's bed?' said the small, high voice.

'Who are you?' Hammersmith said.

'Bradley.'

'Bradley Shaw?'

'Yes.'

'Is your mama named Penelope?'

'Yes.'

'I'm in her bed?'

'Yes.'

'I thought you were at the park with your governess.'

'I was.'

'How long have you been back?'

'Just now.'

'Where is your mother?'

'She's downstairs.'

'Did she send you to get me?'

'No.'

Hammersmith waited for more, for an explanation, but it didn't come.

'Did she tell you to wake me up?' he said.

'No.'

'Did you come looking for me?'

'No. I just came in.'

Hammersmith waited, letting his skin adjust to the sudden stimulation of the air.

'The door was open,' the boy said.

'How long were you at the park?'

'I don't know.'

Hammersmith levered himself up on one elbow and swung his feet off the side of the bed. He blindly arranged the bedsheets as he moved to cover himself. He didn't remember undressing, but he was naked. He sat for a long time, his eyes closed, waiting at the side of the bed for the world to catch up to him.

'Are you my new papa?'

'No.'

He opened his eyes and saw the back of a small boy as he went out by the bedroom door.

'Why would you ask me that?' Hammersmith said.

The boy turned and came back. He might have been five years old. Hammersmith could see that he was sensitive. Bradley Shaw had big ears that stuck out from his face and a cowlick that had arranged his hair in circles around the back of his head so that his face was the epicentre of a hurricane. But his eyes were huge and brown and lively. There were sparkling depths there.

'Because my mama is done with my papa,' the boy said.

'What do you mean?'

'My mama isn't his friend any more.'

Hammersmith looked around the room for his clothes.

'Your clothes are on the chair,' the boy said.

'Bring them to me.'

The boy walked sideways, his eyes on Hammersmith, and picked up a pile of clothing from a wingback chair in the corner. He brought them to the bed and set them within Hammersmith's reach. He stepped back and watched the man on his father's bed as if waiting for violence, ready to run. Hammersmith picked up his trousers and slid them on under the sheet that lay across his lap. He stood up and fastened them at the front. He grabbed his shirt and pulled it on. When he closed his eyes, the room seemed to be rocking under his feet. He sat back down on the edge of the bed.

'Your father is always your father,' he said. 'He always will be.'

He didn't look at the boy.

'I don't care about him,' Bradley said.

Hammersmith looked at the big brown eyes of the little boy.

'Does he hit you?'

The boy shook his head.

Hammersmith pulled his boots on over bare feet.

'Then you've no reason.'

He grabbed his hose and garters, stuffed them in his jacket pocket and then stuffed himself into the jacket. He noticed now that his shirt fitted better than it had and he smoothed it over his chest. It was not the same shirt he'd worn into the Shaw house. It seemed Penelope had given him one of her husband's shirts after all.

'Where is your water closet?'

The boy pointed to a door on the far wall. Hammersmith made his unsteady way across the moving floor. Behind the door, he found a room larger than the bedroom. A claw-footed bathtub shared space with a toilet, a washbasin and a conversation suite, including a Chesterfield and a vanity table. The Shaws had clearly followed the lead of most middle-class Londoners and converted an existing bedroom into an indoor washroom. The paintings on the walls looked to Hammersmith as if they were of a set with the valuable art in the downstairs room. A bay window overlooked a small garden and served as a light source for the room. The sun was low on the horizon. He closed the door behind him so that the boy wouldn't follow him and he leaned over the basin. He stuck a finger down his throat and brought up the contents of his stomach.

He emptied the bowl into the toilet and pulled the brass chain, watching the sad remains of that morning's penny pie whirl away from him. The poison in Penelope's tea, however much of it was left in his stomach, went with it.

He sat on the Chesterfield, wiped his mouth on the sleeve of Charles Shaw's borrowed shirt and waited for his stomach to settle. He wondered whether the boy was still waiting outside the door. After a few minutes he stood and made his way across the room. He felt steadier on his feet.

He cracked the door open and peered out into the bedroom. It was empty. He stumbled through to the hallway and paused at the top of the stairs, but heard nothing anywhere in the house. The boards creaked under his feet as he descended to the ground floor. The parlour was dark and cool and he almost didn't see Penelope Shaw sitting in the shadows of the high wing-back chair.

'I'm sorry,' she said.

Hammersmith couldn't see her face.

'Thank you for the shirt,' he said.

'It looks good. At least it fits you better than the one you were wearing.'

'What was it? The poison, I mean?'

'Benzene, just a drop of it, from the laundry.'

Hammersmith nodded. He had seen benzene used to remove stains from upholstery and curtains, things too cumbersome to be washed properly. He had no idea what the long-term side effects of benzene poisoning might be, but he knew that if he stayed awake and on his feet, any poison should eventually work its way through his body.

'What if I'd died? Killing a police officer wouldn't have gone well for you.'

'It's not lethal,' Penelope said. 'At least not in small doses. My husband uses it on his patients to calm them.'

'Did he tell you to use it on me?'

She raised a finger to her mouth and bit her knuckle.

'I was supposed to . . . I just needed to put you in my bed. Elizabeth had to help me with that part of it. Charles was going to come in and catch you there.'

'I don't understand.'

'It would give him something, some way of controlling you. The scandal would have ruined you. You would know that and you would leave us alone. Leave him alone.'

'The boy in the chimney.'

'Charles tried to remove him, but he couldn't. The body was stuck. Charles said we had to go. But we hadn't the money to go far and he didn't know what to do then. Someone was supposed to come and remove the body while we were gone. An associate of Charles. But when we came back, you were waiting for us here and Charles knew that you'd been inside.'

'He might have talked to me.'

'You might have talked to him.'

Hammersmith nodded. 'Where is he?'

'I don't know. I didn't give you as much benzene as he told me to. You woke early.'

'Why would you want me to wake early?'

'I don't . . . I hoped you might deal with him when he arrived.'

Hammersmith walked slowly – he was still dizzy and didn't want to stumble in front of Mrs Shaw – through the arch to the entrance hall and opened the front door. He paused there, unable to see Penelope.

'I will be back. Don't leave the house. You may want to send your son away. Send him to visit relatives. It wouldn't be good for him to see his parents taken into police custody.'

He didn't wait to hear her response. He stepped out into the late afternoon air and took a deep breath. He closed the door behind him, vomited in Penelope Shaw's rose garden, and made his unsteady way down the crowded street.

He didn't notice when Charles Shaw emerged from behind a vendor's wagon half a block behind and followed Hammersmith away from the house.

49

'We're missing something, aren't we?' Kingsley said.

'We are?' Day said.

'Yes, I'm sure I've touched that razor. We'll need my thumbprint to compare.'

He unstoppered the bottle of ink and stuck his thumb inside. He wiggled it around and pulled it back out, then pressed it firmly against the piece of paper. When he pulled his thumb away, a wet black smudge sat next to the other three marks on the page. There were no ridges visible in the doctor's mark.

'Too much ink, I suppose,' Day said.

'Yes. Perhaps the bottle is too large a reservoir. In future, it may be prudent to use some sort of inkpad instead.'

He moved his thumb to the other side of the row of marks and pushed it against the paper once more without re-inking first. This time he left a clear print. He smiled at it.

'Now, why didn't I take the amount of ink into account in the first place? Let's see the razor and the . . .'

He trailed off.

'What is it?' Day said.

'It's just occurred to me that there's absolutely no reason to continue working in a store cupboard. Could we possibly reconvene at your desk, Inspector?'

'That would certainly smell better. Henry appears to have left a stain in the air here. But I'm afraid my desk is completely covered with reports at the moment.'

'Then what say we find another place to work?'

Kingsley gathered up his bag, the ink bottle and the paper with its four fingerprints. Day carried the razor and the shears, and the two of them left the store cupboard. As soon as they hit the relatively fresh air of the squad room, they both breathed deep.

'Oh, my, I had no idea I was becoming so accustomed to that rank atmosphere. This smells wonderful.'

'We can use Detective Gilchrist's desk. He's out at the moment.'

'Actually, if you don't mind, I'd like to check in with Sir Edward. I'd like him to be aware of this process and his office might afford us some privacy.'

Blacker rejoined them. He made no mention of the dancing man.

'I'm sure I wouldn't bother Sir Edward,' Blacker said. 'Until we have concrete results.'

'Nonsense. He's a thinking man. He'll appreciate this.'

'Then I will respectfully wait here,' Blacker said.

'Suit yourself. Day, are you with me?'

'I am.'

'Good man.'

'I'll look through these files and await your good news, then,' Blacker said.

Kingsley led the way across the room and knocked on Sir Edward's office door. After a moment, they heard the commissioner's voice.

'Come.'

Kingsley smiled and turned the knob and Day followed him into the office. He closed the door after them. Sir Edward stood and came around his desk. He held out his hand to Kingsley. His other sleeve was folded and pinned up at shoulder height and Day imagined Sir Edward's wife ironing that sleeve so that it would lay flat against his side.

'Doctor. It's good to see you again so soon.'

He turned and nodded at Day. 'Detective,' he said. 'Making progress?'

'Dr Kingsley has made an interesting discovery.'

'I'd like to show you something,' Kingsley said, 'which I think might make the process of criminal identification much easier in the future.'

'By all means.'

Sir Edward gestured towards his desk, which was far neater and more organized than Day's own. Kingsley set his bag on the desk and opened it. He laid the piece of foolscap in the centre of Sir Edward's blotter and held out his hand to Day, who handed over the razor. Kingsley set that down nearer to the three men than the paper and took the shears from Day as well. He picked up the ink bottle and handed it to Day.

'I believe that's yours. Thank you for the use of it. May I trouble you now for a pen?'

Sir Edward took a pen from his top desk drawer and handed it to Kingsley. Kingsley nodded at the ink bottle and Day opened it. Kingsley jabbed the pen into the ink and leaned over the desk.

'I should have labelled these immediately, but I believe I remember the order of them.'

He scratched a name under each of the four useful marks on the paper: Day, Blacker, Mayhew, and finally his own name.

'Who's Mayhew?' Day said.

'Isn't that the name of the unfortunate man from the store cupboard?'

'He said his name was Henry.'

'Yes, Henry Mayhew.'

'He never gave a family name, only Henry.'

'Well, for some reason, the name Mayhew sticks in my mind. Regardless of whether it's correct, we shall know that it stands here for that same man.'

Day nodded and indicated that Kingsley should continue.

'Now, Sir Edward,' Kingsley said. 'As I showed your detectives yesterday, each and every citizen has a pattern on the skin that is different from that of anyone else in the city.'

'Do you mean skin colouring? Brown and white and freckled, and so on?'

'No, sir, a pattern of ridges. Look carefully at your fingertips.'

Sir Edward held his hand up to the light and stared at his fingers.

'You mean the wrinkles here at the knuckle?'

'Even smaller. If you'll look at this piece of paper, you'll see that the application of ink brings the patterns out and records them for future comparison. Here we have fingerprints made by two of your detectives, a street person, and myself. None of them are exactly the same. There are minute differences in them all. And if you were to record this same sort of mark from the tip of the thumb or finger of everyone for miles around, none of them would match exactly.'

'That's impossible. A fingertip is too small. Eventually you would come across an exact likeness.'

'It would seem so, but I believe this is one of nature's many little miracles. Now, as fascinating as this is in theory, I'm about to put it into practice.'

He reached into his open bag and removed a brightly decorated tin that had once held snuff, but when Kingsley opened it Day could see a quantity of black powder inside.

'You've already shaved the charcoal,' Day said.

Kingsley smiled. 'By keeping a certain amount of charcoal dust prepared and ready, I believe I might save time in the future. Now let's see what evidence we can find on these two instruments of murder.'

He tapped a small amount of dust out on to his hand and blew it across the surface of the shears, then did the same with the straight razor. He picked them up, one at a time, and shook off the excess dust, then set them next to the paper and got his magnifying lens from the bag. He peered through it at the razor, moved over to the shears, back to the razor.

'Here,' he said. 'And here. You see?'

He turned around and pushed the lens into Day's hands. Day bent over the weapons and looked at the magnified marks. He played the lens over the paper and then back to the shears.

'Remarkable,' he said. 'Unless I'm mistaken, I see Mr Blacker's prints on these scissors. These, right here, may be yours. But there are more that don't match any on the paper.'

'Those are undoubtedly the marks of Inspector Little's killer,' Kingsley said.

'You don't say,' Sir Edward said. 'May I?'

Sir Edward bent over the items on his blotter and spent several minutes looking through the lens before straightening back up. He was frowning.

'I see it. I do see it. Mr Day, you've handled this razor, as has the good doctor and, it would seem, Mr Blacker. This other mark, this Mayhew fellow, his marks aren't visible on the razor. At least not to my eyes, but perhaps Dr Kingsley has a more well-trained ability of perception. These shears, on the other hand, have all four sets of markings, and at least three other patterns.'

'Yes,' Kingsley said. 'Very observant, sir. I'm going to assume that at least one of the sets of prints on the razor belongs to the victim, since we're going on the theory that his own razor was used to shave and kill him, but I won't know until I have a chance to retrieve fingerprints from the body in my laboratory and compare them.'

'Grizzly work, that.'

'Simply a part of the job, sir. A new part of the job. I believe I'll institute this step in all future examinations. It might even be possible to build some sort of repository of finger marks to compare against.'

'That sounds dreadfully tedious.'

'But if a suspect were to be winnowed out by other methods, then this sort of evidence might prove the clincher, mightn't it?' Day said.

'And I can imagine other uses for this,' Kingsley said.

'I've been considering it for quite a while now. Think of how useful it might be in helping to find missing persons. Or identifying bodies. You have no idea how many bodies come through my laboratory in a week that are not claimed, that end up being buried anonymously.'

'I understand how frustrating that must be,' Sir Edward said. 'I'm not entirely convinced, but there does seem to be enough merit here to explore this.'

'Thank you. Let me dust the opposite side as well, the side lying against the table now. There may be surprises awaiting us there. But at the moment, these finger marks do provide us with some clues.'

'Such as?'

'You already knew that Mayhew, the dancing man, has handled the shears. But he did not handle the razor. That points to his innocence in the murders committed by . . . what did Mr Blacker call it?'

'The Beard Killer.'

'Right. The Beard Killer is not your dancing man. At least, I don't believe he is. This doesn't excuse him from possible suspicion in Inspector Little's murder.'

'I have some trouble believing Mr Little would have been surprised and overpowered by the dancing man.'

'Nevertheless, it is at least a possibility. But the extraneous set of marks on the shears does not match any of the marks on the razor.'

'We already suspected that the Beard Killer and Little's killer were not the same man.'

'But this confirms it.'

'If we can somehow find more prints to compare with both weapons . . .'

'The trunk. I will dust the entire trunk and we may discover something helpful there.'

'Indeed.'

'I wish we'd known of this even yesterday,' Sir Edward said. 'I can see how it may be quite useful in the future. But for now, please continue along traditional lines of investigation and use this as a last resort until we know more. I would like to have some confirmation that these finger patterns are always different. I won't see a man convicted and imprisoned solely on the strength of his fingertip marks.'

'Of course, sir.'

'But by all means let's keep this in mind as a means of narrowing down the pool of suspects in a case.'

'Thank you, Sir Edward,' Kingsley said.

'Now . . .'

Kingsley and Day jumped at the sound of a knock at Sir Edward's door.

'Yes?' Sir Edward said.

'Sir, there's been a development,' Blacker said.

'Well, open the door and talk to me face to face, man.'

Blacker came in and bowed his head.

'Sorry, sir.'

'Like the Crystal Palace in here today, all this traffic in and out of my office. What is it, man?'

'There's been another murder.'

'There's always another murder.'

'Another body was found in a trunk, sir. I'm afraid it's another policeman.'

50

'His name's Sam Pizer,' Blackleg said.

Hammersmith was sitting with the criminal at a small round table in a pub five streets from the Shaw residence. He had been late arriving and Blackleg seemed impatient. Judging by the number of empty mugs on the table, Blackleg hadn't waited for Hammersmith before he began drinking.

'The chimneysweep, you mean?'

'Yeah. You been tippin' the bottle already, copper? Y'act like yer on the deck of a sinkin' ship. Yer weavin' about on yer chair.'

'I was poisoned earlier today.'

Blackleg sat up and leaned forward.

'What'd they use?'

'Benzene.'

'Aye, I've had it myself. You'll be shipshape by the day after tomorrow. Plenty a sleep, plenty a water. That'll do the trick fer ya.'

'I feared I might not wake up if I slept. I had a great deal of trouble the last time I awoke.'

'I never said it'd be fun to wake up. But unless you was already dead afore you come in here, you'll wake up again.'

Blackleg gestured to the serving girl to bring another mug. He shook his head at Hammersmith.

'You'll wanna be avoidin' the drink, though, or your head'll shoot clean off and to the moon.'

'Tea sounds lovely.'

'You'll drink water.'

When the girl brought Blackleg's ale, he asked her to bring his friend the biggest glass of water she could find. As he watched her go, Hammersmith noticed two whores at a table across the room. They seemed familiar to him and it appeared they'd been looking his way, but he couldn't be sure. He turned his attention back to his table-mate.

'You said you'd discovered the chimneysweep's name,' Hammersmith said.

'Right. Not easy to track down, neither.'

'Well, how did you do it?'

'You did the right thing, you did, settin' a gonoph to find a gonoph.'

'A gonoph?'

'Somebody don't mind gettin' a little dirty in the pursuit of coin, right?'

'Oh. Understood.'

'I asked around a bit, here and there, nothin' too indiscreet, you understand. Pressed a little of the coin you gave me into the right palms.'

Hammersmith winced. He'd given Blackleg half the grocery money for the month in order to help the criminal track the chimneysweep. He hoped Pringle would be able to come through with groceries for them both or Hammersmith would have to tighten his belt again.

'Anyway, I found him in a flash house down the road apiece. He's been talkin' up his business, askin' about for a kid might do as a climber. Seems he lost the climber he had.'

The girl interrupted them with Hammersmith's water. She plonked it down on the table, rattling Blackleg's empties, and turned on her heel before Hammersmith could thank her. Clearly, she wasn't impressed by men who drank water. Hammersmith saw the whores across the room looking at him again and finally recognized them as the same two from the previous evening. The tall one had a distinctive scar across her face. He was still certain they had set the younger woman to bait him. He was surprised because this pub seemed a good bit nicer than that other one had. He smiled at them and raised his glass. The two women abruptly stood and hurried down a hall at the back of the pub. They were quickly out of sight.

Hammersmith shrugged and took a drink. The water burned his throat going down and, still unable to breathe through his broken nose, he felt a sudden panicky sensation as if he were drowning. He set the glass down on the table and left it there.

'Where can I find him?' he said. 'The chimneysweep. Where is he?'

'You don't wanna go where he is, Mr Hammersmith.'

'I can handle myself.'

'Oh, no doubt of that. But you'd be outnumbered afore you got two words out and I don't like yer chances.'

'You go with me, then.'

He watched Blackleg size him up, taking in the ripped and soiled clothes, the broken nose, the eyes that wouldn't focus properly. At last, the criminal nodded.

'Yes, I guess I'd better go along, hadn't I? Come with me.'

51

'He knows.'

'He don't know.'

Liza and Esme were in the alley behind their favourite pub. It seemed to be deserted except for dozens of broken crates stacked against the wall behind them.

'But that's two times we seen him.'

'Did you hear his name?'

'I heard the other one call him it. I walked right by their table.'

'He's on the beat is all. Or havin' a drink afore he goes home.'

'He ain't drunk nothin', though,' Esme said. 'And Jonny's on the beat round here, not him.'

'Could be Jonny's ill.'

Esme gave Liza a look that said she wasn't going to argue about it any more.

'Fine, then,' Liza said, 'if he knows, he knows.'

Esme threw her hands in the air, clearly exasperated. She opened her mouth to speak.

'How much?'

Liza turned to see a man shambling out of the shadows behind the crates. He smelled like rye, and the four front teeth in his upper jaw were missing, leaving a gaping pink maw of need.

'I said how much,' the man said.

Esme's lip curled and she turned away, leaving Liza

to deal with the potential customer. The man didn't have a beard or moustache.

'We're done for the night,' Liza said.

'Can't be. It's early yet.'

'We're done when we says we is.'

'When I says you is, is when yer done.'

He reached out and Liza slapped his hands away.

'Hard to get, eh?' the man said.

But then he suddenly backed away from Liza, his hands up, and Liza turned to see Esme holding a pistol. The man tried to smile, his lips quivering, the black hole of his mouth twisted in a leer.

'No need for that, little lady. I was innerested in yer friend, anyhow. Don't go in for big scars like the one you got there, not that you ain't fetching. Let's all be friends.'

'I have enough friends,' Esme said.

She pulled the trigger.

The three of them stood for what seemed a lifetime, waiting for the echo of the gun's report to fade down the stone walls of the alley. When they could hear silence again, the man blinked at the two women and then collapsed, his knees buckling under him. He fell gradually, straight down and from the bottom up so that he appeared to be shrinking in on himself. When he had reached the ground, he finally slumped back and Liza could see the blood, flowing from his gut faster than his clothes could soak it up. The black fluid spread out, free of the flesh. The man sputtered once and did not move again or make another sound.

'You didn't have to shoot, Esme. He was harmless enough.'

'I didn't mean to.'

'Well, accidents happen. We'd best move on afore Jonny comes runnin'.'

Liza took the gun and shoved it to the bottom of her bag, then she grabbed Esme by the elbow and dragged her through the door back into the pub. The back passage was empty, nobody running to investigate the sound of a gunshot. Liza let go of Esme's arm and turned to face her.

'I really didn't mean to shoot him, Liza.'

'I know, love. It don't matter. Lord knows we done worse.'

'He didn't have no beard like the others. Like . . .'

Esme closed her mouth, bit off the next word. It didn't matter. Liza knew what she was going to say. *Like him.* Him. Saucy Jack, the great bearded beast of Whitechapel. He had left his mark on Esme's face and on her chest and she still waited for him to return and claim her.

'He was a man, wasn't he?'

'Yes. He was.'

'Then the beard don't matter, whether it's there or not.'

'The other ones, the ones we done up, they had the beard.'

Like him.

'The bluebottle don't have it neither.'

'Are we gonna do him up, too?'

'If we don't wanna get caught we will.'

'He might not know.'

'You're the one said he does.'

'That was afore I kilt that man back there. I don't wanna kill no more, Liza.'

'We started somethin'.'

'I think it's enough. None of 'em with beards was the one. And I don't feel so mad no more.'

'What if I still do?'

'Oh, Liza.'

Esme stepped in close and put her hand on the back of Liza's neck. She drew her in and Liza breathed the smell of her, sweat and smoke and mint, and Esme's mouth was on hers and her body pushed in close. Warmth radiated out from Liza's core. Her face flushed and she shut her eyes to contain it.

Esme broke the kiss and stepped away. Liza took a moment before opening her eyes. She smiled.

'All right, love,' she said. 'Unless someone else gets in our way, the bluebottle will be the last one.'

'Only 'cause he knows it was us done the others.'

'Only 'cause he knows.'

'Good. Liza?'

'Yes, love?'

'What's his name? The bluebottle, I mean. You said you heard the other one say his name.'

'Hammersmith. The other one called him Hammersmith.'

Esme nodded.

'Then he'll be the last one. We'll kill Mr Hammersmith and be done with it.'

She smoothed her dress and led the way back into the pub.

52

'We've come to see Inspector Little.'

Sergeant Kett looked up at the couple standing in the door of the back hall. The man had his hat in his hands and the woman had clearly put on her Sunday best to come round to The Yard on a Wednesday afternoon.

'Inspector Little's unavailable,' Kett said. 'What's this regarding?'

'Our son,' the man said. He stepped forward just a bit, half a step. 'Inspector Little was trying to find our missing son. We just wanted to know . . .'

The man broke off and smiled, but there was no warmth in it. That smile was the last vestige of hope on an otherwise thoroughly disappointed face.

'He's our only boy,' the woman said.

'We got three girls,' the man said. 'Only the one boy. We been waitin' to hear, like the detective said to, but we need some news, sir. It's got us torn up.'

'Inspector Little was moved to the Murder Squad not long ago,' Kett said. 'That might be why you never heard nothin'.'

With so many missing in London every year, there was virtually no chance their son would be found. They hadn't received news because the overworked detectives rarely had any news to report in cases like theirs.

'Murder Squad? Is our boy murdered?'

'Nothin' to do with yer boy.'

'Who do we talk to, then?' the woman said.

'I'll take you back there.'

Kett rose and came around the desk. He gestured for the couple to follow and led them down the short corridor. Off to his left, at the end of the hall, the Murder Squad room was mostly empty. Oliver Boring sat munching on a biscuit and reading a file, but the place was otherwise empty, everybody away looking for Little's killer. Kett pointed at the bustling hive of detectives in the bigger room to his right.

'You'll be wantin' one of them,' he said.

'But . . .' the man said, 'But who?'

Kett pursed his lips. He gestured for them to follow and led them to Inspector Gerard's desk. Gerard was one of the better detectives who hadn't been tapped for the Murder Squad. Kett made introductions all around.

'You'll need to ask Inspector Day for the file,' Kett said. 'He's got all of Mr Little's things.'

'Why's that?' the father of the missing boy said.

'We're reshuffling a bit,' Kett said.

If they hadn't read the papers and didn't know that Little was gone, Kett saw no reason to alarm them. Learning that the detective was dead might kill their spirits. And their spirits were all they had.

He left them with Gerard, who had taken a pen and was writing down information about their boy. The only word Kett heard was 'Fenn', but he didn't know if that was a name or a marsh where the boy had disappeared. He shook his head and returned to his desk just inside the door of The Yard.

53

'That's him there.'

The bartender pointed to a short man who was just now drawing one of two chairs up to a low table in the corner of the room near the fireplace. Hammersmith thanked the bartender and followed Blackleg to the man's table.

'You'd be Sam Pizer?' Blackleg said.

The man looked up and pursed his lips. He nodded slowly and drew a blunt, used cigar from his shirt pocket.

'And who'd you be, then?' he said.

'Never mind who we are.'

'Well, I can guess at your game. And that one's a bluebottle.' He pointed at Hammersmith. 'I've no business with either of you.'

'Could be we've got business with you.'

Blackleg pulled up the other chair for himself and left Hammersmith to find his own seat, which he did by dragging a stool over from a nearby table.

'What ya want, then?' Pizer said.

He chewed on the end of his stubby cigar.

'Where were you three days ago?' Hammersmith said.

'Who knows? Where were you?'

'I suggest you treat this seriously.'

'Why? You gonna arrest me? For what?'

'Where's your climber?'

'My what?'

'You know very well. The boy you employ to climb chimneys. Where is he?'

Pizer made a show of looking around the room.

'Don't look like he's out for a drink.'

He laughed and fished a small metal device from his pocket. It looked like a miniature pair of scissors. One end resembled a pair of tongs. There was a rivet in the centre. At the opposite end from the tongs were two crescent-moon-shaped cutters. Pizer snipped the end off the old cigar with the sharp end and turned the device around. He gripped the short cigar with the tong end and held it to his lips. Blackleg produced a match, struck it and held it to the end of the cigar. Pizer leaned forward and puffed until the cigar was lit. He leaned back.

'Thanks.'

Hammersmith pointed at the device.

'Had that long?'

'Got it off a sailor. Handy little cigar cutter, ain't it?'

Hammersmith jumped from his chair. His hand shot out like a snake and grabbed Pizer's arm. Pizer dropped the cigar and the cutter clattered on the table. Hammersmith snatched it up with his free hand.

'I've seen this shape.'

He held the crescent blades under Pizer's nose. The chimneysweep looked at him, his eyes wide, a crumb of tobacco stuck to his bottom lip.

'You branded that boy with these, didn't you? There was a scar on his arm this exact shape and size. You heated it up in the fire and you burned it into his skin.'

Pizer shook his head. He pulled away from Hammersmith and pushed his chair back. Standing, he was a full head shorter than Hammersmith.

'Don't know whatcher talkin' about, bluebottle.'

'You left that child to die in the chimney. You walked away and left him.'

'Did no such thing.' Pizer's eyes narrowed. 'And if I did, you got no proof of it. Nothin' you can do to me, bluebottle, so why don't you go aboutcher business.'

He straightened his shirt, pulling it back down over his ample belly.

'You're under arrest,' Hammersmith said.

He clasped Pizer's wrist. Blackleg cleared his throat and Hammersmith looked over at him. The older man shook his head.

'You can't,' he said.

'No, you can't,' Pizer said.

Hammersmith let go of Pizer's wrist and took a step back. The two criminals were right. They knew the law and they knew its limits. Pizer had done nothing illegal and nothing provable.

Pizer picked his cigar up off the table, brushed it off and stuck the wet end back in his mouth. He grabbed his cigar cutter and grinned.

'Tell ya what. You seemed to like this well enough. You have it. A gift from yer old friend, Sam. So you don't forget me.'

He took Hammersmith's hand, pressed the cutter into his palm and closed Hammersmith's fingers around it.

He winked and walked away. The door of the pub slammed shut behind him.

Hammersmith threw the cutter into the fireplace and turned on Blackleg.

'You didn't help.'

'What should I have done, bluebottle?'

'I don't know, but . . .'

'The law can't touch someone like that. He'll eventually end up dead, and it won't be pretty, but it won't be the law what does him in.'

Hammersmith pulled up Pizer's chair and sat down hard. The poison was still working on him, although it seemed to be slowly dissipating. He felt tired and frustrated and the adrenaline rush of anger was fading. He looked around at the other people in the pub – the bartender, the waitress and four other men deep in their drinks. Nobody was paying attention, nobody cared that the chimneysweep had escaped justice.

'He can't just walk away like this. There must be something someone can do.'

'Oh, there is,' Blackleg said. 'But you needed to see that he's outside yer reach, Mr Hammersmith.'

'What are you implying?'

'You can't do anything to him, but that don't mean he can't be touched, do it?'

'You mean you can do something, even if I can't?'

'I didn't say that, exactly.'

'What would you do?'

'I would do what needs doing.'

'I can't condone that.'

'Didn't say you needed to.'

'What if I stopped you?'

Blackleg chuckled.

'Shame you threw that cutter in the fire. It was a nice one. You coulda give it to me, you didn't want it fer yerself.'

'I want to be the one who brings him to justice, Blackleg.'

'You can't.'

'I know.'

'Best you can do is know it was done without knowin' how. Cause yer still the law and that scum ain't worth losin' yer job and yer freedom.'

'I want more than that.'

'Thought you might feel that way. Could be there's one way you can be a part of what needs to happen.'

'How?'

'Be a part, without bein' involved, I mean.'

'How?'

'Hire 'im. Give 'im a chimney to clean. I don't got a chimney, but you do.'

'How did you know that?'

Blackleg smiled, but didn't answer.

'My chimney's small,' Hammersmith said.

'Size don't matter. He won't get a chance to actually clean it.'

'But if he knows it's small to begin with, he'll press some other child into service to bring with him. We don't want that.'

'Well, we don't need to tell 'im it's small, do we?'

'And when he comes, we'll be on hand. I can have my flatmate there, too. He'll help.'

'What then? He'll laugh in yer face again. No, you don't need to be about and neither do any other bluebottles.'

They stared at each other for a long moment.

'Can you live with not knowin', but knowin' anyways, Mr Hammersmith?'

'I don't know.'

'I s'pose you'll find out soon enough.'

'Why?' Hammersmith said. 'Why do you care enough about the death of a child to involve yourself in this?'

'You said it yerself. It's the death of a child. Someone's gotta care. Hell, we should all care.'

'Use my flat.'

'I thought I would.'

'But how do I hire him? Put an advertisement in *The Times*?'

'I've already taken the liberty,' Blackleg said. 'The notice is runnin' in the morning's edition.'

54

When Hammersmith left the pub, he kept a hand on the outside wall and concentrated on putting one foot in front of the other. He walked carefully towards a cab rank and never looked behind him. If he had, he might have seen Charles Shaw leave his shadowy post beside the pub's front door.

Shaw trailed Hammersmith down the street and hovered near the stand until Hammersmith had boarded an omnibus. Hammersmith made his way to the back of the bus and Shaw jumped on, heading for the top deck, where he'd be able to see Hammersmith disembark.

Like Hammersmith, Shaw never looked behind him, and so he didn't see the two women who were already following Hammersmith at a discreet distance. Shaw was already climbing the ladder to the top of the bus when the prostitutes paid their ha'pennies and found seats near the front, behind the horses.

When everyone was safely aboard, the driver shook the reins and the bus rumbled off in the eventual direction of Hammersmith's flat.

55

She answered the door herself and so he assumed that she was the housekeeper. She was very young and very pretty, but she had a haggard air about her as if she had been worked to the bone by a harsh mistress.

'Is the lady of the house in?' he said.

'I am the lady of the house, sir.'

'Oh, my. I do apologize.'

'No need to apologize. The housekeeper has left for the day or your question would make perfect sense.'

'Were you the housekeeper I should worry about the state of your mistress's marriage. Her husband would no doubt be unable to take his eyes off you and she would discharge you within a fortnight.'

'How charming. Thank you, I think.'

'I apologize again. I've reached too far for a compliment and embarrassed you instead.'

Cinderhouse took her hand and kissed it.

'My name is Bentley,' he said. 'Inspector Richard Bentley. I'm an associate of your husband's. We work closely together at The Yard.'

Her eyes grew wider and her smile disappeared.

'Is Walter all right?'

'Oh, of course. Of course he is. I didn't mean to alarm you. I continue to start on the wrong foot here. May I come in?'

'Please do. I shouldn't leave you out on the doorstep. I'm so unused to receiving visitors, you see.'

She stood aside and allowed him into the house. It was small, but well appointed and tidy. He took off his hat and gloves and handed them to her, but kept his coat on.

'I won't be staying. I just had a question or two.'

'I'm afraid my husband isn't home.'

'That's just as well. It's you I want to talk to.'

They were interrupted by the sound of a whistling kettle.

'I was just preparing tea,' she said. 'Would you join me?'

'I'd be delighted, Mrs Day.'

'Please, call me Claire.'

She smiled and hurried away through a door on the other side of the room. He got a glimpse of a tidy kitchen before the door swung shut again, leaving him alone in the front room. The parlour was cosy: a faded Oriental rug over polished floorboards, bright florals on the walls, a fire in the hearth with a red-striped Renaissance revival chair pulled up in front of it. The lady's sewing basket was open beside it and a white shirt was draped over one arm of the chair. Claire Day was obviously mending her husband's shirt. From where he stood, Cinderhouse could already see problems with the repair job.

He edged closer and peered into the basket. A pair of red-handled shears sat atop a jumble of thread spools and a card of needles. A small jar of buttons had tipped over inside the basket, spilling its wood and ivory contents. He picked up the shears and hefted them.

They were good shears.

He realized that Claire had been silent for some time. He pushed through the kitchen door, still carrying the shears. She was across the small room, cutting bread into small triangles. Cinderhouse stepped silently up behind her. Finger sandwiches and pastries had been laid out on a silver tray, part of a matching tea service with a pot and two cups, tongs and a creamer.

Claire turned and nearly bumped into him.

'Oh!'

'I apologize,' he said. 'I didn't mean to startle you. I thought you might want some help.'

'Thank you. Would you mind carrying the tray?'

'Not at all.'

He put the shears down on the counter and picked up the tray, carried it out of the kitchen and set it on the small oak table in the corner of the parlour.

'You needn't have gone to any trouble for me, Mrs Day.'

'I asked you to call me Claire. And it's no trouble at all. I'm glad of the company.'

'Well then, I'm happy I stopped in.'

He pulled a chair out for her and she sat. He took the chair across from her and she poured for them both.

'Milk?'

'Lemon, please.'

He waited for her to take a sandwich and then he took one himself and bit into it. He controlled the impulse to spit it back out. He wondered how anyone could ruin a cucumber sandwich, but he smiled and swallowed and took another tiny bite of the tiny sandwich.

'Delicious,' he said.

'Thank you, but I think you're being kind. It's awful, isn't it?'

'Not at all.'

'You're a gentleman.'

She set down her sandwich and folded her hands in front of her on the table.

'Tell me,' she said, 'what did you want to ask?'

'Pardon me?'

'You said you had a question for me and I'm on tenterhooks to hear what it could possibly be.'

'Ah, that. Yes, well, your husband, Inspector Day, has been sent out suddenly on a new assignment and I'm to take over the case he was working. Only . . .'

'What is it?'

'I hate to speak ill of him in his own home, but his notes are a shambles. I have no idea where he's gone and I'm at my wits' end. I wondered if he might have told you anything about his investigation.'

'Oh, I doubt it very much. He rarely talks about his work.'

'This particular case is rather sensational. A detective was murdered and your husband is tracking the killer. I wonder if he mentioned any suspects to you? Anyone he might be focusing on?'

'A detective was killed?'

'You didn't know?'

'How concerned should I be about my husband, Mr Bentley? Is he in danger?'

'I'm not sure.'

'You mean there might be more murders?'

'It's a possibility. I'm being perfectly frank with you, Mrs Day. I'd hoped that you might shed some light on things for me. I have no idea which way to turn. I'm afraid more murders are a very real possibility.'

'Oh, I wish he had told me something. Now I shall go mad with worry until the killer is arrested.'

'I shouldn't have been so forthright with you. I apologize.'

'No, don't be sorry. I'm glad you told me. I do so hate being kept in the dark. I just wish there were something I could do to help.'

'Perhaps there is something.'

'Yes, anything.'

'If you could persuade your husband to abandon the case . . .'

'But I thought he was already working on another case.'

'He is. But that's only temporary. He'll be back on this one as soon as he's finished.'

'Unless you solve it, you mean.'

'Yes, but it seems hopeless. The thing is, I have every reason to believe that the murderer won't kill again if he's left alone.'

'How could you possibly know that?'

'Some of the clues he's left. I can't tell you anything exact, you understand. That's secret departmental business. But there are indications that the killing is done. But if your husband were to stir this beast up again . . . Well, I'm afraid that it might go poorly for our dear Inspector Day.'

Claire sat back and regarded Cinderhouse over the top of the tea set. Her eyes had narrowed. He couldn't see her hands. They were below the edge of the table. All he could see was the reflection of his own gleaming pink forehead, huge and distorted in the surface of the teapot.

'You seem to know a good deal about this killer, Mr Bentley.'

'Please, call me Inspector Bentley. I've worked quite hard for my title.'

'Very well. Inspector Bentley, how could you possibly know whether the killer will do it again? And why wouldn't you want him brought to justice?'

She was smarter than he'd assumed she would be and he had overplayed his hand. Women these days were overreaching themselves. He smiled, took a sip of tea. It tasted like brown water.

'You misunderstand, Claire. I do want him brought to justice, but I don't want Inspector Day to be the one to do it. He has much more

to lose than I do and might be harmed if he pursues the case. I, on the other hand, am unmarried. My family is long gone. It would be better if I were the one placed in danger, rather than him.' He set his cup down and spread his hands. 'I'm only trying to do some good here,' he said.

She leaned forward in her chair and pursed her lips. He saw the trace of a smile on her face.

'This is an important case, isn't it?' she said.

'I suppose it is. In fact, I believe it's the most important case The Yard has ever undertaken.'

'Surely not more important than the Jack the Ripper investigation.'

'Well, no, not more important than that. But important, nonetheless. And, I think, equally unsolvable.'

'And yet you want the glory of solving it yourself, don't you?'

'Beg pardon?'

'You want my husband to step out of the way so that you can solve this unsolvable case and win the admiration of your peers. Perhaps of all London? Paperboys shouting your name at every street corner? Is that it?'

Cinderhouse was startled into silence. He took another sip of tea and thought. He concluded that the lady herself had given him the best way out of the sticky situation he'd blundered into. He set the cup back down on the table and laughed.

'You've found me out, Claire. I'm afraid I am a self-aggrandizing heel. Yes, I very much want the respect of my peers. Like your husband, I'm new to The Yard. But he's caught on so quickly and is doing so well there. I feel I'm competing with him.'

He leaned forward and raised his eyebrows.

'Please forgive me? I thought this might take nothing away from

him and yet, perhaps, do me some good. I only want my son to be as proud of me as you are of your husband.'

'You said you had no family.'

'Did I? I'm sorry. My wife died so recently that I'm unsure of how to describe myself now. I have no wife, but my son . . . well, my son is my family, if you understand me.'

He saw her relax and his own smile became genuine.

'I do understand,' she said.

'Oh, thank goodness.'

'I'm sure you needn't have resorted to all this in order to gain respect. Hard work is its own reward, don't you think?'

'You're right, of course.'

He stood and adjusted his coat.

'Well, I've rather badly embarrassed myself. I should take my leave.'

'Please don't feel embarrassed. I'm sure you meant Walter no harm.'

'Still.'

'As you please. Let me fetch your hat.'

When she turned away, he noticed a monogrammed handkerchief on the floor, partially hidden under the edge of the chair. She must have dropped it from her lap when she stood to answer the door. She brought his hat and gloves and he feigned clumsiness, dropping his gloves on the floor near the handkerchief. When he picked them up, he grabbed the cloth, too, and quickly pocketed it.

He pointed at the arm of the chair.

'I couldn't help but notice that shirt.'

'Oh, I do wish you hadn't. It's become something of a puzzle for me. I can't get the buttonholes to line up.'

'How have you been marking them out?'

'Oh, I couldn't mark the shirt. I've been using my eye.'

'You mean you've been guessing at the measurement of the holes?'

'Well, yes.'

'Oh, dear me. What you need is a washable tailor's marker. I have several and would be happy to give you one.'

'You have several tailor's markers? Why would that be, Inspector?'

'Yes, well, you see we use them occasionally to mark bodies. Washable, remember? We wouldn't want to leave traces of our work for mourners to see.'

'How fascinating. I never would have guessed.'

'But the markers are readily available at any general store and would be quite useful to you.'

'Thank you for your kind advice. Perhaps the next time I visit my husband at work, you'll be gracious enough to lend me the use of one.'

He moved to the front door and opened it. He donned his hat and stepped out on to the doorstep, then turned back towards her.

'Please stop in at The Yard any time and I'll make you a gift of one. Only . . .'

'Yes?'

'I do wish you wouldn't mention today's visit to your husband. It might go hard on me at headquarters.'

Claire smiled and nodded.

'I don't see that there's any reason for me to bring it up.'

'Thank you so much.'

'No, thank you. You've livened my afternoon considerably.'

'Then my visit has not been a waste of time.'

He grinned at her, tipped his hat and walked down the steps to the street. His cab waited at the kerb and he stepped up into it. As the cab rolled away from the Day house, he took the handkerchief from his pocket. It was a lady's cloth with the initials 'CC' in one corner. Claire's maiden name must have begun with the letter 'C', and she hadn't yet ordered new handkerchiefs with the initials of her married name.

He touched it to his face. It smelled of apples and smoke.

His visit to the Day house had not gone as he'd hoped, but a new possibility presented itself. He folded the handkerchief neatly and put it in his pocket and settled back against the seat. The cab bounced over ruts in the road and jostled this way and that, but Cinderhouse didn't notice. He was deep in thought.

56

'Who is he?' Sir Edward asked.

'I don't know, sir,' Day said. 'But he looks familiar.'

'Then he's definitely one of ours?'

'I think so. When Sergeant Kett gets here he may be able to tell us.'

'Where is Kett?'

'Organizing the men, sir. We're doing a better job this time of keeping the onlookers out of the way so the doctor can do his work on the spot. The discovery of Mr Little's body yesterday caused a bit of a circus, but the park's been secured. Nobody here but police this time.'

Day and Sir Edward stood back and watched Dr Kingsley work. The trunk was concealed in a stand of lime trees on the outer edge of St James's Park. The scent of the limes partially hid the odours of the canal and the animals and the people. The body in the trunk had not yet begun to stink.

'This is quite recent,' Kingsley said. 'Not more than a few hours old, I'd say. Who found it?'

'A little girl who chased a duck into the trees.'

'She might have seen the murderer.'

'Agreed. Inspector Blacker is making enquiries now. He'll try to find the girl.'

'Why wasn't she detained and questioned?' Sir Edward asked.

'The man on the beat apparently felt she'd been sufficiently shocked by what she saw. He instructed her mother to take her home and put her to bed.'

'Understandable, but in future let's hold on to our witnesses until an inspector can talk to them. It's a waste of effort and time to have to track down the girl when we should be tracking the killer. That's already one less man we have for the hunt.'

'Yes, sir.'

'Doctor, do you –? Good Lord, man.'

Kingsley was unpacking the trunk. He lifted out a severed arm and set it in the grass. He reached back in and brought out another arm. He sat back on his haunches and stared in at the dead man's face for a long moment, then stood and carried the arm he was holding over to the detectives.

'Feel the severed end here,' Kingsley said.

Sir Edward said nothing but stared at Kingsley until the doctor looked away.

'Very well,' Kingsley said. 'But the blood's fresh. Tacky, but still wet. The killer's barely ahead of us.'

Day closed his eyes and nodded.

'Did you bring the shears, Mr Day?'

'I did.'

'Good. Give me a few minutes and we may learn something useful.'

Kingsley returned to the trunk and set the severed arm carefully back inside, closing the lid. He opened his black bag and took out the little pot of charcoal dust. He tapped a mound of it into his palm and blew it over the lid of the trunk. He repeated the process on the front and sides of the light brown box. The setting sun cast an orange glow on the trunk's hinges and seams.

'We're more fortunate here than we were with Inspector Little's trunk. It was impossible for me to make out any marks on the black surface of it.'

'Do you see anything on this one?'

'Yes, several good ones. Bring those shears over here, please. And a lantern.'

A constable approached and set his lantern on top of the trunk. Day averted his gaze and handed over the shears. Kingsley took them without looking and Day stepped back to stand with Sir Edward. Kingsley found a grease pencil in his bag and circled several spots on the trunk. He held the shears up next to each of these spots and examined first one, then another, with his magnifying lens. It took him several minutes and, as he was working his way around the back of the trunk, Sergeant Kett joined Day and Sir Edward under the trees. Sir Edward gestured for him to stay put. Kett nodded and stood silent.

'It's him, all right,' Kingsley said.

'Him who?'

'I don't know the name, but I know his mark now. The same man handled these shears and this trunk. His prints are all over the lid and on both sides. Aside from the victim, another man or woman, and what appears to be a small child, nobody else has touched this trunk.'

'A child?'

'Yes, I think so. Or possibly a dwarf. But that's not likely. I should think a dwarf would have been noticed here in the park.'

'Well, how do we know that one of them is the killer?'

'The child, or dwarf, left a single print. Here, you see? The unknown second man left marks on the lid and the handle, but only on one side of the trunk, which indicates to me that he probably helped to carry it. The overwhelming majority of prints are from the same person who held the shears both before and after the murder. Those prints are under and on top of the layers of blood on the weapon and some of his marks on the trunk display trace amounts of blood in them. This constable was put in the trunk and it was latched shut before the killer cleaned himself up.'

'Which of my boys was it?' Kett said.

'You may be able to put that matter to rest for us, Mr Kett.'

Kett nodded, took a deep breath and went to the trunk. He opened the lid and stood over it for a long time before coming back to the trees and lighting a pipe. Both Day and Sir Edward were silent. They waited for Kett to get the pipe lit and take a deep drag. Smoke curled from his mouth when he finally spoke.

'I was gonna yell at 'im when he shewed hisself today. I was mad as a wet hen 'cause he missed his shift and the whole of the time he was settin' here under the trees in little pieces.'

Day opened his mouth, but Sir Edward laid a hand on his arm to quiet him. He moved his head almost imperceptibly from side to side. *Let the sergeant talk.*

'He was always a bit of a dandy, he was. Always worryin' that his jacket din't fit right across the shoulders or the cuffs of his trousers was showin' wear. Used to drive me batty. But he did the work. I couldn't never fault him for that. He weren't in the league of his mate Hammersmith, but he were a fine young man, that one.'

Kett turned his back to the other men and stood smoking. Day noticed that Sir Edward looked away towards the canal while Kingsley busied himself with the trunk, doing things Day thought he'd already seen him do, circling the same spots again with the grease pencil. Finally, Kett wiped his eyes on his sleeve and turned back, but he kept his face down.

'Someone needs to find Hammersmith and tell him what's happened here. He'll wanna know Mr Pringle's gone and got hisself killed.'

57

Claire Day watched until 'Inspector Bentley' was in his cab and away before she put on her gloves and hat and left, locking the front door behind her. She hopped on to an omnibus three streets from the house and a kind gentleman yielded his seat to her.

Whoever the man was who had visited her, she was deeply suspicious of him. He had thought himself cunning, but his eyes were furtive and there was something in his bearing that suggested a weak man. He reminded her of that long-ago acquaintance Percy Erwood, who had received daily beatings from his father. Percy had told her in confidence, because he thought they were to be married, that he feared his father and secretly wished he could . . . well, what Percy said was between the two of them and she would never tell anyone, not even dear Walter.

It was clear that this 'Bentley' character had set himself against Walter. She had no intention of getting underfoot or embarrassing him, but her husband needed to be armed with all the information he could get if he was going to succeed at his new career.

She settled back on the bus, listened to the horses clop along the street, and did her best to ignore her rising gorge.

She would reach The Yard soon enough and, regardless of what happened after, it would at least be a relief to see her husband.

58

He sat back and looked at his handiwork. The note was poorly written, of course. He had carefully considered his misspellings to be sure they were still decipherable, but would lead the detectives to believe that the writer was illiterate. He chuckled at his last sentence '. . . the wurst will hapinn.' Ridiculous.

Still, the message was clear. If Day continued to investigate the murders, he would be endangering everything dear to him.

Cinderhouse leaned forward again and stopped with his pen poised above the paper. Should he sign the thing? Not with his real name, of course, but it vexed him to send it off without claiming any credit. It would be a simple matter to sign some pseudonym, something that would sail over the heads of the police, but would serve as a private amusement for the tailor. The Ripper had claimed credit for his deeds in just such a fashion and look how famous, and how feared, he had become.

Saucy Jack.

No. He set the pen aside and stood up. Cinderhouse wasn't after infamy. As nice as it would be to feel that glow of ownership for his clever plans, he really did want to be left alone. His cat-and-mouse game with Inspector Day was satisfying in its way, but there was a boy to be raised properly and a shop to look after. The tailor had his hands full. Drawing extra attention wasn't necessary.

He fetched the handkerchief he'd brought from Day's house and put it in an envelope along with the note. He took the entire package out to the waiting coachman to have it posted. Then he went to check on his son.

59

Hammersmith stepped off the omnibus and waited for the horses to huff past him before he crossed the road and leaned against the wall outside his flat. The sun was setting and the light had turned purple. He thought that he might vomit there in the street, but the feeling passed and he was able to pull himself upright again.

He gazed through the large picture window at cakes and chocolate truffles, caramel apples and fudge and dainty flowers made of sugar, all arrayed under a gas lamp on a tiered counter for passersby to see. He smiled to think that he smelled like chocolate and wondered why nobody before Fiona had pointed it out to him.

He found his key and entered through the unmarked green door next to the beckoning chocolates. Up the narrow staircase, past the landlady's flat and finally to his own front door. All was dark and still in the flat. Hammersmith lit a lamp by the door and went to the mantel. The tea box was nearly empty, which meant that Pringle had neglected to do the shopping. Hammersmith had no money for tea – he had given all the money he had on him to Blackleg – and anyway he didn't want to leave the flat again.

Pringle's bedroom door stood open. Hammersmith assumed that his friend was finishing his shift or entertaining a lady friend somewhere, but the flat felt hollow and it seemed to Hammersmith that his footsteps echoed louder than usual.

Hammersmith's own room was spartan. There was a narrow bed, a single straight-backed wooden chair and a nubbly round rug that had been there when he moved in. Nothing on the walls, two changes of uniform hanging in the closet alongside a single pair of civilian trousers and three white shirts. A lamp rested on the windowsill above the head of the bed, but Hammersmith didn't need it. He knew the room in the dark.

He kicked off his boots and stripped off Charles Shaw's white shirt, draped it over the back of the chair. He would find a way to return it tomorrow without revisiting the Shaws' home. He remembered that Penelope Shaw still had Dr Kingsley's shirt. He had no idea how to get that back from her, but he knew he'd need to find a way. He couldn't afford to buy the doctor a new shirt. At least not this month. He wasn't sure he'd even be able to eat for the rest of the month unless Pringle came through with groceries for them both.

Hammersmith wondered if he could live for a month on nothing but recycled copper-tasting tea.

He fell into bed without removing his trousers and followed the darkness down into sleep.

60

Charles Shaw waited until Hammersmith got off the bus and it started rolling again. When Hammersmith had crossed the road, Shaw hollered at the driver and hopped down before the horses had stopped moving. Hammersmith didn't turn around, but Shaw had to wait in the shadows of an awning while his quarry stared into a shop window across the street from him. He didn't know if Hammersmith could see him reflected in the glass, but he felt reasonably secure in the dying light of the day.

'Excuse me, sir.'

Shaw turned to see two women standing behind him. Their dresses were shabby and had been inexpertly dyed in bright Easter colours. Their faces were thickly painted and their hair hung in ropes from loose buns at the backs of their heads. The taller one had a scar across her face.

'Not interested,' he said. 'Get along now.'

'Weren't asking.'

'What is it, then? I'm very busy.'

'Well, obviously, sir. Any time we sees a man standing about on the street, we know right away there's big business afoot, right?'

'Ah, sarcasm,' Shaw said. 'The lowest form of humour unless you count limericks.'

'Well, I like a good limerick,' one of the ladies said.

'Of course you do.'

He turned back in time to see Hammersmith enter through a green door across the road.

'We was just wondering about that lovely beard you've got, sir.'

'My beard?'

'Yes, sir. It's impressive, is all we wanted to say.'

Shaw turned and smiled. He had Hammersmith cornered. There was time enough to be polite.

'It is impressive, isn't it?' he said.

'Oh, very. It must take you some time to get those beautiful curls just so.'

'Would you believe it takes me four hours. Four hours, twice a week.'

'Cor, I don't doubt it, but what an awful lot of time to spend,' the first lady said.

'Not that it ain't worth every minute,' said the other.

'Oh, of course, of course,' the first one said.

'Well, I'm glad you appreciate it.'

'You wouldn't let us touch it, would you?'

'I'm afraid not. I'm sure you understand.'

The second, friendlier, whore frowned and sighed. She reached out and touched his chest with her fingertips.

'Well of course we understand. Just disappointing, is all.'

'There's other things we might touch,' the first one said.

She winked at him.

'Wouldn't cost a thing for a man with a beard like that one neither, would it, Esme?'

The second one, whose name was apparently Esme, moved her hand down Shaw's chest and stomach.

'Not a thing,' she said. 'For either one of us. Or both at once, if the gentleman prefers.'

Shaw felt his face redden and he swallowed hard. He glanced once more at the green door across from him and then back at the ladies. They looked more attractive than he'd first thought and he wondered whether he'd misjudged them or if it was merely a trick of the shadows.

'Where do you live?' Esme said.

'I'm afraid I'm rather far from home at the moment.'

'Well, that's no problem for us. We know a place.'

'Unless he ain't interested.'

'Oh, no, I'm . . . I assure you I'm interested.'

'Of course you are, aren't you,' Esme said. 'I've got the evidence in my hand.'

She did. Shaw looked around, up and down the street, but few people were about and nobody was looking their way.

'Come with us,' Esme said.

Charles Shaw allowed himself to be led away.

61

'Hello, Sergeant,' Claire said.

It took a moment for Constable Jones to look up, but when he did he smiled at her and stood up from his seat behind the desk.

'Ma'am,' he said. 'Thank you, but Sergeant Kett's out tonight and I'm sittin' the desk for a bit. I'm Jones.'

'I'm sorry, Mr Jones, I should have realized. My husband's only just started on the Murder Squad and I haven't had a chance to meet everyone yet.'

'You'd be Mrs Day, then? If you're here to see yer mister, I'm afraid he's out and about, same as Sergeant Kett. It's been a bit of a day round here. But I'll tell him you stopped in.'

'Please do. But, if I may impose, I'd like to ask a question of you.'

'It's no imposition at all.'

'Is there, by chance, an Inspector Bentley working with my husband?'

Jones frowned. 'Bentley, did you say?'

'Yes, Inspector Richard Bentley.'

'No, ma'am, there's no Bentley here. Never since I been here.'

'I see.'

Claire felt the hairs at the back of her neck rise and pinpricks of sweat bead her upper lip. So the friendly bald man who had come to the house was not a detective at all. He'd been playacting. But why?

'There's a Benton, though,' Jones said, 'if that's who you mean.'

'Is he a part of the Murder Squad?'

'No, ma'am, he's helping keep the peace on the docks. Good fellow. I can see if he's in.'

'Oh, would you?'

Jones nodded and smiled and walked away down the short passageway behind him. He turned to his right and passed out of Claire's line of sight.

Perhaps, Claire thought, she'd been mistaken about his name. Perhaps he'd said 'Benton' and she'd heard 'Bentley' and all that time cooped up in the house with nothing to do and nobody to talk to had made her suspicious and fidgety. Now Constable Jones would tell Walter that she'd come visiting and he would worry about her.

She skirted the desk and hurried down the hall. She just needed a glimpse of Inspector Benton to be able to tell if he was the same man. If he was, then she would apologize and be on her way.

And if he wasn't? What then?

She saw Jones at the other side of a massive room, talking to an old man with a long, droopy handlebar moustache and a fringe of grey hair at the back of his head. Jones turned and came to her. 'That's him. You can go on over if you like.'

Claire shook her head. 'No, thank you. I've changed my mind.'

The old man was not her visitor. Claire's stomach turned over and her vision blurred. She stumbled against the rail behind her and, through a cloud of bright floating specks, she saw the young constable rush towards her.

'Ma'am? Mrs Day, are you all right?'

She waved him off. 'Of course, thank you. I'll be fine, Mr Jones. Just a momentary spell.'

'Constable!'

A tall man stood up from a desk behind Claire, in the area behind the railing where she knew Walter worked. The man was square-jawed, handsome in a vague way, with an impressive mane of dark hair.

'Constable Jones,' he said, 'can we please have some peace in here. We can't accomplish anything with the public coming through on these asinine tours and banging into the fixtures.'

'I beg your pardon,' Claire said. 'I can't have disturbed you as much as all that.'

'Inspector Tiffany, sir,' Jones said, 'may I introduce Inspector Day's lovely wife.'

Inspector Tiffany sniffed and smoothed his necktie. 'Ah,' he said. 'I hadn't realized. I'm a bit distracted with work, I suppose.'

'That's hardly an apology,' Claire said. 'You've been quite rude.'

Tiffany raised an eyebrow at her and almost smiled. 'Then I do apologize.'

'Apology accepted, Mr Tiffany. I'm sure I'm pleased to make your acquaintance.'

She held out her hand and he stepped to the rail and took it.

'And I yours,' he said. 'Please, call me James. But I'm

afraid if you're here to see your husband he's stepped out. It's just me and Boring here right now.'

He gestured to a fat detective, who raised a hand in greeting without turning around.

'Thank you. No, I came to report a suspicious man.'

'That'd be for one of the others to hear about,' Jones said. 'Inspector Tiffany and the other Murder Squad isn't to deal with nothin' but murders. Instructions from the commissioner hisself.'

'It's all right,' Tiffany said. 'I can hear the lady, Constable.'

'Sir Edward won't like it none.'

Tiffany smirked. 'I supposed he won't, will he?'

Jones shrugged. 'Then it's you who'll get an earful from 'im. I done my duty. Mrs Day, it's a pleasure to meet you.'

Jones hurried away in the direction of his temporary post in the back hall.

Tiffany gestured for Claire to follow him through the gate and into the squad room. He pulled a chair over from another desk for her to sit and took his own seat across from her.

'Have you a disagreement with Sir Edward?' Claire said.

'I preferred Commissioner Warren,' Tiffany said. 'He let us do our jobs and kept his nose out of it.'

'I see.'

'But that's hardly your concern, is it, Mrs Day? Let's hear about your suspicious character.'

He picked up a pen from his desk and toyed with it, as if prepared to write down what she said, but he leaned back in his chair, away from his desk. She could see that, despite his pretence, he had no intention of writing anything down or pursuing anything she might have to say to him. She was nothing but a diversion for him.

Still, she needed to tell someone.

'I had a man come round the house earlier today,' she said. 'He presented himself as a detective and told me that he worked closely with Walter. But Constable Jones has just confirmed for me that there is no such person here at The Yard. I'm worried that Walter may be in some danger from this man.'

'It sounds to me as if you're the one in danger.'

'He didn't threaten me or make any move towards me at all. In fact, he acted the perfect gentleman.'

Tiffany sat back in his chair and tossed the pen on his desk.

'Then you've nothing to worry about, have you? I suspect you've just let nerves get to you. Happens to women all the time. Go home, have a rest, and you'll be right again in no time.'

'But what could his purpose have been? He seemed to want information from me regarding one of Walter's cases.'

'And did you give him information?'

'Well, no, of course not. I don't even know about Walter's cases.'

'Good. This sort of work isn't anything a woman need trouble herself with. Your husband's done the right thing by keeping you well out of his business.'

Claire wasn't sure she wanted Inspector Tiffany to

approve of her husband. Walter and Tiffany were different men entirely and Claire was glad of it.

'Are you married, Mr Tiffany?'

'I hardly see how . . .'

'I didn't think so.'

'Thank you, Mrs Day. I believe we're done here.'

'One more thing, please. That pen you're using is one of Walter's, isn't it?'

'Why, yes, I think it is.'

'I know because I gave it to him. I suppose he shared it with you?'

'Mine wasn't working.'

'That's right. Thank you, Mr Tiffany. I'll show myself out.'

She stood and left by the back hall, stopping just long enough to thank the kind constable for his time and trouble. Claire resolved to tell Walter about her strange visitor as soon as she saw him. He would listen to her.

He had always listened to her.

The world was full of men like James Tiffany. There was only one Walter Day.

62

Somewhere in the dark house, Saucy Jack called out to him.

'I won't hurt you,' the Ripper said. 'Come out and watch me play.'

Hammersmith remained quiet. He was in a drawing room with no lamps, but he could see dust motes floating through the air around him, backlit by the blue light of a picture window. The furniture was covered with white sheets, but the sheets were stained, brown and red, spattered with the blood of Jack's victims, who lounged about, blocking Hammersmith's exit.

There was Annie Chapman, sitting on a Prince of Wales chair, her uterus in her lap. She smiled at Hammersmith. Elizabeth Stride and Catherine Eddowes were together, leaning against the empty fireplace, talking in hushed tones. Stride raised a hand in greeting and her throat opened with the effort, fresh blood pouring out and over the front of her party dress. Mary Kelly relaxed on the day bed. Her heart beat slowly next to her. Mary Ann Nichols stood at the window and Hammersmith noticed for the first time that it was snowing outside the room. Mary held a finger to her lips, hushing him, and Hammersmith realized the snowflakes were grey ash, drifting past the window.

The Ripper had been busy, Saucy Jack had not stopped with those five women. Or started with them. Jack was London itself and London had always been a killer.

Eight-year-old Johnny Gill played with a tin train set beside the divan. He grinned at Hammersmith and a thin smear of blood slid across his teeth. The train continued around its track and Johnny's attention returned to it. Elizabeth Jackson sat by Johnny, brushing her hair, one hundred strokes before bed every night. She turned her decapitated head this way and that in her lap, blindly moving the brush, her shy face tucked away in the crook of an elbow.

The drawing-room door was closed and the key was in the lock. Hammersmith could see it from where he stood. The key moved as someone worked the handle. Then a great fist struck the door and Jack's voice echoed through the hall outside.

'You're too small, Nevil,' Jack said. 'I'm everywhere and I always find my little boys and girls. You can't hide from me.'

Hammersmith looked down at his body and saw that he was a child again.

He was almost five, and he was still smaller than the other four-year-olds.

Elizabeth Jackson picked up her head and stood. Her face peered out from under her arm and a single eye focused on Nevil. It winked.

Nevil grabbed the white sheet from the divan and threw it over his head. Under the sheet, the air was thick and the darkness was complete and Nevil felt safe. If the door broke down and the Ripper came in, he would tramp right past the sheet-clad boy and he would never ever find him. Jack would only see another ghost.

He was blind, but he could still hear as, across the room, the key fell out of the lock and clattered to the floor. Hinges creaked as the door opened and deliberate footsteps thumped across the floorboards and over the rug and stopped in front of the policeboy under the cloth.

Jack's lips pressed against the other side of the sheet and Nevil felt the Ripper's breath, hot and moist, against his cheek. A kiss.

'Thank you, Nevil,' Jack said. 'I couldn't do any of it without you.'

The lips drew away and Nevil heard the Ripper's footsteps retreat, and the room must have grown because the footsteps went on and on.

Nevil closed his eyes – there was no change in the quality of darkness – and he wished that the footsteps would stop, that Jack would reach the door and leave, but the sound of the killer continued, pounding against the floor, pounding.

He awoke in a sweat, his bedsheet tangled about his throat. His room was nearly as dark as the dream had been. He could still hear the distant pounding.

'Hammersmith,' someone said.

The voice was faint, coming through the hall door. Someone was out there knocking.

'Are you in there? Answer the door, man, or I'll break it down.'

Hammersmith sat up and stumbled out of his bedroom to the front door. He threw the latch and opened the door and Sergeant Kett blinked at him, his arm raised to knock again. Hammersmith's landlady, Mrs Flanders, was behind the sergeant. Beside her, Inspectors Day and Blacker stood with their hats in their hands.

'I couldn't find the key, Mr Hammersmith,' Mrs Flanders said. 'I've told you not to lock the door.'

Hammersmith said nothing. He stared at the old lady and the three policemen, and he tried to remember why he had felt so safe with a sheet over his head.

'I'm sorry, lad,' Kett said. 'We was worried perhaps you'd been done in, too.'

Hammersmith shook his head. He didn't step back from the door, didn't make way for anyone to enter the flat. Day and Blacker appeared uncomfortable and Kett was red in the cheeks.

'He's dead, lad. Little's killer done him.'

Hammersmith found his voice.

'What time is it?'

'It's not late,' Blacker said. 'Did we wake you?'

'No,' Hammersmith said. 'Of course not. Who's died?'

But somehow he already knew.

DAY THREE

63

Forty-one hours since the discovery of Mr Little

The sun was beginning to rise, but its rays had not yet reached the alley where Sam Pizer waited. He mashed the lit end of his cigar between his thumb and forefinger and put it in his pocket to enjoy again later. The rattle of wheels on stone grew louder, echoing up and down the alley, then slowed and stopped.

Pizer leaned against the alley wall and waited. After a long moment a voice came from atop the hansom cab.

'You the sweep?'

Pizer spat on the stones and nodded, realized the coachman couldn't see him in the pre-dawn gloom and cleared his throat.

'Aye, I does chimneys.'

'Heard you was in the market for a climber.'

'Where'd you hear it?'

'Round and about.'

'Maybe I is and maybe I ain't.'

'Well, make up your mind about it.'

'I'll think on it while you climb down here so's I can see you ain't got a pistol aimed at me bean.'

The coachman grunted.

'I ain't got a pistol on you.'

'How do I know it?'

'I'm tellin' you.'

'Your word, eh?'

'Aye, my word.'

'Don't mean squat if I don't know your name, even.'

Another grunt and then, after an extended silence, Pizer heard the other man shift his weight. The coachman's cloak rustled as he swung out on to the side of the cab and hopped down with a clatter of boot heels to the alley floor. He stepped forward, his hands held out to show they were empty. The coachman's face was hidden in the murk.

'Have a cigarette?' Pizer said.

The coachman hesitated and reached into the cloak, pulled a dull silver case from the blackness and opened it. Pizer took a cigarette and waited for a light, the stub of his old cigar heavy in his breast pocket. In the flare of the match, he caught sight of a prominent nose, ungroomed muttonchops and a high hat before the orange flame sputtered and the two men were once again swallowed in shadow.

'Thanks,' Pizer said.

'So, is you?'

'What, in the market for help? Might be.'

'What're you payin'?'

'Tell me . . . you know a fella name of Blackleg?'

'Blackleg? Ain't heard of him.'

'You sure?'

'Sure I'm sure. Who's he to you?'

'Just heard he's been nosin' round about me.'

'That might be why you're such a hard man to find.'

'You found me.'

'Took some work, though, I'll tell ya.'

'Yeah, well, I don't wanna be found by this fella Black-leg. And neither do you. I heard stories.'

'Why's he want you?'

'Got no notion and don't wanna find out.'

The coachman said nothing. Pizer took a drag of the cigarette. He blew the smoke up and watched it shimmer away.

'So you got a climber for me, then?' he said.

'Might have.'

'You the child's parent?'

'No. I work for a gentleman who done recently acquired a boy what ain't his.'

'Ah, and he's ready to dispose of the kid, that it?'

'Wrong again. He'll keep this one for a good while, I'm guessin'.'

'Then what?'

'I get paid to procure them poor wee children for the gentleman.'

'So you sell the boy to me for my climber and then you get another payday when you replaces 'im.'

'Could be.'

Pizer nodded, even though he knew the other man couldn't see him. At least this made sense. He understood the coachman's motives here, which made him trustworthy as far as this particular arrangement went. The coachman was entirely motivated by profit. He made money by locating and helping to procure a child for his employer. Eventually, the coachman would make sure the child disappeared. His employer would pay him to help look for the child. And then he would pay him again to help find a new child. And the cycle would repeat.

Whatever money he could chisel from Pizer in the process was nothing but gravy and that gave Pizer the upper hand in this negotiation.

'How big is he? The kid?'

'Smallish, I'd say. Maybe half the size of a man and big around as my leg. Skinny thing, he is.'

'Hmm. What'ya want for him, then?'

'Ten quid'll do it.'

Pizer snorted.

'Ain't worth ten. I'll find me own climber.'

'You will, eh? You'll do that while you're hidin' from this Blackleg fellow? You'll rummage about the neighbourhood for a child to snatch? Take a young person from the bosom of his family and none the wiser?'

'I get around all right.'

'Good night, then.'

Pizer heard the coachman's cloak rustling again as he turned away.

'Wait. I gives ya two pounds eleven.'

'You'll give me five.'

'I'll gives ya two an' eleven.'

'You need this boy or you don't work.'

'But you need to get loose of the boy more'n I need 'im.'

'An' how's that?'

'You got another kid lined up already, don't ya? Don't bother to say no. You got another kid, but ya can't put the finger on 'im 'til you lose the one you already got.

You could kill the kid you got already, but that might cause you some problems. You need a patsy and that's where I comes in.'

'You're not a . . .'

'No, you don't got to pretend anythin' ain't what it is. I got no problem bein' the patsy in this here case, long as you don't bring the law round.'

'I wouldn't.'

'Course you wouldn't. Too much to answer fer yerself.'

'Four pounds.'

'To do you a favour? Yer already makin' a bundle, I'm guessin', offa findin' yer master a new boy to do . . . well, to do whatever he does to them boys you grab.'

'He is a perfect gentleman.'

'Course he is. Listen, sir, once you and me finishes up this fascinatin' conversation, I can toddle on down to any embankment in this here city, sidle up under a bridge and find me at least a half a dozen starvin' urchins be only too happy to go wiv me fer the price of a hot meal or a biscuit even.'

'Might also find this fella you're worried about, this Blackleg fella, under there.'

'Aye an' I might at that. But ol' Blackleg can't be everywhere, can he?'

'Three pounds, then.'

'Tell ya what, two pounds eleven an' I'll take the next boy offa you too, when the time comes.'

'You think you'll have need of another climber?'

'Risky business climbin' up the flue. Bound to get stuck, sooner or later. 'Specially if you take it upon yerself to keep growin' alla time.'

'That's . . .'

''Tis what it is. An' yer in no position to go castin' stones.'

The coachman was silent, but Pizer knew he had him. He really had no other choice.

'Done,' the coachman said.

'Good. Bring 'im round here tomorrow night, this time.'

Without another word, the coachman sprang to the top of his hansom cab and flicked the reins. The cab lurched forward and rolled down the alley, turned left at the mouth and was gone. Pizer fished the remains of the old cigar from his pocket and lit it from the dying embers of his cigarette. He took a drag of the stale cigar and leaned back against the alley wall.

Two pounds eleven was still a lot to pay for a new climber, but the coachman had been right. Sam couldn't do his own scouting when there was Blackleg to think about. All things considered, he was getting off lucky. No question about it, things were looking up for Sam Pizer.

The bald man, Cinderhouse, hadn't stayed to watch his work being discovered this time. He wasn't stupid and he didn't want to be caught. He had derived some satisfaction from watching the detectives find Little's body, but if he had been noticed then and was noticed again when Pringle's body was discovered, there would be suspicion. He would have liked to experience that final step in the process, but it wasn't essential. He could guess what was happening tonight as the Metropolitan Police Service was mobilized. As the panicky prey huddled together, knowing that the hunter was out there somewhere in the night beyond the fire.

He knew now that he would kill again. It was only a matter of time. He'd had no idea how right it would feel to strike back at the universe, at the city, at the police, for everything they'd taken from him. He'd played the good citizen for most of his adult life and it hadn't worked out for him. That was all, it just hadn't worked out and it was time to move on. The city had taken his family and the police had done nothing to find them and now the scales would be balanced.

For all Cinderhouse knew, his family was still alive somewhere. They had left the house one day and they had not come back. No bodies had been found. So perhaps they were in a different city, with new names. Perhaps they thought of him sometimes and wondered how he was doing. The idea was disturbing, but sometimes it comforted him to imagine his wife and son living a separate life far away.

That fantasy never lasted long. He knew they must be dead. The city swallowed nearly ten thousand people every year. Ten thousand people simply disappeared, Cinderhouse's family among them. There was nothing the police could do. He'd gone to them and they had listened to him and taken notes and done nothing.

But here he was, finally taking matters into his own hands. Killing the police wouldn't bring his family back, he knew that, but it quietened the angry voices in his head. It wasn't quite justice, but it felt good, just the same. Maybe he would kill Sir Edward Bradford, the commissioner of police himself, the very embodiment of the useless Metropolitan Police Service.

But one thing at a time. Cinderhouse was letting himself grow angry again and it would be all too easy to take that anger out on the wrong person. He needed to be calm. He had family matters to deal with.

He made his way across the back lawn in the dark. The old

carriage house loomed up, blocking the moonlight, and he found the latch on the side door. He hadn't been back here in months, but he still knew the place. He stepped inside and smelled the damp and the rot and the musky animal scent that tickled the back of his throat. He tried not to think about the cause of that odour. Three empty horse stalls were directly ahead of him and he felt along the wall until he came to a set of brackets hung at eye level. Something small scurried across his foot and he kicked at it. His hand closed on the thing in the brackets and he pulled it up and away. He felt along the length of it and held it to his nose. The leather hadn't rotted away and the animals had left it intact.

He cracked it against his leg and felt the familiar sting, the tingle that travelled down to his toes and back up to his loins. He cracked it again and groaned. His breath quickened and the old memories of discipline returned at once.

He exited the way he had come and relatched the side door. Back across the lawn and into the house. He set the riding crop on the butcher block while he fetched an extra lantern from a cupboard in the kitchen and lit it. With the crop in his right hand and the lantern in his left, he moved through the back hall to the storage cupboards near the pantry.

The boy had stopped banging on the walls and kicking at the door of his cupboard. Cinderhouse hoped that Fenn had managed to get some rest. He still had a long day ahead of him.

A boy must be taught to respect his father.

Philippa Dick hated Claire Day.

She hated her so much that she had taught her the wrong way to sew buttons on a blouse, the wrong way to clean an oven, the wrong way to boil a sheep's head . . .

She had done everything she could to foul Mrs Day's marriage.

Her tactics had not, of course, made even the slightest dent in the Days' marriage.

The husband, Mr Day, was an uncommonly handsome man, Mrs Dick thought. His broad shoulders, dark eyes and kindly manner never failed to quicken Mrs Dick's heart. Her own husband had been a small, ratty tortoise vendor who had spent most of his life walking up and down Oxford Street calling after passing housewives to come and take a look at the best tortoises in London. Upon selling one of the slow-moving beasts, Mr Dick had hied himself to the nearest pub for the remainder of each day, until money was once more tight. He had spent the entirety of their married life shuttling back and forth, from street to pub, leaving his wife to keep a roof above their heads with the meagre profits she earned by cleaning houses.

She had never, strictly speaking, been a full-time servant, which would have required her to keep a room in her employer's house, but instead had returned to her own home every evening after tea. Upon her husband's death Mrs Dick had received fifty pounds from his life insurance policy and had paid off the mortgage on her house. She had the relative luxury now of working only a few hours a day for food money.

Perhaps surprisingly, her opinion of other women's husbands had not been curdled by personal experience. Mr Dick could not have fallen further in her esteem, but other husbands were judged on their own merits and Mr Day was considered too good for the pampered likes of Claire Day.

Claire spent the majority of her time that was not taken up with household responsibilities curled by the hearth reading novels. And not just novels, but mystery novels replete with scandal and murder and intrigue – all subjects a good wife ought to avoid at any cost. She never dressed for company until her husband was expected to arrive home and she was clearly unable to budget the weekly stipend her husband set aside for the household.

She was fortunate that Mrs Dick had so much experience with parsimonious budgeting. Philippa Dick still bought soap by the pound, soft and gritty and sliced from the end of a long bar by the grocer. It was more fashionable these days to buy individual paper-wrapped soaps, but Mrs Dick's old ways saved the Day family two pennies a week. There were countless other ways that Mrs Dick scrimped and saved, and the total savings to her employers amounted to nearly a crown a month, but Claire Day seldom spared Mrs Dick a kind word. The younger woman avoided contact with her housekeeper unless there was some special skill she wished to learn so as to impress the master of the house.

Still, Mrs Day did not dog her servant's heels the way that some employers did. She allowed Mrs Dick to carry out her duties without watching over her shoulder and Mrs Dick was grateful enough for that.

The routine of the household had been unusual of late, with Mr Day working all hours, sometimes missing tea and supper, sometimes arriving home at dawn only to change his shirt and leave again. To Philippa Dick this could only mean that the man was keeping another woman somewhere, but she had limited experience with hard-working men and, anyway, she considered it to be none of her business. She had been given a key to the back door of the Day home and she let herself in every morning before dawn. If Mr Day had left his boots by the kitchen door, she scooped them up on her way in and cleaned them as the fire drew up. She put on the kettle and, while she waited for it to boil, she gathered the previous day's damp tea leaves, carrying them to the parlour where they were strewn over the rugs to help collect the dust there.

She opened the curtains in all the rooms at the front of the house and started a fire in the parlour, then swept up the scattered tea leaves and returned to the kitchen to prepare breakfast.

She changed into a clean uniform and put the breakfast things on a tray which she carried up the stairs and set on a low table outside Claire Day's bedroom. She rapped twice on the closed door and continued down the hall to Mr Day's bedroom. The bed was untouched, which might mean that Mr Day was visiting his wife in her own room this morning, but Mrs Dick presumed that he had not yet returned home.

Nevertheless, she stripped the bed and hung the bedding to air. The Days had an indoor toilet and there were no chamber pots to empty, but Mrs Dick was of the old school and kept up the old ways of airing sheets and blankets to ensure that there was no build-up of unsavoury emanations in them.

She swept and dusted the room, cast an experienced eye over the floor and decided it would not need to be scrubbed yet. She returned to her mistress's room and was surprised to discover that the breakfast tray was still on the hall table and had not been touched. It was true that Mrs Day's appetite had not been strong lately, but the water had gone cold in the pot and the tea leaves were dry.

Philippa Dick rapped on the door again and waited. Finally, she turned the knob and cracked the door open.

'Forgive me, missus. I beg yer pardon, but is there somethin' else you'll be wantin' to eat this mornin'?'

There was no response. The room was dim, the curtains still drawn over the windows. Mrs Dick swung the door open and entered.

The stench rocked her on her heels. She pulled the end of her apron over her nose and tiptoed to the window on the other side of the room. She pulled the curtains back and in the dim light saw Mrs Day on the floor next to her bed. The younger woman was lying on her stomach with her nightshirt hiked up so that a sliver of lace panties was visible. Ordinarily, Mrs Dick would have been scandalized, but this was clearly not the time for shock or judgement. She bent over the body and turned her mistress face-up. A long tendril of spit and vomit snaked down Claire's cheek. Her skin was grey and cold, but she was breathing. Mrs Dick put her ear to Claire's chest and listened for a beating heart. When she was sure that Claire was alive she made her as comfortable as possible, bringing pillows from the bed to put under her head. She covered her with a thick quilt, taking care to keep the edge of it out of the puddle of sick.

The carpet would have to be thrown out.

Mrs Dick hurried downstairs and threw open the front door. It was early yet and there was little traffic, but a young boy was walking a bicycle over the kerb and Mrs Dick called him over.

'Go fetch a doctor. Do it quick and there's a ha'penny in it for you.'

The boy studied her face and set his jaw.

'Looks like you need 'im round here pretty bad, lady.'

'Just do as I tell you, boy.'

'Aye, I will. But not for less than a penny.'

'Why, you little demon.'

'Suitcherself.'

He began to turn away but Mrs Dick grabbed him by the shoulder.

'Very well, then, you'll get your penny, but if the doctor's not here within the hour I'll not be givin' you a thing, you hear?'

'You bet, ma'am. I'll get 'im round here right away, you wait and see.'

He hopped on his bicycle and rode off, pedalling furiously. Philippa Dick watched until he was out of sight and then turned back inside, shut the door and waited.

64

St James's Park was quiet and cool. The gas lamps along the footpath pulled their yellow light in close, jealous of the rising sun, ignoring the police who tramped through the grass with their lanterns held low. Day stood next to Hammersmith in the darkness under the lime trees. He couldn't look at the constable. Instead, he watched the bobbing lanterns as every available policeman in the city searched the park for evidence, going over the same ground that a hundred other men had already scoured.

'Here?' Hammersmith said.

'Yes,' Day said. 'Another trunk, same as with Little.'

'We should have caught him already. We should have caught him after Little.'

Day nodded. There was nothing to say. It had been only two days since Little's body was found, but Hammersmith was right.

'What about his face?'

'Sewn shut, same as before.'

'Colin would've hated that.'

'I doubt he felt it. He was probably already gone by the time the sewing started.'

Hammersmith was silent so long that Day finally looked over at him. Hammersmith was gazing at the rectangle of flattened grass.

'Where's the body now?' he said. 'Where's the trunk?'

'Kingsley's got him at the laboratory.'

'When he's done, Colin will want a new uniform. He wouldn't want to be in something wasn't clean and fresh.'

'I'm sure that will be arranged.'

'Do you have a lead?'

'There was a little girl playing by the water who said her friend's father deposited the trunk here.'

'Her friend's father.'

'I know. It's a slim clue, but there were no other witnesses.'

'So there's nothing else?'

'We're working on it. Kingsley thinks his finger patterns will narrow the suspects down for us.'

'You said it happened yesterday.'

'I think so.'

'He was awfully tired yesterday. Colin was. Up all night on a case.'

'None of us have slept much these last few days.'

'No. But if I hadn't pushed him so hard . . . And on a thing that, on a case that nobody wanted me working on anyway. He did it, though, he came along and he helped and he was tired and probably distracted.'

'You didn't kill him.'

'But I didn't help him. I wasn't there when he finally needed me. He was always there when . . .'

Hammersmith's voice broke and Day looked away into the trees and pretended not to notice the constable's grief. There was no sense in embarrassing the man.

They stood like that for a long time and then Hammersmith took a deep, rattling breath. When he spoke his voice was soft and low. There was something deadly behind his words.

'We'll get him.'

'We will,' Day said.

'Do you think Kingsley's still up and about?'

'I imagine he's worked through the night on this. One murdered policeman is a disaster, two policemen is a war.'

'Then let's get to his laboratory. If there's news, if he finds something, I want to know about it immediately.'

'You should get some rest, so as to be ready when there *is* news.'

'I've had some rest.'

'Then we'll go.'

The two of them headed up the footpath to where a fleet of wagons waited at the street. Behind them, the lanterns of the police bobbed like fireflies over the park's tainted meadow.

65

Kingsley slid the jacket sleeve down Pringle's left arm and dropped it in a bin. He did the same with the left shirt sleeve. He set the bare arm on the table next to the constable's body and used a long, metal skewer to pin it in place against the left shoulder. He dipped a rag into a basin of cold water and washed Pringle's torso, dipping the rag in the basin again and again. The water in the basin turned pink, then red, then black, and Kingsley dumped it out, refilled it. Bits of blue and white thread from his uniform had been embedded in the constable's skin by the force of the murder weapon. Kingsley bent over the body with tweezers and pulled out each thread.

He stepped back and bent his head first to one side then the other until his neck popped, then went back to work separating the man from his uniform.

'Father?'

Kingsley turned and blocked his daughter's view.

'I don't need you for this yet,' he said.

'You don't need to hide it from me. I'm sure I've seen worse.'

'I'm sure you've seen similar horrors, but you needn't see everything that comes through here.'

'Is it another policeman?'

'Why would you guess that?'

Fiona pointed to the shredded jacket on a nearby table and Kingsley nodded.

'Yes, it's another policeman.'

Fiona's hair was unbrushed and her nightshirt was too short. Her ankles showed beneath the hem. *She's still growing*, Kingsley thought, *still a little girl*.

'Let me get my sketchpad,' she said.

'I'll sketch this one.'

'You can't draw, Father.'

'True, you're much more skilled than I am with the charcoal, but I can still mark out the positions of these injuries.'

'Not as well as I can.'

'Have I done the wrong thing, Fiona?'

'What do you mean?'

'All the horror you've seen, all the death and murder and evil. I recently met a man named Henry who was driven mad by it all and I'm . . .'

He couldn't think how to phrase the doubts he had. The same doubts that had been with him since he'd first decided to include his daughter in his work.

'Death is there, whether I see it or not, isn't it?' she said.

'Of course.'

'Then I'd rather see it and know it. I'd rather not be ignorant of it.'

'But I think you're supposed to be ignorant of it. I think your mother would have kept it from you.'

Fiona nodded.

'I could have sent you to school with your sister,' Kingsley said.

'I didn't want to go.'

'I know.'

She stood there in the doorway until he relented.

'Get your sketchpad,' he said. 'I'm a tired old man and this city seems to get worse every day.'

'I like this city, Father. And you shouldn't worry so. For all the bad we see, you've shown me how to look for the good.'

There was the faint sound of a bell and Kingsley snapped to attention. They had early visitors.

'Thank you,' he said. 'Now go put on a proper dress. That will be the police, come to see their friend.'

66

'I've brought tarts,' Blacker said.

He came through the railing and into the murder room, holding a brown paper parcel done up with string. Day looked up from his report. Blacker set the parcel on Day's desk and unwrapped it. A dozen tarts lay on the grease-soaked paper.

'I missed breakfast and thought the same might be true of you,' Blacker said.

Day smiled his thanks and went back to the report he was writing. Hammersmith didn't look up from his own paperwork or acknowledge Blacker in any way. Blacker shrugged and bit into a tart. Inspector Oliver Boring wandered over from his own desk. He was a large man and moved like a horse with an overburdened cart.

'Are those for all of us or just for you and Day?' he said.

'Anyone, I suppose.'

'Fantastic. Many thanks, Blacker.'

'Don't mention it. These two haven't.'

Boring took a tart and returned to his desk, passing Sergeant Kett along the way. Kett stopped at Day's desk and folded his hands in front of him.

'Don't mean to interrupt, Inspector,' he said. 'It's nothing important.'

Day looked up again and set his pen down.

'What's that?'

'All the excitement, I forgot to mention you had visitors yesterday. While you were out, I mean. Your wife was one.'

'I never had a chance to speak with her last night. She was asleep by the time I got home. And I was hardly there long enough to change clothes. I'll have to look in on her today.'

'And the tailor dropped by. The supplier we use for uniforms and the like. Seems to want to help with your investigation.'

'Good of him. Perhaps we'll drop by and get his opinion then. Is he reliable?'

'Odd bloke, but friendly enough.'

'This the strange bald fellow we're talking about?' Blacker said.

'He's the one,' Kett said.

'Rubs me the wrong way.'

'Still, good of him to offer his assistance,' Day said. 'We meant to talk with him yesterday, but it slipped my mind in the excitement. Thank you, Sergeant.'

Kett nodded and left by the gate. His shoulders were slumped and the life appeared to have gone out of him.

'Poor Kett,' Day said. 'I think he feels like a father to some of them here. Pringle's death has hit him hard.'

'Any word from Kingsley's laboratory about that?' Blacker said.

'We've only just come from there. We were with him all morning. There's very little to report, but we do have a few promising leads. There's the witness, of course, the little girl in the park. We've determined her identity, but we don't expect much from her.'

'Is that all we've got?'

'No. Kingsley found a multitude of clues on the body. There's the thread used to sew poor Pringle's mouth and eyes shut. It matches exactly the thread used on Little. So we're dealing with someone who has a fair supply of thread at hand.'

'I suppose that narrows things down a bit. But not much.'

'It's something. Particularly since we're assuming a man did this. We're not going to be looking for a seamstress or a housewife here. It also appears, from the force and depth of the blows, that the killer worked in a sort of frenzy. It's likely he took Pringle by surprise the same way he did Little. Both policemen probably knew their murderer well enough to trust him.'

'Well, we have Hammersmith here to help us narrow down that list.'

Hammersmith finally looked up at Blacker.

'That's what I'm doing now, sir. Writing up my impression of Constable Pringle's daily routine and acquaintances.'

'There's also the matter of the finger marks,' Day said.

'Finger marks,' Blacker said. He rolled his eyes.

'I know your feeling on that matter,' Day said. 'Nevertheless, the doctor feels they may be helpful and Sir Edward himself concurs.'

'He doesn't.'

'But he does.'

'I'm astonished. He's such a reasonable sort.'

'Kingsley kept the trunk from Little's murder and is comparing the two. He's been keeping a shed full of evidence from previous cases that he thinks might be revisited one day. He suggested that we do the same here.'

'Why would we keep old evidence?'

'I think it's a good idea. In a case like this, evidence from one murder may reflect on a later case.'

'It would accumulate until it toppled and crushed us.'

'It would require a lot of space.'

'Not to digress but, speaking of valuable space and the scarcity of it, we need to take up the matter of your dancing gentleman. He's spent the night in our cell and we're going to have to decide soon what to do with him.'

'I know it.'

'Fair enough. He'll keep for the moment. So, then, Pringle's murder . . .'

'Right. Finger marks on Little's trunk, and on Pringle's trunk, and on the shears found by the dancing man, all the same. There's another, unidentified set of markings that belong to someone else. Those are on both of the trunks and may be those of an accomplice. Someone probably helped carry the trunks, which would have been too heavy for one man. Marks matching those of the possible accomplice weren't found on the shears. So the markings found only on the shears have to be those of the killer.'

'I'll begin rounding up every person in the city so we can match those markings against everyone's fingertips.'

'You're sarcastic, but I really think we'll be able to match them up if we find someone we suspect of these murders.'

'Won't ever hold up in front of a judge.'

'No, but it may help to focus us on the right suspect.'

'Perhaps. I'm willing to budge on that a bit, but I'm still not completely convinced.'

Day shrugged.

'Well, at any rate, it seems Kingsley did a fine job for us,' Blacker said.

'There was one more thing. He found something else when he brushed Pringle's trousers.'

'He brushed the man's trousers?'

'He did. And he found long, white hairs. A good many of them.'

'We're looking for an old man?'

'Animal hairs, not human. He thinks a cat.'

'Did Pringle own a cat?'

'No,' Hammersmith said. 'He disliked cats.'

'That seems like a far more promising clue than your finger marks.'

'Oh, for pity's sake,' Oliver Boring said.

His voice carried throughout the murder room. He was standing by the railing, talking over the top of it with a group of constables who seemed quite animated about something. Day looked over at the fat detective and back at Blacker. Whatever Boring was up to, it was none of their business.

'What?' Blacker said. 'Oh, I see. So if Pringle disliked cats, then the hairs didn't come from his own home and it's unlikely he stopped to pet a stray.'

'Right.'

'So the cat might have been at the scene of the offence and might have brushed against him after he died.'

'It's a possibility.'

'Then we're looking for an acquaintance of both Little and Pringle, someone who owned a white cat. Were cat hairs found on Little's clothing?'

'The doctor allows for that possibility, but he says Little's hygiene was such that he might not have noticed animal hair.'

'Well, we can't rule it out, then. This feels good, doesn't it? It's not a sure bet, but it feels right, like we've got a chance at catching this blighter.'

'I think there's reason to hope,' Day said.

'Oh, we will catch him,' Hammersmith said. He was staring across the room at the jackets hanging on the far wall. Day couldn't see his face. 'This one won't go unsolved,' he said.

'Of course it won't, old man. Of course.'

Oliver Boring ambled over from the railing and stood in front of the tarts on the desk.

'Have another tart,' Blacker said.

'Thank you,' Boring said. 'These men being offed in their water closets. That's already on one of you lot, ain't it?'

'The Beard killer,' Blacker said. 'You're talking about the bloody Beard killer. That's my case.'

'You're welcome to it. I don't want it, no how.'

'Well, what about it?'

''Nother one of 'em found. Some doctor from up the East End's been shaved and left for dead in an empty flat. Thing of it is, they didn't quite finish the job on him.'

'Where is he?'

'In hospital now. Can't talk. Throat's slit wide open and they're stitching it up. But it seems he can still write if you want to drop round and see for yourself. Name's Charles Shaw.'

67

Cinderhouse sat at the edge of the bed and watched the boy sleep. The sun shone through the freshly mortared bars in the window and cast a long, grey grid across the bed and up the opposite wall. Finally, the boy tried to stir. He opened his eyes when he found he couldn't move.

Cinderhouse smiled at him.

'You're a deep sleeper,' he said. 'I carried you from the cupboard without waking you.'

Fenn said nothing. He stared at the shadowy bars on his wall.

'I'm afraid I've had to tie you down. When the mortar in the window dries, I might consider letting you sleep without the ropes again, but you'll have to convince me that I can trust you.'

Fenn closed his eyes, but Cinderhouse could tell the boy wasn't sleeping.

'I'm sure what happened yesterday was difficult for you to witness. I wish you hadn't made me do that. You realize you're the one who killed that policeman, don't you?'

A tear appeared at the corner of Fenn's eye and rolled down his cheek.

'He would still be alive if you hadn't involved him in our family affairs, you know? Won't you answer me? I need to know that you understand the consequences of your actions.'

The boy nodded. His head barely moved, but Cinderhouse saw it.

'If you promise it won't ever happen again,' he said, 'that you'll

always listen to your loving papa, then you'll be forgiven. And God will forgive you, too. You know His most important rule, don't you? "Honour thy father." Can you promise me that you'll listen and obey me from now on? Can you promise God that you'll honour His commandment?'

The boy nodded again. More tears made their way down his face and through his hair, pooling in his ears. The tailor smiled. It was good that Fenn was taking this so seriously. Perhaps he really had learned a lesson. Cinderhouse felt his chest swell with love for the boy and he thought he might start crying too.

They sat like that for a long time. Finally, the boy opened his eyes.

'What's that?' he said.

Cinderhouse raised the crop from his lap. He had forgotten he was holding it.

'This? Haven't you seen a riding crop before?'

'It's for horses.'

'Yes, it is. And it's also for naughty boys. My own papa used this very crop on me whenever I was bad. This exact one.'

Fenn began to cry again, and this time a choking sound from deep in his chest accompanied the tears. Cinderhouse barely noticed. He was wrapped in memories thick as a blanket.

'The old man next door had trees, then, when I was a boy. There's nothing there now. The trees didn't survive. I've outlived them by years and years. But back then there were still trees, and a great many of them. Plum trees. Damsons, I think. And one morning, very early, I got myself over the wall between our houses and I stole three ripe plums from that old man's trees.'

The tailor smiled at the memory, the smooth feel of the plums, the rubbery flesh between his teeth, the purple juice spilling from his lips.

'We didn't have money for fruit then. My papa did his best, but plums were dear and I had never tasted one. He beat me, of course. Beat me with this crop. Took me to the carriage house and made me fetch it to him, which in a way was worse than the beating. Because of the fear, you understand? The fear grew and grew until I couldn't stand it and the beating came as a release from that band of terror that had tightened around me.'

He looked over at Fenn, sharing the experience of being a boy with him. Fenn had quietened, but tears still spilled on to the pillow under his head.

'He beat me, my papa did, until I couldn't lie down to sleep. And then that old man came round with the police. They took me off to the boys' detention house and they put me in a hole that was so dark I couldn't see my hand when it was this close to my face.'

He held his hand an inch from Fenn's nose, but the boy flinched and wouldn't open his eyes to see. That was all right, the tailor thought – that was the darkness he meant to convey.

'I was there for a month. At first, I couldn't sit or lie down on the rocks and dirt in that cell because the scabs on my back would break and bleed. But after a week or more, I lay down and I slept. I slept for days and days, and when I finally woke I felt stronger and I knew that I had learned the lesson that my father had set out to teach me and that I would be a good father myself when I grew up.

'And I was a good father. My son, my boy, he was a good boy. He was a good boy. I didn't get to be his papa for very long. He was taken away from me because I must have done something wrong. I must not have been a good papa to him because God took him away and I don't know where he is.'

Cinderhouse swallowed hard. He felt his own tears gathering behind his eyes. He cleared his throat and stared at the bars over Fenn's window.

'But that came much later. I remember, when I was still a boy myself and I left that cell after a month, the light stung my eyes and the air burned my skin, but I grew used to it. It was easier then. Children can grow accustomed to anything over time.'

He nodded at the boy, hoping he understood. A boy will adapt and forget what came before. Children were made to do that.

'I never stole again. And I obeyed my father. I learned his trade from him and I became a tailor and took over his business and made it so much more successful than he ever did. And when he was dying, dying at my feet, he reached out to me and he told me that I was a good boy. He knew that a boy takes his father's place. He knew that what I had to do to him was the right thing.'

Cinderhouse thought that perhaps he ought not to have told the boy this last part of his story. Perhaps this wasn't a lesson he wanted the boy to learn yet.

'I'm going to untie you so you can eat. If I do that, will you try to run again?'

Fenn shook his head.

'Say it,' Cinderhouse said.

'No, sir. I won't run.'

'Good. Good lad. We can't have you starving to death. And we can afford fruit. I have fruit downstairs for you. No plums, but a fresh, ripe apple for you. Things are different now.'

The tailor realized he had muddled his own childhood with that of the boy in the bed. Fenn hadn't stolen the plums. He frowned and reached out to ruffle the boy's damp hair.

'Anyhow, you'll need to eat.'

'Please don't hit me.'

'What, you mean this?'

Cinderhouse chuckled and lifted the crop from his lap. He sat back and regarded his son.

'I was only telling you a story about this. I wouldn't hit you. I'm not like my father. I'm completely unlike him.'

He leaned forward again so that his son would see the intent in his eyes and understand that the time for play had passed.

'But if you run from me again, I will use this and the skin will fall from your back in sheets and you will stand until your feet swell and throb with pain and you will try to sit and there will be nothing to lean against without your back feeling as if it's aflame and you will try to lie down and scream in agony and leap to your feet again and the torture will be unbearable.'

Fenn's eyes were huge with fear.

'Do you understand me, son?'

The boy nodded.

'We'll have no more of this foolishness, then, will we?'

Fenn shook his head.

'We'll have no more running away from your dear papa, will we?'

Fenn shook his head again and swallowed hard.

'No,' he said.

'No, what?'

'No, papa.'

'That's good. That's a good boy.'

Cinderhouse felt his chest ache with sudden pride and love for this boy who had come back to live with him again.

'I forgive you, son,' he said.

And he began to untie the ropes so that he could embrace the boy at last.

–

68

University College Hospital squatted at the corner of Gower Street, Bloomsbury. It was an unexceptional brick and stone building, surrounded by an iron fence. The hospital had been built in 1834 and had expanded twice since then, but it was still too cramped to accommodate the hundreds of patients passing through its doors every day.

Inside, it was a madhouse, with great open wards, each holding the maximum number of beds possible in long, starched rows along each wall. Nurses, doctors and white-clad assistants glided from bed to bed over the blanched and bloodstained floor.

Penelope Shaw was stationed at the open door to one of the wards when Blacker, Day and Hammersmith arrived. She had clearly been crying, her eyes and mouth blotched and puffy, but her hair was up in a perfect swirl, her posture straight and elegant in a bright red dress. A rose standing tall among thistledown.

'Oh, Mr Hammersmith. Thank God you came. I was hoping it would be you.'

'Mrs Shaw,' Hammersmith said.

Blacker gave Hammersmith a suspicious glare, but Day grabbed Blacker by the elbow and steered him past Penelope Shaw before he could speak. Hammersmith held up a finger, asking Day for one moment alone with the victim's wife. Day nodded and disappeared into the chaos of the ward with Blacker in tow.

'It wasn't my choice,' Penelope said. 'I mean, what I did to you. He made me do it. You do believe me, don't you?'

'It hardly matters now, does it?'

'Will you arrest him?'

'From what I've heard, I doubt he's healthy enough for me to bother.'

'What about me? Will you arrest me?'

'I haven't made up my mind. I have more important things to worry about.'

'I'll understand if you have to arrest me.'

'What is it that you want, Mrs Shaw?'

'I want . . .'

'Go on.'

'I want to be free of him.'

'Did you do this? Is he here because of something you did to him?'

Her eyes widened and she put a hand to her mouth.

'Oh, no. No. How could you even ask me that? You haven't seen him, haven't seen what was done to him. I could never. Not even to him.'

'You have reason to want him injured or dead. You've just told me as much.'

'Not like that. I only hoped . . . I hoped that you might act against him.'

'You've made a mess of things, Mrs Shaw. I've only met your husband once. Almost everything I know about him has come from you. Right now, I have more reason to act against you than against him.'

'I know. And I don't blame you for feeling that way. But he's . . . he was following you. He meant to do you harm.'

'What kind of harm?'

'I don't know. He wanted to be able to stop you. You wouldn't go away, even after he visited your commissioner.'

She looked down at her hands. Hammersmith took a step back from her and watched the nurses bustling to and fro at the end of the hall.

'I still don't understand why he didn't simply report the dead child. I wouldn't even know who he was if he'd done the right thing in the first place.'

'He didn't want it to reflect upon his reputation. Why is that so hard to understand? You threatened to cause a scandal that would have ruined his practice.'

'I never cared about him. It's the chimneysweep I want. He's the one who left the boy's body there. I want to see justice done. I don't care about scandals and reputations and all this ridiculous social claptrap.'

'Do you care about me?'

Hammersmith took a step back. He looked away at the open door of the critical ward.

'I . . . I need to see your husband now,' he said. 'Wait here.'

He started to pass her, then stopped and spoke without turning around, without looking at her.

'Maybe you'll get lucky and he'll die.'

69

Dr Charles Shaw lay on his back with pillows under his shoulders and neck. Between this arrangement of pillows there was a plank that held a shallow metal tray, there to catch the blood and pus that drained from his throat. Heavy black stitches spiderwebbed across his neck, but fluid seeped through and ran down both sides under his ears, dripping into the pan. A copper tube snaked out through a small gap in the stitches and Day could hear air being drawn through it as Shaw's chest rose and fell.

As Day and Blacker approached Shaw's bed, a nurse quickly slid the full tray of gore from under his head and replaced it with a fresh tray. The movement jostled the pillows. Shaw made no sound, but his hands clawed at the sheets, and Day knew that no matter how efficiently the nurse acted, the procedure must be painful for Shaw.

The two detectives stood side by side at the edge of the bed and looked down at the doctor's swollen purple face. The elaborate curly beard was gone. Shaw's naked chin was weak and pale. The wound across his throat nearly separated his head from the body below and Day wondered that Shaw was still alive.

'Can you hear us, Dr Shaw?'

Shaw's eyelids rolled up and his bloodshot eyes worked to focus on Day.

'Can you say who did this to you?'

'He can't talk,' the nurse said. 'His voice box is just, well, it's just gone.'

'We'll need to ask him some questions. Will he improve?'

She shook her head. The pan under Shaw's head was already filling up again with brown and yellow waste.

'He needs to rest,' she said. 'There's nothing anyone can do now but let him rest.'

Day sighed and began to turn away, but Shaw reached out and grabbed his wrist. Shaw's grip was so weak that Day almost didn't notice. He looked down at the doctor's wide and pleading eyes.

'Get me paper,' Day said. 'Any kind. Something to write with.'

The nurse glared at him.

'Sir, I shouldn't say this in front of the patient.'

'Say what?'

'I shouldn't say.'

Day took her elbow and moved her away from Shaw. They stood at the end of another bed, where a man with no arms was crying for a drink of water. Day tried not to look at the man.

'What don't you want to say?'

'He won't live through today.'

'Then you must allow us to talk to him.'

Hammersmith entered the ward and saw Day. Day nodded to him across the room and Hammersmith joined them. The nurse glared at Hammersmith, too, clearly resenting police intrusion on her premises. Day decided that she was the kind of petty bureaucrat who revelled in whatever small amount of power they had, and she clearly ruled the critical care ward. Her attitude towards the police had no doubt been coloured by the Ripper murders. So many people who might once have been glad to see the police were now immediately scornful.

'You should leave now,' the nurse said. 'Any exertion at all will speed the process of that man's death.'

'Please forgive how plain this must sound,' Day said, 'but what does it matter if he'll die today anyway? Let us talk to him now. We'll be easy on him, but he may be able to lead us to a murderer, someone who has killed before and who we believe will kill again. Don't you think he'd want to help us with that? To help us find the man who murdered him?'

'Every moment of life is sacred. Let him spend his last moments in peace.'

'Every moment of life should be spent accomplishing something,' Hammersmith said. 'Could someone get this poor man some water?'

He pointed to the man in the bed who was still screaming for a drink.

'He's just had a drink of water. He wants attention, that's all.'

'Then perhaps someone should pay attention to him.'

Hammersmith fetched a pitcher from a nearby cart and poured a small amount of it into a shallow bowl. He stepped around Day and lifted the crying patient's head, holding the bowl to his lips. The man grew quiet and sipped at the bowl of water.

The nurse stomped away and Day saw her talking to a doctor at the far end of the room, pointing back at them.

The doctor broke free of her and waved his hand at the nurse to stay where she was. He had dark pouches under his eyes and his tie was askew. This wasn't a man who was accustomed to sleeping well. When he approached them, Hammersmith handed him the empty water bowl. The doctor took it and nodded.

'There's too many of them,' he said. 'We do what we can for them, but the men in this ward are just waiting to die. We're not cruel, but we haven't the time.'

'I'm not asking for your time, sir,' Day said. 'I apologize if we've distressed anyone. I am a friend of Dr Bernard Kingsley, who works here in the hospital if you'd like to enquire about my discretion and habits.'

'I know Dr Kingsley. I'm sure it won't be necessary to trouble him. What is it we can do for you?'

'You have a patient. Also a surgeon. Dr Charles Shaw.'

'I don't recognize the name. Does he work here?'

'I don't know, sir. But he's lying in that bed, with a wounded throat.'

'Oh, my. Yes. I wasn't aware he was a doctor. I've done what I can for him, but I'm afraid there's no hope. All we can do at this point is pray.'

'We've no use for idle praying,' Hammersmith said. 'We need information from this man.'

'I'm afraid he can't talk to you. By that I mean he's incapable of any speech at all.'

'Then could we have a small notebook and a pencil?' Day said. 'He may be able to write something down that could help us.'

'I don't see any harm in that, if he's awake. But he won't be able to sit up.'

The doctor snapped his fingers to get the nurse's attention and made a scribbling gesture in the air. She nodded and hurried from the room. The doctor shook their hands, made sure they were satisfied and returned to his futile rounds. The nurse came back a moment later with a small, brown, cardboard-covered notebook and a wooden pencil, sharpened at both ends. Day took them and thanked her. She nodded curtly, spun on her heels and retreated to the far side of the room.

'I don't believe we're making friends here, Constable,' Day said.

'Were we here to make friends?'

Day raised his eyebrows.

'No. But I've found that the more friends I have, the easier my life seems to be.'

Hammersmith nodded, but didn't speak.

'I don't know about you, but I became a policeman because I care about people. We're under a lot of pressure and you've suffered a horrible loss,' Day said. 'But you can't let it change you or you'll be no better than that hard-hearted nurse over there.'

'I'll keep that in mind, sir.'

Day turned away. He wasn't accustomed to being called 'sir' and had no idea how to respond. He didn't like it much and realized he had now created a certain formal distance between himself and the constable. He resolved to bridge that gap later. For now, he led the way to Dr Shaw's bed, where Blacker had kept vigil. Blacker shook his head at them as they approached. Shaw was asleep. The sound of his breath as it echoed up through the copper tube was irregular and wet.

'He's been in and out of sleep,' Blacker said. 'I don't think he has long.'

'We heard that from the doctor, as well,' Day said. 'Perhaps one of us should stay here and monitor him. When he wakes, he may be able to write something for us.'

'*If* he wakes,' Blacker said.

Hammersmith reached out and jabbed Shaw in the side. Day and Blacker looked at him, their eyes wide, but Shaw started awake and a deep, rasping sound vibrated the copper tube. Day leaned over the dying man and held out the notebook.

'Can you hear me, sir?'

Shaw blinked twice at the three policemen.

'We're sorry to intrude upon you, but we'd like to find the man who did this. Do you have the strength to write?'

Shaw tried to shake his head from side to side, but the effort appeared to cause him pain and they stood for a long moment, letting him recover. Finally, he took the paper and pencil from Day's hands. He laid the pad flat on his stomach. Even moving his hand was clearly an effort and Shaw didn't lift the tip of the pencil from the paper as he wrote. Day watched him scrawl curlicues across the paper. Since Shaw couldn't see what he was writing, the strokes didn't link up properly and the continuous line made unintended connections between letters. When Shaw finished, Day took the paper from him and held it out so that Blacker and Hammersmith could help decipher what was written.

'No,' Blacker said. 'This first word is "no".'

'What's this next bit, then?'

'Turtles? I think it says turtles.'

Day sneaked a glance at Shaw. He seemed frustrated, but it was hard to read an expression on his blood-caked face. The tray under his neck was brimming with fluid.

'No, it's two words,' Hammersmith said.

'Yes, I think you're right,' Blacker said. 'And the first word is "two", isn't it?'

'Does it actually say "two words"?

'No, that second word has an "h" in it.'

'Whores.'

Hammersmith said this last word too loudly and the nurse at the end of the row of beds looked up and glared at them.

'Two whores? Is that what you mean to say?'

Shaw blinked rapidly and Day put the paper and pencil back in his hands. He wrote again.

Yes.

'So, it wasn't a man who did this to you? It was two women?'

Yes, again.

'But how were you overpowered by women? Even two of them?'

This time Shaw didn't write on the pad. Day saw Blacker and Hammersmith look away from the bed. They seemed uncomfortable.

'Did they first render you unconscious?' Day said.

After a moment of hesitation, Shaw wrote again. *Yes.*

'I see.'

'Why did they accost you, sir, do you know?'

No.

Another furious bout of writing and Shaw handed the

paper to Day. Shaw's hand fell back against the bed and he seemed to collapse in on himself, exhausted. His eyes closed and he was instantly asleep again.

'What does it say?'

'I can't . . . This first word may be "flow".'

'Let me see,' Blacker said.

He took the pad from Day.

'I think it says "ploughing tool". But that makes no sense.'

'Let's wake him and ask,' Hammersmith said.

He reached out to poke Shaw again, but Day grabbed his hand.

'Show some mercy. He's done in. I don't think there's anything else he can tell us this way.'

Hammersmith stared down at Shaw.

'Maybe Kingsley will be able to tell us more once he gets hold of this.'

Day understood what Hammersmith meant. When Shaw died, his body would be transported to the basement of the hospital and Kingsley would take him apart. If there were physical clues to be found, they would only come to light upon Shaw's death.

'You act as if you hate this man,' Blacker said.

'I don't hate anyone,' Hammersmith said. 'But this creature isn't among my favourites.'

'What did he ever do to you?'

'Yesterday he nearly had me killed.'

'You jest.'

'He had me poisoned. And he used a good woman whose only mistake was in marrying him.'

'Why didn't you tell me?'

'It had no bearing on your case.'

'I think I'd better be the one to determine that.'

'Yes, sir.'

'Clearly,' Day said, 'there are a great many things going on at once and it might be a good idea for the three of us to talk.'

'Agreed,' Blacker said.

They stood at Shaw's bedside until he drew a last rattling breath and passed away. None of them made any move to try to resuscitate him, and when they left they did not inform the nurse that she had one less patient to care for.

70

'I hardly know what to say.'

Colonel Sir Edward Bradford stared at Patrick Gilchrist's empty desk as if it were a coffin. He didn't look up at the assembled Murder Squad, but kept his eyes on the stark desk top. His voice, when he spoke again, was soft and low and thoughtful.

'You all know by now that we have lost another fine officer,' he said. 'Many of you knew and worked with Constable Pringle. I did not get a chance to know him well. I regret that.'

He paused and no one interrupted him. The detectives found themselves looking down at Gilchrist's desk as well, though none of them knew why.

'It would appear that someone is targeting the police. The morale of London has not been good for some time now. The police are out of favour. Now someone is killing you.'

He took a deep breath.

'I will not lose another policeman. If just one more of you men is harmed in the course of this, whatever this is, I will tender my resignation. You must be able to perform your duties without fear and without violence done to you. You are the hope of this city. I believe that.'

He cleared his throat and looked up. He regarded each of his men in turn before he began to talk again.

'Mr Day and Mr Blacker have been working together on this case and they remain unharmed, despite being most at risk. So I would like all of you to work in pairs for the foreseeable future. Not only is it safer for you men, but it's possible that each of you brings a different perspective to the same situation. Perhaps it will help us to solve crimes more quickly. Speed is of the essence. And so is your safety. When you leave this building, unless you are going home, you will partner with someone else, another detective, a sergeant, a constable, I don't care who. But there will be no exceptions. If you cannot find someone to accompany you, tell Sergeant Kett and he'll find someone.'

He nodded and looked at Inspector Day. 'Catch this villain, Mr Day. And do it today if you can.'

'Sir,' Day said. 'I will.'

'There will be a service for Mr Pringle the day after tomorrow. Before that, I expect to see you all at Inspector Little's funeral tomorrow. Let these be the last two funerals I ever have to attend for my police. Mr Day, I would like to see you in my office now. Please bring the others involved in this with you. That includes Constable Hammersmith.'

He turned and went into his office and gently shut the door. The click of the latch echoed like a thunderclap through the silent squad room.

71

Sir Edward sat behind his desk, the tiger glaring down from its post on the wall above his head.

'Where is Mr Blacker?' Sir Edward said.

'He seemed to think you only wanted to speak to the two of us.'

'I asked for those of you involved in the investigation of Mr Little's murder and that includes Detective Blacker.'

Sir Edward pulled a cord that ran along the top edge of the wainscoting and out of the office through a small hole near the door. A moment later, the door opened and Sergeant Kett stuck his head in the room.

'Yes, sir?'

'Please find Mr Blacker.'

'Unless I'm mistaken, sir, I just saw Mr Blacker leavin' by the back hall.'

'You are rarely mistaken, Sergeant. Do you think you can catch him?'

Kett smiled.

'I'll get 'im in 'ere straightaway, sir.'

The door closed again. Sir Edward busied himself with the paperwork on his desk while Hammersmith and Day stood at awkward attention. Long minutes went by before they heard a knock at the office door. Sir Edward looked up from his papers.

'Yes?'

'Detective Blacker here, sir,' Blacker said.

His voice was muffled by the closed door.

'Open the door, Mr Blacker. I'd like to be able to see you when you talk to me.'

The door cracked open and slowly swung on its hinges until there was enough room for Blacker to squeeze through. He moved sideways into the office as if he were being pulled along, a tired fish on a line. Sir Edward put on a patient face until Blacker had completely entered the room.

'I hope you move more swiftly in pursuit of your cases, Mr Blacker. Please close the door behind you and join your colleagues.'

Blacker did as ordered. He kept his eyes on the floor.

'Detective Blacker,' Sir Edward said, 'do you know why I'm always right?'

'I'm sorry, sir. I never meant . . .'

'It's because I have no left.'

Hammersmith averted his eyes from Sir Edward's empty left sleeve. He looked at Day, but Day was staring at a spot near the ceiling, seemingly oblivious to what was happening. Hammersmith fixed his gaze upon the same spot.

'There was no disrespect intended, sir,' Blacker said.

'I still have both of my ears, Mr Blacker, and if you insist on circulating jokes about me I will hear them.'

'Of course, sir.'

'So you knew that I would hear them?'

'I . . . I understand it now, sir.'

'You understand? So you must have imagined that the

loss of my arm was a richly humorous affair for me.'

'No, sir.'

'You may relax, Mr Blacker. I do have a sense of humour and it's unlikely that you'll invent a joke that I haven't already heard.'

'Of course, sir.'

'In the future, if you insist on risking your career, at least come up with better jokes. Here's what you'll do . . . The next time you believe you've formulated a wonderful *bon mot* about me, or about my missing arm, I want you to come to me immediately. You come straight here and tell it to me and I'll help you decide whether it's funny enough or not. There's no sense spreading a joke until you've refined it. We'll work on these jokes together, you and I. Does that sound agreeable?'

'Yes, sir. I'm sorry, sir.'

'Of course you are. From all I've seen, you're a good detective. Don't let your personality get in the way of that.'

Blacker nodded at the floor.

'I hope you fully understand what I'm saying to you, Constable Blacker.'

Blacker looked up, his eyes wide, his mouth open. Sir Edward shook his head.

'What did I say? Did I call you Constable Blacker? My mistake, Inspector. Perhaps I was imagining a future conversation. I hope that conversation never happens.'

'It won't, sir.'

'See that it doesn't. Now, with that out of the way, let us discuss something more serious. How does the Little murder case progress?'

Hammersmith looked at Day, who was already looking at him. It was clear that neither of them wanted to be the first to speak. Hammersmith wasn't easily embarrassed, but he felt some of Blacker's humiliation and couldn't figure out why Sir Edward had reprimanded Blacker in front of them. Surely Blacker would now feel uncomfortable around them, knowing what they had seen and heard. Of course, Blacker's jokes about the one-armed police commissioner had been told behind Sir Edward's back, in public. Perhaps Sir Edward had simply given shame for shame, making Blacker's humiliation nearly as public as his own. He had spent years outside of England and away from the social norms that governed proper Victorian society. It was possible, Hammersmith thought, that the ways of Indian society were more direct.

'If none of you is willing to talk, I could select someone.'

Day cleared his throat and stepped forward.

'Sir, we do have some clues. You saw for yourself the demonstration of Dr Kingsley's finger marks and he discovered a great many of them on the trunks and the weapons that may have been used.'

'Yes. But that was yesterday and another police officer has been murdered since Dr Kingsley was in this office.'

Sir Edward turned his attention from Day to Hammersmith.

'I'll be addressing the entire squad momentarily, but I wanted to talk to you three first. And especially you, Mr Hammersmith. I understand Colin Pringle was an especially close friend to you.'

'Yes, sir. We joined the force together.'

'If you need the day off . . .'

'No, sir.'

'Good. Keep your head in the game then.'

'I will, sir.'

'Should I enquire about your appearance?'

Hammersmith looked down at his ensemble of dirt and sweat and blood and tattered fabric.

'Sir, I would prefer that you let me bathe and change my clothes first.'

'Very good. Now then, what of this Charles Shaw fellow? Was he involved somehow?'

'We don't think so,' Day said.

'Is this the same Charles Shaw who visited me with a concern about you, Mr Hammersmith? Do you have any light to shed on this?'

'It was, sir. He won't be visiting again.'

'He's dead, then?'

'He is.'

'Murder or accident?'

'Murder, sir. Throat slashed almost to his backbone.'

'I see. Same person killed Little and Pringle?'

'We don't think so.'

'Sir,' Blacker said.

It was the first time he'd spoken since Sir Edward had given him a dressing-down.

'I respectfully disagree with my colleagues, Sir Edward.'

'You think Shaw's death is related to the other two murders?'

'I'm not certain. But I'm suspicious of coincidences.'

Sir Edward nodded and leaned back in his chair.

'As am I,' he said. 'But I have experienced a great number of them anyway. What is the coincidence in play here?'

'We're agreed that the same person killed both Little and Pringle. The methods are nearly identical.'

'Yes?'

'And we have three other murders, at least three, that are also similar to each other.'

'Are they similar to the murders of Little and Pringle?'

'No, they're not. But I have trouble believing that there are two completely unrelated murderers at work in London who kill again and again, and seemingly at random.'

'Whether the killings are random or not remains to be seen. That fact is up to you men to discover, is it not?'

'It is, sir. But to kill in this sort of repeated pattern isn't the work of any kind of murderer we're used to seeing.'

'There was Jack.'

'Yes.'

'But we don't think this is him, do we?'

'Right, sir,' Blacker said. 'I mean, no, sir.'

Sir Edward almost smiled, but raked his fingers through his beard and scowled at the desk.

'I think,' he said, 'that Jack was the first of a new breed of killer. I think he opened a door to certain deranged possibilities and there will be more like him. These cases you're currently pursuing may well be connected, but if they're not – or even if they are – this department, The

Yard itself, is going to have to adapt. We're going to have to stop struggling against the idea of the mad killer and instead take steps to anticipate such a person. There are still patterns in the crimes they commit. We have to be able to see those patterns. I have great faith in you men and I'm encouraged by the new techniques that Dr Kingsley and others are discovering.'

'I think . . .'

Sir Edward held up his hand. 'I understand your misgivings, Mr Blacker. I do. But we are living and working in the largest city in the entire civilized world. There are more people packed together within London's borders than anywhere else. And I think it's that very closeness, that utter lack of privacy, that has caused a new kind of perversion to flower in the minds of some deviant people. I saw things in India that would shock you, all of you. But I also saw kindnesses among the people there that I don't see here. London is locked in a sort of dance of propriety and it seems to me that it has led to desperation among certain elements of our society.'

He took a deep breath.

'And that is as much as I want to say on the matter. I would much rather hear from you detectives.'

'Should I leave, sir?'

'No, Hammersmith. You're involved in this and I'd like you to have a hand in, so to speak.'

He looked at Blacker as he said it and smiled. Blacker blushed and looked down at his shoes.

'For now, let's treat Dr Shaw's murder as a separate case, but to be handled in conjunction with the Little case. Work them both and compare notes. As I told you,

Mr Day, all of the detectives out there are at your disposal, but I regret that I have nobody to assign Shaw's case to as a separate matter. I hope that you'll rise to the challenge.'

'I will do my utmost, sir.'

'Back to Shaw, then. Were you able to learn anything from him?'

'He couldn't speak, but he was able to write answers to a few questions before he passed away.'

Day took the small notebook from his jacket pocket and opened it to the page Shaw had written on. He laid it on Sir Edward's desk.

'Anything useful here?'

'It's hard to tell,' Day said. 'Most of what he wrote consisted of answers to specific questions we asked. That last bit at the bottom of the page was spontaneous, though.'

Sir Edward held the pad up close to his face and squinted at it.

'I can't make it out.'

'Neither could we. It seems to be a reference to ploughing something, but we don't know what. He wrote it just as he died.'

'He certainly didn't appear to be a farmer when I saw him.'

'He was a surgeon, sir.'

'It may have no bearing on his case at all then. Just the delusional last thoughts of a man in great pain.'

'That's possible, sir.'

'Still. Be nice to know what it says. Give me a moment.'

He opened his top desk drawer and rummaged inside

before finding a small glasses case. He held the case against his chest and removed the glasses, perched them on the end of his nose and picked the notepad back up.

'I've had occasion to decipher the handwriting of Indian doctors,' he said. 'Their penmanship was better than this, but perhaps I can bring a fresh pair of eyes to it.'

He didn't look up as he spoke, but continued to gaze at the paper in front of him. There was a long moment of silence as the three policemen watched the commissioner. Finally, Sir Edward pursed his lips and shook his head.

'I don't think that's a "p". It looks like an "f" to me.'

He laid the pad on his desk, removed his glasses and pointed at the paper.

'Look here.'

Day leaned in.

'If that's an "f",' Sir Edward said, 'then this word isn't "ploughing," I think it says "following". What do you think? See the "w"?

'Yes.'

Day looked up at the others. His face was flushed with excitement.

'It says "following". That's exactly it. And this second word has to be "you". "Following you".'

'Following who?' Blacker said.

'Was Shaw following you, Mr Day?'

'We were discussing his killer.'

'His killer was following him.'

'He doesn't say here that anyone was following him. This says "following you".'

'He also wrote that his killer was two women,' Blacker said. 'He called them whores.'

Hammersmith stiffened and grabbed Day's arm.

'He was following me. Shaw was following me. This must be a confession.'

'What makes you say that?'

'His widow told me as much. Remember I told you that he had me poisoned?'

'That's a large leap to make from two words scribbled on a page.'

'I know. But I think I'm right.'

'But why would he confess to following you?' Blacker said. 'What good does it do him as he lays dying to tell you that?'

'If he was confessing his sins, why not confess all of them?' Day said. 'Why this one?'

'Perhaps he ran out of time,' Hammersmith said, 'and this was merely the first of many confessions. I do believe he had more wicked sins to talk about.'

'Wait a moment,' Sir Edward said. 'Did you say that he poisoned you?'

'Yes, sir.'

'Why wasn't I informed?' Sir Edward said. 'The man came to my office to complain about you. If I'd known . . .'

'Sir, Mrs Shaw was involved and I wanted to think through the possible repercussions before bringing anything to you. I believe she was coerced into helping him and the scandal would be . . .'

'Mr Hammersmith, the health and safety of my officers is of great concern. You should have brought the matter to me.'

'I apologize.'

'Well, I imagine the murder of Mr Pringle rather occupied your thoughts. But in the future . . .'

'Yes, sir.'

'So, you're feeling quite all right?'

'I am now, sir.'

'Good. Well, then, back to the matter before us. If this man Shaw wasn't confessing a sin, then do you think it possible he was delivering a warning?'

'A warning?'

'Yes. Think about it from the killer's point of view. He's been killing police and now the police are on his trail. Isn't it possible he's been following one of you? He might even be planning to make one of you his next victim.'

'It's possible.'

'And if Shaw was following you, Mr Hammersmith, perhaps he saw the killer, also following you. Perhaps you're the next target.'

'Following *me*? Why would the killer be following me? Mr Day or Mr Blacker here, they're the ones investigating him.'

'Maybe you saw something.'

'Nothing I'm aware of.'

'It's a thought. We still don't know why Little or Pringle were killed. You're as logical a target as any of us. You said Shaw's wife is involved in this somehow?'

'Yes.'

'Let's have a talk with her, then.'

'I'll pay her a visit.'

'No, not you, Mr Hammersmith. It sounds to me like you're already chin-deep in a situation there.'

'But, with all due respect, sir . . .'

'I've made my decision. Mr Hammersmith, I want you to you keep your distance from the Shaw home. Help Mr Day as he pursues Pringle's killer. You should find that a satisfactory outlet for your energies. Mr Blacker, you'll visit the Shaw woman. Take someone with you. And Mr Hammersmith?'

'Sir?'

'That's not a suggestion, it's an order. You worry me. I don't want you doing anything alone, and I mean anything at all. You will stay with these other men at all times.'

'But I'm perfectly capable.'

'Of course you are. Indulge me. I am not prepared to lose any more of my men.'

72

'He won't return.'

'Hammersmith?'

'Yes, him.'

'Of course he'll return. He likes the lady.'

'He's had her already.'

'Hasn't. She's a proper one. And, anyhow, her husband's only just dead. But once our Mr Hammersmith finds the body, he'll be round here to call on her, I promise.'

They looked at each other and both burst out laughing at once. Then they lapsed into easy silence. The two women sat side by side under the willow tree on the same low wall that Constables Hammersmith and Pringle had occupied two nights before. The sun had moved behind a blanket of fog and did nothing to warm them. Liza leaned her head against Esme's shoulder.

'Do it still bother you he don't have hair on his face?' she said. 'That there's no beard to shave?'

'They all have beards,' Esme said. 'This one keeps it down, is all.'

'Less work for us, I suppose.'

'He done the work for us. Partly.'

'Partly. Not all.'

'You really think he'll come here.'

'If he doesn't, we know where to find him.'

'Not done it to a police afore.'

'You done it to plenty a police, girl.'

Esme laughed. 'Ain't done the other thing, though. Ain't killed one.'

'Don't matter he's police. What they done fer us, huh? They din't catch him.'

'Let the Ripper do what he done to Annie.'

'And the others.'

'Yes.'

They were silent then and the fog rolled over the wall and up the trunk of the willow behind them and swirled down. It was cool and damp and the short one closed her eyes and felt it on her face.

'He'll come,' she said. 'Patience, love. He'll come.'

73

'Should I be worried about this woman poisoning me?' Blacker said.

'You're not her type,' Hammersmith said.

'Excuse me?'

'A joke. I thought you liked those. Penelope Shaw was a victim of her husband's cruelty and manipulation. She won't cause any trouble for you.'

'Michael and I seem to have hit a dead end with Little's murder,' Day said. 'Now that we have your notes, Nevil, I'd like to follow Constable Pringle's movements in the last few hours of his life.'

Hammersmith nodded.

'You know,' Blacker said, 'that I have the utmost respect for Sir Edward.'

'Of course.'

'The jokes . . . about his arm? They weren't meant to hurt.'

'Perhaps joking makes the job easier for you.'

'Sir Edward knows you meant no real disrespect,' Hammersmith said. 'If he didn't, I believe you'd be back to walking a beat today.'

The creak of the opening gate caused the three men to turn towards the rail where Sergeant Kett was entering.

'Some news for you gentlemen,' he said. 'Mr Day, I'm

afraid we needed the room in lock-up and I was forced to send your prisoner to the workhouse.'

'The dancing man?'

'He wasn't dancing when I saw 'im last.'

'Which workhouse did you send him to?'

'Hobgate.'

'Damn.'

'I had little choice.'

'No, I understand, but I don't think he's well equipped to survive long there.'

'Well, who is?'

'Granted.'

'I brung it up 'cause the good doctor sent round askin' about 'im.'

'Kingsley?'

'That's the one.'

'What did he want with the dancing man?'

'The student he sent din't say. Prob'ly din't know.'

'Of course. I'll look into it.'

'Yes, sir. And Mr Hammersmith, there's been another dispatch from hospital. It's your father.'

'My father can wait.'

'No, son, it don't sound like he can.'

'I'll get round to see him when I have the time.'

'If you want to do that today, I can handle the investigation on my own for a bit,' Day said.

'No, you'll need me to point out Colin's habits.'

'Your notes will steer me in the right direction, I'm sure I can . . .'

'I don't care to see my father.'

'Ah.'

'He doesn't know me. He's half the size he once was and he coughs blood on to himself and I have no desire to watch him die. If it's quite all right with you lot, I will do my job and I will remember my father the way that I wish to remember him.'

The other policemen looked at each other, but remained quiet. Finally, Kett reached out and clapped Hammersmith on the shoulder.

'Well,' he said, 'you lads have a busy afternoon ahead of you. I'll let you get to it.'

Kett stepped through the gate and disappeared down the back hallway.

'Well, then,' Day said. 'Let's get started, shall we? Where would Pringle have been yesterday morning?'

Hammersmith was grateful to Day for giving him something constructive to think about, a goal, no matter how wretched the circumstances surrounding that goal might be. His head throbbed and the room span slowly around him, the poison working its way through his system. He closed his eyes, thinking, waiting for the walls to stop moving.

'He was headed to the tailor's shop,' he said. 'I forget the name. It's the one used by the department for uniforms and the like.'

'Cinderhouse,' Blacker said.

'That's it. Colin had new trousers being made and he was anxious to have them fitted.'

'He was anxious for a pair of trousers?'

'He was quite . . . well, he was immaculate in his ways and in his appearance. He liked to impress the ladies.'

Hammersmith allowed himself a wistful smile at the

thought of all the disappointed women who would never again receive a compliment from Colin Pringle. Some of them, Maggie especially, deserved an explanation. Hammersmith could see that the days ahead would be busy. He would need to track down and inform Pringle's friends – the friends that Hammersmith knew about – that their social circle had been diminished.

'Then Cinderhouse should be your first stop,' Blacker said. 'You were going to pay a visit there anyway. We can share a wagon, at least that far, before I have to head for the Shaw home.'

'The scarcity of police wagons is alarming. How can we hope to track anyone down when we have no transportation?'

'The tailor's shop won't be open yet,' Hammersmith said.

'What say we roll past it and take a look. I don't want to wait another day before questioning him. If he's not in there, we'll try again after we see this Shaw woman. Meanwhile, Mr Hammersmith looks particularly rough this morning. Perhaps we could all do with a spot of tea and a fresh change of clothing.'

'I'm fine,' Hammersmith said. 'Perhaps not as rested as I might be, I'll admit, but I won't be able to sleep again until this monster is in our dungeon.'

'Of course.'

'Then what say, after the tailor's shop, we pay a visit to Shaw's widow together?' Blacker said. 'We're supposed to stick together anyway and I'll feel a bit less likely to be knocked off by her.'

Day looked at Hammersmith.

'I'll wait outside her home,' Hammersmith said, 'in the wagon.'

Day chuckled and clapped Blacker on the back.

'Very well. Perhaps the presence of three of The Yard's finest will convince Mrs Shaw to keep her poisons locked up.'

The gate creaked again.

'Your pardon,' Kett said, 'but there's a gentleman out here who says he's got to talk to Mr Day.'

'To me?'

'Well, not by name, but he said it was regarding the dancin' man and that's your special interest.'

Day looked at Hammersmith and Blacker. Blacker shrugged.

'I can spare a minute,' Day said, 'but no more.'

'Aye, sir.'

'Wait. Who is it?'

'Never seen 'im round before, but he says he's the dancin' man's brother.'

74

Dr Bernard Kingsley looked past the body of Dr Charles Shaw. Most of the tables in the large, spotless room were full and two nurses were busy bringing in more bodies. Next to Shaw was the body of a girl who couldn't have been much older than Fiona Kingsley. Much of the girl's jaw was missing, her tongue lolling down the length of her neck. A belated victim of the white phosphorus used to make matches, and a clear holdover from London's 'Matchstick Girl Strike' of the previous year. Kingsley had seen scores of similar bodies, but fewer of them since the strike. The young women who had worked in Bryant and May's matchstick factory had breathed phosphorus fumes. They had touched their faces when they lit their cigarettes, scratched their noses and wiped the sweat from their brows, transferring phosphorus from their fingers. Their skulls had turned to jelly.

He pronounced the cause of death for the poor girl at a glance and the nurses cleared the table to make room for a new corpse. There were many more waiting. There always were.

The man next to her had been ill. He had come from somewhere upstairs in the hospital and had been worked over by another doctor. There were small purple wounds on the man's chest, abdomen, legs, arms and forehead where leeches had been applied. It was an old method of treatment and Kingsley had no use for it. Patients who had been bled were invariably weaker and thinner and sicker than when they were first admitted to hospital. Kingsley would have to decide whether to credit the man's death to illness or malpractice. In similar cases in the past, he had marked 'bleeding' as the cause of death, but the hospital frowned on that. Doctor Kingsley had been encouraged to keep his progressive thinking to himself.

There was a bin next to the only empty table in the room. The bin was filled with disembodied limbs, heads and torsos. There was no mystery as to the cause of death. A man in Mayfair had wheeled the bin in to a police station and had confessed to chopping up his entire family in a fit of pique after too much drink. Kingsley had already pronounced cause on the woman and two children whose body parts were mingled in the bin. But he had decided to stitch the three people back together, to make them whole again, before their burial. It seemed only proper.

The bodies of children always bothered Kingsley most.

Many of the other tables' occupants had been struck down by horses, or wagons, or stray building materials as they walked in the streets near the hospital. Here a man's head was stoved in and unrecognizable, there a woman's arm was separated from her shoulder. She had bled to death while the omnibus that hit her had rolled on to its appointed rounds.

Victims of consumption occupied three of the tables near the far wall. They were all razor thin, their skin marble-grey, their clothing spotted with blood. They had slowly coughed up their lives. Kingsley's own wife had suffered this way and he avoided looking too closely at their faces, afraid he might see the same dull animal fear that had transformed Catherine. He had carefully suppressed the memories of his wife on her deathbed, the bloodstained linens, the long nights, the hoarse moans that had echoed through their home every night. He preferred to remember her as she had been in her prime.

He moved on as he always moved on when those memories surfaced.

The last table in the corner of the room held an old woman's body. Her throat had been cut as she passed through an alley, her bag stolen. Kingsley had no idea what might have been in that bag. The mugger and murderer had not been caught. Kingsley stood by that table and looked down at the old woman. She seemed peaceful, sleeping, as if she might wake at any moment and ask for a cup of tea. He took her hand and gazed at her untroubled face and allowed himself a moment before turning and unloading the bin of body parts on to the empty table beside it.

There was much to do and the work never ended.

Interlude 3

Charing Cross, London. Two years ago

Dr Bernard Kingsley stood in the open doorway and surveyed the room. It was long and narrow like a potting shed, with more than thirty tables flanking a tight centre aisle. There was just enough room between the tables for a man to walk sideways. There were no windows in the room and only the single door. The ivy that grew along the outside walls of the tiny morgue had pushed through crevices in the wood and moved inside, where its tendrils spilled in streamers across the low ceiling. Street sounds echoed through the odd-shaped chamber like the bustle of an open-air bazaar, but the room lacked the breeze or sunlight of such a place. No one had yet noticed Kingsley standing there.

Two men in dirty smocks wandered aimlessly at the back of the room. One of them had tied a kerchief around his mouth and nose, presumably to filter the stench, which was considerable.

Kingsley took a step further into the room, letting his eyes adjust to the gloom. He resisted the impulse to gag and reached inside his coat for his pipe and tobacco. Disguising the odour of the dead was the only reason he ever smoked. He blew through the stem and added a pinch of an American blend to the bowl, catching the leftover tobacco in his pouch as it fell. Hard to do in the semi-dark. He tamped the bowl with his thumb and sucked air in through the dry tobacco, tasting it.

One of the men, the one with the kerchief over his face, saw the flicker of Kingsley's match and moved towards him as Kingsley drew on the pipe and got a decent flow going. It was a false light; the pipe went out. He tamped again, and lit another match. This time smoke billowed around his head. His own private and portable atmosphere.

The man with the kerchief waited patiently as Kingsley made the matches and tobacco pouch disappear back into the recesses of his coat. Kingsley took a long drag and held it. He looked back out at the street then turned and plunged into the morgue facility.

'Beg pardon, sir,' the man with the kerchief said. 'Not s'posed to be reg'lar folk in here while the work's goin' on.'

'What's your name, fellow?' Kingsley said.

'Francis Mayhew, sir. Call me Frank. That over there's my brother Henry.'

'Francis and Henry. Are you doctors?'

Francis let out a guffaw. The sudden gust of air blew his kerchief up over his eyes. When it had drifted back down over his mouth and nose, Francis bowed and tugged on his forelock.

'No, sir. Not hardly. No call for doctors round here. Patients in here's all dead, don'cha know.'

'Are you assisting a doctor, then?'

'Like I said, sir, no doctors come round here, mostly ever. Ain't no ways to bring these 'uns back to life.'

Kingsley brushed past Frank Mayhew and walked down the row of corpses. The tables, three dozen of them, were short, each barely more than a yard long. The young children in that room fitted the tables well, but the adults lay with the tops of their heads butted against the walls and their legs dangling off the tables into the corridor. As he walked, Kingsley was unable to avoid brushing against them, setting the legs in motion. He looked back at the rectangle of light that led to the street outside, dead feet swaying back and forth in front of it as if on the verge of escape. Rigor had passed in most of the bodies. They had been lying there long enough for their muscles to become pliable once more.

'This is monstrous,' he said.

'Well, yes, sir. No argument from us there.'

'If you agree, why do you allow these conditions?'

'Due respect, we don't allow nothin', sir. Ain't our place. We does the job as told.'

Kingsley pointed at the one called Henry, who cowered at the back of the room.

'You. Are you in charge here?'

'He don't talk much no more,' Frank said.

'Well, who's in charge here, then?'

'Nobody.'

'What do you mean, nobody?'

'Well, somebody, I s'pose, but they ain't come round here in as long as Henry and me's been here, which is goin' on a couple of months now.'

'Then how did you come to be here?'

'Got choosed out the workhouse.'

'Why were you chosen? What was your experience?

Were you a doctor's aide? An apprentice or student of some sort?'

''At's a lotta ways of askin' the same thing, sir. I don't mean no disrespect, but you gettin' worked up past where you oughtta. It ain't good in here, 'at's for sure, but Henry and me's doin' what we's told. We ain't lookin' for no trouble and we don't no ways wanna go back to the workhouse.'

Kingsley took in a deep breath of pipe smoke and coughed. He held up a hand until the coughing spell had passed, then nodded.

'I didn't mean to besmirch your work or your reputation. But I want to speak to someone in charge, and this all seems a cruel joke.'

'No joke, sir. And it's like I said, there ain't nobody in charge round here 'cept me and my brother. We's just doin' our best to get along, 'at's all.'

'Yes, you said as much. Let me ask again. What did you do that you were chosen for this job?'

'Well, we dug ditches for a time and 'fore that we helped on that retaining wall was built down the river.'

'Dug ditches.'

'Dug us a few graves, too. Might be called experience with the dead. Might be why we was choosed.'

'Good Lord,' Kingsley said. He glanced back at the doorway and sighed. 'Well, in the absence of anyone more qualified, perhaps you can help me. I'm looking for a woman.'

Frank released another kerchief-rattling guffaw. He waited for the cloth to settle back over his face before he spoke.

'No offence meant, sir, but we don't want no part o' that.'

Kingsley finally lost his composure. He pushed past Francis and stalked deeper into the morgue. The darkness was broken only by that double row of pale grey legs swinging gently back and forth. A neglected market with the dead laid out on display. Kingsley felt disoriented already. A hand grabbed him by the arm and swung him around.

'You can't be in here, sir.'

Francis's face was expressionless, backlit by the open door. Without a thought, Kingsley swung at the ditch digger and missed. Francis took a step back and Kingsley grabbed him by the collar and dragged him forward. Francis was the larger man, but Kingsley was determined.

'Beg pardon, sir,' Francis said.

'My wife is here. Somewhere in this hellhole. Show me where.'

Arms reached around Kingsley from behind and lifted him into the air. Startled, he let go of Frank Mayhew's shirt. The ditch digger rocked back on his heels and the arms released Kingsley. He turned and saw Henry retreating again to the back of the room.

'Sir, all due respect,' Frank said, 'you're a right gentleman and all, but I ain't s'posed to let you in here. An' my brother don't let nobody touch me 'cept hisself.'

'I'm a doctor, you halfwit.'

'Oh, well 'at's different then, ain't it?'

Kingsley straightened his shirt and tie. He ran a hand over his hair, but it was always unruly and his hand did nothing to tame it.

'Catherine Kingsley,' he said. 'That's my wife's name. There must be some record of her having been brought in?'

He said it as a question, not at all convinced that anything that resembled recordkeeping went on in this place.

'Henry's got charge of the papers and such.'

Francis motioned to his brother and Henry came forward with a wad of greasy papers in his fist. Kingsley took them from him and went back to the door to look them over in the sunlight. He realized that he was clenching his pipe so tight that his teeth hurt. He squatted, his back against the jamb, rubbed his jaw and took another puff, then smoothed the papers out against his knee. There was no organization visible in the notes, no standardized form, just a haphazard recording of whatever had been relayed when the bodies were brought in. Half of the reports were missing the deceased's names. He shuffled through them quickly and saw nothing about his wife. He stood and turned and thrust the handful of paperwork back at Henry, who took it wordlessly.

Kingsley left both brothers standing at the door and plunged back into the gloom, the bubble of smoke around his head keeping pace.

Kingsley found his wife after some searching. Catherine was on a table halfway down the aisle on the right-hand side. She was nude, lying on her back atop a dirty blanket, her legs dangling like the rest of them. Her eyes were open and unblinking, staring up into the dark. He wondered where she had gone and what she was looking at.

He took her hand and stood there. The pipe fell from his lips and he didn't notice.

After a time, the silent brother Henry appeared at his side and moved the edge of the blanket over her, covering Catherine, giving her back some modesty. He reached out and closed her eyes and then was gone again, swallowed by the shadows. Kingsley hardly noticed.

When Henry returned, he was holding a sprig of ivy, plucked from the wall. He laid it on Catherine's chest. He nodded at Kingsley and backed away. That small gesture was enough to break Kingsley and his grief poured from him in great choking waves.

When it had passed, he leaned in and kissed his wife on the lips for the last time.

He picked up his pipe, stood and turned around.

'My name is Bernard Kingsley. I am a surgeon with University College Hospital in the West End. I will send people later today to help you pack up this operation and you will move it all, every corpse in your care, to my facilities.'

Francis looked alarmed.

'All of it?'

'Just the bodies. You may keep these ridiculous tables and this horrible reeking shack.'

'But the bluebottles send boys round here with the bodies. This place'll fill back up in no time at all.'

'I will notify the police that they may deal with me from now on. This is not the way a civilized society cares for their dead. This is the way of animals and savages.'

He shook his head.

'No, not even savages. Even they practise ritual and ceremony in order to show respect. This is ruin. This is horror.'

He walked past Francis. Henry was standing in the doorway with his back to them, his face in the sun. Kingsley put a hand on the bigger man's arm.

'Thank you for your kindness towards my wife.'

Henry looked at him, but said nothing. He turned his head and looked back at the sky. He rocked back and forth as if listening to music only he could hear. Kingsley couldn't tell if his words had even registered with the former ditch digger.

'But, mister, what will me an' my brother do now?' Francis said.

Kingsley didn't turn around, didn't address the man directly.

'Go back to the workhouse,' he said. 'Go find occupations better suited to your skills.'

'We can't go back again, sir. Henry won't last there. Ain't much left of 'im now.'

Kingsley stepped off the kerb and, still keeping his back to that house of death, he let some warmth enter his voice.

'Then find something to do outside in the fresh air and sun. Your brother shouldn't be cooped up in a place like this, anyway. Nobody should be. Not even the dead.'

He used the sole of his shoe to tap the tobacco out of his pipe, put it back in his pocket and walked away down the street. He didn't look back.

75

He woke from his reverie and looked at his handiwork. A lattice of stitches ran pell-mell over the surface of the little girl's body, linking her arms and legs and head like a hideous human quilt. He raised his head and regarded his laboratory. It was clean and open and the bodies were stretched out full-length on long tables, with adequate drainage. The sunlight through the windows at ceiling level was filtered through bubbling green gasogenes, lending everything a sickly glow, but Kingsley liked that. It meant that work was going on.

And now he remembered where and when he had met the homeless man, the dancing man who had found the shears thrown from a killer's carriage. He'd known the name, but his connection to the man had been lost until now.

'Henry Mayhew,' he said.

His voice echoed.

Kingsley looked down at the little girl's body. In a dress with a high collar, nobody would ever see the black stitches that kept her from falling apart at the seams. She was, at least, presentable.

He put down the forceps and the thread and rubbed the back of his neck with his bloody hand.

There were two more bodies that needed to be sewn

together, but Kingsley knew that he had to find Henry Mayhew again before the police returned him to the workhouse or, worse, the asylum.

He owed the former ditch digger something and he was ashamed that it had taken him this long to remember and to act.

He rinsed the blood off his hands in the basin on the counter, grabbed his jacket and left the room. The people on the tables could wait. They had all the time in the world.

76

He had gone out the previous night while the boy slept, but he dared not risk it again. He could lock the boy up again, but he didn't want to. He felt they'd made real progress in their relationship since Fenn's escape attempt. To imprison him again, even for the hour or two it would take him to run his errand, might cause the boy to resent him again.

But he had offered to take his catalogues to the police. If he failed to make good his promise Sergeant Kett – or worse, Inspector Day – might begin to wonder about him.

Cinderhouse left Fenn at the dining table with a bowl of soup and went from room to room in the tidy house, gathering what he could find. Most of his catalogues were at the shop, but there were a few that he'd brought home, for one reason or another. They were all horribly out of date, but the police wouldn't know that. In all he found eight catalogues. That ought to do.

He checked on the boy, made sure he was still eating, and stepped out the front door, locking it behind him.

His hansom was outside, the coachman bundled up on top, snoozing. Cinderhouse wondered at the fact that the man could sleep while sitting up, but supposed that it came with long practice. The horse whinnied at Cinderhouse as he approached and he stroked its muzzle.

'Somewhere to go, Mr Cinderhouse?'

He jumped at the sound of the coachman's voice.

'Thought you were asleep up there,' he said.

'Was. But nobody gets close to my horse without me knowin' it, even you, sir, no disrespect.'

'Not at all. Quite admirable, really. We must take care of our own, mustn't we?'

'Exactly right, sir.'

'I've an errand for you.'

Cinderhouse held up the small stack of catalogues. The coachman jumped down and took them from him.

'There's a detective at Scotland Yard who's expecting me to deliver these. Inspector Day's his name. Would you bring them round to him and apologize for me? Please tell him I had a family matter to attend to, or I would have brought them myself, but assure him that I will pay a visit to The Yard just as soon as I am able. That I'm anxious to finally meet him. Within the next day or two.'

'Easy as can be, sir. Inspector Day, you say?'

'That's right.'

'Anywhere else today, sir?'

'I don't think so. I may need to go to the shop a bit later, but unless it rains I could do with a bit of a walk. Why don't you take the rest of the day off?'

'Thank you, sir. I'll take these straight round to the police, then. If it begins to look like rain, I'll head back here and fetch you.'

'Only if it rains.'

'Very good, sir.'

The coachman leapt to his perch and cracked the reins. The horse snorted and jerked forward. Cinderhouse wondered at the fact that he trusted the man. The coachman had been present, even helped, during the commission of uncounted crimes, and yet there was no question in the tailor's mind that he was loyal. He was paid handsomely for his dedication. Cinderhouse imagined that the world would be an easier place to navigate if everyone's principles were for sale.

He let himself back into the house where Fenn was still eating soup in the dining room.

With a bit of luck, Inspector Day would be satisfied with the catalogues and wouldn't call on the tailor today. By tomorrow things might be different. By tomorrow Fenn might be more settled into his new life with his new father and Cinderhouse might even be able to bring the boy with him to call on the police. The tailor smiled at Fenn and was pleased to see the boy smile back at him. Despite all their recent troubles, things were beginning to come out right at last.

77

'He ain't gonna last in there.'

'The dancing man, you mean?'

'I mean my brother. Henry's his name.'

'Of course. I apologize. Your brother has spent a great deal of time here, or rather in the street outside of here. We didn't know his name until quite recently.'

Frank Mayhew waved the apology away. He was a lean man, tall but shrunken, slumped in the straight-backed wooden chair next to Walter Day's desk. He had the appearance of a once-larger and perhaps more intimidating man, but there was little evidence left of that past life. His hair was plastered to his forehead with old sweat, he had not shaved in at least a week, grime caked the creases of his neck and forehead. His eyes were bloodshot and rheumy, tears welling up at the corners. His hands trembled as he took a filthy handkerchief from his shirt pocket and dabbed at his blood-encrusted nostrils.

Frank Mayhew was clearly not long for the world.

Inspector Day locked eyes with Constable Hammersmith who nodded back at him. Hammersmith stood and motioned for Blacker to follow. Blacker raised an eyebrow, but allowed himself to be led to the far end of the Murder Squad room.

Day cleared his throat.

'As I said, I meant no disrespect towards your brother.'

Mayhew folded a clump of dried blood into the handkerchief and slipped the cloth back into his pocket. He wiped his face with a filthy paw and sighed.

'I know he's a strange one, sir. But he's a good kid. I been lookin' after 'im a long time now, since our mama died on us, and I'm here to tell ya he's got a sweet heart, a big heart, goes along with that big body o' his.'

'I will admit to being fond of him. Despite his best efforts to alienate me and everyone else.'

'He don't mean to do that. He loves people. Wants to make 'em happy. Just don't like to be touched or pushed around none.'

'He's made that clear on at least one occasion.'

'Sure he has.'

'Frank, I'm afraid I don't know why you're here. Your brother has been taken to the workhouse, where qualified people will care for him and help him re-enter society as a productive citizen. It's entirely out of my hands.'

Mayhew levelled his gaze at Day and, for a moment, his eyes cleared. Behind the blood and tears, there was the angry twinkle of wit.

'You believe a word yer sayin'?'

'About the workhouse?'

'Yes. 'Bout that.'

Day hesitated, then shook his head.

'No. No, of course I don't.'

'Then let's you an' me be honest, each with t'other. Henry stays in that workhouse, he ain't comin' back out alive. They treat 'em rough in there and he ain't equipped no ways to deal with those folk. Nor with the work they'd be puttin' him to.'

'I don't disagree with you, but as I said, it's out of my hands. I have no jurisdiction over the workhouse. Whatever meagre authority I have is strictly tied to the investigation of crime and not at all to the welfare of . . . well, not to social inequities, at any rate.'

'That don't mean nothin' to me. A policeman goes in there and takes him out, nobody's gonna stop 'im. 'Specially a policeman's got no uniform, in a posh suit like you got.'

'There's nothing posh about . . .'

'I'm sayin' you could help Henry if you put your mind to doin' it.'

'But why?'

Day was impatient now. He sat on the edge of his desk and leaned forward, breathing through his mouth. Frank Mayhew smelled like death.

'Why should I do that, Mr Mayhew? Your brother . . .'

He broke off, unsure of how to point out the obvious without insulting the dancing man's brother. Frank looked away, at the piles of paperwork on Day's desk, all the unsolved cases.

'I know it. I understand about my brother. I know he don't contribute much of nothin' and he don't know how to relate to folk and he don't make much sense when he do try to relate. But that don't make him a bad person. He deserves better'n he's got.'

'So many people deserve better, Mr Mayhew.' Day said. He spoke quietly. 'This city is full to the brim with people who deserve better.'

Day held the other man's stare until the spark went out of Mayhew's eyes, leaving them once again watery and grey. Mayhew closed them and hung his head.

'Well, I can't argue with that,' he said.

'I'm sorry, Mr Mayhew. Truly I am.'

'It was a stupid idea anyhow. Police don't do nothin' for nobody ain't got two ha'pennies to rub together.'

'That's not fair.'

''T'ain't fair, but 'tis true. I'll clear outten yer way now.'

Mayhew coughed as he rose. He turned, stumbled and then fell, toppling over the chair, but keeping his feet. He tripped forward again, trying to catch his balance, dragging the chair under him as it banged back into him. His gaunt body finally crumpled and he lay still beside Inspector Tiffany's desk.

Tiffany stood and grabbed Mayhew around the waist. He yanked him to his feet.

'Suspect or witness?' Tiffany said.

'Neither,' Day said. 'A concerned citizen.'

Tiffany's expression softened and he set Mayhew on his feet. Mayhew staggered, but stayed upright.

'Are you all right?' Day said.

Mayhew held up his hands, palms out, and nodded.

'Be right as rain. Need a moment's all.'

He coughed again. And again. And then his body shook with convulsions as he barked and hacked, pitching forward and rocking back. Tiffany jumped out of the way as a thick clot of gore spewed from Frank Mayhew's mouth. Blood, black as tar, spattered the floor. Hammersmith and Blacker rushed from the other side of the room, but Tiffany held them back, giving Mayhew room. Constables and sergeants queued up on the other side of the rail and watched Mayhew work, coughing his life up and out.

Finally, Frank Mayhew straightened. He stood quietly with his back to the detectives and took the handkerchief from his pocket again. He wiped his lips.

'You have consumption,' Day said.

'I do.'

'You're dying.'

'Not too long now.'

'Let me take you to hospital.'

'So I can die there?'

'They can make you comfortable.'

'You know better'n 'at.'

Mayhew turned to face him. The front of his shirt glistened and Day realized that what he had taken for dirt was actually layer upon layer of dried blood.

'What you said. There's too many deservin' of help in this city? That's true enough. But you could maybe help just one of them that's deservin' and that's somethin' and that's true enough, too.'

Day was quiet.

'I can't look after my brother no more. And I know you can't, neither. But you can maybe get 'im outta that place and give 'im a fightin' chance on the street where he can breathe some air and do a dance again. Ain't nothin' wrong with a little dancin', Mr Police, sir.'

Mayhew nodded at him, sniffed and turned. He walked away through the gate, and the uniformed men on the other side of the railing moved to let him pass. Mayhew disappeared down the back hallway. He would, Day knew, be swallowed up by the city and he would die in an alley or under a building somewhere within the week.

'Well, this is quite a mess,' Tiffany said.

'It is.'

'We'll get someone to clean it.'

'Thank you.'

'Day?'

'Yes?'

'If you try to handle more than you can you'll drive yourself mad. My advice to you is to concentrate on the job. Anything else will only get in the way of that.'

Day nodded, but said nothing. After a moment, Tiffany clapped him on the shoulder and went to open the gate for a boy who was lugging a bucket of suds and a mop. Day stepped back and let the boy get to work scrubbing the floor.

'What now, old man?' Blacker said.

'I believe I'll let you and Mr Hammersmith handle the interview with Penelope Shaw by yourselves, if you don't mind.'

'What Tiffany said just now . . .'

'No. He's right, of course, but that's not the way I'm made.'

'So you're headed round the workhouse, then?'

'Of course I am. I'll check in on the tailor first. It's on the way. I'll catch up to you at the Shaw house as soon as I'm able.'

'With any luck we'll see you there soon.'

78

'Our Mr Day has taken the last wagon.'

'Considerate of him.'

'Fancy a walk?'

'That's a long walk.'

'Aye.'

Inspector Blacker sighed and looked at the sky.

'More rain today, I think.'

'Even better news.'

'Yes.'

'I've forgotten my hat,' Hammersmith said. 'Wait for me?'

'Of course.'

Blacker watched Hammersmith duck past a pair of bobbies and disappear through the back door of Number Four Whitehall Place. When Blacker turned around, a black hansom was pulling up to the kerb.

'Well, that's a stroke of luck,' Blacker said.

The two bobbies looked at him expectantly and he waved them on.

'Talking to myself,' he said. 'It'll be the nuthouse for me next.'

They smiled and nodded and moved down the pavement as the hansom's coachman alighted and reached into the cab for something. He emerged with a short stack of books and approached Blacker.

'Pardon me, sir,' the coachman said. 'I'm to deliver these to an Inspector Day.'

'I'm afraid you've just missed him,' Blacker said. 'What have you got?'

'Catalogues from Mr Cinderhouse.'

'The man's name pops up at every turn. Tell you what, take those in to Sergeant Kett. He'll be right inside there. Tell him that Inspector Day needs them left on his desk and he'll take care of you.'

'I'll need a receipt of some sort.'

'Kett's your man.'

'Thank you, sir.'

'I say. When you've done with that, I don't suppose you're up for giving me a ride?'

'A ride, sir?'

'It's a short distance. Can your employer spare you the few minutes?'

'I'm sure he'd be happy if I was of service to you.'

'Excellent. Hurry yourself, then. Remember, Sergeant Kett's the fellow you're looking for.'

The coachman tipped his hat and carried the stack of catalogues into The Yard, passing Hammersmith, who emerged from Number Four with his hat in his hands. Hammersmith scowled at the sky. Heavy clouds were rolling in, the colour and texture of over-boiled spinach.

'I'm too tired to be wet today,' he said.

'There's good news in that department, old man. I've arranged a ride for us in this shiny beast of a cab.'

'That is good news. I don't believe I'd have made it halfway there on foot.'

'Then hop in and we'll be talking to this Shaw woman in mere moments.'

Hammersmith climbed into the cab and shut the door behind him. Blacker stood on the kerb until the coachman came back out.

'Did the sergeant fix you up, then?'

'He did. Thank you, sir.'

'Then we're off.'

'My pleasure. Where to, sir?'

'Here.'

Blacker wrote the address in pencil on the back of a calling card. He handed it to the coachman, who squinted at it.

'It's not far,' Blacker said.

'Not at all. No trouble, sir.'

'Good man.'

Blacker clapped the coachman on the shoulder and clambered into the cab. He felt the hansom shift as the coachman settled into position above. There was the sound of reins snapping and the cab lurched into motion.

Blacker looked over at Hammersmith. The constable had pulled his hat down over his eyes and was snoring softly. Blacker smiled and pulled the curtains closed over the windows. In the darkness he leaned his shoulder against the wall of the cab and shut his eyes. Within moments, the gentle rocking of the hansom had lulled him to sleep as well.

79

Sergeant Kett was so buried in his paperwork that he didn't notice when the postman rapped twice on the doorjamb. The mail sat in its box for more than an hour before Kett's internal clock reminded him that the post was overdue.

He fetched the mail to his desk and looked through it, quickly sorting it into piles for the runners to deliver about the building. He always looked through the messages to the squad room himself, though, to be sure there wasn't anything that might disturb his detectives. The Ripper fiasco had led to a fair amount of hate mail and even, once, a letter bomb.

There was an envelope addressed to Inspector Day. No return address. Kett slit it open. Inside was a lady's handkerchief and a note. The handkerchief had the initials *'CC'* embroidered on one corner. Kett opened the note. It said:

> *Inspektor Day, you no who this belongs to & I can get at her agin. Stop what your duing and declare it insolvible or the wurst will hapinn.*

The note wasn't signed.

Kett read it again. It was nonsense, clearly meant as a

threat, but so vague as to be pointless. Just one more crazy Londoner.

He tossed the envelope, note and handkerchief in the wastepaper basket next to his desk. His duty was to serve and protect the detectives who, in turn, served and protected the great city. Inspector Day didn't need to be heckled by anonymous citizens.

Kett bundled up the remainder of the mail for the runners and returned to his paperwork.

80

It had been a long morning and he had barely slept the night before, but there was work to be done, so he locked up the house and took the boy to the shop with him.

He had just entered the shop when he heard a carriage roll slowly down the street and stop outside the door. But he wasn't expecting clients today. He pointed at the boy and Fenn nodded. Fenn moved to the back wall of the shop and stood still, waiting. Cinderhouse watched him with pride. The boy was learning.

Cinderhouse quietly turned the bolt on the front door, easing it into its casing in the jamb, and watched through the smeary picture window as Inspector Day alighted from the carriage and approached the shop. Cinderhouse noticed an oily handprint on the glass, no doubt left there by Constable Pringle the previous day. He cursed under his breath and pulled back into the shadows.

What was the detective doing here now? Had he already received the note? How could he know who sent it? Unless he'd talked to his wife. She was entirely too smart for her own good. Or maybe there was a question about the shears. Maybe they had somehow been traced back to Cinderhouse. Had his driver talked? Why would the coachman betray him? More money?

There were too many questions.

He could slip the bolt, open the door and welcome the detective, show him in, maybe even serve tea. If luck was with him, he might learn more from Day than the detective learned from him. But Fenn was here and the situation would be tense. Suppose the boy spoke up?

Day tried the front door and, when it didn't open for him, he peered in through the window, past Pringle's handprint, shading the glass with his own hands. Cinderhouse froze in the shadows. From the corner of his eye he watched Fenn. If the boy moved or called out now, Cinderhouse would have to take drastic action again. He wasn't sure he could overpower the policeman, but he could move fast enough to reach Fenn and make sure that his son wasn't taken from him. If he couldn't keep the boy, he would make sure that nobody else would either.

The detective moved away from the window. He shook his head and clambered back into the carriage.

Cinderhouse leapt across the room and grabbed Fenn by the upper arm. The boy protested, but there was no time to explain things. He shoved Fenn into a cupboard under the long counter with a slit in the top for cutting fabric. A small padlock fitted through two iron loops set into the wood and fastened the cupboard tight. He had used this cabinet to seal away the bleaches and dyes he used so that his first son wouldn't find them and hurt himself. It would work as well to keep the new son in place.

If there had been time, he would have given Fenn food and water, but he would be back within the hour.

He grabbed his hat and a pair of shears from a nearby drawer, then hurried out the door and locked it behind him. He looked for his regular hansom and remembered that he'd sent it away. A bright red coach rolled past and he flagged down the driver. He gave terse orders and hopped into the back as the horse was whipped into motion. Up ahead, the wagon carrying the policeman was still visible. The smaller, faster coach would have no trouble catching up to it.

Why had Day come to the shop? Had Cinderhouse overplayed his hand by going to them in the first place? Did the men of The Yard finally suspect that their official tailor was a murderer?

Cinderhouse shook his head. There was nothing to connect him to the murder. He would follow Day and, if necessary, dispatch him. If he had learned anything in the last few days, it was that the police were just as vulnerable as anyone else.

81

Fenn heard the tailor leave and he immediately began to explore. There wasn't a lot of room to work with in the cramped cupboard. He pushed on the door, but it only budged a fraction of an inch. The hinges felt solid. He knocked over a few bottles next to him. There was some sort of liquid in them, but Fenn didn't see how that would help him escape. He kicked at the wall to his left and heard a squeak. A moment later, something furry ran across Fenn's ankle and he jumped, banging his head against the counter above him.

He rubbed the top of his head and scrunched up against the opposite corner, as far away from the furry thing as he could get. After a while he realized that the rat – he was almost certain it was a rat – wasn't in the cabinet with him any more.

Wherever it had gone, maybe Fenn could follow.

He probed the corners of the cupboard with his fingers, feeling for any crack or hole. Nothing. He wiped his hands across the walls and then over the floor, moving from one end to the other, shifting his body to feel beneath himself. Three inches from the back wall he found a small, half-moon-shaped hole in the floor. He poked his finger into it cautiously, worried about rat bites, but there was nothing on the other side that he could feel. Just empty air.

He prodded the sides of the hole and ran his fingers along a crack that ran from the top of the hole to a point three inches from the wall next to him. The crack made a right angle and, three inches from the cupboard door, another right angle. He traced the crack all the way around the floor and established that there was some sort of panel in the bottom of the cabinet.

Fenn bent so that his back was against the ceiling of the cupboard and straddled the panel in the floor, his feet wedged against both walls. He was uncomfortable and his neck cramped, but he was excited too. He reached down, got a finger in the hole and pulled up. There was a wrenching sound and most of the floor came away. But now Fenn was pinned to the counter above by the edge of the trapdoor. He moved it back and forth, trying to find a way to move past it. Suddenly it gained weight as gravity took hold and he couldn't hang on to it any longer. He lost his balance and steadied himself with a palm against the cabinet doors. The trapdoor dropped away from him, down the hole, and crashed to the ground somewhere below.

Fenn eased himself down to a sitting position, his feet dangling through the opening, and turned his head back and forth, working the kinks out of his neck.

He had no idea how deep the hole went. If he dropped through it he might fall too far and be killed. But if he stayed in the cupboard, he knew that the tailor would eventually kill him. That was a certainty. And so the hole in the floor was the only hope he had.

He took a deep breath, held on to the far edge of the floor and scooted himself forward. He plummeted, stopped short by his grip on the floor, but he wasn't strong enough and his fingers were torn away from the narrow lip. He fell down into the darkness.

He hit the ground hard and felt his ankle twist under him. Pain seared up his leg and lodged behind his ribs. He gasped.

The darkness around him was complete, and beneath him was cold, hard-packed earth.

When he had caught his breath, he dragged himself forward and found the trapdoor where it had fallen. It was broken in half. Past it, he found a wall and followed it around the small enclosure. There were no openings that he could find, but mud at the base of the wall gave way to dense crumbly dirt and then to loose stones. Fenn scraped at the stones with his fingers until pebbles came away. He had no idea what was on the other side of the wall. Probably nothing but more dirt. Still, he had to try something.

He crawled back and retrieved half of the broken trapdoor. Back at the wall, he raised the door over his head and struck the splintered edge of it against the stones. More pebbles tumbled out on to the ground. He struck the wall again and larger stones fell away. Again and again he hit the wall with the stout piece of wood. When he felt he had made some progress, he jammed the end of the door into the small gash he'd created in the wall. He pushed down on the other end. Nothing happened. He sat on the edge of the door that was sticking out from the wall and bounced on it, putting his full weight on the makeshift lever. There was a tearing sound and a shower of stone and dirt sluiced away. Fenn breathed deep and smiled.

Another tearing sound. This time the stones above him fell straight away from the wall. Fenn felt a sudden intense pain in his leg and tried to pull back, but he couldn't move. His leg was caught.

He forced himself to remain calm. He closed his eyes and did his best to put the pain out of his mind.

Something furry ran up his arm and he screamed.

Fenn knew that the only person within earshot would be the tailor when Cinderhouse came back to the shop. But Fenn was a little boy and he wanted his parents. And so he screamed again.

82

Blackleg rapped on the door and waited. When there was no answer he took a flat strip of metal from his back pocket and inserted it between the door and the frame. He pushed on it until he heard a faint click. He put the metal bar back in his pocket and turned the knob. The door swung open.

'Here now, what're ye doin'?'

He turned and saw an old woman coming down the hall towards him. She was pointing her finger at him like a weapon.

'That's Mr Hammersmith's flat,' she said. 'And Mr Pringle's, too, only he ain't here no more, God bless him.'

Her finger flitted away from him long enough to make the sign of the cross, touching her forehead, then her heart and, quickly, her left and right shoulders. Immediately, she was pointing at him again. By now she was directly in front of him, her bony finger an inch from his nose.

Blackleg held his hands up, palms out.

'No worries, ma'am,' he said. 'We're friends, him and me.'

'You were a friend of Mr Pringle? I'm so sorry.'

'Don't know the bloke. But Hammersmith's me mate.'

He heard himself and smiled when he realized that he

was telling the truth. Who'd have guessed that he'd ever be friends with a bluebottle?

'Well,' the old lady said, 'I don't know about that.'

She looked him up and down, clearly taking in his grubby clothes and unkempt beard.

'I'm a policeman, ma'am.'

Blackleg had long practice in telling people what they wanted to hear. The lie came to him easily and he saw in her eyes that the old lady wanted to believe him.

'You don't look like a policeman,' she said.

'Thank you.'

He leaned in closer to her, which caused her to back up a step.

'What I do,' he said, 'is I dress up like as if I'm a lowlife and I mix in amongst them. Amongst that sort, I mean. They take me for one of their own and they tells me things as I can take back to Mr Hammersmith and the other police.'

'Why, how clever,' the old lady said. 'You certainly look convincing.'

'Thank you again, ma'am. I do try.'

'Well, I'm afraid Mr Hammersmith isn't at home today. I would have heard him on the stair.'

'Quite all right, ma'am. He gave me the key to the place and tol' me to wait here for 'im. I'm sure he'll be here soon enough.'

'Oh, I see.'

'Unless you has a problem with that. If it makes you uncomfortable, me hangin' about in the flat here lookin' like I do, lookin' I mean to say, like as if I'm a criminal, I understand most complete. I'd be happy to go on outside and wait at the door for him.'

'Oh, no,' the old lady said. 'That wouldn't do at all. No, you stay here and make yourself at home. I'm sure if Mr Hammersmith asked you here, then it isn't my place to say otherwise.'

Of course, she didn't want him loitering outside her building. That might make a bad impression on the neighbours.

'Well, you're uncommon gracious, ma'am. Most exactly like my own sainted mother.'

The old lady blushed and covered her mouth.

'My name is Mrs Flanders,' she said. 'I'm down the hall here, first door on the right. If you need anything at all, don't hesitate to ring the bell.'

'Thank you much, ma'am.'

She smiled and turned away.

'Ma'am?'

'Yes?'

The old woman paused with her hand on the wall.

'There's one more expected here today. 'Nother police like me who looks maybe a bit down at the heels as well.'

'A meeting here?'

'You might call it that.'

The old woman frowned.

'I don't care for business being conducted on my premises,' she said.

'It'll be just the one time. We don't like to meet at the station 'cause someone might see us there and connect the fact that we ain't really criminals.'

'Oh, I suppose that makes sense.'

'Yes, ma'am. So when he gets here, don't trouble yerself none. He can find his own way.'

'You're quite the gentleman, you are, regardless of appearance.'

'Thank you.'

She waved a hand at him and tottered down the hall. When she turned back to look at him, he nodded. She went back into her own flat and closed the door. Blackleg let out a deep breath and pushed Hammersmith's door open. He went in and closed it behind him.

Inside, the flat was even smaller than Blackleg's own place. He chuckled to think that a bluebottle probably made less money in a year than he did. Crime wasn't respectable, but it paid.

He checked the clock above the mantle and saw that he had nearly an hour before his guest was expected. There was a tin of tea beneath the clock and Blackleg opened it. He sniffed the contents and recoiled at the tang of copper in his nostrils. Renewed tea.

'Ah, well,' he said. 'Beggars can't be choosers, can they?'

With time to kill, he went in search of a kettle.

83

Inspector Blacker woke up as the hansom cab ground to a halt. It took him a long moment to realize where he was. His eyes felt gummy. He pulled the curtain aside and saw a low stone wall with a weeping willow drooping over it. The thin light through the window shone on Hammersmith, across from Blacker on the other bench. He was curled up with his neck bent at an awkward angle against the side of the carriage, snoring softly. Blacker grinned and rubbed the heels of his palms against his eyes, trying to massage the grit away.

He pulled the curtain shut again and opened the hansom door, leaving Hammersmith there to catch up on much-needed sleep. The coachman looked down at Blacker and tipped his hat.

'This the place, guv'nor?'

'I suppose it is.'

Blacker fished in his pocket for a coin, but the coachman held up a hand.

'No need, sir. Happy to do what I can for the police.'

'You're a gentleman.'

'You'll be wantin' me to wait till you're done here, then?'

'No need. Inspector Day, my colleague, I mean, will be along shortly with a police wagon. If you don't mind waiting until my friend wakes up, then you can be on your way.'

The coachman squinted at him.

'Sir?'

'He hasn't slept much lately.'

'All right, sir.'

'Thank you again.'

Blacker smiled and patted the side of the cab as he stepped into the street. He hurried across to the Shaw family's house just as the first drops of rain started to fall.

84

The coachman turned up his collar against the rain and watched as the detective crossed the road and knocked on the door of a large house, one of several identical homes joined in a row behind a decorative wrought-iron rail.

After a short wait the door was opened by an attractive woman. She and the detective spoke and the woman moved aside to allow him in. The door shut behind him.

The detective had babbled something about a sleeping friend, but it appeared the household was awake. The coachman didn't see a reason to wait. He had promised Mr Cinderhouse that he'd return to take him to the shop if it began to rain and now the light drizzle was turning into a sudden shower. The downpour was washing the fog away, but visibility wasn't improving and the coachman decided to hurry. Mr Cinderhouse wasn't one to be kept waiting. The coachman wouldn't admit it even to himself, but the tailor's temper scared him. He snapped the reins. The horse snorted and lurched forward and the hansom pulled away from the Shaw home.

The coachman thought about warm fires and dry socks and it never occurred to him that he might have a second passenger asleep inside the cab. Nor did he look back to see two women emerge from behind the drooping willow and scurry across the street in the pounding rain.

85

'Wasn't him.'

'Was, too, him. Saw him clear as day.'

'It's not clear as day though, is it? Can't see yer nose in front o' yer face in this rain.'

'Still, I know it was him.'

'Him wears a uniform like the other bobbies. This'un had a suit.'

'It was a uniform.'

Liza led the way down the steps to the sunken garden below ground level. She reached out her hand to steady Esme.

'Slippery here,' she said. 'Watcher step.'

At the bottom of the steps, Esme knelt in damp cedar mulch and peered into the basement through a tiny window. The room inside was dark. She reached out and pushed on the glass and the window swung up and open.

'Surprised they ain't fixed this yet.'

'Well, it's just her alone now. Somebody done kilt her husband so who's to fix the broken window?'

Esme smiled. She took her friend by the wrists and lowered her over the sill, then hiked up her skirt and swung a leg into the house. She dropped down beside Liza and put a finger to her lips. They both listened, staring at the gloom. Nobody came. Nobody had heard.

They helped each other to their feet and brushed the

wet wood chips from their clothes and wrung water from their skirts, letting it pool on the floor.

'They're up there,' Liza said. 'Hear 'em?'

'Hush,' Esme said.

But she could hear footsteps on the floor above. She smiled and when she spoke her voice was barely audible.

'I suppose we'll find out if it's Hammersmith up there or not.'

'Either way,' Liza said.

She withdrew a straight razor from somewhere in the folds of her skirt. The women held hands and closed their eyes in silent prayer. When they were ready, they approached the staircase on the far wall and started up, still holding hands in the dark.

86

Inspector Day stood outside the forbidding brass gates and looked up at the workhouse on the hill. Many of the city's workhouses were welcoming places where destitute members of the populace could get a simple meal and a berth for the night. In return, they were required to work three hours grinding corn or performing some other menial, and largely meaningless, task.

But Hobgate was for those who were determined to be vagrants, unable or unwilling to work and possibly violent. It was just a step away from the asylum for the poor and mentally crippled in south London, and it resembled a prison more than it did a shelter.

A guard unlocked the gate and swung it open for Day. He held a black umbrella and moved it over Day's head while they talked. Fat raindrops smacked against the waxed canvas above them and Day had to raise his voice to be heard.

'I'm with The Yard,' Day said.

'Pardon?'

'The Yard. I'm a detective with The Yard.'

'Yes, what can we do for you today, sir?'

'I'm looking for someone brought in yesterday.'

'Brought in, sir, or come in voluntary?'

'Brought in by police.'

'Man or woman?'

'Man.'

'Then he'd be in the men's ward. We don't separate 'em out as to how they come so he'd be mixed in with those what come in on their own.'

'Are there many of those?'

The guard chuckled.

'Well, not too many, no. Could be this is the same fellow the doctor's looking for as well?'

'Doctor?'

'Aye, sir. You've barely missed him. Come looking for someone not five minutes before you did.'

'I doubt we're here for the same reason. The man I'm looking for likes to perform. He dances. Have you seen him?'

'Can't say as I have, but I'm out here on the entrance. Might ask inside. Just follow the path up the hill and you'll find someone at the main building. Men's ward's on the first floor. Women and children are upstairs.'

'Thank you.'

'Might think to keep your stick handy. Sometimes they get out of line.'

'You hit them?'

The guard looked away.

'Only if they need it, sir.'

Day didn't know how to respond. He was appalled by the thought that the homeless in Hobgate might be abused, but he had no experience with the workhouse and no idea how dangerous the people here might be. Perhaps it was the guards who feared abuse.

He nodded at the guard and set off up the hill. The path twisted and the workhouse disappeared in the fog. The rain was coming down harder now and Day silently cursed himself for forgetting his own umbrella. The path was lined with small yew trees, all stripped of leaves and bark. Day wondered whether the trees had fallen victim to disease or to the Hobgate inmates. Ahead, the main building hove into view again, a dark stone block against the grey sky. There were no windows in its walls, only a huge oak door wrapped in iron bands.

Another guard was posted outside the door. He was talking to someone as Day approached. The second man had his back to Day and was holding a small black bag in one hand. Both men turned to look at Day.

'Dr Kingsley?' Day said.

'Detective!'

Kingsley seemed relieved to see him.

'What are you doing here?' Day said.

'I suspect I'm here for the same reason you are.'

'The dancing man?'

'Henry Mayhew, yes.'

'I'd like to get him out of here, if I can.'

'As would I.'

'Well, between the two of us . . .' Day grinned. He couldn't help himself. In the wagon on the way to the workhouse he'd wondered whether he was doing the right thing, whether sending a vagrant back to the streets ran counter to his responsibilities as a police officer. But if Kingsley had also made the trip to Hobgate, there must be some logical merit to the idea of letting Henry Mayhew live his life as he pleased.

'I didn't relish the thought of entering this place alone,' Kingsley said. 'I was trying to persuade this gentleman to accompany me inside when you arrived.'

He gestured towards the guard, who raised his umbrella and tipped his hat.

'Against regulations to leave my post here, sir. Unless there's a ruckus inside. Otherwise, I'd be proud to help.'

'I understand. Now that the detective is here, I think we'll be fine.'

'Good luck.'

The guard gave them a look that made Day nervous, then slid back a bolt on the door and opened it. He reached into a small antechamber just inside the open door and came out with two lanterns. He lit them from his cigarette and handed one to each of them.

'You'll need these in there,' he said.

Then the guard stood aside and let the two men move past him into the gloom of Hobgate.

The ground floor of the workhouse was one huge room, partitioned off into smaller chambers. The walls on both sides of the makeshift centre hallway had been hastily thrown up and were rough, so close that splinters snagged at the sleeves of their overcoats. Day inhaled through his mouth to avoid the stench of human waste and body odour. Every six feet there was a hole cut in each wall. A doorway without a door, so small that a grown man would have to crawl through it.

Day and Kingsley divided the hall, each of them

taking a side, and stooped to peer into each room that they passed. The lantern light cast long, moving shadows, but there was little else to see inside the chambers. They were all identical, two long platforms fastened to the walls and covered with straw, a walkway between them that ended at a second door-hole. Each platform was deep enough to sleep three men and the snores echoing throughout the hall were evidence that Hobgate had few vacancies. At the far end of each room was a chamber pot. A single sniff was enough to confirm that the pots were rarely emptied.

'This is inhumane,' Day said.

'Hardly unique in this city,' Kingsley said.

'What do you mean?'

'London is growing too fast for the poor and the dead, the children or the simple-minded to keep up. There is no place for any of them.'

'I hope that's not true.'

'You know that it is.'

Day sighed and changed the subject.

'I don't know how we're going to find him in this labyrinth. There's no rhyme or reason to anything here. Men are stacked like cordwood.'

'Let's try this, then,' Kingsley said.

He set his lantern on the floor and cupped his hands around his mouth.

'Henry Mayhew!' he said. 'Come out, Henry Mayhew!'

'I don't think he'll respond to that,' Day said. 'He's quite timid.'

'Have you another idea?'

Day raised his eyebrows.

'I might,' he said. 'Or at least, an addition to your own idea.'

Several heads had poked out from the holes along the walls. Men peered down the dark hall at them. Day didn't like the looks of most of them. He stuck out his chin and shouted.

'Henry Mayhew, your brother has sent us! We're here on Frank's behalf! Henry, Frank wants you to come out!'

More faces appeared along the length of the hall. From somewhere ahead, a place deep in the shadows, a rhythmic thumping began as something heavy moved towards them. Kingsley leaned close and whispered.

'Do you have your pistol on you, Inspector?'

'I do.'

'Are you a good shot?'

'I've never used it except to practise.'

'That's not particularly comforting.'

Day put his hand on the grip of his pistol but didn't draw it. Kingsley raised his lantern and both men braced themselves as the thumping drew closer. The heads along the passageway swivelled and disappeared back inside their chambers. Finally, a figure emerged from the darkness at the end of the hall and moved slowly forward. The swinging lantern created multiple shadows and Day pulled his gun partially from his belt.

'Where's Frank?'

'Is that Henry there?' Kingsley said. 'Are you Henry Mayhew?'

The dancing man moved into the circle of light cast by Kingsley's lantern and his shadows joined him, pooling at his feet. Without the shadows' imaginary bulk behind him, there was nothing intimidating about Henry Mayhew. If anything, he had shrunk in on himself over the course of the night.

'Where's Frank?' he said again.

'Frank couldn't come to see you today,' Day said. 'He sent us in his stead.'

'You gonna keep me safe from the messenger?'

'The messenger?'

'The messenger of the city. The one what left the scissors for you. He's here to kill me now.'

'Nobody wants to kill you, Henry.'

'The messenger does.'

'What makes you so certain?'

'He looks mad and he scares me.'

'Have you seen him again?' Day said.

'Yes.'

'Where?'

'Behind you.'

The dancing man pointed. Day turned, his lantern swinging wildly in the small space. The yellow light sent shadows looping and veering about the narrow hall, black doors like mouths in the dark. A shadow separated from the others and spun away, taking shape as a man in a dark suit and a tall black hat.

The man raised his hand and lantern light glittered off a pair of shears.

87

The notice in *The Times* was clear and to the point. An elderly couple had lost their chimneysweep and needed someone new for the job. Interested parties were to enquire first thing the following morning at the couple's flat.

Sam Pizer couldn't read letters, but he could read numbers and the bartender's daughter at The Whistle and Flute had read the advertisement aloud to Sam. Now he double-checked the address against the numbers on the kerb.

Lord only knew he needed the money that the job could bring. He had offered the coachman two and eleven for a new climber, but he didn't have it. And everything would be much harder if the police kept coming round to harass him. It might be impossible to find a new boy on his own, which made his connection with the coachman his only real hope.

He hoisted his bucket of brushes and rags and rang the bell next to a confectioner's shop. He heard a shuffling noise and then the door cracked open and a sliver of an old woman's face appeared there.

'What is it you want?' she said. 'It's early yet.'

Sam tipped his hat and smiled.

'Pardon the hour, ma'am, but your notice said to come round about now.'

'Notice?'

'For a sweep? In yesterday's *Times*?'

'Didn't put a notice in. Must've been Mr Hammersmith.'

'Your husband, ma'am?'

The old woman blushed and put a hand to her mouth.

'Oh, my, no. He's a tenant.'

'I see. May I come in?'

She stepped aside, but didn't open the door all the way. He had to walk in sideways in order to get the bucket of tools past her. Looking around, he found himself in a small entrance room with a dark staircase ahead.

'Just upstairs?' he said.

'Yes.'

She peered up at him and stuck a finger in the air.

'I know who you are.'

'You do?'

'You're no sweep at all, are you?'

'But I am, ma'am.'

She winked at him.

'You look like a sweep would look, but there's something not quite right, I think. But never you mind. Your secret's safe with me . . .' She paused and leaned forward, looked over her shoulder at the empty hall behind them and whispered '. . . officer.'

Sam blinked at her, but said nothing. He'd encountered his fair share of dotty old bats in his time.

'Head on up. It's there at the end of the hall. The second flat. He's waiting for you.'

Sam nodded and hoisted his bucket, getting a better

grip. He started up the staircase and turned back when the old lady hissed at him.

'Never mind what I said before,' she said. 'You're quite convincing.'

Sam shook his head and trudged up the remaining stairs to the top. The old lady followed him and broke off to scurry into a flat. Sam moved on to the door at the far end of the hall and rapped lightly on the jamb.

'Come in,' a man's voice said.

Sam Pizer used his free hand to turn the knob and he stepped inside the flat. He closed the door behind him.

88

The coachman pried open a window and let himself into the tailor's house. He checked it thoroughly, but Cinderhouse wasn't there and neither was the boy. He'd hoped to find Fenn in a cupboard somewhere. He could take him, sell him to Sam Pizer the chimneysweep, and Cinderhouse would simply assume that the boy had escaped again. A neat profit for the coachman, and with no consequences to worry about.

Next, the coachman went round to the tailor's shop, but it appeared to be empty as well. Just to be sure, the coachman felt along the top of the doorframe, where he knew Cinderhouse kept a key. He unlocked the door and went inside. He almost locked the door behind him, but decided that he'd only be there for a minute. The shop was clearly deserted.

The tailor's white cat rubbed against his leg. It dropped something at his feet and sat back, looked up at him and purred. The coachman bent to look at the object and recoiled when he realized it was a dead rat. He kicked at the cat and missed, and the damned thing trotted away, its tail in the air.

The coachman ignored the rat at his feet and tried to focus. He couldn't think where the tailor might be. Surely he wouldn't take a walk in the rain with the boy. Of course he could have hired another carriage, but it wasn't the sort of day for an outing, was it?

He had just decided to give up and head back to his own home and a nice warm cuppa when he heard something, a faint and faraway noise. He cocked his head and listened and heard it again.

It sounded like someone yelling for help.

The coachman poked his head out the front door, but heard nothing outside over the rushing sound of the rain. Inside again, he wandered about the shop, keeping his ears open, aware that the sound might be nothing more than the mewling of the white cat. But again and again he heard the small, muffled voice shouting for help.

He opened cupboard doors and toppled mannequins over, ripped curtains from the walls and pulled drawers out of the wardrobes on the back wall. Finally, he pried off a rusted padlock and opened the cupboard doors beneath the long counter in the middle of the room.

There, in the floor of the cupboard, was a large, square hole. He guessed that it was the entrance to some abandoned root cellar. It was possible that the tailor's shop had once been a residence and, when it had been converted to a business, the cellar had been covered over and finally forgotten.

The coachman stuck his head inside the cupboard and yelled. 'Hullo! Is someone down there?'

There was a moment of silence and then a small voice. 'Please help me! My foot is stuck!'

It was the boy.

The coachman smiled. It was his lucky day. The child had been left there alone.

'I'll have you out in a jiffy, boy. Hold tight and I'll be back.'

'Don't leave me,' the boy said. 'There are rats here and I'm afraid they're hungry.'

'They might be at that. Don't you move, now.'

The coachman searched the shop and, when he didn't find any rope, tore part of a bolt of linen into long strips. He tied the strips together and secured one end around the sewing machine that was bolted to the counter. He tossed the other end down the hole in the floor.

'Ready or not, here I come,' he said.

He lowered himself into the coal-black cellar.

89

Mrs Flanders looked up from her magazine. She'd been so absorbed in the story she was reading that she couldn't be sure she'd heard anything at all. She listened carefully. Just as she gave up and returned to the story there came a strangled cry and a thump from the flat next door.

She waited several moments, but heard nothing more.

She clucked her tongue at the wall. *Boys will be boys*, she thought. But she would have to ask Mr Hammersmith to hold his police meetings elsewhere. Hers was a respectable building and she couldn't have riffraff traipsing in and out and horsing about making noise, even if they weren't really riffraff but were actually policemen in disguise. The neighbours didn't know that.

She shook her head and turned her attention back to the latest edition of *Cassell's*. There was a new story about a gentleman thief and it was absolutely thrilling, even if it wasn't particularly true to life.

90

Inside, the hansom cab was dark and dry and Hammersmith came gradually awake, feeling refreshed and more completely himself than he had in the past two days. His mouth was dry and tasted like dirt.

Blacker wasn't in the cab with him. Hammersmith assumed the detective had decided to let him sleep. He pulled the curtain aside and felt immediately disorientated. The rain had picked up and visibility was low, but he could see well enough and the Shaw residence was nowhere in evidence. Nor were the willow tree or the stone wall across the street. Whichever direction the cab faced, Hammersmith felt he ought to see something familiar.

He opened the door and stepped out into the storm. He was immediately soaked to the bone. He turned his face to the sky and opened his mouth, swished the rainwater around and spat it out in the street. His mouth felt and tasted marginally better.

He was in front of the tailor's shop. He'd been here with Pringle many times before. How long had he been asleep? Had Blacker finished the interview with Penelope Shaw and moved on?

He tried the door and it swung open. Inside the shop he shook his overcoat out and ran a hand through his hair to stop the water running into his eyes. The place appeared to be empty. Blacker was nowhere to be seen.

Hammersmith couldn't see many places a grown man might hide in the little shop. He felt something at his ankle and looked down to see a cat rubbing against him. He stooped to pet it.

The cat was white and fluffy and some of its hair clung to his wet fingers. There was a small, hard nugget in the cat's coat and Hammersmith prodded at it while the cat undulated and purred. When he plucked the speck from its fur, the cat yowled. It grabbed his hand between its paws and bit down on the web between his thumb and index finger. He yanked his hand away and the cat ran off.

Hammersmith frowned at the tiny bead he was holding. It was dark brown and there were cat hairs stuck to it. He was certain it was blood.

Day had said something about cat hairs. Something about Pringle's trousers.

He let the crumb of dried blood fall to the floor and stood, wiping his fingers on the leg of his trousers. The stillness of the shop felt eerie to him, now. At his feet, the tangle of white fur bound in blood might well have been an omen. And now the shop came into focus for him, wardrobes flung open, drawers pulled from cabinets, something tied to the sewing machine on the counter.

He approached the sewing machine. A homemade rope of knotted linen was wrapped around its base. He ran his finger under it and traced it across the countertop and to the other side, where it disappeared through a trapdoor inside a cabinet. He knelt by the opening and listened. Nothing.

'Hello?' he said.

Still nothing.

He looked around, but he was alone.

Inspector Blacker had apparently abandoned him in a cab at the kerb. There was no sign of Blacker now, nor were there any traces of the cab driver or the tailor whose shop this was. Something had clearly happened while Hammersmith slept and the only clue he had was this makeshift rope and a trapdoor in the floor. It was entirely possible that Blacker was somewhere below, possibly injured. Possibly worse.

Without another thought he slung his leg over the side of the hole and began to lower himself down.

The coachman's hand was clamped tight over Fenn's mouth and it partially covered his nostrils. He was having trouble breathing and the hand smelled of horses and meat pies and grease.

Above them, Fenn could hear footsteps on the floor of the tailor's shop. He listened, wide-eyed, as someone stomped about the shop and finally came to the trapdoor in the cupboard.

'Hello,' someone said.

The voice echoed down and around the cave under the floor. It wasn't the tailor's voice.

The coachman hissed in Fenn's ear.

'I got a knife here. You make a sound, any sound at all, and I'll cut you ear to ear.'

After a moment, what little light filtered through the cellar entrance was blocked and Fenn heard someone thumping against the wooden floor above.

Fenn knew that, whatever the coachman's plans for him, he wouldn't like them. If he had a chance at rescue or escape, that chance would disappear if he waited. He stuck his tongue out and licked the coachman's hand. The coachman reacted, shifting position just a hair, but it was enough that Fenn was able to get a fold of the man's palm between his teeth. He bit down as hard as he could. Flesh rolled and crunched between his teeth and the coachman screamed.

When the hand was yanked away, Fenn shouted as loud as he could. 'He's got a knife!'

The coachman's other hand covered his mouth again and Fenn couldn't say anything more. He hoped he had been heard and understood.

There was the sound of someone dropping to the ground and the vague outline of a man against the dim grey light from the shop above. And then the man moved to the side and disappeared into the shadows without a word.

Fenn felt the coachman's lips against his ear.

'I'm gonna take care of him and then I'll be back for you,' the driver said. 'You're gonna be sorry you done what you did, boy. I'll get my money for you and then we'll see what's what.'

And Fenn was alone again, his leg still trapped under the stones of the collapsed wall, too scared to call out, unable to do anything except wait.

91

The dancing man was clinging to Inspector Day and he wouldn't stop shouting, his voice echoing in the enclosed men's ward of Hobgate.

'Stop him! Stop the messenger!'

Men had begun to crawl out of their tiny rooms all along the hall, responding to the noise. Day caught a brief glimpse of the man Henry called 'the messenger' before he melted back through an empty doorway at the end of the hall.

'Take Henry to safety,' Day said.

Kingsley nodded and grabbed the dancing man's arm. He led him quickly down the dark hall, away from Day and away from the messenger. They were quickly swallowed by shadows.

Day raced in the opposite direction, dodging past men in their nightshirts. He ducked through the hole the messenger had gone into. A man with one ear and a slit for a nose was sitting up on his bunk, his eyes wide. On seeing Day, he pointed at the door in the opposite wall. Day nodded and darted through into a hallway that was identical to the one he'd just left. He heard the clatter of running footsteps and held the lantern up. He saw the swirl of a dark cloak, a tall hat, and then the messenger passed beyond the reach of the lamp's light.

Day found his whistle and blew a warning note that echoed down the hall, gathering in volume. The sound brought men to add to the swelling mob in the hall. Day rushed forward, elbowing his way down the narrow hall, and caught glimpses of the messenger moving ahead of him, weaving through the crowd.

Someone shouted, 'I got him!' and there was a shriek.

The milling men moved aside and Day stopped suddenly, a dark shape on the floor at his feet. He held his lantern up. A bleeding man was slumped against the wall. He was pale and silent, trembling. He looked at Day, his eyes wide and darting.

'Are you all right?' Day said.

The man nodded.

'Let me see it.'

The man held out his arm. There was a deep puncture wound through his forearm. Blood trickled out, but it didn't gush. It wasn't a fatal injury.

'Put your other hand here where mine is. Hold it there. You . . .'

Day pointed at one of the other men who stood watching.

'Help him. Take your shirt off and press down on the wound.'

He moved aside and let the man kneel next to his peer.

'There's a doctor here on the premises,' Day said. 'Somewhere here. I'm going to find him and send him back here to help. Just wait until he gets here.'

The bleeding man nodded again and Day stood.

'You others, spread the word. Everybody needs to stay in their rooms. Don't crowd the halls. I know you want to help, but you'll only be underfoot. This man is armed with a sharp weapon and he will use it.'

There was a murmur of assent, but nobody moved. Day shook his head.

'Did anyone see which way he went?'

Several men pointed at one of the many interchangeable dark openings in the wall. Day crouched and moved through the hole into a room. It was empty. There was yet another hole in the opposite wall and beyond that, darkness.

He realized he was completely lost now, turned around in the labyrinthine interior of the workhouse. There was nothing to do but move forward. He crossed the tiny room and edged out into the darkness of the second hallway beyond.

92

Hammersmith heard someone shouting. A woman – or was it a boy? – yelled, 'He's got a knife!' There was a scuffling sound and silence.

Hammersmith dropped from the linen rope and moved sideways into the darkness of what seemed to be an abandoned root cellar. There were at least two people in the cellar with him. He pulled the truncheon from his belt and held it down at his side. He squatted against the stone wall, making as small a target of his body as he could, and he listened.

He heard scuffling across the dirt floor, but before he could pinpoint the direction of the sound he felt something furry brush against his ankle. In an instant he was little Nevil Hammersmith again, miles underground in a tunnel, surrounded by rats and by the never-ending dark.

He drew his knees up to his chest and held them against his body. The furry thing rubbed against him, doubled back and rubbed against him again. He reached out for it.

The cat pressed up against his hand and purred. He rubbed its back and felt its tail coil around his hand as it turned in circles. He listened for the cart coming down the tunnel with its load of coal, the pony plodding ahead of it. He would need to open the trapdoor when it arrived.

Instead, he heard the scuffling sound again and it

brought him back to the present. He was a policeman in the biggest city in the world. He had realized his childhood dream of escape and would never have to enter a coalmine again in his life. He shook his head, willing the past away, along with the last lingering effects of sleeplessness and poison.

The cat would give away his position. He picked it up and stroked its head by way of apology and then threw it across the cave. He heard it land and scamper away, and he hoped that his unseen opponent had heard it too.

Crouching, he crept towards where he'd heard the cat land. He kept his hands out in front of him, moving them slowly back and forth, sliding his feet forward a few inches at a time so that he wouldn't trip over anything. He concentrated on breathing, quietly, deliberately. He was a shadow among shadows.

After what seemed an eternity his hand brushed against something solid and he pulled back just in time. He heard a person turn and felt a breeze beside him as something whistled by, missing him by a whisker.

He struck out and hit nothing but air. Off balance, he stumbled forward and caught himself before he fell. He grunted as his knee came down hard on the packed dirt.

Immediately he felt the breeze again. It was followed by a burning sensation in his forearm. Something warm and wet ran down his arm. He was cut.

He rolled to the side and stayed low, crawling as quietly as he could around and back to where he'd been. He swept the area near him with one foot, keeping his centre of balance low and stable. Nothing. He moved to his right and tried again. This time his foot hit something solid. There was a cry and someone hit the ground hard.

Hammersmith was on the other man immediately. Here was a torso and Hammersmith quickly found the man's arms, pinning them to the ground with one forearm before the knife could cut him again. The man grunted and tried to roll away. Hammersmith jabbed down as hard as he could with his free elbow and felt ribs give way beneath him. The other man cried out and Hammersmith aimed his fist at the sound, hitting something solid enough to be a skull. There was another grunt.

From his semi-sitting position Hammersmith sprang up and came back down on the man's body. He heard a crack and a cry of pain and lashed out at the man's head again. This time, he felt his own knuckle break, but the other man's skull snapped back and he went silent.

Hammersmith found the man's throat and felt for a pulse. It was strong. He sat back against the stone wall and caught his breath. He kept his good hand on the unconscious man to make sure he didn't move. His other hand felt like it was on fire and his arm throbbed, but he was alive and when he checked his arm he found that the wound had already stopped bleeding.

'Is someone there?' he said. 'I know there's someone else down here.'

He waited, but there was only silence. When his own breathing had calmed, he listened and heard someone else's breath there in the cave.

'I can hear you,' Hammersmith said. 'The man with the knife is unconscious. He can't hurt anybody. You're safe now.'

'I'll be good,' came a small voice from the other side of the cellar. It sounded like a young boy. 'Don't hurt me.'

'I won't hurt you. I promise. I'm a policeman and I'm here to help you. What's your name?'

'Fennimore.'

'Fennimore, do you know the name of the man with the knife?'

'No.'

'Was he threatening you?'

'I won't run any more. You can tell him.'

'He can't hear us. He's asleep.'

'Not him. Tell the other one, the bald man. Tell him he can be my father for ever if he wants.'

'Fennimore, were you being kept down here?'

'No. I ran down here and now I'm stuck.'

Hammersmith removed his shirt and used it to tie the unconscious man's hands together. It occurred to him that he was running out of shirts. It also occurred to him that he was beneath a tailor's shop. There would be more shirts above. He ought to be able to make himself presentable again once he left the cellar. It wouldn't do to be seen in his undershirt.

He patted the ground in widening circles, searching for the knife that had dropped during the scuffle. When his fingers touched cold metal, he found the handle and picked the knife up and stuck it in the waistband of his trousers, against his back.

He crawled towards the sound of the boy's steady breathing. When he touched what felt like the boy's shoulder, there was a cry of fear.

‘It’s all right, Fennimore. Do your friends call you Fennimore?’

‘They call me Fenn.’

‘Is it all right if I call you Fenn, too?’

‘Yes.’

‘Just now you said that the bald man could be your father. Do you know the bald man’s name?’

‘It’s Cinderhouse, sir. His name is Cinderhouse.’

‘The tailor?’

‘Yes, sir. Please tell him I won’t run away any more.’

‘Is he your father?’

‘He can be. It’s okay now.’

Hammersmith hesitated. He wasn’t sure what was going on, but he didn’t like the sound of it.

‘Are you tied up, Fenn?’

‘No, sir. My leg’s stuck under some rocks.’

‘Is it all right if I touch your leg and try to free it from the rocks?’

‘Yes, sir.’

Hammersmith nodded, though he knew the boy couldn’t see him. Fenn’s ankle was lodged under a small landslide of rocks and dirt. It would take some effort, but the stones were loose and Hammersmith began to work at them, moving them aside one at a time.

‘Do you have another father, Fenn? Someone before Cinderhouse?’

‘Yes, but I’m not supposed to talk about him. Or about my mother, neither.’

‘Fenn, did they sell you to the tailor?’

‘No, sir. He took me in the street.’

Hammersmith sighed and worked harder on the stones trapping the boy.

'Fenn, that was a bad thing to do. When I get you free from here, we're going to find your father, your real father, and your mother, too, and return you to them.'

The boy sat perfectly still. He began to breathe faster.

'And we're going to put Mr Cinderhouse in jail. He won't bother you again.'

'He won't get out of jail?'

'I won't let him get out.'

'Are you really a policeman?'

'Yes, I am.'

'The other policeman didn't help me. But the fat one tried to. Mr Little tried to help me before Mr Cinderhouse done him.'

'Did you say Mr Little?'

The stones were coming loose faster, now that he'd moved the largest of them out of the way.

'Yes, sir. It's my fault I didn't tell him about Mr Cinderhouse. Don't let Mr Cinderhouse stab you, too.'

'I won't, Fenn. Mr Cinderhouse won't ever hurt anyone again. Sit still and I'll have you free in another moment and then we'll get out of here.'

The boy wiggled his ankle and dirt sifted away from his leg.

'I'm almost free already,' Fenn said.

'We'll have you back with your parents in no time at all,' Hammersmith said.

He took a deep breath and yanked another stone loose.

93

'I know you,' the dancing man said.

'Yes,' Kingsley said. 'We've met on several occasions now.'

They were wandering down a dark hallway in Hobgate workhouse. Kingsley held up the lantern and watched ahead of them as shadows played up the walls and disappeared into the dark hollows of low open doorways that led into too-small rooms. Kingsley had allowed himself to get turned around and had no idea where the exit was or how long they had been zigzagging through the make-shift tunnels of Hobgate. They had seen occasional faces peering out from the open doors, furtive men who disappeared immediately back into darkness. The great crowds of men had scurried into their rat holes as soon as word spread that police were on the premises.

'Did I dance for you?'

'No,' Kingsley said. 'You haven't danced for me. Why do you dance?'

'Because I have to help. Dancing helps make people happy.'

'You want to be of use? Is that it?'

'Helping, yes.'

'Henry . . . May I call you Henry? Henry, you were once very good to me. You showed me a small but significant kindness when I came to the morgue, or rather to where the morgue used to be. My wife had only just passed away of consumption and I was very sad. Do you remember that?'

'I remember the dead people.'

'Yes, one of them was my Catherine.'

'That was a bad place. The people had no room. There was no room for dancing there.'

'I agree with you. The dead are in a new place now, a place where I help their families find them and, perhaps, find some justice too.'

'That's good. I do remember you. Your lady wanted a flower.'

Kingsley smiled.

'Yes, you gave her a sprig of ivy and you covered her with a blanket.'

'That made you happy.'

'It did.'

Kingsley cleared his throat, unsure of how to proceed. Henry Mayhew was a large man, but his mind was that of a child. Kingsley wanted to make him an offer, but he wasn't sure if Mayhew would understand what was being given and wasn't even sure it was a good idea to make the offer in the first place.

He opened his mouth to speak and was interrupted by a gunshot somewhere behind them. Henry jumped and clung to the wall. Kingsley spun around and held up the lantern, but could see nothing. Two more shots echoed through the workhouse and Kingsley turned again. He took Henry by the elbow and guided him down the hall as quickly as they could move.

Kingsley was holding his black bag and his lantern in

the same hand and the bag was causing the lantern to swing back and forth, creating treacherous shadows and knocking the bag back into his ribs with each step. He had just come to the conclusion that he didn't need to guide Henry Mayhew down the hall and could free that hand up to carry one thing or the other, when he tripped over something and dropped the lantern.

The something he had tripped over hollered and he realized it was a man, sprawled out on the floor. Kingsley reached for the lantern, which was miraculously still lit.

'You should be in your room,' he said. 'There's a madman on the loose here.'

'Heh. Yeah, there's a lot of madmen on the loose here, mister. One of 'em got me already.'

Kingsley held the lantern up and let the pale light wash over the man on the floor. He was young and burly and unkempt, and lying in a small pool of black liquid that Kingsley took to be blood.

'What's happened?' Kingsley said. He was already on one knee in front of the young man, his black bag open. He rummaged through it, setting one thing after another on the floor between them.

'Mad bloke stabbed me with a scissors and ran off. The policeman gave chase after helpin' me a bit. After a while everybody sort of wandered off and left me here to bleed. Don't blame 'em. Not too interestin' to watch a man bleed after the first few minutes.'

'That policeman is my friend. Was he all right? Was he stabbed, too?'

'Don't think so. I was tryin' to help him out, what got me stabbed.'

Kingsley washed out the puncture wound and dressed it.

'The wound is deep,' he said, 'but you haven't lost too much blood.'

'You a doctor?'

'You'd better hope I am.'

'How bad is it?'

'You're lucky inasmuch as the instrument used, the shears used to stab you, seem to have been reasonably clean of dirt or rust, so that may help with your recovery. And it was sharp enough that you may avoid getting lockjaw.'

'Lockjaw?'

'Yes. A dull weapon may sometimes bruise a nerve and cause excruciating death. We call this lockjaw.'

'But I ain't gonna get that?'

'We'll know soon enough. It's imperative that we get you back to my hospital so I can dress that wound properly. It needs a poultice. For now, the detective did a good job of staunching the blood and this wrap will keep it from bleeding too badly.'

'You gonna leave me here?'

'Certainly not. Let's get you to your feet.'

'I don't know if I can.'

'The injury wasn't to your legs. You can stand and walk.'

'Mr Doctor?' Henry said. 'I can carry him.'

Henry bent and lifted the injured man as if he were an empty suit. The man yelped and sucked in a quick lungful of air.

'Careful with him, Henry. I'd like to keep this one alive.'

Henry nodded and stood waiting. The man put his uninjured arm around Henry's thick neck while Kingsley repacked his bag. He lifted the bag and the lantern and, with a nod to Henry, turned and led the way down the hall, this time with renewed purpose. There was an injured man relying on him to find a way out of the workhouse.

In moments they came to a low door. The door was bolted and the bolt had been padlocked. It was the first true door Kingsley had seen since they'd entered Hobgate – the entrances to the men's rooms were nothing but open holes in the walls.

'If this isn't an exit, we've reached a dead end,' he said. 'So I'm going to assume for the sake of sanity that it's an exit. But I'm afraid we'll have to turn back anyway.'

Without a word, Henry set the injured man down and grabbed the bolt with both hands. He braced his feet against the jamb on either side of the door and pulled. There was a low groaning noise that reverberated through the walls and down the hallway behind them.

'I think it's too strong for you,' Kingsley said.

Henry looked at him and grinned. He tensed his shoulders, set his feet again and heaved backwards, his entire upper body pitched out into the hall so that he was nearly horizontal with the floor. The bolt wrenched away from the door with a terrific rasp and a crack and a shower of splinters.

Henry stumbled, but didn't fall. He tossed the fractured bolt into the darkness behind them and stopped to pick the injured man back up. Kingsley threw the door open and smiled at the grey-filtered sunlight and the spattering rain outside.

'Look what you did,' he said.

He turned, blocking the exit. He wanted to say the thing he'd come here to say before he lost his nerve. 'Henry, I'd like to put you to work.'

'I'm at the workhouse already and I don't like it.'

'No, I don't see how anyone could like it here. But I don't mean the workhouse. I mean that I'd like you to come to my laboratory. There are things I could have you do there.'

'Would I dance?'

'If you wanted to. But there are more substantial things you could do, too. You showed respect for the dead on that day I visited you. That kind of respect isn't something I see in most people.'

'Can they sleep at your laboratory? The dead, I mean. Can they sleep? There wasn't enough room for them at the morgue place and they couldn't rest.'

Kingsley remembered the short tables and the breeze moving through the open shed where the bodies were stored. He remembered the cold, pale legs hanging down in the central aisle, moving in the wind, running in place.

'Yes, there's room for them to rest now.'

'I'll look at it.'

'Good. I can't pay you much. My current assistant is my daughter and she takes no salary, but I'd like to find something else for her to do. I'm not sure it's a good place for her to be any more.'

He realized he was speaking to someone who didn't understand and wouldn't care. He chuckled.

'Anyway,' he said, 'I'll bring you to the place and you can decide for yourself. I think having you there might be good for us both.'

'You should do it,' the injured man said. 'Can't be any worse'n here.'

Henry nodded and smiled.

'It's settled, then,' Kingsley said. 'Now, let's get out of this place.'

He stepped aside and waved Henry through into the fresh morning air. Before he followed, he blew out the flame and set his lantern on the floor.

94

'What's all this, then?'

Inspector Day turned and held his lantern up. The guard from the entrance of the workhouse was approaching with his gun drawn.

'I'm a detective with The Yard,' Day said. 'Do you remember me?'

'Yes, that I do, sir. What's happening in here?'

'There's a homicidal madman somewhere in the building. He's extremely dangerous and armed with scissors.'

'Did you say he has scissors, sir?'

'Yes. He's a killer and he's already injured at least one person here.'

'What can I do to help?'

'The injured man is somewhere back there, behind me. Do you have any medical knowledge? Or is there a doctor here somewhere?'

The guard shook his head.

'Only the one doctor what come in with you, sir. I've got this pistol though, if that can be of service to you.'

'Perhaps it can at that. The man we're looking for has escaped down this hall. I don't know in which direction he's gone. He's tall, dressed expensively in a dark suit and cloak. He has a tall hat, if it hasn't been jostled off by now. His appearance is quite different from that of anyone else you'll find in this place. You go that way and I'll go this. Fire your pistol if you encounter him and I'll come running.'

'Yes, sir. Good luck, sir.'

'And to you.'

Day watched the guard hustle away in the other direction and he shook his head, wonderingly. At least there was one person in all of London who respected the bloody Yard.

He drew his Colt from his pocket and moved down the hall. The lantern light didn't penetrate far into the warren of cubbyholes. His whistle and the screaming of the injured man had turned the rest of the inmates shy. There weren't many men showing themselves in the narrow tunnel. At every opening where there wasn't evidence of a tenant, Day thrust the lantern inside and surveyed the room. It was slow going.

He was finishing his search of the fifth room on the westernmost side of the tunnel when he heard a gunshot somewhere behind him. He listened, waiting for the echoes to subside, and heard another, followed immediately by a third. He dashed out of the room and retraced his steps.

He found the young guard face down in the hall near the entrance. He knelt and turned the guard over, but the man was dead. Blood seeped from a series of deep stab wounds up and down his torso. As Day watched, the flow of blood slowed to a trickle. He closed his eyes and said a short and silent prayer for the soul of the slain guard. A moment later, he was on his feet and running. There was a trail of blood, small dots that glistened yellow in the light of the lantern. They grew smaller as the trail lengthened and Day guessed that the killer had not been wounded. The blood was dripping from his scissors.

But Day hadn't found the guard's gun and that could mean the messenger had it now. The danger had doubled.

The bloody trail ended at the entrance to one of the small rooms. Day kept to one side and reached slowly into the room. He set his lantern on the floor and put both hands on his gun. He ducked into the room and swept the gun back and forth. It was empty. Something silvery glinted in the lamplight. Day moved some straw aside on the right-hand berth and found a pair of bloody shears. He wrapped them in his handkerchief and stuck them in his back pocket. Like the other rooms, there was a door on this side and another on the far wall, leading to yet another hallway. Day picked up his lantern and crept past the parallel berths to the second door. He crouched against the wall and peered out into the hall.

There was a sound behind him and he turned in time to glimpse the swirl of a dark cloak as a man leapt out from under the straw that covered the other berth. The guard's gun went off and Day ducked. The lantern shattered. Day was already moving as he heard the crack of the shot and the tinkle of glass. He leapt forward, but the killer was gone.

Day rushed into the hall he'd come from. Up ahead, he could hear the clatter of shoes against the rough wood of the floor. There was a muffled cry and a thump. Day hurried forward and tripped when he came to a staircase that led up into more darkness. At a landing halfway up he found a guard, slumped unconscious, his head sagging off a step. Day checked and found a faint pulse. He adjusted the guard's head, hoping to make him more comfortable, and moved carefully up the stairs, sliding his back against the wall, his gun ready at his side.

At the top of the stairs was a closed door. Day reached out and slowly turned the knob. When he heard the latch disengage, he flung the door open and threw himself through the doorway on to the floor.

The room Day found himself in was lit by dozens of candles on every side and an open window on the far wall. Outside, the day was grey and rain pattered against the windowsill. Curtains stirred softly and a cool mist wafted in on the breeze.

He was in the upstairs ward for women and children. The guard on the stairs had no doubt been put there to keep the men below from paying unwelcome visits. Mothers were backed up in a semicircle, hiding their little ones behind their skirts. Day looked the room over quickly, his weapon at the ready. There were beds set up in rows along the walls, plain straw mattresses, but nicer than the men's barracks downstairs. Day dropped to one knee and glanced along the floor under the rows. Nobody hiding under a bed.

'A man,' he said. 'Was a man here?'

One of the women, her eyes wide with fear, pointed to the open window and nodded.

He stood and went to the window and looked out. Inside the workhouse, he had nearly forgotten that it was still daytime. Beneath him, a wet stone path ended at a dark line of trees only a few paces from this side of the building. There was no sign of the killer. Day cursed himself silently and slipped the Colt back into his pocket.

Three men, one of them carrying another, came into sight below. The smallest of the men was carrying a black bag. He stepped out on to the path and looked around, then up. He saw Day peering over the sill and smiled.

'Inspector,' he said.

'Dr Kingsley.'

The big man looked up now, revealing himself to be Henry Mayhew. The dancing man grinned and nodded. Day half-heartedly nodded back. The third man looked familiar, but Day couldn't place him until he noticed the stained bandages around his arm. It was the fellow who had tried to stop the killer and been stabbed for his trouble.

'Did you catch him?' Kingsley said. He was shouting. 'The madman with the shears? Did you catch him?'

'I think he jumped out of this window just moments ago. He's long gone by now.'

Day pointed at the trees and Kingsley turned to look.

'Well,' Kingsley said, 'if he dropped from that window, he may well have hurt himself.'

'Still, he's too far away by now.'

'Maybe you can catch him when he comes back,' Henry said.

'Why would he come back? He's got clean away.'

'But he left his hat. Maybe he'll come back for it.'

Henry set the injured man down against the side of the building so that Day could no longer see anything of him but his legs. Henry stooped and reached for something there out of Day's line of sight. He held up the tall black hat Day had seen the killer wearing.

'Without this,' Henry said, 'the rain will make him extra wet.'

'Why is that, Henry?'

'Because he's bald. Didn't you know?'

95

'But why come to The Yard looking for you?' Kingsley said. 'Why follow you to Hobgate?'

'I don't know,' Day said. 'Perhaps he was checking on my progress, worried that we might break the case and catch him.'

'Or perhaps you were his next intended victim.'

Day nodded, but didn't say anything. The thought had occurred to him and he preferred not to dwell on it.

'I nearly forgot,' Day said. 'I found these in one of the rooms.'

He produced his handkerchief and unwrapped the pair of shears from the workhouse.

'They appear to be an identical match to the first pair,' Kingsley said. 'Two pairs of shears. A tailor indeed. May I keep these?'

'Of course. I'd hoped you could tell me something about them when you have a chance to return to your laboratory. You know, if he'd only kept to himself we might never have found him, but the fool keeps throwing evidence at us.'

'You'd have found him regardless.'

'Perhaps.'

'Thank you for not leaving me there,' Henry Mayhew said.

'Of course,' Kingsley said. He deposited the shears

in his black bag and turned in his seat so he could see Henry more easily. 'I could hardly leave my new assistant at the workhouse.'

'I wish this carriage would hurry,' Day said.

As he spoke, the carriage ground to an abrupt halt. Kingsley peered out through the curtains.

'I believe this is the place,' he said.

The three of them alighted from the police wagon and Day took a moment to instruct the driver. Then he held up a hand to stop Kingsley, who had stepped up to the door of the little shop.

'You wait here,' Day said. 'If he's come back here, there may be danger.'

Kingsley nodded and backed up. He waited in the dancing man's shadow as Day tried the door. It swung open easily. A white cat darted through the door, skirted a puddle and disappeared around the corner. Day raised his eyebrows and entered the shop, his Colt drawn and ready.

Inside, the room was dim and cluttered. Clearly, someone had ransacked the shop, tipping mannequins over and pulling drawers out on to the floor. Day moved quickly and quietly through the place. When he was sure there was nobody else there, he put his weapon away and opened the front door again, beckoning Kingsley in. Henry followed his new employer.

Kingsley took a deep breath and set his black bag on the main counter, next to a sewing machine that had a length of fabric tied around its base. From the bag he drew the pair of bloody shears.

'Shall we see if there are finger marks on these?'

'Did you bring your powder?'

'I did.'

With a flourish, Kingsley produced the little tin of charcoal dust. He opened it and blew a pinch of the black powder on the sewing machine.

'Look at this,' he said. 'Several marks on this machine, clear as day. If there are marks on these shears we'll know for certain whether this tailor was the man following you and whether he stabbed that man at the workhouse.'

'It won't prove he killed Little.'

'No, but if we compare these shears to the pair used on Pringle and then compare them to the marks here on this sewing machine . . . well, if they all match, I think we'd be reasonably safe in pinning the blame on this fellow. What's his name again?'

'Cinderhouse. The marks of his fingertips still won't be enough to convict him.'

'Perhaps not, but they'll be enough to convince you of his guilt and, with your case narrowed so precisely, you'll find the proof you need.'

Day smiled. 'That I will.'

Kingsley went about the task of comparing fingerprints, humming quietly under his breath while Day poked about the shop, looking for anything that might be construed as evidence of a crime. Henry Mayhew bobbed about in a corner of the shop, dancing to the tune Kingsley hummed.

'Inspector,' Kingsley said.

Day looked up from a red smear he had found along a crack in the floorboards.

'This sewing machine,' Kingsley said, 'appears to be moving.'

Day trotted over to the counter. The machine, though bolted to the countertop, was rocking back and forth, almost imperceptibly, as if being tugged by something. Day followed the length of fabric tied around its base. The makeshift rope was pulled taut across the counter and ran down into a cupboard on the other side. In the base of the cupboard, there was a square hole. The fabric disappeared into the darkness below the shop. Day squatted outside the cabinet. He drew his gun again and shouted.

'Hello. Is someone down there?'

After a moment, an answer echoed up and into the cupboard.

'Who's that?' the voice said. 'I warn you, I'm armed.'

Day frowned.

'Hammersmith?' he said. 'Is that you, man?'

96

Blacker followed Penelope Shaw through the entrance hall and into a well-appointed parlour. He whistled.

'Lovely.'

He meant that the lady herself was lovely. He had never seen such a creature in his life. Her scent filled the room and he felt lightheaded. No wonder Hammersmith had been so eager to spend time in her company. He would need to focus on the task at hand. He reminded himself that the most beautiful women were often the most dangerous.

'I mean your home,' he said. 'You have a lovely home.'

'Thank you,' Penelope said. 'My son, Bradley, and I are happy here. Would you care for tea?'

'Oh, good Lord, no!'

'Well, all right.'

She looked hurt.

'I'm sorry,' Blacker said. 'That was a bit emphatic of me, wasn't it?'

'Yes, a bit. I take it you've spoken with Mr Hammersmith.'

'I do apologize.'

'No, it's perfectly understandable. I made a horrible mistake with him. I should never have . . .'

'Think nothing of it. Water under the bridge and all that.'

Blacker was mortally embarrassed for having made things so awkward between them. He had no idea how to bridge the resulting silence, so he decided he would take his leave and return another time.

'Well,' he said, 'I'm sorry to have disturbed you today. Perhaps I could . . .'

'Mother?'

Blacker turned to see a young boy standing under an arch by the staircase.

'Oh, I'm sorry, Mother. I didn't know you had company.'

The boy was perhaps seven or eight years old and his tiny pointed face was creased with worry. He looked as if he'd always been worried. Blacker was glad of the distraction. He smiled and waved him over.

'Not at all,' Blacker said. 'Come here, lad.'

The boy glanced at his mother and dragged himself over to them.

'What is it, Bradley?' Penelope said.

'It's raining and I can't go outside today. I thought perhaps we might play a game of chess.'

'You always beat me.'

'I won't beat you this time.'

'Maybe when I've finished with Mr Blacker.'

'Call me Michael,' Blacker said. He turned to the boy. 'And your name is Shufflebottom, correct?'

'No. It's Bradley.'

'That's an extremely silly name.'

'Is not. It's quite common.'

'It's silly and I should know because I collect silly names.'

'It's not a silly name at all.'

'I beg your pardon. Shufflebottom is a very silly name indeed.'

'But I didn't say Shufflebottom. My name is Bradley.'

'I'm certain you said Shufflebottom.'

'And I'm certain I didn't!'

'Well, perhaps you didn't hear yourself say Shufflebottom. Honestly, I don't see how you can hear anything at all when you're walking around with that thing in your ear.'

'What thing in my ear?'

The boy looked alarmed.

'You mean you didn't put it there?'

Bradley shook his head.

'Then let's see if we can't fish it out.'

Blacker reached behind the boy's ear and, with a flourish, drew forth a penny. Bradley gasped.

'Your ear is hardly the best place to keep money,' Blacker said. 'Perhaps you should find somewhere better for it.'

Bradley took the penny and stared at it. Then he looked up at Blacker and grinned. He turned and held the coin out for his mother to see.

'Look, Mother, it's a magic penny.'

'That's wonderful,' she said.

She smiled at Blacker.

'Bradley,' she said, 'why don't you go and show your new penny to Elizabeth.'

'Yes, ma'am.'

'And have her put the kettle on for tea, would you? I'm in the mood.'

Bradley ran out of the room with the penny cupped

in his hands, as if afraid it would vanish as easily as it had appeared.

'Thank you for that,' Penelope said. 'I can't remember the last time anything made him happy.'

'My pleasure,' Blacker said. 'I rather like making people happy.'

Penelope smiled at him and Blacker decided that making her smile again might be the most worthwhile task he could take up.

'That's a nice thought,' Penelope said. 'Bradley's had a rough time of it lately. But I don't think being a child is ever particularly easy.'

'It's not particularly easy being an adult either.'

'No.'

There was an awkward silence, but the tension in the room had dissipated and Blacker decided he didn't want to leave after all.

'Ma'am, I'm sorry to do this, but I have to ask you some official questions.'

'Of course.'

'The person or persons who . . . well, who murdered Dr Shaw have, I believe, killed several others. I think they plan to continue killing unless they're stopped.'

Blacker and Penelope both turned at the sound of a woman's voice.

'You ain't far wrong.'

Two women emerged from the entrance to a short hall at the back of the parlour. One was short and the other tall, with a long scar running down her cheek. They both wore too much make-up. The tall one had a pistol in her hand and it was pointed at Blacker.

'But you're wrong about stoppin' us,' the short one said.

'He ain't the one,' the scarred one said.

'True. He ain't the one. But he'll do. Look at that silly ginger moustache.'

97

‘Up you go,’ Day said.

He let go and the little boy, Fenn, was pulled upward through the shaft of light. The twisted linen rope held tight under the boy’s arms. Day stepped back and he and Hammersmith watched the boy disappear into the tailor’s shop above as Henry Mayhew, the dancing man, hauled on his end of the rope.

‘I’m a bit nervous,’ Hammersmith said. ‘Can this fellow handle the weight of a full-grown man?’

‘He’s unnaturally strong,’ Day said. ‘I believe he’s perfectly able. Handy bloke to have around, to tell the truth, but he badly needs a hot bath.’

Hammersmith moved away into the darkness of the cave and Day followed him. He felt about until he encountered what seemed to be an arm. He grabbed it and pulled. Hammersmith had the other arm and together they dragged an unconscious man across the dirt floor until they had him under the trapdoor above. A minute later, an end of the makeshift linen rope was tossed back down and they tied it under the injured man’s arms.

‘Well, if your dancing man can’t handle the weight, better he should drop this load than either of us,’ Hammersmith said. ‘I wouldn’t mind seeing this one take a bit more punishment after what he put that boy through.’

'Who is he?'

'I think he's the tailor's coachman. Regardless, he's good with a knife.'

Day glanced at Hammersmith's wounded arm.

'Kingsley's up there too.'

'You brought everyone.'

'We do seem to have converged. Good thing. Although we've misplaced Mr Blacker.'

'I have no idea where he went. I fell asleep and he was gone when I woke up.'

'He'll turn up or I'll find him when I find the tailor. Time's of the essence, so I'm afraid I need to leave you here. The doctor will wrap you up and I'll have the carriage take you to hospital.'

The coachman's inert body jerked, then rose smoothly up and away. The two men watched the soles of his shoes until they were reeled through the bottom of the cabinet.

'This arm isn't going to kill me,' Hammersmith said. 'I'm not done until we find the man who put this all in motion.'

'Rest assured, I'll catch him.'

'I have no doubt of that. But it's a bit personal for me now. If you don't mind, I'll stick it out.'

The end of the rope hit the ground in front of them again. Day picked it up and pulled it around Hammersmith's chest.

'First, Kingsley takes a look at that arm,' Day said. 'If he says it's all right, then I'll be glad of your company.'

Hammersmith nodded. He rose into the air and disappeared from view the same way the other two had gone.

Day looked around him at the black empty cave and shook his head. It was amazing what they'd all gone through in the past three days.

He stepped back as the end of the rope descended once more.

98

Kingsley talked to Day while he wrapped Hammersmith's arm.

'The marks on the shears match the marks on the sewing machine,' he said. 'I'm confident that the tailor's your man.'

'But how to find him?' Day said. 'He's not here, we don't know where he lives, and he knows now that we're on to him. We have no idea where he's gone to ground.'

'I know where he lives.'

The three men turned at the sound of Fenn's voice. The boy was standing at the door of the shop, hiding behind one of Henry Mayhew's massive legs.

'Will you write his address for us?' Day said.

'I don't know his address,' Fenn said. 'But I can show you where he lives.'

'We wouldn't ask that of you,' Hammersmith said.

Day looked at him, eyes wide, but Hammersmith shook his head.

'You never have to see that man again,' he said.

'I don't have to see him to show you his house,' Fenn said. 'I don't mind. Really. Just don't let him take me again.'

'There is no chance of that,' Day said. 'If you're sure you're up to it, we'll go for a carriage ride.'

'What should we do with him?' Kingsley pointed at the unconscious coachman.

'We'll tie him up and send someone round for him,' Day said. 'We don't want him near the boy if he wakes.'

'Fenn stays in the carriage at all times,' Hammersmith said.

'We'll do even better than that. Once he points the place out, you and I go after Cinderhouse and Dr Kingsley takes the boy away. We won't put him in danger for even a moment.'

'I'll take him to my laboratory,' Kingsley said. 'It will be safe there and my daughter would be delighted to entertain him until you can catch this fellow and take the boy home.'

Hammersmith looked at Fenn. The boy nodded and Hammersmith smiled at him.

'You're a brave lad,' he said.

99

Day and Hammersmith stood on the kerb and watched until the carriage had rolled out of sight. Once they were sure that Kingsley, Fenn and Henry Mayhew were safely away, they turned and approached the big house. It was a tidy two-storey home, well looked after, nothing ominous about it at all. Day imagined it rented for upwards of forty pounds a year, more than his own house in Kentish Town.

The front door was locked, but Hammersmith found a window at the side of the house that had been jemmied.

'When do you think that was done?' Day asked.

'Looks fresh to me.'

'That's what I was thinking as well. Pried open some time after the rain.'

Hammersmith nodded and drew his club from its belt loop. His injured arm hung useless at his side, but he looked determined and Day was glad to have him there. Day held up a hand and, with his Colt drawn, sat on the sill and manoeuvred himself through the window and into the house. He crept through a dark drawing room to the front door and opened it. Hammersmith was waiting on the other side. He stepped through, quietly closed the door behind him and the two men made their way through the rooms at the front of the house without finding a sign of the tailor.

They split up at the staircase. Hammersmith slid through an open arch, headed towards the rooms at the back of the house, while Day edged up the stairs to the next floor. He poked cautiously through every doorway until he was certain he was alone upstairs. Then he put his gun away and went back through the rooms, more carefully this time, hoping to find some evidence.

At the end of a hallway, near the water closet, there was a small bedroom. The window had been barred. He approached it and looked out. The top of a retaining wall was directly under the windowsill and, beyond that, a tall tree. Day put his cheek to the bars. There was nothing in the yard except an old carriage house that looked like it might fall down the next time it rained. He sniffed and pulled his head back. The iron bars cast a long shadow across the bed. There were leather straps on both sides of the bed and a coil of rope hung loose at the foot of it. Day tested one of the straps and it came loose. The strap looked new and Day guessed that it had been purchased to replace the rope, but had not yet been installed or used.

He looked around. A straight-backed wooden chair sat in the corner. He approached the chair and squinted at the dark shape lying across the seat. He went to the door and shouted out into the hall.

'Hammersmith, have you found anything?'

Hammersmith's voice came back, surprisingly close to the staircase.

'Nothing. You?'

'Up here.'

Day stepped back into the room. Hammersmith's

footsteps clattered up the stairs and Day heard him checking the rooms along the hall.

'Back here.'

A moment later Hammersmith joined him.

'What is it? Not the tailor.'

'No, he seems to be out. But look at this.'

He pointed at the chair.

'A riding crop?' Hammersmith said.

'What is a riding crop doing in a bedroom?' Day said.

'I shudder to think.'

'Yes, but where might you be more likely to find a riding crop?'

'I don't follow you.'

Day pointed to the window and Hammersmith looked out into the yard. He turned back to Day.

'A carriage house.'

'Let's go.'

100

There was a thump-thump-thump on the stairs and Mrs Flanders put aside her book. She hurried to the door and stepped into the hall in time to see one of the disguised policemen, the one with the bushy black beard, struggling through the downstairs door to the street. He was carrying something bulky wrapped up in a blanket. She scurried down the stairs and caught the door before it closed.

'Are you leaving already?' she said. 'Mr Hammersmith hasn't come back yet.'

The policeman jumped, clearly startled. He turned, staggering under the weight of the huge bundle on his shoulder.

'Ah, ma'am, you oughtn't to come up on me like that.'

'Dreadfully sorry, sir.'

'Not at all. Just worried my police training might kick in and I'd do you harm. Wouldn't want that, would we?'

He smiled and winked at her. Despite his rough appearance, Mrs Flanders found him utterly charming. She smiled back at him.

'No, we wouldn't want that,' she said. 'Where is the other policeman? The one dressed as a chimneysweep?'

'He left already.'

'I didn't hear him on the stair.'

'He's very sneaky. Got to be when you're in disguise as a dipper like he is.'

'Do you mean to say that he picks pockets?'

'Yes, he does.'

'But he's dressed as a sweep.'

'That's a disguise on his disguise. Makes him double good at it.'

'Well, if he steals wallets, doesn't that make him as much a criminal as the real criminals?'

'He's got to blend in, you see, but then he always goes and gives people their things back, he does.'

'Oh, well that makes perfect sense, then. He returns what he steals.'

'Yes, that's exactly what he does. Very sneaky one, that.'

'I don't mean to seem curious, but may I ask what's in the blanket?'

'Blanket?'

'The one you've got over your shoulder.'

'Oh, you mean this blanket?'

'Yes.'

'It's police supplies in here, ma'am. Constable Hammersmith was savin' 'em fer me. Gotta get 'em down to headquarters.'

'It looks very heavy.'

'Well, they're not lightweight supplies, I'll tell you that, ma'am. Not the easiest thing to have slung on me whilst I stand about in the street.'

'I'm sorry. I'm keeping you.'

'Not at all. It's a sheer pleasure talkin' with you, and that's for sure. Did I mention you remind me of me mum?'

'That's very dear of you to say.'

''Tis the God's truth, ma'am. But now I'd better get this over to Scotland Yard afore it's too late.'

'Too late?'

'Yes, ma'am. Big rush on it from the commissioner of police hisself.'

'Then I mustn't keep you any longer. Only . . .'

'Yes?'

'Do promise you'll come back for a visit?'

The rough-looking policeman grinned at Mrs Flanders and bowed slightly at the waist, keeping the bundle on his shoulders carefully balanced as he did so.

'I guarantee that I will, missus.'

And with that he tottered off down the road with his heavy burden and turned the corner into an alley halfway along the block.

Mrs Flanders put a hand on her heart and stepped back into the building. She closed the door to the street and went back up to her own cosy flat. Strange, she thought, that she hadn't heard the second policeman leave. They were obviously very good at their jobs. She had not subscribed to all the recent condemnation of the police. It made her feel safe knowing that she had them as tenants in her own building.

She sat down with her novel and found her place again. She had read only two sentences when it occurred to her that the nice policeman had never actually told her what supplies were in the bundle he was carrying.

She made up her mind to ask him about it the next time he paid a visit to Mr Hammersmith.

101

Day looked over at Hammersmith, took a deep breath and swung the carriage house door open. Something hot whistled past Day's right ear and there was the sudden crack of a gunshot. He fell backward and waited for another shot, but none came. He crawled to the side, away from the entrance so that the building's wall would block any more bullets that were fired his way. Hammersmith was already on the other side of the door, against the wall.

'Cinderhouse?' Day said. 'Stop shooting.'

He waited for a response. He was about to call again, when the tailor answered.

'Have you been to my shop?'

'I have.'

'Did you find the boy?'

'Yes.'

'Is he all right? He was under that counter for quite some time. Longer than I intended.'

'He's fine.'

'Good.'

There was another long silence.

'Who am I talking to out there?' Cinderhouse said. 'Is that Inspector Day?'

'Yes.'

'Are you alone?'

Day shook his head at Hammersmith. He put a finger to his lips.

'I'm alone,' Day said.

'Good. It should be the two of us at the end. Cat and mouse. But which is the cat and which is the mouse?'

'I don't take your meaning, sir.'

'Which of us,' Cinderhouse said, 'I mean, which of us will come out of this? We won't both live through this day, you know.'

'Why do you say that?'

'If I let you live, you'll keep the boy from me. I can't let that happen.'

'You plan to kill me, then?'

'I don't think I have a choice.'

'But I have you trapped.'

'True.'

'So perhaps you should lay the gun down and come out where we can talk, face to face.'

'That won't do, Inspector.'

'Why not?'

'I told you. The only way I'll get to keep the boy is if you die here.'

'Have you killed before?'

'No.'

'What about Inspector Little?'

'Who?'

'Or Constable Pringle?'

Day saw Hammersmith shudder and he shook his head again. He didn't want Hammersmith's emotions to get the better of him. Day still hoped that the situation might end without further death.

'It's sad about Pringle,' Cinderhouse said. 'I rather liked him. He was an excellent customer.'

'Then why kill him?'

'I didn't. He was going to take the boy and so he had to go away.'

'Go away?'

'Yes. He disappeared. A shame, really. I had a new pair of trousers ready for him.'

'He didn't go away, Mr Cinderhouse. You murdered him.'

'Certainly not. I did have to discipline him, of course. He was out of line. I only did what I needed to do to keep him from talking about the boy. He would have told everyone.'

'So he disappeared?'

'I haven't seen him since.'

'Who else has disappeared, Mr Cinderhouse?'

'Oh, now . . . now, I don't want to . . .'

Cinderhouse stopped talking and Day could hear a choking sound deep inside the carriage house. He wished he had a lamp, anything that might allow him to see further than four feet into the building.

Quietly, he slipped his boots off and edged around the back of the carriage house. The building had no windows. The only way in or out was through the big door. When he got to the other side, he drew Hammersmith close and whispered in his ear. He handed Hammersmith his gun. The constable nodded and hurried quietly back around the way that Day had come. In a few minutes he appeared on the other side, where Day had been. They'd switched places.

Day got down on his stomach in the short, brown grass and crept forward until the top of his head was even with the edge of the doorway. A few feet away, Hammersmith cleared his throat.

'Mr Cinderhouse, are you all right?' Hammersmith said.

The choking noise inside the carriage house tapered off. Cinderhouse sniffed.

'Inspector?' Cinderhouse said.

'It's me,' Hammersmith said.

Day winced. With his broken nose, Hammersmith's voice was huskier and more nasal than his own. And more Welsh, though he was clearly trying to disguise the lilt of his accent. Fortunately, the tailor didn't notice. The big, empty horse stalls and vaulted ceiling served to flatten and amplify every sound.

'You don't know what it is,' Cinderhouse said, 'to have people disappear. People you care about.'

'I don't know about that,' Hammersmith said. 'I've known people who have disappeared.'

'Who?'

'My friend Pringle, for one.'

'That's not the same. Mr Pringle was a grown man. They disappear all the time. But the children . . . That's not fair, is it? My boys keep disappearing.'

'Your boys?'

'All the boys. Starting with my very first boy. His mother, too. Both gone. One day, just gone.'

'And that justifies all you've done?'

'You don't understand.'

'I might. At least a little.'

Day was uncomfortable, his neck bent up so he could see and his elbows digging into the dirt. There was a small rock under his left elbow, but he was afraid to move it, afraid of the sound it might make. He kept perfectly still. Hammersmith was doing a better job than Day had thought he would. If he kept Cinderhouse talking there might be no need for more violence.

'No,' Cinderhouse said. 'You can't understand.'

Another shot. The carriage house held on to the sound of it and shook it, vibrated it. It seemed to Day that the earth under him trembled with the noise of the gun. He instinctively put his head down. From the corner of his eye, he saw Hammersmith drop to one knee and fire through the door. Day crawled forward and rolled through the doorway. He was almost instantly in the dark. He lay still inside the doorway, back against the wall, the light streaming past him and fading into nothingness.

'Did I get you?' Cinderhouse said.

'No,' Hammersmith said.

'I got this gun from the guard at the workhouse. I have no idea how many bullets it contains.'

'I don't imagine you've got many left.'

'Then perhaps I should rush forward before shooting at you next time.'

'If you do, I'll shoot you.'

'That might not be so bad.'

'I'd rather not do it.'

Either Hammersmith was playing the part of Inspector Day to a fault or he was considerably less violent than Day had realized.

'You said you understood,' Cinderhouse said. 'Just a moment ago, before I shot, you said that people had disappeared on you. Have you lost a child, too?'

Hammersmith didn't respond. Day waited in the dark so long that he had almost given up and decided to make his move, when he finally heard Hammersmith's voice again, echoing faintly through the length of the carriage house and back again.

'No, not a boy,' he said. 'My father has disappeared.'

'Your father?'

'Yes,' Hammersmith said.

'How sad. Were you a good son?'

'I hope so.'

'That's all a father asks.'

There was another shot, but Day couldn't tell whether Hammersmith or Cinderhouse had fired. While the shot still echoed, he moved forward in the pitch black. Another gunshot, horizontal lightning that left spots on his vision, and then a third shot, the noise covering the sound of his steps on the brittle old straw underfoot. There was no way for him to tell where the shots were coming from. Inside the carriage house, the racket was staggering. Blind and deaf, he stumbled ahead.

Something brushed against his leg and, impulsively, he threw himself sideways. Somebody grunted and pushed back against him and Day was suddenly wrestling with the tailor, still unable to see what he was doing.

'Hammersmith,' he said, 'I've got him. Come quickly.'

He felt the guard's gun in his ribs and heard a click. The gun was empty. Day lashed out and his knuckles hit bone. Cinderhouse yelped. The tailor abruptly jerked away from Day and began screaming. Day reached out, but the screaming tailor was moving rapidly away and, knocked off balance, Day fell back against the wall.

In the patch of sunlight at the door, Hammersmith hove into view, his injured arm hanging useless, his other arm extended into the darkness. A moment later, he hauled Cinderhouse into the light, his fingers jammed deep in the tailor's nose. Day got his feet under him and hurried to the door. He grabbed Cinderhouse's arms and twisted them behind his back. Hammersmith let loose his grip on Cinderhouse's nose, which had already turned a deep purple.

Hammersmith frowned at his fingers and wiped them on his already filthy trousers.

'His nose?' Day said.

'I was trying to get him by the hair,' Hammersmith said. 'I forgot the bastard was bald.'

102

'Get behind me,' Blacker said.

He stepped in front of Penelope Shaw. She grabbed his shoulders, frightened, and despite the seriousness of their situation he felt an electric thrill run through his body.

'Put the pistol down,' he said.

The short woman laughed at him.

'You give me your pistol, mister,' she said.

'I know you won't shoot me. You didn't shoot any of the others, did you?'

'What do you know about the others?' This was the tall one talking, the one with the scar. She looked worried.

'Did you get them to sit still and let you shave them because you had the pistol? Or did you make them shave themselves?'

'How do you know that?'

'Don't matter how he knows it, Liza,' the tall one said. 'He won't know it much longer.'

'I won't let you shave me. And I won't shave myself. I know that if I do, you'll cut my throat. So you have no bargaining power here.'

'Then I'll shoot you now.'

'Well, I suppose you do have that one bit of bargaining power,' he said.

He pointed at the arched entryway behind the two women. 'Get back to the kitchen, Bradley.'

The tall woman laughed again. 'You ain't gonna fool me so easy,' she said.

'Leave him alone,' Bradley said.

Surprised, the short woman – the other one had called her Liza – turned around. The tall one glanced at her friend for a fraction of a second, but it was long enough for Blacker to make his move. He leapt forward and as he did he felt his pistol come free from his belt. He landed on the tall woman, knocking her on her back against the floor. Liza attacked him, beating Blacker on the back with her fists. He ignored her and grabbed the tall woman's arm, shoving it up and away as she fired the pistol. The bullet smacked into the wall by the staircase and Blacker felt his stomach lurch as he looked for Bradley, afraid that he'd been hit.

A plain, dark-haired woman ran from the room beyond the arch and gathered Bradley in her arms. The boy seemed frightened but unharmed. Blacker heard Penelope's voice, coming from somewhere behind him.

'You! Stop hitting my friend.'

Blacker turned to see her holding his own pistol. She had it aimed at Liza.

The short prostitute backed away from Blacker and stood pouting against the wall. Blacker picked up the tall woman's pistol. He stood up and moved away from her, keeping the weapon casually aimed in the direction of the two killers.

'Elizabeth,' Penelope said, 'please take Bradley to the

kitchen and get him something warm to drink. When you have a moment, send someone round to fetch the police. Ask them to bring a carriage.'

'My colleague is asleep in the wagon outside,' Blacker said. 'Let's wake him.'

'Beg pardon, but there's no wagon outside, sir,' Elizabeth said.

'He's gone?'

Elizabeth nodded.

'Well, fancy that. He's an odd duck, Hammersmith is. I suppose you'd better send a runner for the police after all, then.'

Elizabeth mumbled something that Blacker couldn't hear and took Bradley by the hand, leading him out of sight.

The tall prostitute stood up and brushed herself off. She moved over next to Liza against the wall and sneered at Blacker.

'Bet you liked that, eh? Up on top of me like you was?'

'Not especially,' Blacker said.

'You woulda had your way wiv me if she didn't interrupt us. I saw you wanted to.'

'Not in the slightest,' Blacker said. 'And you might be wise to keep quiet for the time being.'

'Or what? You'll hit me? Smack me a good one? Show me who's in charge?'

'I don't hit women.'

'I, on the other hand, have no problem hitting women,' Penelope said. 'Nor do I have a problem shooting them, so keep quiet until the police arrive.'

'You won't shoot me,' the tall one said.

'I believe she would,' Blacker said. 'She's remarkably unpredictable.'

'I will take that as a compliment,' Penelope said.

'It was meant as one. Might I have my pistol back before the other police get here?'

'Of course.'

She turned the gun around and handed it to him and he put it back in his belt where it belonged. He kept the women's gun aimed at them.

'We may have a bit of a wait ahead of us,' Blacker said. 'Wagons are in ridiculously short supply at The Yard.'

'Then are you sure you won't have a spot of tea?' Penelope said.

'Thank you. Actually, tea sounds lovely.'

He winked at her and she smiled back.

103

The grounds of the tailor's house reminded Day of the railway station two days before. Dozens of police milled about, digging up flower beds and prying off cellar doors. There was a chance that Cinderhouse had taken other boys and that their remains were still somewhere nearby.

The tailor himself sat at the kerb in a padlocked wagon with a guard of Sergeant Kett and three constables. Nobody was taking any chance that he might get away from them. Hammersmith had broken the tailor's nose and the police were in no particular hurry to have it set for him. Sir Edward, who had arrived moments ago, reprimanded two constables who had spent a few happy minutes pushing Cinderhouse about in the dirt.

But he didn't relieve them of duty.

Sir Edward approached Day and Hammersmith where they sat on a low stone wall at the side of the carriage house.

'Well done, you two.'

'Thank you, sir.'

'Mr Day, if there was any confusion about whether you were up to the job, I believe you've proven yourself beyond a doubt.'

'Sir.'

'And Mr Hammersmith. You surprise me.'

'How so, sir?'

‘You didn’t kill him.’

‘No, sir.’

Sir Edward smiled.

‘Come see me once you’ve had that arm looked at, Hammersmith.’

Hammersmith nodded and Sir Edward walked away, already barking orders at his men.

‘Let’s take a wagon and get you to hospital,’ Day said.

‘Not yet,’ Hammersmith said. ‘Something I have to do first.’

‘What’s that?’

‘There’s a scared little boy has to be returned home.’

Day grinned.

‘Ah,’ he said. ‘That duty would be a pleasure after all this. May I accompany you?’

‘I wish you would.’

They stood and made their way to the street where at least a dozen police carriages were nosed in against the kerb. For once, there was no shortage of vehicles.

104

'Fiona found some things for him to wear. His clothes were filthy.'

'Thank you for watching after him,' Hammersmith said.

'Not at all,' Kingsley said. 'He's a delightful boy. As brave and helpful as my own children.'

'We'll take him back to his family now. I imagine he'll sleep for a week after all he's been through.'

'I'd like to ride along, if you don't mind,' Kingsley said. 'We can take my carriage. It's a bit nicer than the police issue.'

'There's no need to trouble yourself.'

'To be honest with you, these past few days have broadened my horizons some. I find that I rather enjoy getting out of the laboratory.'

'Well, you're welcome to come.'

'Fiona,' Kingsley said, 'Look after things here, will you?'

'Of course, Father.'

The girl smiled at Hammersmith and he smiled back. He was suddenly aware of his broken nose, bloody arm, soiled clothes. He was bothered and had no idea why.

He tipped his hat and hurried after Dr Kingsley, Inspector Day, and the little lost boy, Fenn.

105

Hammersmith knocked on the door and stepped back. He put his hand over the wound in his arm, covering as much of the bloodstain as he could manage.

He looked down at Fenn, standing next to him on the stoop. The boy had been cleaned up some, but he looked almost as bedraggled as Hammersmith did. The shirt Fenn was wearing – one of Kingsley's – was much too large for him, he had no shoes, his hair was matted to his head. He raised his eyes from the door and smiled at Hammersmith.

'Thank you,' Fenn said.

Hammersmith smiled back and put his hand on the boy's shoulder. He remembered his father's hand on his own shoulder, so many years ago. Was this how his father had felt then, some mixture of melancholy and gladness and nearly overwhelming pride?

After a long moment, the door opened. A woman stood there, all in black. She had been crying. Her face was red and her hair was a mess, and she didn't seem to care.

Hammersmith stepped to one side and Day pushed Fenn forward so that the woman could see him. The boy didn't wait for a reaction from his mother. He ran to her and launched himself into her arms.

The woman's eyes closed and her mouth opened, but

no sound came out. She went to her knees, the boy clutched tight to her, fresh tears streaked down her face.

'Mattie,' a man's voice echoed down the hall behind her. She didn't react to it, just rocked back and forth, holding her son.

'Mattie?'

A short man with his shirt-tail untucked from his trousers came up the hall behind her. When he saw Fenn, he ran forward and embraced both his wife and his boy at once.

Hammersmith stepped off the porch and looked at Day, who shrugged and smiled. Nobody in the tiny family took any notice of the two policemen and the doctor at their door. They were locked in a silent reunion and no outsiders were necessary.

It didn't matter to Hammersmith in the least. He knew that he had failed the unidentified chimney climber, the boy nobody had cared for, but, he thought, perhaps he had made up for it in some small way by bringing Fenn home.

'Goodbye, Fenn. Always be brave.' He said it quietly and nobody heard him.

He was startled by yet another boy whom he recognized as one of Kett's runners. The boy hurtled at them on a rickety bicycle and jumped off as he reached the kerb, bringing the bicycle to a shuddering halt.

'One of you Inspector Day?' the boy said.

'I am,' Day said.

'Sergeant Kett said to find you. Been by way of two other places, sir.'

'What is it, son?'

'He said to tell you,' the boy said, 'your wife's taken sick, sir. You're needed home at once.'

'How bad is it?'

'Don't know, sir. I guess she took sick early this morning.'

'Thank you.'

Kingsley gave the boy a penny and touched Day on the arm.

'I'll take you,' he said.

'We only have the one carriage and Hammersmith's in a bad way,' Day said. 'He needs a hospital.'

'No,' Hammersmith said. 'We'll get you home. My arm will wait.'

'Where do you live?' Kingsley said.

'Kentish Town,' Day said.

'St Thomas's is on the way. It's not the hospital I'd choose, but it'll do if Mr Hammersmith will permit.'

Hammersmith snorted. The sudden air through his broken nose brought tears to his eyes and he put his head down. St Thomas's Hospital. He chuckled to himself and, when he raised his head, he saw that the others had stopped walking and were staring at him.

'St Thomas's would be fine,' Hammersmith said. 'Anything that gets Walter to his wife as quickly as possible.'

Day smiled at him and Hammersmith smiled back. He had balanced the universe by saving one boy when he couldn't find justice for another. Apparently, the universe wanted to repay the favour.

He straightened his shoulders and hurried to the carriage.

106

Hammersmith sat at the edge of the bed and carefully pulled the fresh white sling off over his head. He reached for the shirt that was draped at the foot of the bed and inched it on over his damaged arm.

'That's a bad cut there,' the patient in the next bed said.

'Not too bad. It's the broken knuckles that bother me most.'

'Got the same damn thing myself,' the patient said. 'Other arm, though. And me knuckles are good.'

He held up his arm to show Hammersmith the bandage.

'Some mad bugger did me with scissors. You believe it?'

Hammersmith clucked his tongue and pulled the other sleeve over his good arm. He concentrated on buttoning the shirt with his good hand. The shirt fitted well. He'd found it at the tailor's shop and didn't think anyone would complain that he'd taken it.

'Lucky for me there was a doctor at the workhouse today. Just visitin', he was, pure coincidence. Except not a coincidence at all, was it?'

'Wasn't it?'

'He was there with the police, chasin' after the madman

what stabbed me. Anyhow, it was a lucky break. He fixed me up and sent me on here.'

The patient propped himself up on one elbow so he could lean in towards Hammersmith.

'Glad it happened. Know why? Food's better here!'

The patient broke into loud peals of laughter. Hammersmith nodded and put his sling back on, adjusting it across his chest. He stood and surveyed the area for anything he might be forgetting.

'Here now,' the patient said. 'Yer not s'posed to leave 'til the nurse comes an' says it's all right.'

'I'm sure she'll be glad for the empty bed. Anyway, I've things to do. Can't lie about all day.'

'Me, I'm happy to have a reason to lie about.'

'Then enjoy yourself. Glad to have met you.'

Hammersmith walked out of the ward and nobody stopped him. He got his bearings and turned to his left, walking down a long hall until he found a staircase. At the top of the stairs, he asked a harried-looking nurse for the men's critical ward and followed in the direction she pointed until he came to a large room at the end of the hall. Twenty beds lined the walls and in each of them lay a dying man.

He took a deep breath and entered the ward. He found his father in the sixth bed from the end, asleep, an old man with thin white hair and bony shoulders. He no longer resembled the strong coalminer who had ruffled his son's hair as they'd walked home in the starlight so many years ago.

Hammersmith pulled up a stool and sat. After a while, the old man's eyes opened and he looked up at

Hammersmith. There was a long silence and, when his father finally spoke, Hammersmith had to bend over him so that he could hear.

'Look how you're growing, son,' his father said. 'You won't be the smallest boy in the village much longer.'

He smiled and Hammersmith smiled back. He reached out his hand and smoothed his father's hair back from his forehead. After a moment, the old man's eyes closed again.

Hammersmith waited until he was sure his father was asleep and then he rose and left the hospital.

He was surprised to find Penelope Shaw waiting for him when he arrived at Number Four Whitehall Place.

'I heard that you rescued a child,' she said.

'It was luck.'

'You're too modest.'

'No, only honest.'

'Your arm?'

'It will heal.'

'Your nose is healing already.'

'Yes. I noticed it's a different shade of purple today.'

'I came to apologize to you again.'

'There's no need.'

'I want to, anyway.'

'Very well, then. You've apologized. Now it's done and behind us.'

'And I want to say goodbye to you.'

'Goodbye? I don't understand.'

'Perhaps I'm assuming things I shouldn't, but it felt as if there was something between us.'

'How could there be? You've been a widow for a day and a half.'

'And you would never presume, would you, regardless of my feelings for my husband? Or, I should say, my lack of feeling for him.'

'I don't understand why you're here.'

'I told you.'

'And yet I still don't understand.'

'That's the problem, isn't it? So I'm going to marry your Inspector Blacker.'

Hammersmith's eyes widened and he cast his eyes about the room, looking for Blacker.

'What did he do?'

'Michael? Why, nothing at all.'

'He's proposed marriage already?'

'No. He doesn't know.'

'What do you mean, he doesn't know?'

'When enough time has passed so that it seems proper, I will let him know of my intentions and then he will propose to me.'

'But he doesn't know?'

'No.'

'Then how do you know that he'll propose?'

'Because I do.'

'You can't have feelings for him. You've only just met him.'

Penelope looked away.

'I have a child, Mr Hammersmith. I have responsibilities.'

'I don't understand.'

'How will I care for my son by myself? How could I possibly afford to keep Elizabeth on?'

'You'll get by.'

'I don't want to get by. I want to be taken care of.'

'I'll help you find a solution. Marrying Inspector Blacker solves nothing.'

'It solves everything. And besides, I like him.'

'You don't love him.'

'I like his jokes.'

'But you don't love him.'

'He makes me laugh.'

'You *like* his jokes?'

'I do.'

Hammersmith blinked.

'Huh.'

'My son smiled for the first time since . . . well, for the first time in a very long time. Michael made my son smile, Mr Hammersmith.'

'I see.'

'Do you?'

'I think I do. But I would ask that you give this more thought.'

'It would never have worked between us. With you and me.'

'I haven't even considered the idea.'

'Yes, you have.'

He rubbed the back of his neck and looked away from her.

'Well, obviously *you* have,' he said.

'You are already married to your job, Mr Hammersmith. You have no time for anything or anyone else.'

'I don't think that's true.'

'It is. And my problem is that I can't be alone.'

'And so you want to be with Inspector Blacker.'

'He is attentive to people.'

'Well, you like his jokes.'

'Yes.'

Hammersmith shrugged. Penelope reached out to touch his chest, then drew her hand back. She turned and walked away. Hammersmith waited for her to look back at him, but she didn't.

He felt as if he'd gone another round with an enraged bartender.

'Constable?'

Hammersmith turned to see Sergeant Kett hurrying towards him.

'The commissioner wants to see you in his office soon's you arrive. Looks to me like you've arrived.'

'Yes, sir.'

He swung open the gate to the squad room and made his way across to Sir Edward's office. He noticed that Inspector Day wasn't at his desk. Blacker nodded to him as he passed and Hammersmith returned the gesture. He knocked on Sir Edward's door.

'Come.'

Sir Edward was looking through a sheaf of papers and laid them down on the desk when Hammersmith opened the door. He motioned for Hammersmith to close it behind him.

'Mr Hammersmith.'

'Yes, sir.'

'A commendable job. You helped subdue the murderer and his accomplice. And you rescued the boy that set all this in motion. I am impressed.'

'Thank you, sir.'

'The boy may be called to testify, but Inspector Day has amassed enough evidence against the tailor that he may not. It would be good if the boy were left alone now. His family's been through enough, I think.'

'Where is Inspector Day, sir?'

'There was an emergency at home. I've given him the day. And I'm giving you the day as well.'

'That won't be necessary. I'm ready to work.'

Sir Edward chuckled and shook his head.

'You are ideally suited for police work, Hammersmith.'

'Thank you, sir.'

'But . . .'

Sir Edward hesitated and scowled at the top of his desk.

'Sir?'

'You also acted beyond the pale, overstepping your responsibilities at every turn, disobeying the spirit of my orders and displaying a remarkable amount of independence.'

'Yes, sir.'

'It is fortunate for you, Sergeant Hammersmith, that I admire a certain degree of independent spirit in my men. But in future you will exercise better judgement and find ways of applying your zeal that do not step over the bounds of your proper duty, do you understand?'

'I do, sir.'

'Good. How's the arm?'

'The wound was shallow. My hand's broken, but should knit well enough.'

Sir Edward nodded.

'Go easy on it. I want you back in fighting form sooner rather than later.'

'Yes, sir. But, sir?'

'Yes, Mr Hammersmith?'

'Didn't you call me "sergeant" just now? I mean, I believe you may have misspoken.'

Sir Edward nodded.

'It is certainly possible. But in this case I did not. As of today, you are promoted to the rank of sergeant within the Metropolitan Police Force.'

Hammersmith stood absolutely still.

'Hammersmith, are you quite all right?'

'I don't know what . . . Sir, this is most unexpected.'

'I imagine it is. Beginning tomorrow, I would like you to assist Inspector Day on his cases. We need to begin filling the void left by poor Inspector Little.'

'Yes, sir.'

'I believe you and Mr Day will balance each other nicely. I have high hopes.'

'I won't let you down, sir.'

'No, I don't think you will.'

Sir Edward picked up the sheaf of papers from his desk and studied the top page. Without looking up, he said, 'You are dismissed, Sergeant.'

107

'You needn't trouble yourself, Doctor,' Day said. 'I'm sure everything's fine.'

'It's no trouble at all. Your house is on my way home.'

'Well, I appreciate your company,' Day said.

Walter Day opened the front door and Kingsley followed him inside. Mrs Dick greeted them in the parlour.

'She's upstairs, Mr Day. The doctor's in there with her. It's bad, sir.'

Day didn't bother to introduce Mrs Dick and Dr Kingsley. He took the stairs three at a time with Kingsley right behind him. Claire's bedroom door was closed and Day knocked. The door was opened almost immediately and a stout, white-haired man in shirtsleeves and waistcoat stood there barring entry. Day craned his neck to see past the stranger.

'Claire,' Day said.

'I'm sorry,' said the old man. 'Who are you?'

'I'm her husband. Who are you?'

'I'm her doctor.'

'She doesn't have a doctor. We've only just moved to the city and we have no doctor yet.'

'I am Philippa's doctor. She summoned me when your wife took sick.'

'I don't know who Philippa is.'

'Philippa Dick. Your housekeeper. Surely you're aware of your household staff.'

'I didn't . . . I don't know her first name. What's wrong with Claire?'

'Your wife is gravely ill. I fear the worst.'

'Let me in.'

Day pushed past him. The room was dark. It smelled stuffed-up and acidic and smoky. There was a row of small glass jars on the dressing table across from the bed. The jars were turned upside-down over burning candles and smoke moved over the inside surfaces of the glass. Claire lay on her bed, propped up by pillows. She smiled weakly at her husband.

'I'm so sorry, Walter. I don't know what happened to me.'

He went to her and took her hand. It was cold and when he gently squeezed her fingers, she didn't squeeze back.

'It's all right. You're going to be just fine.'

'Of course I will be, dear. Don't trouble yourself over me.'

Kingsley had been quiet and Day didn't realize that he had followed him into the room until he spoke.

'What is all this?' Kingsley said.

'I'm going to cup her to try to reduce the fever,' Mrs Dick's doctor said.

Kingsley looked aghast.

'You'll do no such thing,' he said.

'Will it help?' Day said.

'Cupping will not help anyone with anything,' Kingsley said.

Day glanced at the jars on the dressing table. He had

seen people cupped before. It was a more drastic treatment than leeches. Incisions were made in the patient's flesh and heated cups or jars were placed over the fresh wounds. As the glass containers cooled, blood was naturally drawn up into them. Pints of blood could be quickly extracted from points all over the body.

'It's barbaric,' Kingsley said. 'A relic of the past. There's no place for such mumbo jumbo in this modern age.'

'It's hardly "mumbo jumbo", sir. I'll ask you to keep your lay opinions to yourself and leave me to my work.'

'My opinions are not lay opinions. They are not even opinions. They are fact.'

'Unless you are a doctor, sir . . .'

'I am,' Kingsley said. 'What is your name?'

'Entwhistle. Dr Herbert Entwhistle.'

'I've never heard of you. You don't practise at either of the hospitals where I teach.'

'I'm in private practice. Not that it's any of your business.'

'It is my business now. Tell me you haven't begun to cut this woman up.'

Entwhistle pulled back his shoulders and thrust out his chest. He looked from Kingsley to Day and back to Kingsley, clearly not accustomed to being confronted.

'No, I haven't begun making the incisions yet,' he said.

'Good,' Kingsley said. 'Inspector Day and his wife were just about to employ me as their family physician.'

He looked at Day, who nodded.

'That's done, then,' Kingsley said. 'And now that I'm in charge here I'll ask you to leave.'

'Well, I never!' Entwhistle said.

'Then it's about time you did,' Kingsley said. 'Out you go.'

He made a shooshing motion and Entwhistle left the room, protesting.

'I'm afraid you'll need to go too, Inspector. Your wife will want her privacy.'

'I'll be just outside that door,' Day said.

'I'm sure that will be a comfort to her.'

Day smiled at Claire and patted her hand.

'Don't you worry. Kingsley's a very good doctor.'

'I'm not worried, Walter. Don't you be worried, either.'

'I have complete faith in you both.'

He gave one last look at his wife as he left the room and Kingsley closed the door after him. Day was left in the hall with Entwhistle and Mrs Dick, who shot baleful stares in his direction but said nothing. A moment later, the door opened again and Kingsley thrust an armful of jars and candles at Entwhistle.

'Take these antiques with you,' Kingsley said.

He closed the door again.

Entwhistle narrowed his eyes at Day.

'You'll regret this,' he said. 'Don't beg me to come back here if that quack makes her worse.'

'I'm sure I won't.'

'You're a fool, Mr Day,' Mrs Dick said. 'Dr Entwhistle has been my physician for more years than I can count. He's brilliant, he is.'

'And yet he's been unable to cure your sour disposition.'

'I beg your pardon.'

'Do you imagine that my wife and I never talk? That she hasn't told me about your attitude towards her. You're meant to be helping her about the house, not belittling her at every turn.'

'Your wife is a foolish, spoiled child and it's about time someone put her in her place.'

'You may leave with Dr Entwhistle. We won't be requiring your services any longer.'

'You can't discharge me from my duties. Only the missus can do that.'

'At this moment, Mrs Dick, you do not want to argue with me. Leave my home and never come back here again.'

She opened her mouth to say something more, but saw the look on his face and checked herself. She turned on her heel and marched down the stairs. Dr Entwhistle shook his head and followed after her without another glance at Day.

Day heard one of the glass jars fall from the doctor's arms and tumble down the stairs, but he didn't hear it break. A moment later, the front door opened and slammed shut. Day leaned against the wall next to his wife's bedroom door and listened to the rainfall against the roof. He had no idea how long it might be before Kingsley finished with Claire.

As it turned out, he didn't have long to wait. The door opened after a few minutes and Kingsley stepped into the hall, wiping his hands on a white towel. He patted Day on the shoulder and smiled. There was a twinkle in his eye.

'I have some rather good news for you, Inspector. Your wife isn't "gravely ill" at all. She's with child.'

'She isn't.'

'She is.'

'You're serious?'

'I am nearly always serious. She's pregnant.'

'And that's made her sick?'

'Yes, a bit. But her situation has been compounded by that damned girdle she wears. She'll need some bed rest and she'll need to stop wearing girdles for the duration of the pregnancy as they can only complicate matters for both her and the baby.'

'She's really going to have a baby?'

'She really is. You both are, but she'll be doing most of the work.'

A wave of relief washed over Day. He grabbed Kingsley's hand and pumped it up and down.

'Thank you, Doctor.'

'Well, I couldn't leave you at the mercy of that Entwhistle creature. Cupping, indeed! He would have killed her!'

Day stepped back and swallowed hard. He slumped against the wall.

'But I've only just realized,' he said. 'We can't have a baby here. I've let the housekeeper go. Not half an hour ago. We've nobody to help with a baby.'

'You needn't worry about that yet. You have a few months to find a solution.'

He paused and pursed his lips as if a thought had just occurred to him.

'In fact,' Kingsley said, 'I may know a young woman who would be glad to help with a baby. She's only fourteen, but that's old enough, I think.'

Day smiled.

'Send her round, then,' he said. 'But I'd like to see my wife now, if I may.'

'Oh, of course.'

Kingsley stepped aside and Day rushed into the room. Claire held out her arms and Day went to her.

'Can you believe it?' Claire said.

'I've scarcely had time to think about it yet.'

'Nor I.'

'All I can think of is my happiness, now that you're all right.'

'I have to stop wearing my corsets.'

'That's what the doctor tells me.'

'I'll be fat and ugly.'

'You will never be any such thing,' Day said. 'You will always be the most beautiful woman in London.'

And he meant it.

Epilogue

London. Five hours after Mr Little's funeral

They stood in Trafalgar Square in a light drizzle. Henry Mayhew, the dancing man, was not dancing. He was watching a rainbow formed by the hazy light of the lamppost. Next to him, Walter Day moved from foot to foot, nervous. He'd been anxious since the previous afternoon when he'd found out that he and Claire were expecting a baby. He still wasn't sure about London. Devon might be a better place to raise a child. But Walter had caught a killer and he no longer questioned his place in the city. He was a detective and he was helping to make London safe.

He drew the flat black pouch from his pocket and opened it. The brass key was still there, atop the ugly, more utilitarian skeleton keys. He took it out and closed the pouch and put it back in his pocket.

'Henry,' he said.

Mayhew turned his attention to Day.

'This key I'm holding?'

Day showed it to the dancing man, who nodded.

'It fits this door. I'll wager you didn't even notice that there was a door here.'

'I did notice it, Mr Day.'

'Well, I never did. At any rate, this is the key to it.'

He put the key in the lock and turned it, opened the door and stepped to the side so that Henry could enter ahead of him. With both men standing inside, the kiosk seemed much smaller than it had the last time Day had been there. Henry's head nearly brushed the ceiling.

'Dr Kingsley mentioned that you might be going to work for him.'

Henry smiled.

'You'll need a place to live,' Day said. 'Until you save some money.'

Henry looked suspiciously around the tiny room.

'I know it's not much,' Day said. 'It's not warm and it's not all that comfortable, I'm sure, but it's dry and it's safe and you won't have to spend the night in a heap on the pavement. And, if you decide you want to dance, there's a much larger audience for it out there on the gallery. This is a square. You should dance in a square, Henry.'

'You want me to stay in here?'

'You can come and go from here as you please. I'm sort of giving you this place. As a home.'

'A home?'

'Yes. So far as I know, this is the only key to this place. And I'm giving that to you. When you eventually get something larger, a flat of your own, I'd appreciate it if you returned the key to me, but . . .'

Henry picked him up and squeezed him in a massive bear hug. Day put his hand atop his head in case he should bump against the low ceiling.

'I say. That's not necessary.'

Henry set him back down on his feet and gave him a shy smile.

'Nobody's been as nice to me as you and the doctor's been since Frank went away.'

Day cleared his throat.

'Yes, well, here's the key.'

He put it in Henry's outstretched hand.

'Thank you, Mr Day. I was wrong before. The city's messenger is you. It's been you all along.'

'I don't know about that, but you're welcome,' Day said. 'I think . . . I think the city would want you to have this. That seems right to me.'

Henry looked around the space as if deciding where to put the furniture. Day thought that the milk crate would look the same no matter where he positioned it.

'I'll leave you to it, then,' he said. 'I imagine I'll see you the next time I'm by Dr Kingsley's laboratory.'

'I'll be there,' Henry said. 'Thank you again.'

'You take care of yourself, Henry.'

Day stepped out into the crisp morning air and pushed the door closed behind him. He would sleep much better at night knowing that the dancing man was safe. He pulled his watch out and checked it. He needed to hurry or he'd be late to work. There was much to be done if London was going to be made safe enough for the new Day to come.

Hammersmith had treated himself to a small bag of chocolates from the confectionary shop downstairs. He had never been in the place, but his new promotion to sergeant was an occasion that called for something more than coppery tea to mark it.

On his way down the hall, he heard the creak of a door behind him and turned to see Mrs Flanders standing on the landing.

'Oh, Mr Hammersmith, it's you. I thought you might be someone else.'

'Someone else on the way up to my flat?'

'Well, I thought you might be the other policeman. Your friend. I never caught his name, but he was most gracious. A very nice man.'

'My friend?'

'Yes. The man who came round yesterday. Well, I should say there were two men who came yesterday, but I didn't spend time talking to the second one. It was the first policeman to arrive at your meeting that I mean.'

She waved her hand in the air and shook her head. 'Oh, why am I talking about either of them?' She leaned towards him and whispered. 'If anyone heard me, it might ruin their disguises.'

She put a finger to her lips, winked, and backed into her flat. The door closed.

Hammersmith stood for a moment, wondering whether she would come back out and explain herself. When she didn't reappear, he let himself into his flat and set the bag of chocolates on the table in the small sitting room. He looked around to see if anything had been disturbed. He had been so tired the night before that he had fallen into bed and been asleep nearly the instant he came through the door. There might have been a marching band in his flat and he wouldn't have noticed. Now, he checked the place carefully.

His own bedroom was as spartan as it had always been, but Pringle's room was cluttered. Fresh laundry was draped over a clothes horse in the corner, uncounted pairs of shoes were lined up next to the bed, ready to be shined, a lightly worn shirt was draped in front of the open window to air out. There was something dull and lifeless about that collection of things, as if the room had shut down in Pringle's absence. It smelled dusty. Hammersmith averted his eyes and shut the door.

He found three things in the parlour that he did not think had been there the previous day. There was a small, reddish-brown spot on the rug under the table. It might have been jelly, but it looked to Hammersmith like blood. There was also a piece of paper folded on the mantle, held in place by a new tin of tea.

He opened the tea first and smelled it. There was no scent of copper.

He unfolded the paper and read what was written on it:

Dear Mr Hammersmith, our mutual friend has retired from business. You won't be hearing about him again. Your tea was undrinkable. I took the liberty of replacing it. Perhaps we'll meet again. Your friend.

The note was unsigned, but Hammersmith understood who had left it and what it meant.

He started a fire and put the kettle on. When the tea

had brewed, he took his cup to the window and silently toasted Colin Pringle's memory.

He took a sip. It was the best tea he had ever tasted.

Dr Kingsley put down his scalpel and put on his overcoat. He left his laboratory and locked the door behind him. Fiona was in the hall, hurrying towards him with her pad and charcoal.

'I'm sorry I'm late, Father,' she said.

'Not at all. I was thinking I might take today off and spend it with you.'

'But there's so much work to do.'

'There will always be more work. But you will be grown and gone away before I know it.'

Fiona grinned and set her pad of paper on the low table in the hall.

'What shall we do, then?' she said.

The rain had turned to a light mist and they strolled aimlessly away from the hospital until the sky opened up again. They hopped aboard an omnibus and by the time the rain let up they found themselves at Hyde Park. The park was nearly deserted and it glimmered with fresh raindrops. The landscape smelled of fresh greens and flowers, and they drifted along in companionable silence, content for the moment to be alone together.

Finally, Kinglsey broke the stillness. 'Fiona,' he said, 'I've decided something.'

'Is it bad?' she said.

'Whatever would make you ask that?'

'You never leave your laboratory. And now suddenly . . . I'm afraid you have something awful to say, some news that has to be broken to me outdoors where I won't scream and make a spectacle.'

'Not at all.'

'You're not sending me away to school, then?'

Kingsley chuckled.

'No, I'm not sending you away.'

'Good. I should hate boarding school and I would get bad marks just to spite you for sending me there.'

'I shall keep that in mind in case I ever do contemplate such a thing. No, I've decided that you spend too much time among the dead. It's not healthy.'

'I don't mind, Father.'

'I know, but I do mind. I've arranged for you to assist an expectant young mother. And when she has her baby, I'd like for you to stay on and help her care for it. She seems to be quite over her head about everything and you are a very capable young lady.'

'A baby! Oh, that would be wonderful.'

'The Days are kind people and Claire Day might be just the female influence you need at this point in your life. You don't want to be trapped in a laboratory any more with an old man.'

'You're not old at all, Father.'

'You flatter me. So you'll do it?'

'Of course I will. Only who will help you with the bodies?'

'I've already arranged for your replacement.'

'It's settled, then.'